Twin Treasures

Ethan Fox Book 2 &

Its Puzzling Companion

2 Books in 1

TWIN TREASURES

ETHAN FOX BOOK 2 &

ITS PUZZLING COMPANION

2 BOOKS IN 1

BY

E. L. SEER

COVERS ILLUSTRATED BY JOHN COLLADO

The Ethan Fox Books Company
an imprint of The Ridge Publishing Group

Twin Treasures: Ethan Fox Book 2 & Its Puzzling Companion 2 BOOKS IN 1
Copyright © 2024 by E. L. Seer

To meet the author and learn more about the Ethan Fox Books original series and E. L. Seer's books, please visit us at https://www.EthanFoxBooks.com. Ethan Fox Books is an exciting new website from E. L. Seer that can be enjoyed alongside the Ethan Fox Books series. You can discover behind the scenes information about the author, learn more about your favorite characters, play games, enter contests, and much more. It is FREE to join and use and is designed to be safe for people of all ages. Subscribe to our mailing list, join our Caretaker World Newsletter, join our KidsStagramCLUB, read all about us in The Residential Daily Star, see updates at Ethan Fox Books KidsStagram blog at https://www.KidsStagram.com, "like" us on our Facebook.com/EthanFoxBooks page, or "follow" us on Twitter @EthanFoxBooks.

Cover designed by: John Collado
Editor: Felicity Carter

Library of Congress Control Number: 2024920977

Twin Treasures: Ethan Fox Book 2 & Its Puzzling Companion 2 BOOKS IN 1 / by E. L. Seer

ISBN 978-1-956905-24-3 (paperback)

1. Young Adult Fiction / Action & Adventure. 2. Young Adult Fiction / Fantasy. 3. Young Adult Fiction / Mysteries & Detective Stories. 4. Young Adult Fiction / Science Fiction. 5. Young Adult Fiction / Coming of Age. I. Title. II. Series.

Print copies printed in the United States of America

This book is dedicated to my wife, Lori. Without her coaxing and INSPIRATION, it would never have made it past a couple of wacky dreams and an old high school poem. She has been my wife, confidant, and cheerleader – she is my taletaddler.

Thank you, sweetheart.

ALSO BY E. L. SEER

Ethan Fox and the Eyes of the Desert Sand

Wordly Pagemore's Early Worm Activities & Games:
The Eyes of the Desert Sand Edition

Ethan Fox and the Shadow Princess

Wordly Pagemore's Early Worm Activities & Games:
The Shadow Princess Edition

Ethan Fox and the Kraken's Fury
Coming Soon

Mayhem in the Moongarden
Chapter Book

Received Mom's Choice Award, Moonbeam Children's Book Award,
Story Monsters Award, and Global Book Award.

CONTENTS

BOOK

Ethan Fox and the Shadow Princess

ONE
A Bite of the Big Apple · 1

TWO
Back to The Residence · 15

THREE
Stravis' Bunker · 41

FOUR
Creatures of the Dark Realm · 60

FIVE
Escape to New York · 80

SIX
The Drone Wars · 103

SEVEN
The Oracle · 123

EIGHT
Pandora's Box · 155

CONTENTS

N I N E
A Grim New Start · 177

T E N
The Nibblewarts · 201

E L E V E N
The Pyramids of Never · 218

T W E L V E
The Sayers · 240

T H I R T E E N
Medusa · 258

F O U R T E E N
The Nibblewart Prophecies · 271

F I F T E E N
A Grisly Discovery · 296

S I X T E E N
The Day of Reckoning · 315

E P I L O G U E
A Kraken's Fury · 330

CONTENTS

BOOK

WORDLY PAGEMORE'S
EARLY WORM ACTIVITIES & GAMES
THE SHADOW PRINCESS EDITION

Ethan Fox Books
Character Word Search Puzzles

ONE
Ethan Fox · 337

TWO
George Fox · 341

THREE
Betsy Fox · 345

FOUR
Hayley Ravenwood · 349

FIVE
Daavic Ravenwood · 353

SIX
Damien Ravenwood · 357

SEVEN
Victor Qruefeldt · 361

EIGHT
Jordanna Ravenwood · 365

NINE
Odin Ravenwood · 369

CONTENTS

TEN
Vanessa Ravenwood · 373

ELEVEN
Blair Trabblemore · 377

TWELVE
Caden Stanley · 381

THIRTEEN
Roman Trabblemore · 385

FOURTEEN
Gaylord Trabblemore · 389

FIFTEEN
Jason Crowley · 393

SIXTEEN
Heldrik Vonn Grim · 397

SEVENTEEN
Jasper · 401

EIGHTEEN
Albert · 405

NINETEEN
Linus · 409

TWENTY
Newton · 413

TWENTY-ONE
Kepler · 417

TWENTY-TWO
Irvin McGillicutty · 421

CONTENTS

TWENTY-THREE
Melvin McGillicutty · 425

TWENTY-FOUR
Gruggins McGhee · 429

TWENTY-FIVE
Wordly Pagemore · 433

TWENTY-SIX
Dorkin Drumbles · 437

TWENTY-SEVEN
Tinx · 441

TWENTY-EIGHT
Pixie-Devils · 445

TWENTY-NINE
Azron · 449

THIRTY
Nicholas Knight · 453

THIRTY-ONE
Norell · 457

THIRTY-TWO
Alexander Sturgis · 461

THIRTY-THREE
Tiffany Sturgis · 465

THIRTY-FOUR
Brianna Tanglewood · 469

THIRTY-FIVE
Medusa · 473

CONTENTS

THIRTY-SIX
Bella Wentworth · 477

THIRTY-SEVEN
Boris Wentworth · 481

THIRTY-EIGHT
Mrs. Moongarden · 485

THIRTY-NINE
Grubner and the Trowel Brothers · 489

FORTY
Dakota Drakelan · 493

FORTY-ONE
KaaFoo · 477

FORTY-TWO
Balder, Gilly, and Skronk · 501

FORTY-THREE
Fin Drenchler · 505

FORTY-FOUR
The Seers · 509

FORTY-FIVE
The Sayers · 513

FORTY-SIX
The Shadow Princess · 517

FORTY-SEVEN
The Nibblewarts · 521

FORTY-EIGHT
The Residence · 525

CONTENTS

FORTY-NINE
The Caretaker City of Zen · 529

FIFTY
The Drone Wars · 533

Ethan Fox Books
Who Said That?

Match Characters to their Sayings · 537

Ethan Fox Books
How Well Do You Know the Story?

290 Trivia Questions – Book #2
Ethan Fox and the Shadow Princess · 241

Ethan Fox Books
Answers

Who Said That? · 569

Trivia Questions · 571

Meet the Author

Meet the Author · 606

Ethan Fox and the Shadow Princess
Journey Map

1 After narrowly escaping the Grimleaver attack on Manhattan, Ethan is reunited with his friends at The Residence.

4 Ethan and Hayley sneak away to retrieve his pocket tote.

The Residence

2 Against Jordanna's wishes, Ethan and Hayley embark on a clandestine trip to Stravis' Bunker.

3 Back at The Residence, Ethan learns of a vital clue hidden away in his pocket tote.

HIDDEN REALM OF DESOLATION

5 After uncovering a clue in the Moongarden, the team returns to Stravis' Bunker. But to escape Jordannna's watchful eye, they take a potentially dangerous path.

FINAL SHOWDOWN
After a grisly discovery, and Hayley's sudden disappearance, Ethan frantically returns to Desolation.

Glass Pillars of Nym

Vanishing Dune

Stravis' Bunker

7 Ethan and Hayley accompany Jordanna and CAGE members on a dangerous mission to the Vanishing Dune.

6 After following a tribe of Nibblewarts to a negative door in the Hall of Doorways, Ethan and Hayley make the dangerous decision to follow the nomads backwards through time, destination unknown.

Sand Miser Dunes

??? UNKNOWN REALM ???

Pyramids of Never

Our journey begins here.

Depicts book travel.

Travel by Portal Beacon.

Travel by Portal Plain.

Depicts the Hall of Doorways.

Depicts a Journey back in time.

Travel by Tether Port.

Realm starting points.

The *Ethan Fox Books* Company

Dive into the sands of adventure with "Ethan Fox and the Eyes of the Desert Sand," where every grain tells a story, and every dune hides a secret. As you traverse through Ethan's thrilling escapades, we invite you to extend your journey beyond the pages. For an exclusive peek behind the scenes, visit our official blog at: https://www.KidsStagram.com. Discover the depths of Characters, explore the vastness of Places, unravel the mysteries of Things/Events, and witness the Cutting Floor Scenes that make Ethan's world so vividly cinematic.

Your passion fuels our quest to bring Ethan and Hayley's adventures to the silver screen. If you're captivated by the idea of an Ethan Fox film, join our chorus of voices at our website at: https://www.EthanFoxBooks.com/Fan Page, and let's turn this vision into a panoramic reality!

TWIN TREASURES

ETHAN FOX BOOK 2 &

ITS PUZZLING COMPANION

2 BOOKS IN 1

BOOK

ETHAN FOX AND SHADOW PRINCESS

E. L. SEER

A BITE OF THE BIG APPLE

The cold night air nipped at Ethan's nose as he stepped into a taxi at New York's Times Square. He gazed out at the crowded mass of tourists enjoying the circus-like atmosphere under the bright lights and towering billboards. Street performers were dressed in their usual flamboyant costumes and performing for the city's visitors to vie for their money. While his parents talked beside him, Ethan quietly cataloged his favorite characters in attendance: Spiderman, Superman, Ironman, Godzilla, King Kong, and even a magician masquerading as Harry Potter.

But then a vampire character in the crowd caught his eye, interrupting his fun thoughts. The homemade human costume looked cheesy – but it was enough to jolt his train of thought back to his time at The Residence.

"I wonder what she's doing right now," Ethan thought.

Nearly a year had passed since Jasper lured him and Hayley to The Residence and introduced them to the strange Caretaker world. Things had almost gotten back to normal since he returned home – but that didn't stop him from thinking about his time with the Caretakers and all the friends he had made. Ethan had kept his promise and told nobody, not even his parents George and Betsy, of his adventures. But things could never truly return to normal now that he knew he was the Hybrid Child and connected to the hidden Caretaker universe.

Well, he sort of knew. Nobody had explained what it meant to be the Hybrid Child or where his memories had gone. Ethan's adoptive parents hid his past by explaining away his lost memories and the shiny white symbols etched onto the palms of his hands. Their story was his birth parents were members of an evil cult who marked their children in that manner, and he later suffered amnesia after a car accident. He still had so many questions, and the answers could only come from The Residence – but he felt at ease and had a strange feeling he would see his friends again soon. He settled back into his seat and watched New York flash by.

Miles away and far above the city streets, a dark figure in a black robe stood atop a high-rise building, looking down at the bustling crowded streets. An evil laugh erupted from the silhouette and echoed over the city as his warm breath met the frosty night air and billowed out like smoke from a bull's nose. The stranger's army boots stepped over a dead rat as he made his way to a stone statue of a gargoyle at the corner of the rooftop. He rubbed his hands together, and they began to give off a hot red glow as he reached out to place them atop the cold stone statue.

Moments later, the stone gargoyle moved beneath his touch and slowly animated into a living, breathing monster with a rugged scaly hide where stone used to be. The newborn creature turned and peered up at its master with ruby red eyes that glared with laser-like intensity.

The master turned to face a tall female vampire who stood in front of a dozen more animated gargoyles, drawn from their stone homes around the city. She wore a tattered black robe, slit down the back and sides to allow her batwings to emerge, plus a thick red rope wrapped around her waist to fasten everything in place. She had long pointy ears, dark grayish skin, and deep red eyes. Her long black hair draped down her backside and nearly touched the ground.

"Go, Norell, take our new children and join the others," the dark figure said in a low gnarled tone.

"Will you be joining in on the fun?"

"I wouldn't dream of missing out," the master said. "But our party is not yet complete. I have a graveyard or two to visit before the festivities begin. Join the others and await my arrival."

Norell edged forward as massive batwings grew from beneath the back of her robe. The newborn gargoyle jumped from the side of the building and joined the others behind Norell. She stretched her wings out, and the small battalion of gargoyles did the same.

"All hail the Grimlord," she said and then ran to the edge of the building and jumped off, followed by her gargoyle companions.

The taxi rolled to a stop to drop the Fox family off a few blocks away from their favorite Italian restaurant. Ethan and his parents George and Betsy Fox often went out on the town for a Broadway show, followed by dinner – but tonight was a celebration—Ethan's fourteenth birthday. Their routine was to eat a late dinner after the show and discuss their opinions about the performance. Betsy always asked the taxi driver to drop them off several blocks from their dinner destination. She was a stickler for making sure George got at least a short walk in before what would become a belt-loosening feast followed by at least one dessert.

Saturday night was busy, and the crowded streets crawled with people from all walks of life. The sounds of the city reverberated off the surrounding high-rises; car horns honking, sirens singing, and people shouting above one another filled the air. The Fox family strolled down the busy sidewalk – oblivious to what was happening above.

High above the bright city streets, the light faded to darkness atop the tall buildings that tickled the belly of the skyline. Norell, the female vampire, hopped onto the raised edge of the building and scanned the neighboring rooftops. Hundreds of glowing red eyes glared back. A small army of vampires stood at the edges of the surrounding skyscrapers as the gargoyle battalion circled in the dark sky above.

Norell walked along the narrow edge of the building and stared down at the people walking the streets. But she focused her interests on one particular threesome of people as they entered their favorite Italian restaurant on schedule.

The Fox family entered the restaurant, and the owner greeted them warmly, and escorted them to their usual seats. Ethan's eyes took a moment to adjust to the dim room lit only by the candles from each table. The dining area was nearly empty as usual for this time of night. But Ethan knew that was part of Betsy's plan to minimize embarrassment when George inevitably decided to play the "crack Ethan up game."

Betsy stood to excuse herself for the ladies' room, when a busboy arrived with three glasses of water, each with a slice of cucumber floating on top. George waited for a moment to make sure Betsy was out of sight. He fumbled around in his coat pocket with one hand and plucked two cucumber slices out with the other. A wide grin swept across his face as he ducked under the table. Moments later, a loud wallowing noise rumbled from under the table.

"I am Charlie, the Walrus man of Wiltor. I am here to speak with Ethan Fox!" A loud voice growled as George emerged from beneath the table.

Ethan erupted with laughter at the sight of George's face. A rubber walrus nose with whiskers and tusks covered the bottom half of his face, and cucumber slices stuck to his eye sockets to look like enormous green eyes—George was a Walrus man. Ethan was still laughing when Betsy returned from the ladies' room.

"What's with all the laughter? Is your father being silly again?" She approached George from behind – unaware of his crazy masquerade. Betsy quietly sat down at the table and turned to face her husband. Startled by his face, she let out a high-pitched shriek and turned bright pink. Even in a dark, nearly empty restaurant, George could embarrass his wife.

"Looks like your father's been to the joke shop again. Well, at least one of my men is growing up."

Once the antics were over, dinner arrived, and the Fox's enjoyed a relaxed meal discussing the night's events and how much they enjoyed the show. After dinner, they each ordered only one dessert – but George finished his and half of Betsy's. They paid their bill and left the restaurant for another walk up the street, where Betsy insisted taxis were more abundant.

Norell spotted the Fox's emerging from the restaurant across the street and far below her perch on the roof's edge. She jumped from her roost and walked to the center of the rooftop, where a group of vampires stood awaiting orders.

"I wonder what's keeping him," she said to no one. "If he doesn't arrive soon, we will miss our window."

"CAW, CAW, CAW," the shrieks rang out, announcing the arrival of a sizable raven circling overhead and slowly descending. The raptor had tattered feathers, exposed bones and organs, and the eyes of a dead fish. In fact, this bird was not a raven at all. It was a grimtailed dread and was more dead than alive.

"Poe is here," Norell said, "our master has arrived."

The dread swiftly broke into a dive towards the rooftop and pulled up into a quick loop maneuver causing a small swirling vortex to open near the vampires. The whirling disturbance grew darker and fuller as bright jolts of electricity danced out from its center. A black army boot poked out as Victor Qruefeldt stepped through the vortex to join his Grimleaver army.

Victor Qruefeldt was the master and creator of the Grimleavers and the archnemesis to Ethan's Caretaker friends at The Residence. During their previous encounter, Ethan had outsmarted the Grimleaver leader, making him look foolish. And that left Victor with a particularly strong disdain for young Ethan Fox.

"All hail the Grimlord," Norell said.

"All hail the Grimlord," the vampires echoed from the rooftops.

"Master, you've arrived just in time," Norell said. "The target is on the move."

"Has the devil's swarm arrived?" Victor asked.

"We've seen no sign of them."

"They'll arrive shortly," Victor said with a grin. "Their tiny wings slow them down – but they are eager for their first taste of human blood."

Midnight was approaching, but the streets were still bustling with people as the Fox's strolled towards their destination. An untied shoelace nearly tripped Ethan, so he stepped off the sidewalk onto a small patch of grass in front of a high-rise hotel. His parents kept walking; unaware he had stopped behind them. Ethan knelt and tied his shoe – but as he finished, a sudden eerie quiet overcame him, and time slowed to a crawl. The symbols on his palms started to tingle, and the hairs on the back of his neck felt like crawling ants.

"All hail the Grimlord," voices cried out in Ethan's head.

"He's here," Ethan said aloud. "Victor Qruefeldt!"

An explosion of sound shattered the silence in Ethan's head as a bus roared onto the sidewalk through a crowd of pedestrians, and crashed into a giant lamppost, barely missing him. Victims flew in all directions as a shower of sparks bathed pedestrians now running for their lives. The crash cut Ethan off from his parents, who were now being shepherded away with the frightened mob.

"If they had stopped to wait for me, they'd be dead," he thought.

Ethan gazed at the pedestrians across the street, standing and watching the commotion. Thunderous sounds of shattering glass abruptly filled the air. Ethan gazed up at a formation of stone gargoyles flying kamikaze-style right into the sides of the buildings above the crowd. Shards of glass rained down on the unsuspecting spectators, impaling many of them as chaos overtook that side of the street.

Vampires swooped down and randomly picked people off, hoisting them into the sky, and using them as human artillery to drop on the scattering crowd below. Ethan ducked behind a bush near the crash to hide from their view as he gathered his thoughts. Moments passed, and most of the mob dispersed from the area. The sound of screams slowly quieted, and Ethan emerged from the bush. He backed away from the heat of the now burning bus and slowly scanned his surroundings. A deep sense of angst overcame him as he took in the surrounding carnage. But then his palm symbols tingled, an eerie calm returned to his head, and the voice spoke up again.

"I am not yet finished with you, Ethan Fox. You must stick around for my encore."

"I'm not afraid of you!" Ethan shouted at the sky. "I'm not afraid of you—Victor Qruefeldt."

A mob of people ran back up the street, in the opposite direction from where they had just run. Ethan ducked into the entrance of a long dark alley at the side of the hotel. The sound of the running mob quieted, replaced by a loud, low-pitched hum. Ethan stepped out of the alleyway to look down the street, and his heart skipped a beat. Masses of slow-moving people walked awkwardly down the middle of the road, groaning. The scene reminded Ethan of a *Walking Dead* episode.

"Walkers," Ethan whispered. "Zombies creep me out."

Looking for his parents would have to wait till after he avoided becoming a zombie main course. Ethan turned and ran down the dark alley as fast as he could. Cool bluish light from a lamppost dimly lit the back corner of the alleyway near the backside of the hotel. Ethan stopped when he reached the light so he could scan the area. The alleyway ended but continued left around the back of the building. Ethan strode around the well-lit corner where a lamp hung above a door at the back of the hotel. A spacious trash bin and several random trash cans stood up against a cyclone fence opposite the hotel – but beyond that was more darkness. He turned towards the door and noticed a flyer for an upcoming event posted on the textured concrete wall by the door. But the light flickered a few times and went out, leaving only the lamppost's moon-like glow.

Ethan was reading the flyer when his palms started to tingle, so he raised his hands to look. The bright white light emitted by the glowing symbols bathed his face. The symbols spun in his palms several times and stopped abruptly, pointing to his right – like animated cartoon compasses. Ethan pivoted to his right, and the symbols followed to stay pointing in the same direction. He lowered his hands, and that's when he saw her.

Standing between him and the trash bin was the dark silhouette of a young woman – but this was no ordinary woman. She was pitch black from top to bottom and outlined by a glowing blue aura. Her face, body, and clothing, all consisted of the same glossy substance that caused her shining yellow eyes and blue aura to cast a glow giving her a liquid sheen. A golden necklace wrapped around her neck was clearly visible against her blackness. A swirly eye-shaped pendant hung from the chain against her upper chest.

"It's you," Ethan said and stepped towards her. "I've been seeing you in my dreams."

Her mouth moved like she was trying to speak to Ethan, but he did not understand the unusual sounds she made.

"I'm sorry, I don't understand what you are trying to say."

She raised her arm and pointed up at the wall behind him. He turned to look at what she pointed to and jumped back at the sight. A horde of small dragon-like creatures clung to the wall glaring at Ethan with piercing green eyes. Swarms of them swooped down from the darkness and hovered in front of the others. They were pitch black like the woman but had blue swirl patterns covering their bodies. Ethan backed away as the tiny dragons slowly advanced toward him. Then, all at once, the creatures stopped moving and opened their mouths. The dim yellow glow inside slowly grew brighter and brighter.

The hairs on the back of Ethan's neck crawled as time seemed to slow, and a bright burst of energy erupted from the dragon's mouths like laser beams. Ethan dove towards the woman in black, who promptly vanished and reappeared between him and the tiny monsters. The blasts from the dragon horde absorbed into her blackness like water into a sponge.

"Thank you," Ethan said as he hopped to his feet.

But the menacing horde continued clinging to the walls, glaring at them as they recharged their energy beams. The woman in black spun around and looked at the garbage cans behind Ethan. One of the cans swiftly levitated into the air and launched towards the horde of miniature dragons causing them to scatter and swarm in all directions. The woman looked at Ethan and pointed to the door to the building. It swung open, and a bright light flooded the alleyway as if inviting him inside. He hurried in, but stopped and turned to thank his savior – but the shadow woman was gone.

Ethan shut the door and hurried down a long corridor towards the front of the hotel. He proceeded through a door that led to the hotel lobby, where crowds of people were barricading the doors as others stood glued to the windows watching the commotion outside. He could hear the wailing sirens of ambulances, and the whirring blades of television and rescue helicopters, as the city reacted to what had just happened.

Ethan found a nearby restroom to splash water over his face and catch his breath after his harrowing experience. He finished washing his face and leaned against the sink with his arms as he stared into the mirror.

"Where are the Caretakers?" he whispered to himself. "They must be aware of this."

A small green blob appeared on the mirror, like a wad of gum, and popped off. A three inch tall creature landed on the sink in front of Ethan. Its fuzzy green face looked like a grumpy old man with tall blue Tweety Bird eyes.

"Of course, we know of the situation," Gruggins McGhee said. "I've come to escort you back to The Residence."

Ethan refused to go at first. He was still anxious and insistent on finding his parents before going anywhere. Gruggins tried to reassure him that his parents were already under Caretaker protection and the Grimleavers weren't after them anyway. But when that didn't work, Gruggins resorted to casting a grumpling enchantment on Ethan. It would alleviate his anxiety and temporarily cause him to forget about the plight of his parents. It was Ethan's safety that was of paramount importance – and The Residence was the only place that could ensure it.

Gruggins rode cloaked on Ethan's shoulder and directed him farther down the alley behind the hotel. He widened his eyes to make his way in the darkness of night as the eerie quiet told him they were alone.

"How can you see your way down this dark alley?" Gruggins asked.

"I don't know, I just can."

Gruggins uncloaked himself and held his tiny left hand out. He pointed his right index finger down at his palm and swirled it in a circular motion. A globe of light popped up out of nowhere and hovered over his palm, lighting the alleyway around them.

"You'll have to teach me that trick," Ethan said.

"I'd have to turn you into a grumpling first," Gruggins said as he scanned their surroundings. "A little farther down."

Ethan continued down the alley as Gruggins' glowing orb lit the way.

"Our destination is right up ahead here." Gruggins pointed to a beat-up old tire leaning against the fence at the back of the alley.

"What are we supposed to do with that?"

"Didn't you learn anything during your stay at The Residence? That, my dear boy, is a portal beacon and our ticket home."

Gruggins instructed him to touch the dirty old tire with both hands. Ethan was initially reluctant and wondered if

Gruggins was punking him – but the sound of a distant scream interrupted the silence, reminding him of the dire circumstances of the night. He knelt next to the tire, placed his hands against the cold hard rubber, and they vanished in a flash.

BACK TO THE RESIDENCE

The tire transformed into a hefty crystal ball in Ethan's hands. The glassy sphere balanced on the point of the upside-down cone attached to the bottom. Ethan's eyes squinted shut in the bright sunless blue sky hanging over the black-and-white checkerboard they were kneeling on. Ethan recognized the portal plane from his prior visit to The Residence. He spun around to scan the horizon where tall lifeless trees stood, reaching for the sky with jagged arm-like branches. The portal spheres floated behind him, held in place by colored electric fields.

"Blue for Atlantis, green for Ceres, red for Hades, and yellow for Zephyr," Ethan said as he named the elemental worlds.

"Enough of the history lesson," Gruggins said.

Ethan turned as a doorway appeared out of nowhere and opened slowly. Blue sky, a checkered floor, and a tree-lined horizon framed the outside of the doorway. But inside was the front room of The Residence—the entrance to a world within our own.

They entered the front room, where Ethan's reflection stared back at them from the sizable mirror across the room. He remembered throwing a ball through the mirror and watching it bounce out onto the portal plane when he unlocked the portals.

"Well, kiddo," Gruggins said, "this is the end of the line for me. I'm beat after all the excitement. Time for a well-deserved nap."

"Where is everybody?"

"Dealing with the mess we just left, I'd imagine. Mushmouth will be along shortly, I'm sure. You can wait here or in the study." The front door shut as Gruggins fluttered off Ethan's shoulder. He vanished into a tiny brown box on the table near the study door.

Ethan's eyes were adjusting to the dimly lit front room. He gazed towards a door at the back of the room. The sign above read:

• THE HALL OF DOORWAYS •

Movement near the base of the door caught Ethan's attention, so he moved in for a closer look. Tiny red eyes peered back at him as a hairy black creature came into view. The animal was almost a foot tall with a thick body, short legs, and arms that hung to the ground. Ethan studied its face as they stared back at one another. Horns grew from the sides of the creature's triangular head and curved forward like bull horns. Long sharp canines protruded up from its drooping lower jaw.

A loud bang erupted from the study and startled the creature. It moved towards the door and shrank smaller with each step. Upon reaching the door, the wee-sized critter was tiny enough to squeeze underneath and escape into The Hall of Doorways.

Ethan quietly entered the study to investigate and immediately stopped in his tracks to witness the scene. The fact that RGB were up to no good did not surprise him. Albert, Linus, and Newton, the three mischievous pyrodevlins were collectively referred to as RGB because of their respective red, green, and blue colors – and because they normally stirred up trouble as a unit.

This time, they were at the base of the bookshelf wall that ran the room's length. RGB were looking up at three books hovering over their heads. They were frantically lunging at the books, trying to snatch them from the air.

"I almost got mine," Albert shouted.

"No, you didn't," Linus rebutted.

"I'll catch mine first," Newton insisted.

RGB's antics reminded Ethan of old videos he'd seen of *The Three Stooges*. He stood quietly as one book floated down teasingly close to Albert's head while the other two rose higher. Linus and Newton turned their attention towards

Albert as he lurched up at the book above his head. But the object of Albert's desires swiftly jumped out of his grasp as the other two books came crashing down on the unsuspecting heads of Linus and Newton.

Ethan witnessed the process cycle several times, and RGB fell for the same trick every time. Then something caught his eye. A small green caterpillar stood atop the bookshelves directly above RGB. Its tiny arms moved like a puppeteer's controlling the books. Ethan smiled as the little creature waved his arms gracefully like a maestro conducting a symphony. He laughed and caught the creature's attention.

The books hovering over the pyrodevlins slowly drifted lower and changed shape as they fell. Then, all at once, RGB lunged up and grabbed their prizes.

"Got mine," Albert said.

"Me too," Linus replied.

"I snatched mine first," Newton added.

Albert, Linus, and Newton's yellow eyes grew round as golf balls as they realized what they held.

"Oh no—" Albert yelled.

"Not again," Linus shouted.

"Run for the hills!" Newton screamed.

RGB tossed the reddish marbles into the air, and in a flash, darted past Ethan and out the study door. Ethan recognized the firelyte capsules and dove in a futile attempt to catch them before they could ignite. He crashed to the floor beneath the marbles that hovered in the air and slowly morphed back into books.

"Nothing to worry about," a soft silvery voice said. "I would never give RGB a real firelyte capsule. I wouldn't want them burning down the place."

Ethan hopped to his feet and approached the small caterpillar creature now on a lower shelf directly in front of him.

"Wordly Pagemore, at your service, Master Ethan," he said and extended one of his many tiny arms.

"You know my name," Ethan said as he shook his puny hand.

"Everyone at The Residence has heard of Ethan Fox. I was away on business during your last visit."

Wordly was a four inch bookworm with round nerdy glasses over his baby blue eyes. He was bluish on top, fading to green in the middle, and yellow at the bottom. Oval red rings with yellow centers lined his sides.

"I'm happy to meet you," Ethan said. "That was quite a show you put on."

"RGB are naive and easy to fool."

"Yeah – well – I saw them take down a Hell-Giant last time I was here."

"Good point. I've heard the stories and shall proceed with caution in the future."

Wordly turned towards the still floating books, and with the wave of a hand, they returned to their respective slots on the bookshelves.

"Now then, how may I be of service to Ethan Fox? I'm the resident bookworm. I oversee the Caretaker Arts & Literature archive. If you require information of any sort, I'm your worm. Anything written, drawn, or painted, and I can likely find related information."

"Wow, that's quite the resumé," Ethan said. "Thank you – but I'm only here to wait for Irvin."

"Shnickyrooners and things like that," a voice said from outside the study.

"Speak of the devil," Wordly said. "Until we meet again, Ethan Fox, I will leave you in Irvin's capable hands." He squeezed between two books and disappeared into the shelf.

"Have you ever noticed how big fat toad ears always run through traffic during the leftover pizza underpants?" Irvin ranted as he entered the study. "I've always been amazed at how smart the noodle whiskers sound when they eat frozen beetle lips."

"I wonder that all the time," Ethan answered. "Great to see you again, Irvin."

"Master Ethan," Irvin said, breaking out of his nonsensical rant. "Irvin is happy Ethan Fox is here too!"

Irvin McGillicutty was the butler of The Residence – but his duties didn't end there. He was also the chef, tailor, handyman, and assistant to the Caretaker headmistress. Irvin was a mimic, a species with limited shape-shifting abilities that he used to maximum effect. His appearance reminded Ethan of a living department store dummy wearing a black pinstriped tuxedo with a red rose corsage.

"I've become quite the student of human behavior since your last visit," Irvin said. "I monitor their television channels and follow the news, TV shows, reality shows, and cartoons.

But my favorites are the mini shows played during the breaks."

"The commercials?"

"I guess, they don't have names – but I remember most of them." Irvin's face morphed into a cartoon rabbit. "Silly rabbit, Trix are for kids." Then a leprechaun. "Lucky Charms, they're magically delicious." Then a tiger. "Frosted Flakes, they're Grrrrreat!"

Ethan roared with laughter at Irvin's cereal commercial impressions.

"I am sorry for being late, Master Ethan. I was informing Miss Hayley of your arrival."

"She knows I'm here?"

"Sure does," Irvin said as a grin swept across his face. "Giddy as a flobbyknocker she was when I told her. Asked me to stall so she could get all prettied up."

Ethan's face felt flush and warm, and his heart thumped at the thought of seeing Hayley. Then he noticed Irvin staring at him, his head tilted like a confused dog, and his face slowly turned pink to mimic Ethan's.

"Looks like Miss Hayley isn't the only one who's giddy. Don't worry. She'll be along shortly."

Minutes felt like hours while Ethan waited for her arrival. Finally, the study door swung open, and Ethan's heart skipped a beat as Hayley entered the room. Ethan recognized the white sundress with yellow flowers she was wearing from the day they met at the Santa Cruz Beach Boardwalk. Her golden hair was longer and wavier, but glistened as if the sun shone into the study. Her penetrating bluish-green eyes met Ethan's gaze as she ran across the room. He opened his arms, and she softly fell into them and wrapped hers around him. They hugged for at least a minute before anyone spoke.

Irvin stood quietly watching but then broke the silence.

"I don't understand the hugging thing – but it sure seems all the rage these days."

Irvin wisely decided to give Ethan and Hayley their privacy and left to continue his daily chores.

"I've missed you," Hayley said. "We've all missed you."

"I missed you too. I've thought about you every day since I left – and I've been away almost a year."

"We have so much to catch up on. A lot has happened around here," Hayley said. "Come, we can talk along the way. My mother has summoned us to the Map Room."

They turned towards the exit when Ethan noticed something different about the study.

"The out-door is missing."

"Yeah, it disappeared after you unlocked the door to the portals. We're not sure why, but my brother Damien has a theory. The idea is the lock on the portal plane was causing the duality, and when you unlocked it, the door reverted to normal."

Hayley escorted Ethan out of the study and into The Hall of Doorways. They held hands and slowly walked the hallway under the eerie glow of the light beetle that crawled with them on the ceiling above.

"Wait, I need to get something off my chest," Hayley said as she stopped and faced Ethan. "I haven't had a friend to confide in since you left."

"What's wrong?"

"My mother – she's overly protective and won't let me go anywhere or do anything she deems dangerous."

"Well, she did lose you for a long time. Her reaction is normal for a parent who searched for their daughter for a century."

"Of course, you're right. But when it comes to me, Mother deems everything dangerous – yet I'm ready to start Caretaker training soon."

"Be patient. She'll come around and see things your way eventually."

"You are always able to make me feel better," Hayley said with a smile.

"You do the same for me. I think that's part of our destiny."

Hayley's smile widened, and her cheeks grew rosier.

"While we're getting things off our chest," Ethan said and paused. "I have something that's been bothering me for nearly a year."

"What is it?" Hayley asked.

"Everyone here makes such a big deal out of me being the Hybrid Child. But nobody ever stopped to explain what that means. What the heck is a Hybrid Child, and what's so special about it?"

"I—I don't really know either," Hayley replied. "I always assumed it meant you were half-human half-Caretaker."

"That's what I thought too—at first. But now I'm not so sure. Something tells me there's more to it than that."

"Well, I say we work together and do whatever it takes to find out."

"I was hoping you'd say something like that."

Ethan smiled, glanced down, and noticed the black infinity-shaped ring on Hayley's hand.

"I see you're still wearing the rift-key," he said. "I knew you'd get it back when I saw the look on your face after he stole it from you."

She held out her hand, looked at the ring on her finger, and smiled.

"It hasn't spoken to me since the incident. But that's okay. It's sentimental to me for other reasons."

Hayley grabbed Ethan's hand, and they started back down the hallway.

"So, what else is new?" Ethan asked.

"Well, I am getting some of my memories back."

They walked towards their destination slowly, made small talk, and enjoyed one another's company. They felt like no time had passed since their last time together, and their bond was more vital than ever.

They entered the Map Room and strode over the invisible floor at the midsection of the spherical room. They heard Damien and Jordanna talking as they reached the stairway's base to the crow's nest at the room's center.

"The Grimleavers are honing their craft," Damien said. "They've learned to reanimate dead humans and stone statues."

"If we are to believe the reports," Jordanna said. "They sound far-fetched, even for Victor Qruefeldt."

Ethan and Hayley stepped onto the crow's nest, causing the platform's floor to appear. Jordanna and Damien were sitting in captain's chairs at its center.

"You can believe them," Ethan said, "I witnessed them myself. Reanimated stone gargoyles flew into buildings to shatter windows over the crowded sidewalks – and masses of zombies walked the streets. That's when I ran."

"Ethan, my dear," Jordanna said. "I'm so happy you've come to visit us again."

"Yes, but too bad your visit has come under such dire circumstances," said Damien.

"But that's not all," Ethan continued. "Victor Qruefeldt was there. I felt his presence and was able to communicate with him. It was like some sort of telepathy. I could hear his thoughts, and he could hear mine."

"Has anything like that ever happened before?" Damien asked.

"Kind of, last time I was here," Ethan replied. "But that was nothing like this; this time we were able to talk like we were right next to one another."

"Interesting," Damien said. "I suspect your connection has been there all along. Likely a result of your very first encounter."

"What did Victor say to you?" Jordanna asked.

"Nothing of substance. He was taunting me and told me to stick around for the encore. That's when the zombies showed up, and I bolted."

"Anything else you can tell us?" Jordanna pressed.

"Yes, I saw her," Ethan said. "The woman in black from my dreams. She warned me about a swarm of miniature black dragons stalking me, and when they attacked, she saved me from being fried by their energy blasts."

"He's using the pixie-devils," Damien said.

"Pixie-devils?" asked Ethan.

"Yes, Victor's latest victims were devolved from Tinx's relatives."

"More importantly," Jordanna said to Damien. "The painting that arrived in the Gallery after Ethan's departure has come to pass."

"Indeed, it has," Damien replied.

"The dark spirit woman you encountered," Jordanna said. "You've seen her in your dreams?"

"Yes, I've had the same dream many times since I was last here," Ethan replied.

"Can you describe it?" Jordanna asked.

"I'm in a giant room. It's pitch black, and I can't see a thing until she appears in front of me. Her blue aura and glowing yellow eyes barely light the area around us. I'm not afraid; I feel comforted by her presence. We stare at each other, and she tries to speak, but I can't understand her. Suddenly, I'm able to see in the dark and can see all around us. We are alone in the room – but I feel someone watching.

Something evil is watching us, and I can tell she feels its presence too."

Ethan paused to catch his breath.

"Then what happens?" Damien asked impatiently.

"Then the dream ends and I wake up."

"The evil presence you feel, is it Victor Qruefeldt?" Jordanna asked.

"Before, I couldn't tell who it is," Ethan replied. "But now, after today's encounter, I'm sure it's him."

"Interesting," Damien said, and then the room grew quiet.

Jordanna and Damien exchanged glances and tensed up as if they were hiding something.

"Moving along," Jordanna said. "There is one more important matter to discuss. I must ask you something about your prior stay at The Residence."

"Okay, ask me anything."

"During your visit to Poseidon, Fin Drenchler asked you to stay behind after the briefing. Do you remember?"

"Sure."

"Do you remember your conversation with Fin?"

"Um, uh, not exactly," Ethan answered. "I remember shaking his webbed hand after everyone left. He reminded me of a blue *Creature from the Black Lagoon*, but not as scary. After that, my memory is fuzzy."

"That doesn't surprise me," Jordanna said.

She tapped at the screen of an iPhone-like device called an elemental modulator, or ELMO for short. A holographic window popped up like a theater screen hovering in midair.

"Maybe this will jog your memories," she said as a video of the meeting played.

Fin approached Ethan slowly and asked him to retrieve his pocket tote. Ethan handed the tiny pouch to Fin, who studied the symbols written on the outside. Fin handed it back to Ethan but grabbed his wrist and turned his hand to look at his palm. The symbols on Ethan's palms glowed yellow as he fell into a trance. His eyes glowed yellow too and opened full as he spoke to Fin just as the sound cut out and the recording ended.

"I—I don't remember any of that."

"It appears Fin suspected you were the Hybrid Child," Jordanna said. "But what you said to him remains a mystery."

"As does Fin's whereabouts," Damien said. "Fin Drenchler has gone missing."

"Missing," Ethan repeated.

"Yes, missing," Jordanna said. "Nothing to concern yourself with. We will find him. But if you do remember anything, please tell us immediately."

The long night of danger, chaos, and mystery exhausted Ethan. He was happy to visit his friends at The Residence – but he was also worried about what happened to his parents in the crowd. Damien and Jordanna reassured him George and Betsy were safe and the Caretakers were in control of the situation after the attack on Manhattan.

Hayley escorted Ethan down The Hall of Doorways to his room. She explained, she now had her own living quarters in Zen city, but would stay in her old room next to his while he was around.

Ethan entered his room and found it surprising to see it was identical to his room at home—even his most recent changes were reflected. Irvin made sure to leave Ethan his own ELMO device on his dresser as well. Exhausted, Ethan plopped down onto his bed; it transformed into a soft pillowy cloud, and he fell fast asleep.

Ethan strolled through a dark cave that grew darker as he ventured deeper. An eerie clicking sound echoed out of the blackness in front of him as a tingling sensation crawled down his back like tickling from an invisible hand. He opened his eyes and recognized the ceiling of his room – but the soft pillowy cloud he was on reminded him, he was at The Residence.

Ethan sat upright and stretched his arms over his head when he heard the sound again. The clicking noise from his dream was in his room, coming from under his bed. He moved to the edge and leaned over the side to peek beneath the floating cloud he was on. Two glowing yellow eyes met Ethan's and startled him—sending him crashing to the floor. He hurried onto his hands and knees and peered underneath the now regular-looking bed – but nothing was there.

"Click, click, click," the noise started again – but this time the sound came from above his head and behind him. He glanced up at his dresser, where a small creature stood next to his ELMO device, staring down at him. The critter was nearly eight inches tall with a deep-purple egg-shaped body covered with spikey fur. It had long thin ostrich-like legs, and curving horns that spiraled up behind its bulging yellow eyes at the top of its head. Its body was nearly all mouth, and four tentacle arms covered with hooks protruded from the sides.

"Click, click, click," the sound came from a sizable black insect the creature had trapped in one of its tentacles. The creature's mouth widened into a smile, exposing sharp shark-like teeth as it sprawled open to gobble down the insect in a cacophony of crunches.

Ethan sat frozen on the floor as he and the creature stared at one another for what seemed an eternity. His ELMO rang, startling the tiny monster into hopping off the dresser and landing on the floor by the door. The creature flattened out like a pancake and slid underneath, escaping into The Hall of Doorways.

Ethan quickly jumped to his feet and answered his ELMO. It was Hayley.

"Meet me in The Hall of Doorways, and hurry," he said as he gave chase. He entered the hallway and spotted the creature disappearing into the blackness to his left. Realizing the futility of pursuit, he waited for Hayley to emerge from her room.

"What's with all the excitement?"

"There was a monster in my room under my bed."

"A monster under your bed," Hayley repeated as she crinkled her forehead and furrowed her brows.

"I know it sounds crazy, but this isn't the first one I've seen. When I arrived, there was one in the front room – but that one was a different kind."

"Well, we did have a Ravisher infestation in the Moongarden. But I'm not aware of any monsters lurking around The Residence."

"Come on," Ethan said and started towards the Map Room. "We can tell your mom about them too."

Hayley stopped and gave him a questioning look.

"I need to speak with her anyway," he said. "I remembered an important detail about the dark spirit woman."

"Okay, we'll go speak with her, but please don't tell her about the monsters. She'll never let me near you if she thinks monsters are following you."

"Deal," Ethan said with a smile.

They entered the Map Room and immediately overheard Jordanna and Damien talking like they had never left.

"We control the portal plane," Damien said. "The Grimleavers have limited access to the human world—limiting their attack and retreat options."

"I agree – but we must stay focused and continue searching for the portal prophecies."

They stepped onto the crow's nest platform, and Damien spun around in his chair to greet them.

"Back so soon—"

The Map Room came to life, and its alarm cut him off.

"Incoming transmission, Headmistress," the room said, "I have confirmed the message as level one."

"Onscreen," Jordanna said, and a full holographic screen popped up.

A tall, robed man with angelic wings and vampire teeth stood next to a blue-skinned woman with a snake's body and bright green hair that was alive. Ethan recognized them as Nicholas and Brianna.

"What have you found?" Jordanna asked.

"We've uncovered a base of operations," Nicholas said. "A warehouse in the meatpacking district in New York City. They've cleared out the last of the vampires and other Grimleaver soldiers. But we have found another victim, Boris Wentworth – and he's alive."

"The Grimleavers were holding him captive as Bella had feared," Brianna added.

"What is his prognosis?" Jordanna asked.

"He's weak and malnourished," Brianna said. "But we expect he will make a full recovery."

"That's strange," Damien said. "Why would they take him to the human world and hold him in a warehouse?"

"I agree," Nicholas replied. "There is no rhyme or reason to it."

"Regardless, this is great news," Jordanna said. "Wrap things up and return to The Residence. We will inform Bella of the good news."

"There's one more thing to report," Nicholas said. "We hear chatter of Grimleaver activity in other cities around the globe. The humans have only reported minor disturbances thus far, but they may be planning more attacks."

"Send all updates to the Map Room as they come in," Damien said. "We will monitor the activity in real-time from here."

"Good work," Jordanna said.

The screen disappeared, and the spherical room lit up into a giant globe of Earth with them sitting inside at its center. Yellow blips of light began popping up in random cities on the map surrounding them.

"Well, there you have it," Damien said. "He orchestrates an attack on Ethan's birthday – and now we uncover a secret lair in the human world. As I've been saying, Victor Qruefeldt is planning something."

He pulled a yellow journal from his half-black half-white robe and studied its pages. Ethan recognized Stravis' journal from his previous visit. As he had learned, Earth was created by four Creators from the elemental worlds, and Stravis was the Creator from the yellow world of Zephyr.

"Agreed," Jordanna said, "but your obsession with the journal is becoming a distraction."

"I've been studying it, Mother, and I think I've deciphered some of Stravis' encoded entries."

"The Grimleavers are spreading us thin as things now stand. We can't afford your continued focus on that book."

"But Stravis' journal is not just a book, Mother. It is the writings of a Creator, and we can learn a lot from such a gift if we know what to look for and where to look."

"But that's my point, Damien. We do not have any idea where to look. So we will focus on what is real—the Grimleavers have infiltrated the human world and are attacking humans."

"I won't drop this, Mother. We thought it crazy for Victor to have wanted the portals open—yet he did. The whole notion is crazy unless he had help on the other side. And if I'm right, we will need all the help we can get."

"You are stubborn like your father," Jordanna said as a proud smile slipped onto her lips. "All right, I will indulge you this once—what have you learned?"

"Stravis wanted to protect this information, he encoded some of his entries, and I think I've cracked the code on some of these markings. I believe they are timestamps, and some of them are dated after the Creators locked the portals."

"Interesting," Jordanna said. "That would suggest Stravis stayed behind when the other Creators returned home. But we were already told that by the Council of Elders, so you have learned nothing new."

"Yes," said Damien. "But don't you find it odd that nobody has bothered to question why? Why would Stravis stay behind? We know he is strongly connected to the Seers and helped them save the Hybrid Child."

Jordanna, Damien, and Hayley all turned their gaze toward Ethan.

"I believe some of these encoded entries are about Stravis' dealings with the Seers. I believe he stayed behind to help them – and I think he lived in his desert bunker to serve them."

The room fell silent, so Ethan blurted out what was forefront on his mind.

"Can somebody please explain to me what a Hybrid Child is?"

Jordanna turned towards Ethan and studied the intense look on his face as she pondered her answer.

"We don't know for certain," she said softly. "It is the term used in the writings and stories passed down through the ages. I suppose only the originators of those truths know for certain."

"Great, so in other words, I need to ask the Seers," Ethan said.

"What we know for certain is the Hybrid Child is special," Jordanna continued, "and plays an important role in what is to come. The survival of Earth and the elemental worlds depends on it—depends on you."

"Yet another reason to study Stravis' writings more thoroughly," Damien said. "The answers could be right here in this journal."

"What became of Stravis' bunker?" Ethan asked.

"Humans discovered it," Jordanna said. "They unearthed the bunker and made off with most of its treasures. We may never have found out if not for an unfortunate accident."

"What happened?" Hayley asked.

"A young woman stumbled upon a box. She opened it and found something dangerous inside."

"Pandora," Hayley said. "She found a petrified wood berry."

"Yes," said Jordanna.

"What happened after that?" Ethan asked.

"We sent in a team. Alexander Sturgis cleaned up the mess and ensured no humans would discover it again."

"Alexander Sturgis—" Ethan repeated the name of his birth father.

"Yes," Jordanna said. "Your mother was present as well. Alexander took Tiffany on that mission, and you were born."

Ethan's face felt flush, and he grew antsy. He had tried to avoid thinking about it for George and Betsy's sake. But the mere mention of his birth parents caused a flood of emotions to rush through his mind.

"They might have missed something," Ethan said. "We should go to the bunker and have a look."

"Alexander is the best we have," Jordanna said. "He missed nothing."

"I agree with Ethan," Damien said. "I'd like to examine Stravis' bunker for myself."

"Have you forgotten what we learned during Ethan's last visit?" Jordanna asked. "The portal prophecies are out there somewhere and finding them must be our priority. We cannot afford to lose sight of that."

"But Mother—"

"I forbid you to return to the bunker!" Jordanna commanded. "I have entertained this nonsense for long enough. We have real Grimleaver problems to deal with — and we must find the portal prophecies before it's too late."

The room fell into an uncomfortable silence. Ethan's mind became distracted, so he and Hayley left without discussing what he had remembered. He returned to his room to sulk and ponder his next steps. Hayley's attempts to cheer him up fell on deaf ears, but she understood. He still didn't have the answers he was seeking. Between that, his concern for George and Betsy, thoughts of his birth parents, not to mention his strange encounter with Fin – it consumed his thoughts.

The sound of singing outside his door awoke Ethan from his thoughts.

"Hotdogs, armored hotdogs, what kind of kids eat armored hotdogs," Irvin sang out loud.

Ethan opened the door to witness the spectacle that was Irvin McGillicutty.

"Fat kids, bratty kids, kids with dirty socks. Dumb kids, smelly kids, even kids in cuckoo clocks."

Ethan roared with laughter at the sight of Irvin, who had morphed into a giant hotdog with arms and legs and a smiling face. He was there to cheer Ethan up on Miss Hayley's orders.

"Shnickyrooners," Ethan said.

"Shnickyrooners, and shnackleboxes, and things like that," Irvin said.

"Thank you, Irvin. I needed a good laugh."

"I've been meaning to stop by," Irvin said as he morphed back into his pastie-white self. "I've brought Master Ethan a gift – like the ones on TV." Irvin rummaged through his pocket tote and pulled out a bright orange toy gun.

"A water pistol. Thank you, Irvin. I haven't seen one of these in forever."

"Irvin modified this one himself. Added a hydro-generator so you won't run out of water as quickly as the human ones."

Ethan pointed the toy pistol into the darkness and pulled the trigger. Water squirted out like a kid's water gun.

"Cool," Ethan said, trying to sound convincing.

"That's nothing," Irvin said with a proud grin. "That was on the lowest setting. The knob on the side adjusts the power, and you could put out an inferno with the highest setting."

"Well, I—"

"No need to drone on thanking me. Sorry, but I must run along, Master Ethan—toodles."

Ethan started back towards his room but stopped and knocked on Hayley's door instead.

"Was he able to cheer you up, I hope?" she asked as the door swung open.

"A little," Ethan said. "I'm still worried about my parents, even after all of the reassurances—"

"I understand why you'd feel that way," Hayley said. "Last you saw of them; they were in danger. But I can assure you if my mother says they're safe, they are safe—trust me."

"Yeah, you're right, I guess," Ethan said. "My mind is racing on overdrive after our last discussion with your mom and brother."

"I'll say," Hayley replied. "You even forgot to tell them whatever you went to tell them in the first place."

"Oh yeah, I guess I did," Ethan said. "It wasn't anything major. I just forgot to tell them about the golden necklace the black spirit woman wore. It held a large swirly eye-shaped pendant that glistened against her chest."

"Yeah, that doesn't sound like anything major to me either."

Ethan stared at the ground and grew quiet again.

"Okay, out with it," Hayley said. "What else is bothering you?"

"It's just—seeing that video of my encounter with Fin— it makes me wonder. Maybe something I said led to his disappearance. I don't remember anything – but seeing myself fall into a trance like that makes me feel somehow responsible."

"Well, you shouldn't—"

"Hear me out," he said. "I have no idea where to start, but I need to do something. Somehow, Fin suspected I was the Hybrid Child before anyone else did. And now I learn that Stravis stayed behind on Earth, maybe to help the Seers. I can't shake the feeling that my past is also a part of it."

"Yeah," Hayley said and nodded.

"We know I'm connected to the Seers."

"And?"

"And I was born at Stravis' bunker. That's where everything started for me."

"Are you saying what I think you're saying?"

"If Jordanna isn't going to let Damien investigate the bunker, I will."

Hayley's cheeks bunched into a broad smile.

"I was hoping you would say that. I'm tired of being overly protected. I'm ready for some adventure."

"Really?"

"You didn't think I'd let you go alone," she said. "But how do we find Stravis' bunker?"

"I don't know, but I know who might."

CHAPTER TWO

"Wordly Pagemore," Hayley said.

"Wordly Pagemore," said Ethan.

STRAVIS' BUNKER

After agreeing on a plan of action, all they needed to do was find Wordly Pagemore's whereabouts. Hayley pulled out her ELMO and tapped on the screen. A list popped up with the names and locations of all inhabitants currently at The Residence.

"He's at the archive," Hayley said.

They hurried down The Hall of Doorways and entered a dimly lit warehouse that reminded Ethan of a Home Depot with the lights out. The ceilings were twice as tall as any he'd ever seen, and rows of giant racks lined the floor as far as his eyes could see.

"He's probably in there," Hayley said and pointed to a small office.

"What is this place?"

"A storage facility, where we archive all Caretaker art and literature. The study contains only a small sample of Caretaker literature, chosen by Wordly, of course."

They entered the well-lit office where Wordly stood on a desk under a reading lamp. He was studying a ledger as the pages magically turned by themselves.

"And the art, where does that come from?" Ethan asked.

"The Gallery," Wordly said. "The archive houses all pieces rejected by the Fates. At least that is how things are supposed to work."

Ethan recalled seeing the three old hags in the Gallery on his previous visit. It was the Fates job to use their clairvoyance to determine a painting's significance.

"Hi, Wordly," Ethan and Hayley said in unison.

"How may I be of assistance?"

"Well—"

"I'm studying for Caretaker training," Hayley said, cutting Ethan off. "And one of the questions asks about traveling to Stravis' bunker."

"Interesting, I write the Caretaker training questions and I do not recall writing that one."

"Well—I—um—"

"No need to explain," Wordly interrupted. "I was a rebellious teenager once."

"So, how might someone travel to Stravis' bunker?" Ethan asked.

"You could have just asked that in the first place," Wordly said and smiled.

"Well, how would we?" Hayley asked.

"One would first book-travel to *Sand Miser Dunes*. From there, one must inquire at the nearby shantytown. But beware, as that town is home to thieves and criminals looking to hide from civilization."

"What would one inquire about?"

"One would seek out KaaFoo, a one-armed desert nomad who wears a patch over his eye. KaaFoo will decide if the traveler is worthy of continuing the path."

"Thank you, Wordly," Ethan said.

"Yeah, thanks for the information," Hayley said and then paused. "You—you're not going to tell my mother about this—are you?"

"No. I couldn't even if I wanted to," Wordly replied. "As the resident bookworm, my directive is to disseminate information, no questions asked."

"Really?"

"Yes, really. You are protected by worm-client privilege, and the Headmistress would never ask me to break that trust."

They started to head out of the office when Ethan spotted something on a shelf behind the desk.

"That looks familiar," Ethan said and pointed at a wooden box with cut vines protruding from it.

"Is that—"

"That is Pandora's box," said Wordly.

"The petrified woman in the Moongarden was holding that," Ethan said.

"I remember," Hayley said, "when I nearly shared her fate."

"Yes," Wordly said, "and now we know why. Someone enchanted the box to eject petrified wood berries. We discovered its secret recently – so Mildred had it sealed and moved here for safety."

"What happened?" Ethan asked.

"After a recent infestation, Mildred found a petrified Ravisher in the Moongarden."

"Why would someone enchant a wooden box?" Ethan asked.

"One can only surmise, but Mildred has her suspicions."

"Sure would have saved Grubner a lot of headaches," Hayley said. "If he knew petrified wood berries worked against Ravishers."

"Grubner?" Ethan asked.

"You haven't met him yet," Hayley replied. "Grubner is a dwarf who works in the Moongarden. He's become Mrs. Moongarden's right hand man."

Ethan and Hayley dashed to the study so they could book-travel to *Sand Miser Dunes*. Caretakers often used book-travel to teleport to the many hidden realms scattered throughout the human world. Doing so required the use of special portal books found on a specific shelf in the study. They hurried to the shelf of brown books with golden letters on the cover and perused the titles. Ethan ran his hands over the books on the shelf to his left, pulling some out and looking at them, and then re-shelving them. He searched through more books, faster and faster.

"The book is missing," Ethan said as he frantically scanned the shelf a third time. "We must find it; I need to see where it all started for me."

"Must be here somewhere. I remember seeing the title before," said Hayley.

"Is this what you're looking for?" A petite girlish voice said from somewhere in the room.

Sand Miser Dunes

Ethan scanned the room and saw nothing, but then a tiny, winged dragon fluttered down from atop the bookshelf above their heads. She carried a brown book in her claws and set it down gently on the reading table at the other end of the room.

"Planning a trip, are we?" she asked.

"Tinx, what are you doing here?" Hayley asked.

"Rebelling against an over-protective headmistress," said Tinx. "Does that ring a bell?"

Tinx was a winged pixie-dragon with peach and white swirled lizard skin.

"I remember you," Ethan said. "From the Deadwood Saloon, you served us sugar-pickle soda."

"Likewise," Tinx said as she smiled and bowed to Ethan.

"I don't understand," Hayley said. "You're a CAGE member now. Why would you rebel?"

CAGE was short for Caretaker Anti-Grimleaver Enforcement. A special group of Caretakers focused on fighting against Victor Qruefeldt and his army of evil Grimleavers.

"Yeah, the newest CAGE member due to the atrocities committed against my family. But according to the

Headmistress, I am too small and delicate for the dangers of fieldwork."

"Oh, I understand now," Hayley said.

"After what they did to my family, I can't sit around and do nothing. So, I'm going with you."

"I understand too," Ethan said. "I had a dangerous encounter with the pixie-devils, I've seen what they turned your loved ones into."

"When I learned of your return—when I heard Ethan Fox was back at The Residence—I knew it was only a matter of time before the two of you would be seeking answers. So, when Damien asked me to keep an eye on you, I followed you and listened to your conversation with Wordly. Being small does have some advantages."

"My brother is keeping tabs on us?"

"Yeah, he wanted me to let him know the moment you showed up in the study and book-traveled."

"And are you going to tell him?"

"Of course not. I'm going with you."

Ethan and Hayley gazed at one another and nodded in agreement.

"Well then," Ethan said, "let's get a move on!"

Tinx stood atop Ethan's shoulder as he and Hayley joined hands and fumbled with the brown book to flip its cover open. They stared into its pages as a blinding bright light sent them spiraling into darkness.

They awoke in a field of small, perfectly round dunes of sand. Ethan stood up and scanned the horizon. He spotted a small town in the distance, so they set off on foot. Nearly an hour later, they reached the small village of canvas tents and wooden shacks thatched together for shelter.

They stopped at the edge of town before entering. It reminded Ethan of an old western movie as they started down the street while the town's people eyeballed them intently. They walked into the heart of town – and an unruly-looking gang of locals immediately greeted them. They were tall with tattered brown clothing, whiskered faces, and missing teeth.

"Y'all are not welcome here," the group's leader said.

"We don't want any trouble," Ethan said.

"We are looking for somebody," Hayley added.

"Nice ring," one said and pointed at Hayley's infinity ring.

"We'll be taking that," another said.

"We'll be taking everything," the leader said.

"You're not taking anything from anybody," Ethan said and stepped in front of Hayley to shield her.

Ethan squinted at the bright sun behind the strangers, but a shadow abruptly moved in like a giant raincloud. He gazed up and smiled at the one-eyed giant he recognized standing behind the gang of robbers. Damien stepped in front of Ethan and faced the strangers.

"As the boy said, you'll not be taking anything. Is that understood?"

The gang of thugs turned and peered up at Azron, blocking out the sun behind them. Azron was a one-eyed giant that stood at least twelve feet tall, a member of the soleyed dwarf-giant species. He and Damien were fellow

CAGE members. The thugs turned back to Damien, who stood smirking with his arms folded. His long half-black half-white Caretaker robe presented a look of authority.

"We meant no harm," one said.

"We were only joking," the leader said. "We'll be going now."

The thieves slowly backed away from Damien and Azron, then turned and ran like scared mice.

"Azron, am I glad to see you," Ethan said.

"Robbers no like Ethan Fox. Har, harr, harrr," Azron roared as he gently patted Ethan on the head.

"You were foolish to come here alone," Damien scolded them and then turned to Tinx. "And what have you got to say for yourself?"

"I came along because I'm fed up with being overly protected. I wanted to be a part of something real."

"How did you know we'd come?" Hayley asked.

"I learned from watching you two. When you get together, you don't take no for an answer. So, when Mother forbid us from visiting the bunker, the look on your faces told me all I needed to know."

"That's why you told Tinx to spy on us," Hayley said. "You wanted us to come."

"Well," Damien said with a smirk, "since you two were so foolish to make the trip. I had to come after you. But who's to say you didn't make the journey to Stravis' bunker before we could stop you."

"Who's to say," Hayley agreed and smiled at her brother. "We need to find KaaFoo."

"Follow me," Damien said.

He led them to a brown tent near the end of town and disappeared inside. He emerged with a one-armed man with an eye patch several minutes later. The man handed Damien a small disc-shaped object and pointed behind his tent.

Damien walked into the desert and waved for them to follow. He continued for several hundred feet, stopped, and threw the disc onto the desert sand.

"Our ride will be along shortly," he said.

Moments later, the ground trembled, and Ethan saw a significant disturbance in the sand moving towards them.

"What is that?"

"A giant sand slug, if I'm not mistaken," Hayley said.

"Correct, sis, you've been studying."

The disturbance slowed and drew closer, and the ground calmed as the oblong pile of sand came to rest directly in front of them. The mound grew taller, and the desert poured off the sand slug exposing brown armored scales along its back and sides. The front half of the giant slug held seats saddled into position behind two long antenna-like eyes protruding from its head.

"What about Azron?" Ethan asked. "That's not big enough to carry him."

"Don't worry about Azron," Damien said. "He grew up on Hades and is well adapted for traversing the desert."

"Azron hell-walker," Azron said and thumped his chest.

Damien made sure Ethan and Hayley were adequately seated before seating himself. The sand slug jolted into motion and sailed along the surface of the sand like a jet boat.

Tinx darted around like a playful hummingbird searching for nectar. Azron stood in place to let the rest of the party get a head start.

"What's he doing?" Ethan asked, staring back at Azron as he disappeared into the distance.

"He'll be along shortly," Damien said with a grin.

Azron squatted down and launched skyward like the Hulk. He flew several hundred feet into the sky before falling and landing gently back on the desert surface. Azron continued Hulk-vaulting his way across the desert landscape and caught up with them quickly.

"Look," Hayley said and pointed up at the horizon to an enormous dune.

"What is that?"

"That is the great vanishing dune," Damien said.

"I read about that somewhere," Hayley said. "If you approach close enough, the dune disappears. Some say a desert mirage is the cause; others say the dune is real but protected by the desert harpies."

Ethan's palm symbols suddenly distracted him. They were glowing white and pointing at the giant mountain of sand. His eyes moved back and forth between his hands and the dune as he watched his symbols follow the mirage across the horizon. But then he nearly slipped off the sand slug.

"Whoa there," Damien said as he quickly grabbed Ethan by the arm to stop his fall.

"Are you okay?" Hayley asked. "We almost lost you."

"I—I'm okay." Ethan peeked down at his palms, but they were no longer glowing.

"Here we are," Damien said after nearly an hour of uneventful dune-surfing.

The sand slug stopped to let them off. Tinx landed on Ethan's knee while Azron gently sat on nearby sand. Damien hopped off and pulled out his ELMO device. He tapped the screen and spun around in circles to scan the area. A black metallic pole poked up from beneath the sand and stopped at six feet tall but then shortened and grew into a widening rectangle that repelled the sand. The rectangle continued to shorten and grow until disappearing into the sand and exposing a sizable hatch hidden beneath the desert.

"I could use a hand with this," Damien said to Azron.

Azron approached the bunker door, and Ethan immediately realized he would not be joining them inside. The generous handle appeared small in his hands as he lifted the heavy iron hatch, exposing a dark stairwell into the sand.

"Remind you of anything?" Hayley asked Ethan with a deep grin.

"Hang tight. We won't be long," Damien said to Azron.

"It's getting hot out here," Ethan said. "Will he be okay in this heat?"

"Har, harr, harrr," Azron roared. "Azron from Hades, this desert cold like ice—Har, harr, harrr."

Tinx rode on Ethan's shoulder as he and Hayley followed Damien down the dark staircase. Damien tapped at his ELMO as they reached the bottom, and light shone on the dusty dingy cavern they were now in.

"Doesn't look like much," Damien said.

The room was mostly empty but for an old wooden table and benches. Ethan spotted a small object lying beneath one of the benches.

"What's that?" Tinx jumped onto the table as Ethan bent down to pick up the miniature capsule.

"Be careful, Ethan," Hayley said. "Remember what happened to Pandora."

"Let me see that," Damien said, and Ethan handed it to him.

"This proves Fin Drenchler has been here."

"What is that?" Ethan asked.

"A hydration capsule," said Damien. "Used by hydromorphs when they are away from water for extended periods."

"Why would Fin come here?" Tinx asked.

"Good question," Hayley said. "This is the last place I would expect Fin to go."

Hayley's attention moved to the back of the room, where she spotted something.

"What's that on the wall?"

Damien and Ethan followed Hayley to the jagged rock wall at the back of the cavern. She pointed at a flattened-out area where someone engraved a hand-sized symbol into the rock.

"Interesting," Damien said as he examined the engraving.

Ethan's hands tingled again, so he stepped away from Damien and Hayley to take a peek. His palm symbols were glowing faintly and pointing towards the staircase. Ethan walked to the base of the stairs and glanced up into the bright light of day. A three foot tall blue bunny-like creature with yellow polka dots was standing atop the staircase, waving at him—it was Jasper.

"I—I'm gonna check on Azron," said Ethan and started up the stairs.

Ethan reached the top of the stairs and followed Jasper right past Azron, sitting in the sand. Azron's eye followed Ethan as he continued into the desert – but then he stood and followed quietly to ensure the Hybrid Child's safety.

Jasper continued into the desert for several hundred feet but then stopped and turned to face Ethan.

"They want you to have it back, Ethan Fox," Jasper said in a cartoonish voice. "The Hybrid Child's journey has only just begun."

Ethan was suddenly walking in the middle of a cold, fierce sandstorm. He squinted his eyes as he struggled to move forward but felt compelled to continue as if he was searching for something vital.

Azron stood behind Ethan and watched him stand as if alone in the warm sunny desert. Then Ethan threw his arms up to shield his eyes and slowly stumbled forward. He stopped abruptly, dropped his arms, and spun around to scan his surroundings.

"Ethan Fox feel okay?" Azron asked.

"That sandstorm, you didn't experience it?"

"Azron, no see phantom storm."

"And Jasper? I suppose Jasper wasn't here either."

"Azron, no see Jasper."

"Yeah, I didn't think so," Ethan said, sounding defeated. His head drooped as he looked to the ground and spotted a brown book with shimmering golden symbols on the cover. It lay in the sand between his feet – so he knelt to pick it up. His spirits lifted.

"What about this?" He asked as he held up the book.

"Azron, see book."

"Jasper said they wanted me to have it back."

"Seers speak to Ethan Fox," Azron said.

Ethan and Azron headed back towards the bunker – but along the way, a strange feeling overcame Ethan as the sky dimmed and storm clouds formed overhead. Azron stopped to gaze up at the previously blue sky, and that's when it happened. The black form of a woman appeared from out of nowhere. She was less than twenty feet away, and her shiny black sheen, and golden pendant necklace glimmered in what was left of the desert sun. The sky quickly darkened as the clouds continued to grow. The woman's eyes glowed bright yellow as she motioned at them and pointed into the desert behind them.

"Do you see her?" Ethan asked Azron as he pointed at the black apparition outlined by a blue aura.

"Azron see shadow spirit."

"She saved me before," Ethan said. "I think she's warning us about something."

Ethan spun around to see where she was pointing, and Azron did the same. They saw a significant disturbance dredging up the sand as it moved towards them. It was still far away but approaching quickly.

"Whatever that is," Ethan said, "it's heading this way, and I doubt it's a welcoming committee. We need to warn the others."

Ethan turned to thank the dark spirit woman – but she was gone. He hurried back to the bunker while Azron stayed put and kept his eye on what was coming.

"I think we're all in danger," he yelled into the bunker. Damien, Hayley, and Tinx emerged quickly to witness the commotion.

"Ethan, your symbols, what is happening to them?" Hayley asked.

Ethan glanced down at the symbols on his palms. They had come to life like a cartoon again. They were glowing red and spinning, but when he flattened them out, they stopped and pointed towards the approaching danger like compass needles.

"I don't know. They've been acting strange lately. But there's no time for this now. Danger is approaching." He turned and pointed out the disturbance in the sand. "I think a monsoon is coming."

"That's not a monsoon," Damien said. "It hugs the desert floor too closely."

"Desert harpies," Tinx said.

"But they never leave the vanishing dune," Hayley said.

"Well, they have now," said Damien.

He held up his ELMO and stared at the zoomed-in display of approaching harpies. The desert harpies were hag-faced sand creatures with mermaid bodies. They swam in and out of the dunes like porpoises over ocean waves. Their shapes merged in and out of the churning sand as if formed from the desert itself.

"Shelter," Azron said, pointing at the bunker. "Azron, take care of harpies."

"They're very dangerous," Tinx said. "They bury their victims in torrents of sand. He'll suffocate."

"Azron, be okay."

"We'll have to take that chance—good luck, old friend," Damien said and directed the others towards the bunker.

When the vast school of sand creatures arrived, they concentrated solely on Azron. They circled him and took turns jumping at his head, back, and torso, exploding into shards of glassy sand when they hit. Azron swatted many away with his giant mitt-like hands – but he was vastly outnumbered, and a wall of sand quickly grew around him.

"We've got to help him," Ethan said. "They must have a weak spot."

"Water," Tinx said. "They hate water."

Ethan glanced at Hayley, and his eyebrows arched high.

"Hayley, your copycat! Summon a hydrosphere ejector like you did at Deadwood."

"But I don't have my copycat, and Tabby Cat won't hear me call to her from inside a hidden realm."

The smile drained from Ethan's face, until he remembered something. He handed Hayley the poem book, reached into his pocket, and pulled out the toy water pistol Irvin had given him.

"I hope Irvin's modifications work."

Ethan spun the power dial and took off towards Azron, who was now buried to his neck in glassy sand. Ethan aimed the pistol at the swirling mass of churning desert near Azron's feet and pulled the trigger. A powerful jet of water erupted from the tiny barrel and nearly knocked him to the ground. But Hayley had followed him and arrived just in time to brace Ethan's back and help him stay upright. The small orange toy performed like a water cannon, dousing the harpies until they melted into a mud-like soup of water and sand. The wall of glassy sand melted away from Azron as the harpies wailed in pain, retreated, and disappeared into the surrounding desert.

"Arrrrrr," Azron groaned.

Shards of glass covered those parts of his arms and neck not protected by clothing. He tried to extract them with his giant fingers but was only poking them in deeper.

"Stop your whining," Tinx said as she flew over and gently landed on his shoulder. "Your giant sausage fingers aren't going to help."

Ethan and Hayley spent the next hour scouring Azron's arms and neck, looking for glass shards while Tinx removed them with her tweezer-like front teeth.

"Well, I hate to break up all the fun, but the time has come to return to The Residence," Damien said.

Azron stood and stared down at Ethan.

"Ethan Fox save Azron again," he said.

"You would have done the same for me. Besides, those harpies looked thirsty, didn't they?"

"Har, harr, harrr," Azron roared. "Harpies no like Ethan Fox—har, harr, harrr!"

"That was very brave of you," Damien said.

"That wasn't bravery. Tinx told me about their dislike of water."

"You didn't know if Irvin's modifications would even work – yet you still charged a swarm of harpies with what you only knew to be a harmless child's toy," Damien said. "I call that bravery."

Ethan turned to Hayley with a questioning look.

"Where is your copycat?"

"On a secret mission. I might tell you about it when you tell me where this came from?" Hayley held up the brown poem book for everyone to view.

"I saw Jasper again," Ethan said.

"So, your little friend came bearing gifts, did he?" Damien said.

"Yes."

"What did he say?" Hayley asked.

"He said my journey has only just begun."

"Well, that's an understatement," said Damien. "By the way, did any of you think to bring a portal beacon?"

Ethan, Hayley, and Tinx all shook their heads.

"That's very careless, you're lucky Azron and I were around—this time. Let this be a lesson to you all, the number one rule that all Caretakers must live by, when traveling the protected realms—or anywhere outside The Residence for that matter—always bring more than one portal beacon along. You never know how many you might need in a pinch."

Damien held open the right half of his Caretaker robe to display an array of small pockets stitched to the inside lining. He reached his hand inside a pocket, pulled out a small black cube, and tossed it to the desert floor. The portal beacon morphed into a crystal ball standing atop an upside-down glass cone that grew tall enough for them all to reach.

"I never go anywhere with less than three – but often carry more. Now then, let's get home."

CREATURES OF THE DARK REALM

Ethan's eyes squinted nearly shut in the bright sunless light of the portal plane. The eerie sight of endless checkerboard stretching in all directions under the clear blue sky was an oddity he cherished. They entered the front room of The Residence, and the sound of Gruggins' angry voice greeted them.

"Come back here, you rock-eating roaches," Gruggins shouted as he shook his fist in the air. He was standing at the edge of his table, looking at the ground, but nothing was there.

"What's wrong, Gruggins?" Hayley asked and ran to his side.

Gruggins gazed up at Hayley and the grumpy scowl on his face melted into a smile.

"Those dastardly Nibblewarts are interrupting my nap for the millionth time. They've been on the move lately, coming through in caravans, and they always stop to chant below my table."

"Nibblewarts believe grumplings symbolize good luck," Tinx said from her perch on Damien's shoulder. "Their chanting is a gesture of admiration and goodwill."

"Yeah, well, I'll give them some of my goodwill, all right," Gruggins said and shook his fist again. "Always droning on about the Shadow Princess—"

The beeping of Damien's ELMO cut Gruggins off.

"They are awaiting us in the study," Damien said. "And by the tone of her message, the Headmistress is unhappy."

Hayley, Damien, Tinx, and Azron turned towards the study – but something had grabbed Ethan's attention, and he stood listening to Gruggins' rant.

"The Shadow Princess has returned," Gruggins said as the others walked away.

"Ethan, are you coming?" Hayley asked. Ethan backed his way towards the study but kept his eyes on Gruggins.

"The Shadow Princess delivered us from evil, the Shadow Princess will lead the chosen one, Shadow Princess this, Shadow Princess that . . ."

Ethan reached the door to the study and turned towards the others.

"You can sit this one out," Damien said to Azron, "go take care of those wounds – and I'll cover for you."

Damien opened the door and led the way into the study. Ethan glanced at Gruggins as he stepped into the study.

"If I hear one more word about the Shadow Princess or the Nibblewart prophecies—"

The study door closed.

Jordanna sat behind the desk in the center of the back half of the room. Nicholas stood by her side with his expansive angelic wings on full display, protruding from under his white robe.

"What have you to say for yourself?" Jordanna said, glaring at Damien. "How can I expect others to trust in your leadership if I can't—"

"Damien didn't do anything. I did this, Mother!"

"But I've made it perfectly clear," Jordanna said. "You are not to—"

"Yes—you've made it perfectly clear you will treat me like a child – and I can no longer think for myself."

The room fell silent for several moments as Jordanna and her daughter exchanged glares.

"You've made your point," Jordanna said and turned to Damien. "Fill me in on the details."

"Well," Damien said and hesitated, "After our discussion in the Map Room, I suspected these two would venture to Stravis' bunker. I sent Tinx to keep an eye on them, but when she didn't report back, I learned she went along with them. That's when Azron and I went after them."

"Tinx, what have you got to say for yourself?"

Tinx jumped from her perch on Damien's shoulder and darted over to land on Hayley's.

"I insisted upon joining them because I needed to be a part of something real."

"But I've made you a CAGE member. You are a part of something. Why would you disobey?"

"My reasons are not unlike your daughter's. I'm sorry, Headmistress, but you've been overly protective of me because of my size."

The room fell silent again.

"Continue," Jordanna said to Damien.

"We caught up with them in the shantytown. After that, it was my decision that we continue to Stravis' bunker."

"Of course, you predicted your sister would be insubordinate," Jordanna said and smirked. "I bet you even counted on it – so don't think you've put one over on me."

"I'm sorry, Mother, such a lapse in judgment will not happen again."

"Moving along. What did you find?"

"We found this," Damien said as he showed her the hydration capsule.

"Interesting," Jordanna said. "But what would Fin be doing at Stravis' bunker of all places?"

"That's what I asked," Hayley said.

Jordanna glanced from Hayley to Ethan and the book in his hands.

"It appears the Seers took the opportunity to return their gift to you."

"Yes. Jasper appeared and led me through a phantom sandstorm where I found it buried in the sand at my feet."

"The Seers have reached out to you once again," she said and turned to Hayley. "And the Hybrid Child's exploits will undoubtedly include you. I understand I must come to terms with my motherly instincts."

Jordanna paused then continued.

"Anything else to report?"

"The desert harpies attacked us," said Tinx. "For some reason, they saw fit to leave the site of the vanishing dune and attack us."

"The Shadow Princess," Ethan said. "She appeared again, and this time Azron saw her too."

Hayley's eyebrows bunched as she shot Ethan a questioning look.

"She warned us that the harpies were coming."

"Interesting," Nicholas said. "We've still not received any reports of such a woman—inside or outside of the human world."

"Which brings us to other matters," Jordanna said. "Fill them in on Grimleaver activity."

"Reports are coming in from across the globe. Small random sightings are occurring with regularity. Thus far, they are nothing more than minor annoyances – but the humans have reported seeing vampires, zombies, and otherworldly creatures."

"It sounds like they are trying to spread us thin," Damien said.

"My thoughts exactly," said Nicholas. "They are trying to distract us from something."

"They are distracting us from searching for the prophecies, and they are doing a good job of that. We are spread thin, so I will not tolerate any more rogue missions like today's."

Damien nodded in agreement – but Ethan, Hayley, and Tinx were quiet.

"Might I suggest," Damien said, "we catalog the time and location of each and every event and search for a pattern. No matter how careful they've been, there is bound to be a pattern hidden in the chaos."

"Good thinking," Jordanna said. "Nicholas, task a team of scholars to start immediately."

Hayley asked Jordanna to excuse them from the remainder of the strategizing session – and she agreed. Tinx stayed behind, eager to learn more about what the Grimleavers were doing.

The day had been very long, and midnight was nearing, but neither Hayley nor Ethan had eaten – so they beelined down The Hall of Doorways to the Caretaker cafeteria. The room was dark and empty when they entered, but Hayley tapped at her ELMO and lit up the large white room.

"Irvin's not around to serve us," Hayley said. "But the wall pantry he had installed is always stocked with food."

Ethan scanned the room looking for a pantry and then gazed at Hayley with his eyebrows wrinkled.

"Follow me, and I'll show you," she said.

She walked past the kitchen to an empty area where no tables, chairs, or anything stood. There was only a tall, blank white wall.

"All you have to do," Hayley said, "is concentrate on what you're hungry for and put your hand on the wall like this."

She held her hand against the wall, and a rectangular section lit up around it. When she removed her hand, the lit up area opened like a hatch exposing an opening where a plate of hot spaghetti stood waiting.

"Reminds me of a replicator."

"A what?" Hayley asked.

"The wall pantry is like the replicator in *Star Trek*," he said.

"Star Trek?"

"Yeah," Ethan explained. "*Star Trek* is sort of a universe of its own. It started as an old TV series but has grown into movies, books, and more series."

He placed his hand against the wall, and moments later, his small pizza appeared—just the way he liked.

"Boy would George love to have one of these. Mom rarely lets us eat pizza at home—"

Ethan fell silent. He and Hayley adjourned to a table where they sat and quietly nibbled away at their midnight snacks.

"You seem distracted," Hayley said. "Is something still bothering you?"

"I just keep picturing them in my head," he replied. "My parents, surrounded by a frightened mob, being rushed down the street against their will. They were probably worried sick about me."

"Well, they know you're safe now," Hayley said.

"Yeah, I know – but I just can't shake the feeling."

"I understand," Hayley said. "Let me think about it. I may have an idea."

A meatball rolled off Hayley's plate and Ethan pulled a pizza slice away from his mouth creating a stringy bridge of cheese to stretch between them. They broke out in laughter – but it quickly subsided and silence filled the room as they each took another bite.

"Your mother seemed upset," Ethan said to change the subject. "She tried to hide it – but I could tell."

"Me too. I hate making her sad, but she's become suffocating – and when you came back, I knew it was time to take a stand."

"Yeah, well, you took a stand all right—"

"Why did you call her the Shadow Princess?" Hayley asked, cutting him off mid-sentence. "Before, you referred to her as the woman in black – but this time you called her the Shadow Princess."

"Did you hear what Gruggins was shouting about when we arrived in the front room?"

"Not really. My mind was wandering. I was more worried about what I would say to Mom."

"He was angry with the Nibblewarts," Ethan explained. "They keep disturbing his naps, and all they talk about lately is the return of the Shadow Princess."

"Yeah, so what," said Hayley. "The Nibblewarts are always blabbering about something. Nobody listens to them or takes anything they say seriously."

"A truth that falls upon deaf ears is true to no one," Ethan said.

"Where did you come up with that philosophical nugget?" Hayley asked.

"I—I don't know. It just popped into my head."

"Well, it is a good point. I never thought of it that way," Hayley replied. "The Nibblewarts could be telling us the meaning of life, and nobody would listen."

"Don't ask me how, but I'm sure they are talking about her. She is the Shadow Princess and has returned to lead us to something."

"Lead us to what?"

"I don't know," Ethan said. "But she's trying to tell me something."

"Well, Gruggins seems to hear a lot from the Nibblewarts," Hayley said. "Maybe we should talk to him about them."

"Great idea, we should—" the words froze in Ethan's mouth as he quietly pointed at something moving near the door to The Hall of Doorways.

A tiny insect-like creature squeezed in beneath the door and slowly grew bigger.

"Do you see that?" Ethan whispered.

"What is that? I've never seen anything like that."

"Act like we don't see it," Ethan said.

He and Hayley continued making small talk as they sneakily kept track of the creature out of the corner of their eyes. It was the size of a guinea pig and looked like a black scorpion covered with red lines in a shattered glass pattern. But this was no scorpion. Its head consisted of one giant yellow eye and two small nose slits. Two arm-like appendages grew from the sides of its head, each holding another eye that swiveled independently to scan the area. Instead of a stinger, this creature had a mouth at the end of its tail that reminded Ethan of *Predator*. The fangs clapped repeatedly as sharp finger-like bones outside its mouth bristled inward like inviting fingers.

"Is that what you've been seeing?" Hayley asked.

"That's the third one I've seen, but they've all been different."

"Have they all been this scary-looking?"

"Yeah, but they're not coming to harm me. The one under my bed even smiled at me before it chowed down on a big creepy bug."

Suddenly, the poem book came to life atop the cafeteria table and scared their little visitor away. It flipped open as wisps of golden whimsy wafted from the pages and turned to the first blank page. A poem wrote itself up the page backward. The passage read:

Creatures of the Dark Realm

They revel in the darkness, and hide from view of light.
As they slither, creep, and crawl, while staying out of sight.

Not all of them are evil, and some have earned free will.

They protect the Hybrid Child, from those who've come to kill.

Most Creatures of the Dark Realm were born of ill intent.

But some serve a different master, who's taught them to repent.

Ethan and Hayley read the poem over and over carefully and sat in silence for several minutes pondering the Seer's cryptic words.

"Creatures of the Dark Realm," Hayley repeated.

"Yes, it rings a bell with me too."

"I recall where we've seen something similar before," said Hayley. "The book in the study with your symbols, it was called *Secrets of the Dark Realm*."

"I remember, written by Dakota Drakelan. He lives in the scary old house on the hill outside Deadwood."

"Yeah, he has a reputation for being creepy. He was the master of dark studies when Grandpa Odin was the headmaster. We must pay him a visit," Hayley said.

"I agree," Ethan said. "The poem book wants us to learn about Creatures of the Dark Realm and he is our best place to start. But it's late, so we'll have to wait till morning."

"No, we'll go now," Hayley said. "Dakota Drakelan is a retired dark master. Everything I've read about dark masters says they are night people and normally sleep during the day."

"Even better."

They agreed, there was no time like the present, and they were both eager for answers. They pondered the poem in

silence as they finished their snacks and cleaned their plates—
then they were off.

They stood at the base of the hill and stared up at the
silhouette of the meager house against the blackish-blue
morning sky. Only the light of a half-moon shining from
behind the house lit the winding path leading to the front
porch. Ethan started up the narrow path, and Hayley
hesitantly followed closely behind him.

"This is creeping me out," she said.

"Nothing to be afraid of," Ethan said in as bold a tone as
he could muster. Truth be told, he was a little creeped out
too, but he continued up the hill anyway. As they drew closer,
Ethan saw a small dark blob run into the house through the
front door that was slightly ajar. Moments later, a curtain in
the front window moved.

"Do you see anything?" Hayley asked. She was walking
behind Ethan and held onto his belt loop to help guide her
way in the darkness.

"N-Not yet," Ethan fibbed.

Ethan stepped onto the porch and paused at the partially
open front door to muster his nerves. Hayley joined him and
stood at his side, staring into the black crevice leading into
the house.

"Are you sure?"

Ethan took one step forward and pushed at the door with
his hand. It creaked its way open, slowly exposing the total
blackness of the house's interior.

"Trick or treat," said Ethan. "Is anybody here?"

"Well, well, well," a deep gruff voice said from inside. "Guess I finally got yer attention. Come in, please."

Ethan stepped inside the dark house. A snapping sound clicked, and a series of candles lit themselves one by one around the room. Hayley stepped into the house and stood by Ethan's side. An older man with long grey hair, a goatee, and a bushy mustache sat in a recliner in the corner of the room. He grabbed a beat-up brown cowboy hat and placed it atop his head as he stood to greet them. He wore a long duster-style overcoat and a worn leather vest.

"Good thing too," he said. "I was fresh outta nice ones ta send."

"Are you Dakota Drakelan?" Ethan asked.

"The one and only—last I checked."

"Pleasure to meet you. I'm Ethan—"

"Yeah, yeah, I know who ya both are. Ethan Fox, the Hybrid Child, an yer the long lost Ravenwood kid."

"Well, you don't have to be rude," Hayley said. "Ethan was only being polite."

"You've got your mother's spirit," Dakota said.

But Hayley's attention was elsewhere as she looked around the room at the various oddities. In particular, she focused on the candles burning around the room. Only, they were not candles at all, and they were alive. Small stick creatures with the tops of their heads burning and their arms held up as small flames burned their hands. A look of horror reflected from their tiny faces as bullets of sweat poured down their sides, and they grimaced in pain.

"You're hurting them!" Hayley shouted at the top of her lungs.

"An yer grandmother's," Dakota said.

"Stop it, put them out now!" Hayley insisted.

"Alright, alright, calm down, was only for effect anyway."

Dakota smiled, snapped his fingers, and the burning candle creatures vanished. Various antique lamps around the room flickered on to replace the candlelight.

"Definitely a Ravenwood woman," Dakota said.

"Where did they go?" Hayley asked.

"Back to where I summoned 'em from," Dakota said. "And for your information, those little liars were not'n pain. They're fakin grief to feed off ur sympathy."

"I—I'm sorry," Hayley said.

"Well, that's a first," Dakota said and smiled at Hayley. "I'm told you're quite the promising student. If you read page 115 of my book, you'da learned about candle-grifters."

"Well, I—I'll be sure to put that on my reading list."

"About your book," Ethan said. "The one titled *Secrets of the Dark Realm.*"

"Yeah, what about it?"

"The symbols on the spine," Hayley said.

"Symbols?" Dakota questioned.

"Yes, Stravis' symbols," Ethan said and held up his palms. "Symbols that looked like this."

"Oh, that," Dakota said. "Met him once, made quite the impression."

"That's it?" Ethan asked.

"Yep."

"So, did you send the little monsters?" Hayley asked.

"They're not monsters. They're friends. We categorize many'a the world's creatures as monsters based on appearance alone. It's all'a matter of perception."

"Are you saying there are no monsters?" Hayley asked.

"Oh heavens no. There are monsters in this world as sure as the nose on ma face. But not all scary creatures are monsters. You can come out now—"

Dakota snapped his fingers, and three tiny creatures crept out from beneath a couch, miniature versions of the ones stalking Ethan. They grew as they crawled across the room, growing to about eight inches tall.

"Are they shape-shifters?" Hayley asked.

"Not exactly. I've taught 'em various dark techniques to help 'em help me."

The tiny critters stopped at Dakota's feet and turned to face Ethan and Hayley.

"Balder, Gilly, an Skronk," Dakota said as he pointed to them. "Meet Ethan an' Hayley."

Ethan and Hayley waved and said hello, and the creatures smiled and curtsied to acknowledge them.

"Are they from the Dark Realm?" Ethan asked.

"These ur the ones I rescued. But their kin are still in that god-forsaken place."

"What is the Dark Realm?" Hayley asked.

Dakota tensed up, and his demeanor immediately got serious.

"It—It's whur happiness goes ta die," he said, and the room fell silent.

"Why did you send them?" Hayley asked, breaking up the silence. "Why did you send your friends to capture Ethan's attention?"

"Because he's in danger. There'za dark presence at The Residence. Fact is, they been protecting ya since ya first arrived. That's how they caught all those."

Dakota pointed at a sizable, covered enclosure in the corner of the room. He motioned with his left hand, and the cover flew off, exposing a brightly lit aquarium. Inside, a hoard of at least twenty palm-sized black insects crept over one another. They were black beetle-like insects with protruding thorny legs and barbed appendages angling forward over their sharp giant mandibles.

"Those look like the creepy bug one of your friends ate," Ethan said.

"I told ya not to eat 'em," Dakota said to the creatures. "Okay, spill the beans. Which one a ya ate a death scarab?"

The creatures slowly shrunk smaller at the sound of Dakota's scolding, and then they each raised an arm or leg.

"Did you say death scarab?" Hayley asked.

"I'll deal with ya later," Dakota said to the creatures and turned back to Ethan and Hayley. "Yeah, someone's been releasin 'em in The Residence. Releasin 'em everywhere Ethan Fox goes from the looks'a things."

"I've read about death scarabs," Hayley said as her face paled, "a pinprick of their venom kills instantly."

"It does indeed," Dakota said. "We captured these since ur arrival, not countin the ones they ate, of course. Someone's out to getcha."

The room fell silent again. Hayley paced around the room and appeared deep in thought. She stopped abruptly and studied something in the colorfully decorated fish tank at the other end of the room. Ethan noticed too – and quickly approached the tank alongside Hayley.

There was only one fish in the tank, swimming frantically in circles. But as Ethan got close, he could tell the fish was not a fish at all. It was a tiny porpoise blowing shape bubbles from its blowhole. A string of bubbles blew out and hovered mid-water before slowly floating towards the surface. As they rose, the bubbles morphed into letters spelling out the words: HELP ME!

"I've never seen such a small porpoise before," Ethan said.

"Why is he calling out for help?" Hayley asked.

"Um—oh yeah—about that," said Dakota. "There'za perfectly good explanation fer that."

Ethan and Hayley's eyes stayed glued to the small porpoise that turned towards them and stared directly at them. Its eyes grew larger, and its nose shortened as its skin changed color. The porpoise slowly morphed into a navy-blue colored aquatic humanoid with yellow highlights and bulging orange eyes.

"Is that—"

"What is Fin Drenchler doing in your fish tank?" Hayley asked in a stern, condemning tone. "Let him out of that tank immediately!"

Dakota approached the tank and fished Fin out with a small net. He placed him on the dusty wooden floor. Tiny

Fin hopped out, peered up at Dakota, and shook his webbed fist at him.

"I was fixin to set 'em free soon enough. Held him here fer his own good I did."

"Free him now!" Hayley ordered.

Dakota held his hand out over tiny Fin and mumbled unintelligible gibberish as he moved his hand in a circle. Fin sprouted quickly and grew like a time-lapsed flower. He rose to over six foot tall and turned to face Dakota.

"What is the meaning of this? I will inform the Headmistress of your despicable actions."

"I meant no harm by it. Ya come poking around, asking questions ya had no business ask'n. Trapped ya for yer own good."

"My own good—"

"Was only holdin ya till I could discuss matters with someone. Meant ta let ya go, but then all the commotion started, and Ethan Fox came back."

Dakota pointed at Ethan, and Fin's anger quickly melted away. He bowed his head to Hayley, turned to Ethan, and changed the subject.

"Ethan Fox – am I glad to see you. Do you remember anything about our last meeting?"

"Um—no, but Jordanna showed me part of a video. I fell into some sort of a trance and spoke to you."

"You spoke in tongues," Fin said. "I believe you spoke in the voice of Stravis himself."

"I don't remember any of that. What did I say?"

"I'm not quite sure. You spoke in the language of the Creators, from what I could tell. I couldn't understand what you were saying – but felt a strong presence that I believe was Stravis."

"Is that why you visited Stravis' bunker?" Hayley asked.

"Yes," Fin replied. "Let's just say that after my encounter watching the ghost of Stravis possess Ethan Fox—it piqued my interest. I spent months researching Creator Stravis and his connection to the Hybrid Child. But my efforts came up mostly empty. I couldn't even find a mention of what a Hybrid Child even is."

"Tell me about it," Ethan said.

Dakota seemed very uneasy with their conversation with Fin. Ethan suspected Fin might be more forthcoming if Dakota weren't present. So he suggested to Hayley that they escort Fin back to the Map Room to tell Jordanna of his return. They left Dakota's creepy house, and along the way, continued their talk with Fin.

"Why did you visit Dakota in the first place?" Hayley asked.

"Stravis' symbol on the spine of his book for one," Fin replied. "But you already know that."

"Yeah, but it sounds like you had other reasons," Ethan replied.

"I did indeed. Years ago, when I was first recruited to become the Seakeeper leader—Headmaster Odin summoned me to The Residence to meet with him."

Ethan recalled his visit to Poseidon, the Seakeepers homebase. Seakeepers were the ocean-going equivalent of the Caretakers. Watching over the human world's oceans for the betterment of mankind.

"Upon my arrival," Fin continued. "I witnessed the end of another meeting Odin was finishing. I didn't see all the attendees, but I saw Dakota Drakelan and Creator Stravis—and Stravis was carrying a baby wrapped in a Caretaker blanket."

"That had to have been me," Ethan said.

"I suspect it was," Fin replied. "The timeline seems right, though I found no information on when Stravis received you."

"That also matches the painting we saw in the Gallery," Hayley said.

"Yes, it does," Ethan said. "Which means I still have business to discuss with Dakota Drakelan."

"Be cautious with that one," Fin said. "You saw how he reacted to me asking questions."

"Fin's right," said Hayley. "We can't just go storming up to his house asking questions."

They arrived at the Map Room and delivered Fin to Jordanna. He had been away from Poseidon for too long and was becoming weaker by the hour. But she'd make sure he received a hydration capsule to regain his strength for his return to Poseidon.

ESCAPE TO NEW YORK

Ethan slept like a log after the previous day's events, and by the time he finally woke up, Hayley was gone from her room and not answering her ELMO. He dressed and headed for the study to check if she might be there. When Ethan entered the front room, Irvin was hard at work, dusting and cleaning.

"Hi, Irvin," Ethan said. "Have you seen Hayley? She's not answering her ELMO."

"Miss Hayley is in the Moongarden," Irvin said. "She may have blocked incoming messages. They are performing a very delicate procedure requiring utmost quiet. That is why Irvin is forbidden to join them. Irvin can't keep his big trap shut—as Gruggins always says."

Irvin's face drooped, and his mouth morphed into an exaggerated frown.

"Shnickyrooners and Shnackleboxes," Ethan said. "I heard that loon turtles were walking upside down on the roof of the rabbit's French toast."

Irvin quickly perked up, and the frown on his face spun into a smile.

"Yes," Irvin said, "and they always wash the poopy diapers of the lawn mower's sausage lips by the side of the baker's trousers."

Irvin stood upright, stopped dusting, and turned to face Ethan with a straight face.

"Thank you, Master Ethan. Nobody has ever tried to cheer Irvin up before."

"That's what friends do."

"Ethan Fox is a good friend. But Ethan Fox should be in the Moongarden with Miss Hayley and the others. Go – Irvin is cheered up now—thanks to his friend."

When Ethan arrived at the Moongarden, the entrance area was quiet, and not a soul was around. He quietly entered and walked the path towards a giant red flower on the ground ahead. Right on cue, Wendy, the withering-froo, balled up into a huge bolder of bark to protect her precious frooberries. He continued along the path and gazed up at the skyclimber that fell from the clouds like an enormous rope of vine tethered to the sky. His gaze traced its way down the immense beanstalk to a gigantic figure climbing up its side. He stopped to watch and heard shouting in the distance, coming from the back half of the Moongarden. He ran along the path to a dark tunnel boring through the tall wall of foliage that split the Moongarden.

Ethan emerged from the tunnel and slowed to a crawl as he quietly approached the small crowd of Caretakers gathered at the base of the massive vine. Hayley stood between Nicholas and Mrs. Moongarden while a group of seven dwarfs stood in front of them. They were all looking up at Azron, who Ethan could now tell was the climber.

"What a rosy surprise," Mrs. Moongarden said. "Ethan Fox has chosen to join us – delighted as daffodils I am."

"What's going on?" Ethan asked.

"One of the trembling nomads," Mrs. Moongarden said. "Escaped the pen and wandered up Lois' side. The poor dear has been stuck there for months."

"Escaped. How?"

"Ravishers," Hayley said. "They infested the Moongarden and set fire to the nomad pen."

"Indeed, they did," Mrs. Moongarden said. "If not for Grubner's quick thinking, I wither to guess what else may have happened."

Mrs. Moongarden motioned to one of the seven dwarfs who was fidgeting. He reminded Ethan of one of Snow White's little friends.

"Let me introduce you to Grubner Trowel."

Grubner stepped forward and held his hand up to Ethan as his cheeks turned bright pink.

"Grubner, this is Ethan Fox."

"Grubner has heard the stories of Ethan Fox. Grubner is pleased to meet the Hybrid Child."

"Happy to meet you too. And who might they be?"

Grubner turned and gazed at his brothers as his cheeks flushed a deeper red.

"They are my brothers. Grabner, Gribner, Grobner, Gripner, Gropner, and Daryl."

Grubner's brothers stepped forward and surrounded Ethan, who shook their tiny hands as they expressed their admiration. A thundering sound interrupted the introductions.

"Azron, reach nomad!" Azron's voice echoed over the Moongarden.

"I'll be right up," Nicholas shouted to Azron. He stepped away from the crowd, tied a rope around his waist, and stretched his ample angelic wings as wide as they would open.

"Okay, everybody," Mrs. Moongarden said. "It is important we all remain silent while I entice the little dear into uprooting."

"Ready?" Nicholas asked.

Mildred tapped away at the screen of her ELMO and hesitated.

"Go!"

Nicholas flapped his wings, soared into the sky, and within seconds he was hovering next to Azron, who patiently clung to the side of the skyclimber. They witnessed the operation in silence as the trembling nomad quivered at Azron's side while Mildred stared at her ELMO screen. She raised her hand, and Azron gently plucked the nomad from Lois' side with two fingers. He held it out to Nicholas, who quickly lassoed its trunk legs and secured the rope tightly.

Azron dropped the small evergreen, which dangled from Nicholas' waist as he circled overhead and slowly glided towards the ground. Azron Hulk-leaped from the side of the skyclimber and landed with a thud several feet from the rest of the crowd. They quickly made their way back through the foliage tunnel and stood by the nomad pen when Nicholas swooped in and gently set it down with the other trembling nomads.

"Whip-dilly-doodles," Mrs. Moongarden said.

Most of the crowd stuck around and made small talk as Grubner entered the pen to remove the rope around the lassoed nomad. But Hayley had other ideas and tugged at Ethan's shirt sleeve to draw his attention. She nodded sideways towards the back of the Moongarden where they had just been. They quietly slipped away and headed back through the dark tunnel.

"I need to show you something," she said as they emerged from the tunnel.

Hayley led him past the skyclimber towards the courtyard near the back of the Moongarden.

"I've been doing a little research," she said as they passed the fountain at the center of the courtyard and proceeded into a vast field of ruins. "I've been trying to learn about the history of this place."

"What's to learn from a heap of old stone ruins?" Ethan asked.

"Lots of things," Hayley replied. "What were they before? Who built them? Who destroyed them, and why?"

"But why does any of that matter now?"

"Because whoever built them also built the spin dial Daavic showed us."

"Good point. What have you learned?"

"I haven't been able to find much information on them. It's like somebody erased their past. There are the rumors they're haunted – but that is all anybody seems to know."

"Have you asked Wordly for help?"

"Not yet. So far, it's been my secret. But I may ask him for help at some point."

"What about the spin dial? Have you tinkered with that at all?"

"Yes, I have," Hayley said as her lips widened into a smile. "That's what I wanted to show you."

Hayley led the way to the tallest partially standing structure in the ruins. They entered the dark, musty room and beelined for a flat circular panel glowing pink on the stone wall.

"I don't even bother covering the panel. Nobody comes near the ruins."

A soft pink glow bathed Ethan's face. It emanated from the symbols on the black rings of the spin dial. He stared at the innermost ring containing only four symbols, one of which was his palm symbol.

"I'm sure you recognize one symbol on the inner ring," she said. "But don't you recognize the others too?"

Ethan studied the other symbols for several minutes, trying to place where he had seen them before.

"Yes, I do," Ethan said as he remembered. "They are the four symbols that made up the Creator's crest we found in the lair of the spider gecko."

"Yes. Those are the symbols of the four Creators of Earth – one from each of the elemental worlds. The one on your palms is Stravis from Zephyr's symbol. The other three represent Driveous, Vraitor, and Zamalador from Atlantis, Ceres, and Hades."

"Interesting – so the ruins must have something to do with the Creators."

"You read my mind," said Hayley. "I think the innermost dial selects which creator was using it."

"Okay, but what is it? What is it for?"

"I'm getting to that," Hayley said as she spun the dials. "I tried quite a few combinations – but nothing worked. Then I fiddled with the center arrow and found out it spins too – and that's when I found this."

Hayley spun the center arrow to point to the right, and then she turned the other three but kept her hand touching the panel. The tall stone walls of the dark room abruptly melted away. They were now standing outside, in a beautiful grassy meadow, under the starry night sky. Stars were everywhere, but what dominated the clear night sky was the giant green planet hovering in space. It was the size of a hundred full moons. The spin dial was still visible, hovering midair with Hayley's hand pressed against it.

"Wow! Where are we?"

"I don't know, but I'm sure that is Ceres," Hayley said. "And I suspect this meadow is just like one on Ceres."

"Cool, it's like we are on Ceres and looking at it at the same time," Ethan said.

She turned the inner dial to Driveous' symbol, and the environment changed around them. They now stood atop a turquoise body of smooth glassy water with various forms of aquatic life swimming below the surface. Ethan gazed up at the enormous blue world hovering in the sky above them. Hayley flipped the dial to Zamalador's symbol, taking them to a hellish fiery environment beneath a giant red planet that pulled the flames skyward.

"And last but not least," she said and flipped the dial to Stravis' symbol. They were now standing on a beach of golden sand that glistened under the starry night sky. The giant yellow planet hovering overhead reflected off the ripples in the calm ocean that stood before them. "The spin dial sticks around as long as I continue to touch it." She removed her hand, and the dial vanished into thin air.

"Where did it go? How do we get back?"

"Just like we did with Daavic." She grabbed Ethan by the hand and turned to lead him away from the water's edge. But then she quickly stopped and stared at something in front of them.

"Wait a minute," Hayley said, "That wasn't there before."

She pointed to a painter's easel and canvas that stood on the beach ahead of them. But they could not see the painting, as it was covered by a yellow sheet with a black swirly eye-shaped emblem stamped on it.

"Well, let's have a look," Ethan said.

They walked towards it – but when they got to within ten feet of the apparition, it vanished.

"Whatever that was," Hayley said, "it wasn't here before – so I think it was meant for you."

They continued inland for another fifty feet – and in a flash, they were standing in the Moongarden's circular courtyard.

It took Ethan a moment to wrap his head around what he had seen. They stood in the courtyard for several minutes discussing Hayley's theories about the ruins. But then Ethan grew quiet as his thoughts flashed back to the chaos in Manhattan and becoming separated from his parents.

"You're thinking about them again, aren't you?" Hayley asked.

"Yeah," he replied. "It just feels different this time. This time something terrible happened – and I need to see for myself that they are alright."

"Well," Hayley said. "I've been thinking about your predicament, and I think I've come up with a solution."

"You have!" Ethan said.

"Yes – but traveling to Manhattan will require us to use the portal plane, and we will need a portal beacon to return to The Residence."

Ethan perked up and listened to every word of Hayley's plan. Obtaining a portal beacon would be tricky – but Hayley knew where CAGE kept a stash of them. So they agreed to meet in the front room in an hour. That would give her enough time to sneak in, borrow a portal beacon, and sneak out.

Ethan stood alone in the front room, awaiting Hayley's arrival. His mind drifted back to his previous visit and the events that took place right in this room. But the sound of the door to The Hall of Doorways opening interrupted his thoughts.

"That was a close call," Hayley said.

"I don't even want to know," Ethan said.

"It's probably better that way. Anyway, let's get a move on." Hayley walked to the front door and opened it. Bright light showered into the dim front room as the portal plane reflected on the mirror next to Ethan.

"Beat you there," Ethan said. He stood several feet from the giant mirror opposite the front door and took a few steps towards it.

"Ethan—"

But she was too late. Ethan smashed headfirst into the solid mirror and bounced off like a pinball.

"Ouch! What happened to the out-door?" he asked as he rubbed his forehead.

"Didn't anybody tell you? The out-door doesn't work anymore, ever since you left. My brother thinks it's related to the out-door to the study vanishing." She stepped out the front door onto the portal plane and waved him over. "But this one works like it did before they locked it."

"Nobody said a word," he said, and joined Hayley on the checkerboard plane.

"You sure hit that thing hard."

"Yeah, I'm lucky it didn't break."

Hayley tapped at her ELMO screen, and a small square matrix appeared. She grabbed Ethan's hand and led him farther out onto the vast checkerboard. He could tell where they were going because a beacon of light shone from a square they were moving towards.

"Don't you need my address or something?"

"We know where you live, silly. Damien has been keeping a close eye on you since the day you left. The portal plane won't take us directly to your home but should get us close."

They arrived at the beacon of light, and Hayley's grip on Ethan's hand grew tighter.

"Have you done this before?"

"No, and I am a little nervous. But I'm excited too. I finally get to see where you live."

They continued to hold hands as they stepped into the beam of light that grew broader and brighter around them – and in a split second, they were gone.

Their eyes took a moment to adjust after the blinding flash of light and the dizzying feeling of being whisked away and dropped on a hard surface. They found themselves at the end of a spacious secluded alleyway between two tall buildings. Dumpsters and trash bags lined the sides of the brick alley walls, and the sounds of a bustling city cried out from up ahead.

"The nearest street corner is that way," Ethan said and pointed. "Let's find out where we are so I can get my bearings."

They started walking down the long alleyway that branched off into smaller side alleys in places.

"Is this a maze?" Hayley asked.

"It can sure seem like one," Ethan said with a laugh. "If you've never been here before."

They were near the midpoint of the alley when a bright flash of light strobed directly in front of them, and a tall man appeared with his back to them. He wore a black overcoat, and long silvery-white hair fell well past his shoulders. He spun around, and his pale blue eyes gazed upon them as a smile grew across his face exposing sharp vampire-like canines.

"How did you find us?" Hayley asked.

"I tracked your portal beacon," said Nicholas. "Your mother is not a fool. She was aware of your little trip before it began. She sent me to look after you."

"This was my idea," Ethan said, "if anyone is to blame, it's me."

"You're wasting your time. We can look after ourselves," Hayley said.

Nicholas sniffed the brisk air and scanned the alley slowly.

"Really? Then I suppose you know we've got company."

Ethan and Hayley scanned up, down, and all around the alley but saw nothing.

"Ethan, your symbols," Hayley said as she glanced down at the red glow emanating from his palm.

"I stand corrected," Nicholas said. "Follow me and keep your eyes on what's in front of you."

They continued towards the mouth of the alley but stopped when the black figure of a woman appeared in front of them. Her piercing yellow eyes glowed brightly as she stared at Ethan and waved her arms skyward. Her mouth moved like she was trying to talk – but muffled gurgling noises were all that emerged.

"The Shadow Princess," Ethan said. "She's warning us about the danger."

Ethan noticed out of the corner of his eyes that Hayley was fiddling with the ring on her finger.

"Is it speaking to you again?" he asked – but her attention was elsewhere.

"Yes, I understand what you are saying," she said and took a step toward the woman – and they exchanged stares for several moments.

"Yes, I understand, and I will tell him," Hayley said.

Yellow rays spilled from the Shadow Princess' lips as a broad smile appeared on her face – and she gazed at Ethan and Hayley.

"It's nice to finally meet you," Hayley said. "And this is Ethan—"

Loud screeching sounds flooded down from above. Ethan and Hayley followed Nicholas' gaze up the sides of the surrounding buildings. Dozens of black figures clung to the brick walls and were inching their way down while others swooped in from both ends of the alley. Two groups of vampires landed in the alleyway, blocking them from both sides. Nicholas started towards the group nearest them but stopped cold when he got close enough to recognize their faces.

"Nicole—but you're—dead," Nicholas said. "I was told he killed you to create—them."

"I no longer answer to that name," said Norell. "And as you can see, I'm not dead—I merely serve a different master, one with a higher purpose."

"But there may be something we can do, Nicole. Please, come back to us. We will figure this out together at The Residence."

"We've come for the boy," Norell said as the vampires behind them slowly advanced. "Give us the boy – or you will all die."

"Well, that don't sound much like a fair fight," a voice said behind the advancing vampires. Ethan could only make out his silhouette – but the tall cowboy hat, long overcoat, and gruff voice gave him away.

"Let's even up the odds a little," Dakota Drakelan said.

He knelt and set three tiny creatures free on the concrete alley floor. Skronk and Gilly scurried past the vampires and stopped at Ethan's feet, while Balder slowly approached the vampires and grew a foot taller with each step. He was nearly seven feet tall by the time he reached them. The vampires fearlessly attacked Balder – but their offensive was futile. Balder countered their attacks by whipping at them with his hooked tentacles. He tore holes in their clothing and ripped pieces of flesh from their bodies with his lashing hooks. One unlucky vampire took flight to flank Balder but was quickly ensnared and slammed to the ground for his trouble.

"Skronk, Gilly, tend to the others," Dakota said and pointed at the unattended vampires. They followed his order and grew larger with each step towards Norell and her companions.

"He's using our brothers and sisters against us," Norell said. "The Grimlord must be told of this."

Norell peered skyward and let out an ear-piercing screech. The walled vampires instantly stopped their descent and leaped into the air to take flight. "This won't be our last meeting," Norell said as she and the others opened their enormous batwings and took to the sky.

The last of the retreating Grimleavers disappeared into the clouds. Balder, Skronk, and Gilly shrank down to size and scurried over to Dakota, who scooped them up and stashed them away in his overcoat.

"Almost didn't recognize ya without ur wings," Dakota said as he walked towards them.

"Your wings. What happened to your wings?" Ethan asked.

"Vamprils can shed their wings at will. I can't allow humans to see me wandering around in their world with giant angel wings."

"How very fortunate we are that you showed up," Nicholas said. "What's lured you out of retirement?"

"Let's just say I have a vested interest in their well-bein'," Dakota said and tilted his head towards Ethan and Hayley.

"How long has she had you looking after the boy?" Nicholas asked.

"Let's just say," Dakota said and then paused. "In some ways, I reckon I've been involved from the beginnin'."

"The Headmistress suspected as much," Nicholas said.

"Not surprisin'," Dakota replied. "Ya may as well tell 'er, the arrival of that shadow spirit is a sign. Things've been set in motion—things Vanessa foretold long ago."

"Vanessa—are you talking about my grandmother?" Hayley asked – but they ignored her inquiry.

"If she knows more about the Grimleaver's plans, she must tell the Headmistress immediately."

"If there's anything ta report, we'll be 'n touch," Dakota said.

"Why are you here anyway?" Nicholas asked.

"The boy wants ta visit his folks," Dakota replied and winked at Ethan. "Return to The Residence and tell Jordanna I'll guarantee their safety an escort them from here."

"Will do," Nicholas said. "Though, I'm not sure how comforting that news will be to her."

Nicholas pulled out a portal beacon, tossed it to the ground, and knelt beside it.

"One more thing," he said to Dakota. "Did you know Nicole is alive?"

"We suspected so."

"Who else knew? Did the Headmistress—"

"No," Dakota said. "Jordanna was not told uv our suspicions."

"Why was I not told? I had the right to know!"

"Vanessa had ur best interests at heart. What would ya have done if ya knew? You woulda charged off and gotten ur darn self, killed. Besides, the Nicole you married is dead. I agreed with the decision then and agree with it now."

Nicholas sighed deeply, placed his hand on the beacon, and vanished in a flash.

The second Nicholas was gone, Ethan turned to speak with Hayley as Dakota watched quietly.

"The Shadow Princess, you could understand her?"

"Yes," Hayley replied. "Her name is Adara, and she wanted me to tell you something."

"Tell me what?"

"She seemed confused and wasn't very clear."

"Just tell me what she said, and we'll figure it out together."

"She said she must help you find the hidden desert fortress – but her presence has put you in danger."

"But she's been helping me. Why would her presence be putting me in danger?"

"Because it is the same fortress he seeks. It is why Victor Qruefeldt has been trying to capture you."

Ethan gasped and felt his face flush as adrenaline coursed through his veins. He stood silently, pondering what Hayley had just told him.

"How are you able to understand her?" he asked.

"I—I don't know," she replied. "I just heard a soft, calm voice in my head when she spoke. But I think it has something to do with my ring because it finally woke up."

"Is that'ta—" Dakota said under his breath. "A rift-key?" He stepped forward and knelt beside Hayley to inspect her ring.

"Yes," she said and held out her hand. "I snatched it from Victor Qruefeldt's puzzle box."

"Hmmm," Dakota said, "well if that don't beat all. Answers a few questions too."

"What are you talking about?" Hayley asked. "Do you know something about my ring?"

"Nah. Nothing to concern yerself with."

"You were talking about my grandmother, weren't you? How do you know my grandmother?"

"We been associates fer a long, long time," Dakota replied. "An if ya wanna learn anythin more, yer gonna have to ask 'er yerself,"

Ethan stared at Dakota as he contemplated his next words to the old-timer. Hayley gently reached down and held his hand to calm him.

"Ya got sumthin' ta say ta me?" Dakota asked.

"No," Ethan replied. "I was just thinking. How did they know? How did the Grimleavers know we were here?"

"That's a good question," Dakota said. "It's smellin' more-n-more like we gotta rat at The Residence."

Dakota accompanied Ethan and Hayley to the end of the alley, and they emerged onto a busy city street. Ethan quickly recognized where they were and hailed a taxi to take them the rest of the way. Hayley's eyes scanned up the sides of the tall buildings and became riveted to the sky.

"Reminds me of the Caretaker city of Zen," she said.

"Yeah, in a primitive sorta way," Dakota said.

The taxi dropped them in front of a tall plush high-rise across from Central Park. The doorman recognized Ethan and politely let him and his friends into the building. They took the elevator up to a penthouse near the top of the building. They exited the elevator into a foyer leading to a sizeable living room with huge windows overlooking the park.

"Shhh, stay here. I'll find my parents and explain."

"What are you going to explain?" Hayley said. "Are you going to tell them, Caretakers from a parallel world rescued you?"

"I—I'll think of something," Ethan said and ran upstairs to his parents' bedroom. But he returned moments later because nobody was there.

"I searched every room upstairs, and there is no sign of them. Maybe they're in the game room or George's study."

Ethan headed down the hall to George's study. Light peeked into the dark hallway from underneath the closed door.

"Dad," Ethan called out as he reached the door. "It's Ethan. Are you in there?"

"Ethan, we've been so worried!" George said from inside.

Ethan opened the door as George stood up from behind his desk and gave him a wide-eyed stare.

"George Fox," Dakota Drakelan said as he entered the room and stepped in front of Ethan. "How long's it been? Seems like a hundred years."

George glanced at Dakota, then at Ethan, then back at Dakota.

"Ur all grown up since ur days at The Residence. Up and out from the looksa it." Dakota pointed at George's belly and laughed.

George turned back to Ethan, let out a deep sigh, and sat back in his chair.

"I guess an explanation is long overdue."

"Ya think," Ethan said and held up his open palms. "Are you going to tell me these aren't tattoos from an evil cult?"

"How long have you known?" George asked – but when Hayley entered the room and stood by Ethan's side, he quickly recognized her.

"The Boardwalk. You've known since our trip to Santa Cruz. Your mother sensed there was more to your attraction to the girl."

"Her name is Hayley."

"It is a pleasure to meet you, Hayley," George said.

"Happy to finally meet you too," Hayley said as she stepped forward and held her hand out.

George's face went blank as he took her hand and gently shook it. Ethan could tell he was struggling to grasp what was happening.

"Cat got ur tongue, George? Don't remember ya being the speechless sort."

"I—I've spent years trying to prepare myself for this. Betsy and I tried to envision every scenario."

"Betsy," Ethan said. "Where is she? Is she okay?"

"She is safe. After the attack, Alexander paid us a visit. We decided Betsy would be safer if he took her to stay with family."

"Alexander," Ethan said.

"Yes, Alexander Sturgis, your real father," George said. "I'll explain – but let me start at the beginning."

"Please do."

"When I was a young boy, a taletaddler named Pepper visited me," George said and smiled as he remembered. "We quickly became the best of friends. He would visit me every day like clockwork. But then one day—"

George paused. A serious look crept over his face as his body tensed up.

"I've heard the story," Hayley said. "You were the boy with Pepper when Grimleavers abducted him."

"Yes. They killed my parents and took Pepper."

"I'm sorry you went through that," Ethan said as he hurried to George's side and knelt beside him.

"That's when Alexander arrived and rescued me. He was the Caretaker in charge when they showed up to scrub the site. He took me back to The Residence and raised me as his own."

"Alexander was my apprentice," Dakota said. "The best student a darkness I ever had the pleasure'a meetin, an' e's an even better man."

"Where do I fit in?" Ethan asked.

"They didn't tell me much," George said. "Only something terrible happened – and Alexander and Tiffany's infant son disappeared. Alexander kept your room exactly as it was. Then one day you reappeared at the exact location you disappeared from hundreds of years prior."

"And I had these," Ethan said and held out his palm symbols.

"Yes. After that, Alexander raised us both – and you were like my baby brother."

"What about the picture?" Hayley asked. "We saw a picture of you two with Alexander. You were at a cabin in the woods."

"I was kept in the dark about that too. All I was told is something bad happened – and they moved us from The Residence."

"And you never asked why?" Ethan asked.

"Sure I did. But all they told me was it would be safer if we hid in the human world."

"They, who is they?" Hayley asked.

"I don't know – but Alexander had others helping him," George said as he turned to face Dakota. "And I'm quite sure you were one of them."

Ethan and Hayley turned towards Dakota, who was now fidgeting in place.

"Don't look at me like that," he said. "Question and answer time's over. You've learned as much as ya need to know—fer now."

Ethan stared at Dakota, contemplating whether to question the old-timer about Fin's revelation regarding Dakota's meeting with Stravis and Odin. But he decided to heed Fin's warning and error on the side of caution.

"Well," Ethan said and smiled at Hayley. "While I'm here, I may as well grab my pocket tote."

He walked to George's bookshelf, climbed the ladder, and removed three books from the top shelf exposing a small cubbyhole. Next, he removed a small brown book with shiny gold lettering, and from beneath that he retrieved his pocket tote.

"You found my secret hiding spot?" George asked.

"I've been stashing my pocket tote there for almost a year now."

"That book," Hayley said, "Is that the missing portal book?"

"No," George said, "It's a tether port. That's how they transported you into the future. It's how you disappeared from the Caretaker world. Betsy and I agreed to hide you from the Grimleavers—and it worked. Until now."

"I'll take that," Dakota said. "Workin' tether ports are hard to come by nowadays."

Ethan tossed the book to Dakota. They spent another hour with George discussing whether he should return to The Residence with them. But George was adamant that he and Alexander had a plan. George would stick around as Grimleaver bait just to gauge their interest – but a Caretaker security detail would keep a close eye on him.

All in all, the journey was a success. Speaking with George quelled Ethan's worries, and he learned a little about his past in the process. It was time to return to The Residence—regroup and discuss their next steps. He needed to learn about his real parents, and hopefully, what a Hybrid Child was too.

THE DRONE WARS

They materialized on the checkerboard plane, and Dakota stumbled forward – but Ethan caught him before he could fall.

"Never have gotten used ta these dag-nam portals," Dakota said. "Miserable way ta travel if ya ask me."

When they entered the front door, a short man with four arms stood in front of the tall mirror across the room. He saw their reflection and spun around to greet them.

"Ethan Fox, what great timing," he said.

"Boris Wentworth," said Dakota. "Squirreled your way out of another close call, I gather. I guess even Grimleavers can't stomach the likes 'a you."

"Still sore about that piece I wrote about you," Boris said, and strode across the room with his right arms extended.

Boris Wentworth was a pudgy man in black formal attire, with a pocket watch chained to his vest. He was shorter than his wife Bella, and had grey flattop hair, long sideburns, and a monocle over one of his brown eyes. A fat droopy nose sat in the center of his round face, and a thick bushy mustache covered his upper lip. Boris and his family were members of the four-armed quadroll species.

"How very fortunate I am," Boris said. "I've so wanted to meet the Hybrid Child face-to-face."

Ethan politely shook one of Boris' extended hands. Dakota walked past him and grumbled as he approached The Hall of Doorways – but he stopped and turned back.

"Be careful what ya say ta that snake oil salesman," he said to Ethan. "Choose yer words wisely, or he'll bend the truth till both ends meet."

Dakota slammed the door as he exited, and an uncomfortable silence filled the room.

"Not your greatest fan, I guess," Hayley said to break the silence.

"Pay him no mind. He's still mad about my article for *The Residential Daily Star*. I suppose he wasn't happy about me exposing the dark dealings from his past. But as I always say, a good reporter makes more enemies than friends."

Boris took out his pocket watch and glanced at the time.

"Oh my, I must have lost track of time. I've somewhere to be, so I must be off."

"It was nice meeting you," Ethan said.

"The pleasure was all mine," Boris said and paused. "Tell me, my boy, are you a fan of the Drone Wars?"

"Drone Wars?"

"Well, if you've never experienced them, you simply must join me for tomorrow night's match. I've access to a VIP seating box, and there is plenty of room for the both of you."

"No, thank you," Hayley said and pursed her lips.

"What are Drone Wars?"

"The sport of Caretakers," Boris said. "A head-to-head battle of evolutioneer ability and wits. The Drone Wars are as much a game of chess as a show of raw brutality."

"That sounds dope," Ethan said.

"Brutal and barbaric is a better description – and I will have no part of them," Hayley said and crossed her arms.

"They're not so bad," Boris said to Ethan and winked. "My daughter Blakelyn isn't a fan either."

Ethan's eyes ping-ponged from Hayley to Boris and back a few times as he pondered the invitation – but in the end, curiosity got the best of him.

"Sounds fun," he said, "I'll go with you."

"Splendid, I will drop by your room tomorrow evening and accompany you."

Boris exited the front room. Hayley stood quietly with her arms crossed, staring daggers at Ethan.

"Don't be mad. It sounds interesting to me."

"I'm not mad. Just disappointed you would want to witness something so barbaric."

"And how do you know it's barbaric?"

"Because I went to a match and saw for myself."

"Oh, so you made up your mind after experiencing a match yourself. Is that what you are telling me?"

Hayley unfolded her arms and laughed.

"Good point," she said. "You should witness a match yourself and make up your own mind."

After the eventful visit to Manhattan, they needed time to decompress – so they grabbed a quick bite to eat in the cafeteria. Then Hayley suggested they stop by the Moongarden to ask Mildred if she needed any help. So they spent the rest of the day and half of the next helping Grubner and his brothers replant a patch of creeping tanglers damaged during the recent Ravisher infestation.

It was late afternoon, and Ethan's Drone Wars date with Boris Wentworth was approaching. Time for him to adjourn to his room to shower and get ready for the main event.

"Sorry guys, I gotta be going now," Ethan said to Grubner and his brothers. "But I promise to help more tomorrow if you need me."

Grubner and his brothers smiled and bid Ethan adieu. They were grateful to have his help and assured him they could not have done it without him.

"Where are you going?" Hayley asked.

"The Drone Wars. Remember?"

"Ooh yeah, I almost forgot," Hayley said with a smirk. "Have fun – and I hope you enjoy them as much as I did."

Ethan laughed and left. Along the way, in The Hall of Doorways, he heard Irvin singing from the darkness ahead.

"My bologna has a first name its G-R-U-M-P, my bologna has a second name, its L-I-N-and-G, oh I love to tease it every day and if you ask me why I'll say . . . cuuuzzzz silly Irvin has a way of making Gruggins mad all day."

"Shnickyrooners and things like that," Ethan said as his light beetle merged with Irvin's, and they came face-to-face.

"Ethan Fox, Irvin is happy to talk to his bestie on such a lovely day."

"Nice to see you too, Irvin. You're in great spirits today."

"Oh yes, Irvin is going to view some of his favorite new shows on TV. The Real Housewives always make Irvin laugh. Would Ethan Fox like to join Irvin this evening?"

"I'm sorry, Irvin – I've got plans. I'm going to the Drone Wars with Boris Wentworth tonight."

"Bahhh, Drone Wars are a kiddie show compared to the Housewives. Irvin is thinking of producing his own version here at The Residence—The Real Caretakers of Zen City."

"Good luck with that, Irvin," Ethan said as he choked back a laugh. "Anyway, I gotta be going now."

Ethan returned to his room, showered, and changed. He didn't expect Boris to arrive for another hour – so he sat on his bed and thumbed around with the apps on his ELMO device. He came across one for *The Residential Daily Star* and opened it. He remembered hearing that Boris Wentworth was a senior reporter for *The Daily Star*.

"I may as well check out some of Boris' work," he thought to himself as he perused the app.

He searched all articles by Boris Wentworth, and a long list of Boris' works scrolled down the screen. Ethan scanned his way down the list to some of the older articles when one towards the bottom caught his attention, *The Troubling Truth Surrounding Headmaster Ravenwood's Latest Decisions*. He read from the article:

"Thumbing his nose at popular opinion, new Headmaster Odin Ravenwood has decided against abolishing the Master of Dark Studies position. Created during predecessor Gaylord Trabblemore's tumultuous reign, the position has come under intense scrutiny as calls for its banishment have reached a crescendo. Opponents insist Gaylord's downfall was a direct consequence of him creating the position for his questionable appointee, Heldrik Vonn Grim."

Ethan skimmed his way through the article when another paragraph grabbed his attention.

"As if the groundswell of negativity were not troubling enough, the position is already filled, as this reporter has learned. While not yet announced by the administration, sources confirm Dakota Drakelan, a little-known Caretaker, will fill the position. On the surface, the appointment of Drakelan may seem like a non-event. But this reporter has uncovered the dark and troubling past of the new appointee.

As an orphaned child, young Dakota was captivated by dark and gloomy things. As he grew older, the subject of dark studies absorbed most of Drakelan's time. Then one day, he encountered a man named Heldrik Vonn Grim. The boy's dreary demeanor and thirst for darkness attracted Vonn Grim. And so it was, Heldrik took the boy under his wing as his apprentice. And so it is, Heldrik Vonn Grim's apprentice, one Dakota Drakelan, will become Odin Ravenwood's first appointee. Needless to say, our newly appointed Master of Dark Studies is sure to be mired in controversy."

Ethan sat on the edge of his bed, contemplating the article when a knocking sound interrupted his train of thought. He quickly hopped to his feet and answered the door to greet Boris, who was talking to a colorful figurine attached to his lapel.

"No, no, that won't do for tonight," he said to the pendant shaped like a strange bird. The color drained from the charm as it abruptly came to life, peeled itself off Boris' lapel, and scurried onto his shoulder.

"Let's try something reptilian for tonight's festivities," he said. The bird on Boris' shoulder melted into a goopy metallic puddle and slowly elongated into a tube that forked at one end. Black scales grew along its length as the two fork prongs morphed into serpent heads. Shimmering blue diamond markings painted themselves down the entire length of the two-headed serpent as it slithered down Boris' chest and reattached to his lapel.

"Now that's more like it," he said and winked at Ethan.

"That's so cool. Reminds me of Hayley's copycat."

"Not a copycat. Just my favorite garment frill I fancy to wear on occasion."

"I have cufflinks and a tie clip my dad makes me wear sometimes. He wouldn't even have to ask me to wear one of those."

"Well, it pleases me that you like it. Now, are you ready for some excitement, my boy?"

Boris escorted Ethan down The Hall of Doorways and ushered him to the thirteenth door on the left.

"Isn't the Map Room right across the hall?"

"You have a keen recollection," Boris said with a chuckle. "You might have a future in reporting. *The Residential Daily Star* is always looking for fresh young talent."

They entered an enormous flat square room with vendor booths lining the outer walls. Masses of people lined up to buy food and refreshments. But what caught Ethan's attention was the colorful array of robes these Caretakers wore.

"Their robes," Ethan said. "Why are they all wearing so many different colors?"

They wore the same half-and-half style as traditional Caretaker robes – but these consisted of every imaginable color combination. Some robes even split along the diagonal to allow four different colors.

"Most Caretakers wear formal attire to an event like the Drone Wars. The color combinations represent their elemental origins."

"So purple means one parent is from Atlantis, and one is from Hades," Ethan said.

"Exactly. I'll make a reporter out of you yet."

"What do black and white represent?" Ethan asked.

"You possess a thirst for information, and you're asking all the right questions – but I'm going to let you take a stab at that one too."

"Well," Ethan said as he pondered the question. "I would say good and evil, but Caretakers are all good. Aren't they?"

"Of course – but all creatures possess a natural bias towards either darkness or light. Bats live in dark caves, but it doesn't make them evil. Humans equate darkness with evil – but the truth is, darkness is merely a convenient veil under which evil often chooses to hide."

Boris' philosophical explanation confused Ethan – so he shook his head and smiled.

"Wow, look at all the vendors," Ethan said. "Reminds me of the Boardwalk."

"Would you fancy a refreshment?"

"Sure, do they have sugar-pickle soda?"

"I am sure they do," Boris said as they slowly strode towards the vendors.

"Where is the arena?" Ethan asked. "Where does the match take place?"

"The arena is here. You are not looking in the right places."

Ethan scanned the room around him and slowly guided his gaze upwards. The room walls stopped about thirty feet up, but they did not end at a ceiling like most rooms. Instead, it continued up to an open night's sky filled with stars. Ten enormous concentric rings hovered in the sky several hundred feet directly overhead. The annuli grew wider as their diameters increased – and a giant empty circle of the sky filled their center.

"What is that up there?"

"That is the arena," Boris said as they gathered their refreshments. "Come, they are about to open up the floater ports."

"Floater ports?" Ethan questioned.

He followed Boris towards a crowded queue at the room's center, where a trail of giant bubbles floated skyward with people inside.

"What are those?" he asked.

"Elevation pods," Boris replied. "That, my boy, is our way up to our seats."

The line moved quickly, and within minutes, they stood at the edge of an immense circular divot in the ground. A Caretaker couple stood at the center and waited as liquid goop poured from the edges of the divot. Spherical walls grew around them, forming an enormous bubble that slowly floated skyward. Ethan's gaze followed the bubble as it gained speed and drifted towards the arena.

Ethan glanced down as they reached the empty sky at the center of the arena. The room below looked like an open box with tiny people wandering inside. Their pod continued to rise, and he could now tell the floating rings formed a giant bowl-like stadium in the sky as each larger ring floated at a slightly higher altitude than its neighbor, and formed a self-contained section.

"VIP seating, my boy," Boris said as the elevation pod dropped him and Ethan on a walkway of the innermost ring section. He guided Ethan to a roped-off seating box with eight seats that reminded him of the captain's chair in the Map Room. They sat quietly as hundreds of Caretaker-filled bubbles floated through the arena's center and dropped their fare at the various levels. Ethan spotted Brianna, Damien, and Nicholas in one bubble, followed closely by Azron in another much larger bubble. He tried to wave – but they did not recognize him as their elevation pods sped by and dropped them on the highest and outermost ring.

"Your CAGE friends occupy the uppermost section, and I have a theory as to why."

"What do you mean?"

"Caretakers at The Residence revere CAGE. They should be in their own VIP box," Boris said and pointed to an empty box of seats nearby. "Yet they choose to sit top-side with the commoners. I believe the Headmistress has put them up to it."

"Why would she do such a thing?"

"I believe the Drone Wars threaten or frighten Jordanna Ravenwood – so she has deployed her henchmen to police the events. And what better place to keep an eye on things than up there, where they have a bird's eye view of all that is going on."

Ethan sat quietly, contemplating his friend's choice of seating. Boris spotted something that piqued his interest in the nearly filled arena.

"I'm sorry, my boy – I must step away for a moment to follow up on something. A good reporter is never off duty. But have no fear. I will return before the match begins."

Ethan's eyes followed Boris up a set of stairs dividing the seating boxes. He stepped onto one of the walkways that ringed the various levels of their section. Boris continued around the walkway to the opposite side of the arena and stopped at a box filled with Caretakers wearing half-black half-red robes. A man with long black hair stood and shook Boris' hand. Ethan had never seen him before, but he recognized two of the people sitting next to him. It was Blair Trabblemore and Caden Stanley, and they were leaving so the man could speak to Boris in private. Ethan vividly remembered he and Hayley's previous run-ins with the resident bullies – and those memories were not pleasant.

Ethan perused the rest of their section and moved his eyes up to the levels hovering above. His eyes scanned the ring, looking for anyone he might recognize, but they were too far away. He stood and turned to look up at the closer parts of the sections when something smacked the side of his head from behind. He spun around and found himself face-to-face with Blair and Caden, who were standing on the nearby stairs.

"Look, Blair, the mutant child," Caden said. "He's come to the match all by himself."

Blair laughed as she clung to Caden's side and held his hand tightly.

"Where is your little pet, Malik?" Ethan asked. "Too bad you didn't bring him along so I can sic him on you."

"He doesn't like the stench of mutants," Caden said and stepped towards Ethan with his fists clenched.

"You didn't learn anything from our previous encounter," Ethan said with a grin.

The thundering sound of a gong rang out over the arena, causing Ethan to flinch. Caden and Blair roared with laughter.

"Mutant boy is afraid of loud noises."

"He's probably afraid of his own shadow," Blair said as they continued to laugh.

"That's enough," Boris said from behind Blair and Caden. "Ethan Fox is my guest here – and you will treat him respectfully."

"We were leaving anyway," Blair said as she tugged at Caden's arm to lead him away.

"I said you will treat him with respect," Boris said louder. "Do you understand me?"

"Yes, sir," Caden and Blair said.

"Very well, return to your father. He is wondering as to your whereabouts."

The two troublemakers turned and hurried away towards the other side of the arena.

"I'm sorry they were so unpleasant. But you are the Hybrid Child, and you will require thick skin."

Ethan's gaze followed Blair and Caden around to the other side of the arena to the seating box where Boris had gone. Then he sat in silence, wondering what business Boris might have with Blair's father.

Several moments passed, and most of the crowd sat quietly when a white circular platform grew from nowhere in the empty sky at the center of the arena. A transparent barrier sprouted up like glass around the exterior of the platform, creating a fat cylindrical enclosure.

"What is that?"

"The battle ring, where combat happens."

Two square platforms grew midair to each side and above the circular battle ring.

"And those are the evolutioneer platforms, where the contenders compete."

With all the blanks filled in, he understood what good seats Boris had gotten them. They were essentially sitting ringside. Ethan sensed the electricity in the air as a low-pitched hum of the chanting crowd slowly grew louder and louder.

"And that sound is the call to battle," Boris said with a broad smile. "The first match is about to begin."

Ethan's eyes widened with excitement as he stared at the arena. He did not want to miss anything. Two giant bubbles floated up through the space between the battle ring and the innermost VIP section. They swiftly floated to opposite sides of the battle ring and dropped the contenders onto their respective platforms. Each of them carried a small pouch matching the colors on their robes.

A giant expressionless face appeared in midair over the battle ring. It was half-black half-white split down the middle and reminded Ethan of a blank Halloween mask. At first, the holographic face hovered motionlessly – but then the mouth smiled and began to speak.

"Tonight's first match pairs two first-year contenders," its voice boomed over the stadium. "On the east platform, robed in white and green, contender Artemis Klem." The crowd roared with anticipation as the face continued. "And on the west corner, robed in black and blue, is contender Reginald Simmons."

The roar from the crowd grew louder as the evolutioneers held out their pouches and opened them. A bubble floated out of each and grew as they glided away from their contenders, stopping when they reached their proper place over opposite sides of the battle ring. Ethan studied the small elevation pods, trying to figure out what the small oblong blobs standing inside were.

"What's inside the bubbles?"

"Those are the drones. Lifeless lumps of flesh each contender starts with. The first-years use smaller ones, but the drones vary in size depending upon the evolutioneer's experience level. Study them closely, my boy. Those drones won't be lifeless for much longer."

"Ladies and gentlemen, beasts and banshees, and all other present lifeforms . . . prepare yourselves for battle," the face said, causing the crowd to roar louder. "Evolutioneers, are you ready?" The contenders bowed their heads in agreement. "Combat commences when the drones hit the canvas." The face flashed one last giant smile and vanished.

The crowd quieted with anticipation as all eyes focused on the two small bubbles hovering over the battle ring. The evolutioneers held their hands up and stood, waiting for something to happen. The bubbles abruptly disappeared, sending their drone payloads thudding to the canvas where they immediately expanded.

The white and green evolutioneer clasped his palms together and spun them in a circular motion. The drone nearest him instantly morphed into a spherical shape. Tiny legs grew from the bottom, and a gaping hole appeared in its side where rows of sharp canine teeth began to form. Brown fur sprouted, covering the emerging creature as small eyes bulged from above its menacing mouth.

"Bad move," Boris said to Ethan, "he's tipped his hand and given his opponent a glimpse at his strategy. This match will be short."

The second evolutioneer in black and blue stepped back and waved his arms up and down in opposite directions – and Ethan was riveted. The evolutioneer's drone flattened out and rolled itself into a long stick shape. Four insect legs sprouted from one end while a ball of flesh grew on the other like meat on a skewer. The insect legs moved in unison to lift the ball of flesh, walk towards its opponent, and dangle it like an enticing meal. The ploy worked as the opponent's fat round creature quickly waddled over and chomped down on the skewered meatball with its razor-sharp teeth.

"That's all she wrote for the little ball of teeth," Boris said with a grin.

It confused Ethan initially – but his eyes remained glued to the battle. And then, in an instant, everything changed as four spikes sprang from the skewered meatball, impaling the fat round creature on all sides from within. A crimson river of blood oozed from the losing drone. It no longer looked like a lifeless mass of flesh; but, instead, a dead creature. Ethan now understood why Hayley disliked the Drone Wars. Yet something primal had awakened inside of him, and it excited him.

"That was so cool," Ethan said, "but how did you know?"

"Amateur mistakes like that are easy to spot, my boy. Once you witness the more experienced competitors, you'll understand."

After watching several more matches, Ethan understood what Boris meant by 'amateur mistakes.' As promised, the more experienced competitors used larger drones which meant more complex creatures and strategies. It was time for the main event, a battle of champion evolutioneers, and Ethan couldn't wait. Now that he understood what was going on, and the skill involved, he was having the time of his life.

The championship started like all the rest, with the holographic face announcing the champion contenders and disappearing as the crowd awaited the dropping of the drones. But this time, the drones grew to the size of small boulders as they crashed onto the canvas with a loud bang.

The champions wasted no time making their moves but were sneakier about concealing their strategy. The evolutioneer in black and red stepped to the edge of his platform and turned his back to his opponent, making slashing gestures with his hands as he did so. His drone sprouted two long chicken legs that lifted the rest of the fleshy mass off the canvas. A thick thatch of feathers sprouted from the drone's mass and fanned out like an umbrella blocking the opponent's view of its metamorphosis. The transformation continued, hidden from view, as hooked tentacle-like appendages grew around a snout full of razor-sharp teeth that morphed from the drone's body.

Not to be outdone, the champion in white and yellow took a step back and crossed his hands in front of his chest. His drone shivered like an egg about to hatch and grew as it shook more and more violently. A confused look washed over the champion's face as he lowered his arms and stared at his hands. Blood slowly gushed from his nose as the champion shook like his drone.

Boris fidgeted in his seat – and his arm twitched as he watched with a demented grin.

"Oh, how unexpected," he said.

"What?" Ethan asked.

"Something is going delightfully wrong," Boris answered.

The drone's shivering slowed as it morphed into an egg and continued to grow to three times its original size. The crowd fell silent as the bleeding champion dropped to his hands and knees and fell unconscious.

A crack suddenly appeared on the enormous yellow egg in the battle ring.

"Click, click, click," a noise echoed inside the giant egg.

Chills crept down Ethan's spine as he recognized the sound he was hearing. The egg shattered as a massive black beetle-like insect emerged. The creature had broad jagged mandibles and sharp-pointed front legs that thrust forward like stabbing knives. The enormous death scarab leapt forward and made quick work of the opposing drone creature. Wrapping its giant mandibles around the smaller animal, biting it nearly in half, and popping it like a sack of crimson blood.

"Click, click, click," the noise echoed from the death scarab as it circled the battle ring.

"It appears to be searching for something," Boris said.

Ethan's palms tingled, so he peeked down at his glowing red symbols pointing at the death scarab.

"No, it's looking for someone. It's looking for me."

"Nonsense, my boy, it would be impossible for a drone to attack you here."

No sooner had the words left Boris' lips, then the creature leaped from the battle ring and flew across the gap between them. The scarab landed on one of the walkways circling their section and beelined towards Ethan. The nearby crowd panicked and ran – but the beast quickly impaled two unlucky fans. Ethan hopped to his feet and hurried up the staircase to the walkway. The giant insect slowly closed the distance between them. The shocked audience stared at the scene in silence from the other sections.

"It's after me," Ethan shouted to anyone close enough to hear. "Run away from here while I distract it."

Ethan stood motionless, staring into the creature's black beady eyes as it inched closer. It was nearly on top of him when he finally took Boris' advice and bolted up a set of stairs to another empty section. The creature saw where Ethan was headed and took a shortcut by leaping to the next platform where the staircase led.

Ethan turned as he reached the top of the stairs – but did not see anything chasing after him. He turned back just in time to see the monster directly in front of him. Ethan's momentum was thrusting him headfirst into the creature's giant open mandibles, so he instinctively ducked his head and extended his arms to shield himself. Bright beams of green light erupted from his palms as they touched the beast. Then, in a flash, the creature transformed into a lifeless drone.

Everything fell silent as Ethan fell to his knees, shaking. Boris was the first to arrive at his side.

"You were amazing, my boy!"

"I—I don't understand—I didn't do anything," Ethan said.

"Well, this is another first," Nicholas said as he landed on the walkway alongside Ethan and gave him a toothy smile. "Thought I would fly down and give you a hand, but you've already gotten everything under control."

Above them, the silent crowd erupted in applause at what Ethan had done. Azron, Brianna, and Damien joined Nicholas in the VIP section to help calm the spectators who were still in shock while a steady stream of elevation pods flowed to evacuate the crowd. It took over an hour to empty the floating arena; and by then, Ethan was so tired, he could barely keep his eyes open. He expended a lot of energy to defeat the giant creature, so Azron carried the sleeping Hybrid Child to his room, where Irvin would tuck him in.

THE ORACLE

The time was nearly 11:00 AM when Ethan was awakened by a light tap at his door. He popped out of bed, still wearing his clothes from the night before. He answered the door to a somewhat subdued Boris Wentworth standing in the hall.

"I'm sorry, my boy, I didn't want to disturb your rest after last night – but I wanted you to have this."

Boris handed him a small box with a red bow.

"No worries, I was already getting up," Ethan said. He popped the top off the present – and his eyes lit up as he recognized the small reptilian garment frill from Boris' lapel.

"Are you sure? I thought this was your favorite garment frill."

"You earned it, my boy. Nobody has ever performed an instant de-evolution. Everyone considered the maneuver an impossibility, but I witnessed you perform one firsthand—you gave me the thrill of my life."

"I don't know—"

"I want you to have it. You simply must take this as a token of my gratitude."

Boris explained how the pendant would cling to any garment and take on whatever form Ethan imagined. He even showed him a trick to turn the trinket into a two-dimensional cartoon that would wander around on the surface of his shirt. And then, after explaining the secrets of his gift, Boris left.

As he shut the door to his room, Ethan noticed a small envelope slipped underneath at some point in the morning. He opened the letter and quickly remembered the fragrant scent of Jordanna's note from his previous visit.

Dear Ethan,

I've been briefed on what happened during last night's Drone Wars match and your courageous actions in the face of imminent danger. I'm told your heroics drained a lot of energy from your body, so please sleep until you feel rested and join us in the Map Room when you wake. I am concerned with your safety and that of my daughter. I must ensure your well-being and take measures to do so. We will discuss this when you arrive.

Sincerely yours,

Jordanna Ravenwood

Ethan wasted no time changing his clothes, putting on his sneakers, and turning his new gift into a cartoon gecko on his yellow shirt. He jogged down The Hall of Doorways so fast the light beetle barely kept pace. He reached the door to the Map Room and paused to look at the door across the hall. His mind flashed back to the dreadful spider-like eyes of the giant death scarab as it stared at him – and a tingle crept up his spine like the legs of a centipede.

"I am your mother, and you will do what I tell you!"

The sound of Jordanna's voice boomed from inside the Map Room, jogging Ethan back to reality. Hayley was already inside; and from the sound of it, they were having a heated conversation – so he hurried in.

"I am not a child anymore, Mother," said Hayley. "I'm nearly ready for my first-year of Caretaker training. Do you protect all first-years like this?"

"She has a good point, Mother," Damien said.

"You're always jumping to her defense," Jordanna said. "All first-years are not my daughter – and they are certainly not out gallivanting about with the Hybrid Child. His presence places a target on both their backs."

"That's not fair—"

"Your mother is right, Hayley," Ethan said as he stepped onto the crow's nest platform. "Victor Qruefeldt is after me, and until one of us is dead, I am a danger to everyone. I will leave."

"No! See what you've done now," Hayley screamed at her mother.

"Ethan, my dear, I'm sorry you had to hear that," Jordanna said and strode across the room to embrace him. "Please don't take my words literally and accept my apology.

I don't want you to leave. I am merely suggesting additional measures to ensure both your safety."

"She wants to ban us from leaving The Residence," Hayley said. "And she is going to saddle us with a CAGE babysitter."

"Really?" Ethan stared Jordanna in the eye. "But the Shadow Princess, and everything we've been doing, we must be able to come and go as we please."

"Everything you've been doing," Jordanna repeated. "Let's see – thus far, you've been accosted by thieves in the shantytown, attacked by desert harpies, and nearly abducted by Grimleavers."

"You overlook one critical point, Mother," Damien said. "Ethan is the Hybrid Child. His connection to Stravis, and the Seers, has gifted him abilities we cannot begin to fathom. I would suggest there is no safer place for my sister to be than at his side."

"Exactly," Hayley said. "When we are together, I know I am safe. I can feel it."

Jordanna glanced from Damien to Hayley, then she turned to Ethan and peered into his eyes.

"I need to learn about my past and what it means to be the Hybrid Child," Ethan pleaded. "The Shadow Princess is coming to me for a reason – and Hayley is the only one who understands her."

"Nicholas told me of your encounter with the shadow spirit," Jordanna said.

"She's not a shadow spirit," said Hayley. "Her name is Adara."

"I don't yet know her purpose," Ethan said. "But it is vital, I know it is."

"I can tell I'm not going to win this one," Jordanna said and sighed deeply. "Fine, I will allow you to come and go as you please – but you will have a CAGE escort."

"Tinx," Ethan said.

"Yeah, Tinx," Hayley agreed. "We will take Tinx with us everywhere we go."

"I don't recall saying you would choose your own. Besides, I have yet to discipline Tinx for her previous indiscretion."

"How about this," said Damien. "Tinx will accompany them, but I will remain in close contact and oversee everything they do."

Jordanna's gaze moved from Ethan to Hayley and then Damien as she contemplated his compromise.

"Fine," she said and let out another deep sigh. "I will agree to Damien's compromise only because we are already spread so thin – but I feel like you've all sold me a bill of goods."

"I suggest you track down Tinx," Damien said to Hayley. "You can inform her of her new assignment, and I will be in touch."

"Will do," Hayley said and smiled.

It seemed rehearsed to Ethan. He felt like it was all for show, and Jordanna was right about being hoodwinked by her two children.

"Now then, let us move on to the real reason for this meeting," Jordanna said. "Have we learned anything more about last night's mishap?"

"No," Damien said. "But the fallen champion has died from his injuries."

"How could a drone malfunction like that?" Hayley asked.

"Drones cannot malfunction," Damien replied. "Someone in the crowd must have evolved it."

Ethan gasped.

"Only a very powerful evolutioneer could pull that off," Jordanna said.

"Or de-evolutioneer," Ethan said. "Victor Qruefeldt had something to do with this. That monster was sent after me."

"We can't be sure of that," Jordanna said.

"Yes, we can," Ethan said. "My symbols told me so. They've been coming alive lately. I only wish I knew what they are trying to tell me."

As soon as the words left his lips, wisps of golden whimsy wafted from the book in Ethan's pocket tote.

"I believe we are about to find out," Damien said.

Ethan fished the poem book from his pocket tote, and it flipped open to the first blank page where the words appeared. They read:

Round and Round

Round and round they spin and glow,
and point to what you seek to know.

White for where the unseen lands,
or red for where the danger stands.

Green to ward off ill intent,
or yellow when it's heaven sent.

A gift to help you find your way,
and fight the grim that's come to play.

"Interesting," Damien said. "It appears the Seers have sent you the directions to your gift from Stravis."

"If I'm reading this right," Hayley said. "They turn white to point out something you are not seeing."

"That sounds right," Ethan said. "They pointed to the Shadow Princess the first time I saw her – and then they showed me when Jasper was near."

"I'm not sure about green," Hayley said. "But red points to danger."

"Yes," Ethan said. "They pointed to the harpies, the Grimleavers, and the death scarab."

"Yellow when it's heaven sent," Jordanna repeated. "I believe that is referring to Stravis."

"Your right," Ethan replied. "They turned yellow when I met with Fin and spoke in tongues. He was convinced I was possessed by the ghost of Stravis."

"Green is the only one I can't figure out," Hayley said.

"Yeah, I think I may know what that is referring to," Damien said.

"You do?" Ethan asked.

"Last night, when you spontaneously devolved that creature back into a drone," Damien replied. "Witnesses reported seeing a powerful green burst of light as you heroically charged the beast. I believe they turn green to ward off evil, and that's how you devolved the drone."

"Yes, I—I remember now," Ethan said. "My symbols did turn green. But there was nothing heroic about it. I didn't even know the monster was there till I ran headfirst into it."

"Additional reports say you sacrificed yourself by distracting the beast so others could get away," Jordanna said. "Yet you still refuse to accept that your acts were courageous."

"That sounds pretty heroic to me," Hayley said.

"Indeed, it does," said Jordanna. "I've learned enough to feel comfortable with the company my daughter keeps."

They entered The Hall of Doorways, and Hayley stopped, turned to Ethan, and hugged him tightly.

"When I learned what happened last night," she said and paused. "I realized how close I came to losing you."

"It wasn't a big deal."

"Sure, not a big deal. That's why everybody is talking about what happened. Ethan, you did something considered impossible last night. You spontaneously devolved an evolved creature back to its original form. Now everybody is wondering, if that is possible, maybe you can evolve devolved creatures too."

"If I can do that, it would mean—"

"You can destroy the Grimleavers – and if Victor Qruefeldt finds out about last night, he will want you dead even more than he already did."

"He already knows. He was responsible for last night. I feel it."

"All the more reason to stay the course and find the hidden fortress the Shadow Princess spoke of."

"I agree," Ethan said. "Especially if Victor is searching for it too. But where do we start? It's not like I can just summon her, and she appears."

"Yeah, I know. I guess we'll need to think on it," Hayley said.

"Okay, but don't we need to track down Tinx first?" Ethan asked with a grin.

A mischievous smile swam across Hayley's lips.

"What are you and your brother up to?"

"Follow me," she said.

Ethan followed Hayley down The Hall of Doorways, past Dakota's creepy house on the hill, and into the Deadwood Saloon. All was quiet and the few patrons sitting at the bar didn't even turn around when they entered. They made their way to the back of the room, where Tinx sat perched on a table, sipping from a tiny mug of dragon's breath.

"Well, don't keep me in suspense," Tinx said to Hayley. "Did she go for it?"

"She agreed to my brother's compromise. But she is suspicious, so we must tread lightly."

"It was a ruse," Ethan said. "And I played right into your plan."

"You played things perfectly," Hayley said with a grin. "I thought you had figured us out when you asked if Tinx could be our CAGE escort."

"Aw shucks," Tinx said, smiled, and batted her long eyelashes at Ethan. "I'm flattered Ethan Fox asked for little old me . . ."

"Okay, okay, spill the beans," Ethan said.

"Damien came to my room to tell me about last night's drone incident. He warned me that our mother would likely overreact. So, I confided in him, and we agreed to an arrangement."

"But Damien is second in command," Ethan said. "Why would he help us?"

"For two reasons," Hayley said. "For one, when he was in exile, he kept a close eye on us. He witnessed us in action firsthand and understands what we can accomplish when allowed to proceed unhindered."

"And the second reason?"

"I agreed to check in with him occasionally and keep him in the loop. If we need any help, he will be available to us."

"Great, so where do we start?" Tinx asked.

"I was thinking about that on the walk here," Ethan said. "I think we should start by speaking with Gruggins."

"That's right," Hayley said. "The Nibblewarts have been telling him all about the Shadow Princess."

"Gruggins isn't staying in his box as much lately," Tinx said. "He has secret napping spots all over The Residence. I know a few of them, but if he doesn't want to be found, he won't be."

"You're right," Hayley said. "I suggest we split up. Ethan and I will check his box, and if he's not there, we know one of his secret spots too. If you find him, ELMO us, and we will do the same. If not, we will meet up later."

Ethan and Hayley entered the front room and tapped lightly on Gruggins box, but he was not home.

"I guess we check the secret wishing well next," Hayley said.

Ethan glimpsed at something small, black, and red, barreling down the staircase from the upper levels. A hairy ape-like creature with glowing red eyes reached the floor and beelined towards them. Stopping at Hayley's feet, the tiny beast transformed into a metallic statuette of a cat—her copycat had returned.

"Tabby Cat. She must have something to report."

"Are you finally going to let me in on your secret?" Ethan asked. "What covert mission are you working on with your copycat?"

"Shhhh – you never can tell who might be listening," Hayley said as she bent down to pick up her copycat.

"Follow me," she said and nodded towards the stairs.

Ethan remembered the last time he ascended these stairs and discovered another Gruggins lurking. Of course, Gruggins quickly zapped him with a memory-erasing knock-out dart for stumbling upon his secret.

"Where are we—" Ethan said but was quickly silenced.

Once on the second level, they continued into a short hall leading to more stairs. Ethan stared ahead as they slowly crept up the stairs. The staircase was dark and eerie as they continued up towards infinity. There were no ceilings, and the only light visible was the dim glow of the torches lighting each level. Hayley led him to the third level and stopped to whisper to her copycat that transformed into an ELMO device in Hayley's hands. She stared at the directions on the screen, and they guided her into a hallway to their left.

"I overheard a conversation between Blair and Caden some time ago. They were talking about her father's trip to Hades and how if everything went as planned, the Trabblemores would be returning to power. They hate my family and are up to something – so I've been spying on them to find out what."

"I had a run-in with Blair and Caden last night," Ethan said. "Did you ever find out why they hate the Ravenwoods so much?"

"They hate us because my grandfather, Odin Ravenwood, exposed Gaylord Trabblemore for his crimes against humanity. He was our first headmaster, and his crimes disgraced his entire family."

They continued down the dimly lit corridor leading to a dead end. A square room with a stone floor, stone walls, and two iron doors on each of the three walls. Torches hung beside each door and lit the room. The scene reminded Ethan of a musty old castle dungeon.

"This must be the place," Hayley said as she stooped to set her copycat-ELMO on the floor in the middle of the room.

"What place?"

"I tasked my copycat to follow Blair around. The grindle was perfect for that task – but I also needed to instruct it to record her suspicious activity. At first, I wasn't sure how to achieve that one – but I remembered ELMOs have a built-in proximity encoder."

"Proximity encoder?"

"Keep your eyes open," Hayley said as she tapped the ELMO screen and stepped back.

Blair, Caden, and Malik suddenly appeared out of thin air. They stood facing one of the iron doors. Ethan jumped back at first, but quickly figured out they were the holographic result of the copycat-ELMO's proximity encoder.

"What is that blasted combination again?" Blair asked as she rummaged through her handbag.

"You ask that every time," Caden said.

"I know, but I can never remember these stupid symbols."

Blair pulled a piece of paper out, unfolded it, and turned to face the door. She placed her hand against a grapefruit-sized symbol embossed onto the iron door. A faint red glow appeared beneath her hand as the symbol on the door flattened out into a square grid of more symbols that reminded Ethan of a touchpad on an old-fashioned telephone.

"Let's see what new goodies daddy has left for us," Blair said.

She glanced at the paper, touched a series of symbols, and the door swung open. Malik swiftly spun around and growled, and he appeared to be looking directly at Ethan and Hayley.

"He hears something," Caden said as he and Blair spun around.

The feed from the proximity encoder stopped and the apparitions disappeared. Hayley approached the door and studied the symbol embossed on it.

"This symbol," she said, "I wonder what it means?"

Ethan scanned the other doors in the room and walked to the adjacent door.

"This one has a symbol too, and it's different – but the other four are blank."

"She held her hand against the symbol like this," Hayley said and placed her hand on the symbol. But a small blue arc of electricity zapped her hand away. Ethan put his hand on the other door's symbol, which zapped him.

"Must be some kind of security mechanism," Ethan said. "Probably only accepts Blair's hand."

"Blair's hand," Hayley said as a grin spread across her lips. "Ethan, you're a genius."

"I am—"

"Replay the last encoding," she said into her copycat-ELMO. Blair, Caden, and Malik reappeared, and the scene replayed.

"What is that blasted combination again?" Blair said again.

Hayley studied the scene as it unfolded.

"Freeze encoding," she said into the ELMO before Blair's hand touched the door. The three apparitions froze in place. Hayley walked through Caden and Malik to get to Blair's likeness and stood beside her, studying the piece of paper in her hand.

"Create a hard copy," she said into the ELMO.

Ethan watched as Hayley pried the paper from Blair's now solid hand. Then she tugged at Blair's arm with all her might, but it remained solidly frozen in place.

"What are you trying to do?" Ethan asked.

"I'm trying to move her hand against the symbol on the door," Hayley said.

"Stand back. I have an idea," he said.

Ethan pulled out his pocket tote and retrieved a jeweled dagger from it. Then he walked across the room and proceeded to cut fake Blair's hand off below the wrist.

Hayley watched in horrified silence and stood motionless before deciding to speak.

"That was disturbing," she said. "I think last night had an effect on you."

"Yeah, it almost made me gag," Ethan admitted. "But truth be told, up until the attack, I really enjoyed the Drone Wars."

Hayley remained silent for a moment as Ethan stepped away from fake Blair and put the dagger away.

"Erase replay," she said into the copycat-ELMO, and the apparitions disappeared.

"Anyway, I thought you might need a hand," Ethan said and held the severed hand out to her.

"Very funny, but I'll pass. You give it a try," she said and motioned him towards the door.

"Here goes nothing," Ethan said and held the hand against the embossed symbol. A red glow appeared beneath the hand, and the emblem slowly melted away to reveal the flat keypad. Ethan stepped away to make room for Hayley.

"You can take it from here," he said.

Hayley stepped forward and tapped at the keypad to enter the symbols from the paper. The door swung open, and the embossed symbol reappeared on the door.

Ethan followed Hayley into the dimly lit room. They entered what looked like someone's office—full of boxes and rows of shelves in the dark back half of the room.

"Shut the door," Hayley said. "In case someone comes."

Ethan shut the door, and Hayley tapped at her copycat ELMO to turn on its flashlight. She walked past Ethan as he studied the desk under the light of a small lamp barely lighting the front of the room. She strode down one of the aisles of shelving and started snooping through the junk stuffed onto them.

"Ethan, come here," she said as she stopped at one of the shelves stacked with mostly empty jars. She reached up and grabbed one of the jars and held it under her flashlight to show Ethan.

"A death scarab, like the ones Dakota's friends captured."

"It sure is," Ethan said.

"All of these jars are empty," Hayley said and shone her flashlight at the shelf of empty jars. "Except for this one."

"Blair is the one who has been releasing them," Ethan said.

"It appears that way – but we can't prove it."

"Shhh," Ethan said. "Do you hear something?"

"No."

She turned off the flashlight, and they stood quietly for a moment. The sound of muffled voices from beneath the door barely broke the silence. Ethan grabbed Hayley's arm and guided her deeper down the dark aisle.

"It's so dark back here I can't see anything," Hayley whispered.

"I'm seeing perfectly," Ethan said softly. "Everything looks black and white, but I can see."

They walked through a tall free-standing metal frame and ducked behind a tall box near the back of the room as the door swung open.

"Daddy will be along shortly," Blair said as she, Caden, and Malik entered. "I didn't speak with him last night due to all the interruptions. It's been good to have him back these last few weeks—he was away on business for so long."

"What does he want us to do now?" Caden said as he sat down, reclined, and kicked his feet onto the desk.

"I don't know, but it will surely be the end of you if he finds you sitting at his desk like that."

Caden quickly returned to his feet just as the door swung open again – and someone else entered the room. Ethan and Hayley peeked around the box and down the aisle as Blair approached the tall man with long black hair. He wore a half-black half-red robe split diagonally lengthwise.

"Hello, Daddy," Blair said as she reached up to hug the man. "I'm so glad your back."

"Yes, dear, I know," a deep voice replied. "But I've been back for weeks now, and you keep saying that."

"Is there any more we can do to help, sir?" Caden asked and cowered ever so slightly.

"Have you deployed our little friends?"

"All but one, sir. Unfortunately, none have hit their mark."

"We think he is under someone's protection, Daddy."

"As expected – but it was worth the effort."

"How else can we serve the cause?" Caden asked.

"Put this someplace safe," the man said and tossed a pouch to Caden.

"What is that Daddy?"

"That is the Hadean tanzanite I procured on my trip. Should be more than enough to fulfill our needs."

"I took the measurements and built the frame, sir—as you ordered," Caden said. "It is ready and waiting in the back room."

"Good work," Blair's father said. "I will be hearing from the supplier any day now. I will send orders when it is ready for pick up."

"Yes, sir."

"Good, he will be pleased to learn his plan is coming together on time."

"Do you think his plan will work, Daddy?"

"Of course, it will," Blair's father said. "And when it does, it will shock everyone at The Residence to their core."

A cacophony of corrupt laughter filled the room as Caden and Blair cheered her father's prediction. Caden made several more failed attempts to kiss up to him but quickly ran out of material. Blair filled in the awkward moments by reminding her father how missed he was while away. Ethan and Hayley sat silent until the lights finally dimmed and everyone left the room.

"Blair's father was there last night," Ethan said. "Boris left to speak with him about something."

"His name is Roman Trabblemore," Hayley said. "He blames the Ravenwoods for killing the Trabblemore legacy. But I wonder what Boris would need to discuss with him."

"Boris is a reporter," Ethan said. "Maybe he's working on a story."

"Maybe," Hayley replied. "It sounds like Roman is working for someone. He didn't name any names – but when Caden asked if he could serve the cause, a chill crept up my spine."

"Me too," Ethan said. "I'd bet anything it's Victor Qruefeldt."

Ethan and Hayley quietly exited and made it to their rooms before either of them spoke a word.

"I don't know about you, but I'm hungry," Ethan said. "I'm craving pancakes."

"Me too," Hayley said as her stomach growled on cue.

Ethan and Hayley beelined for the dining hall, where Irvin displayed his mad chef skills to the early Caretaker dinner crowd. But he was happy to whip up a batch of pancakes for his two favorite customers—even if it was breakfast food.

"So, where do we start?" Ethan said after slopping down a sizeable fork full of syrup-drizzled hotcakes.

"Good question," Hayley replied. "And since we can't find Gruggins, I've been thinking about anything we may have missed."

"We still haven't looked in the secret wishing well," Ethan said.

"No, we haven't," Hayley said. "Spying on the Trabblemores sidetracked us – so I sent Tinx a message and she agreed to check there."

"So we're back to square one," Ethan said.

"Not yet, we aren't," said Hayley, "I remembered something that gave me an idea."

"What did you remember?"

"When I saw that swirly eye pattern on the yellow sheet it looked familiar," Hayley replied. "Then I saw the Shadow Princess' necklace and I knew I'd seen it before."

"You've seen her necklace somewhere?"

"Yes—but it wasn't till Nicholas and Dakota mentioned my grandmother Vanessa that I knew where I'd seen it. She has one exactly like it."

Ethan's eyes widened and he straightened up.

"We need to speak with your grandmother," he said.

"It's not that simple," Hayley replied. "She left The Residence a long time ago, and I've not been told where she lives. But there may be another way."

"And what might that be?"

"It may be a long shot, but we can start at the Caretaker city of Zen."

"Isn't that where you said you lived now?"

"Yes—but I'm not talking about my place, I'm talking about my grandparents. We may find clues about where she lives now – or maybe even the necklace itself."

"That sounds like it's worth a shot," Ethan said. "Who's living there now?"

"Nobody. My grandmother abandoned the place shortly after my grandfather's death. But my mother has kept it maintained in case she ever returns."

"Dakota said the shadow spirit was a sign of things to come, things that Vanessa foretold. Do you know what he meant by that?"

"Maybe," Hayley said. "My grandmother is an oracle. When grandpa Odin was headmaster, something happened, and she gained second sight. They say she has visions of the future and has never been wrong."

After refueling on their delicious breakfasts, Ethan and Hayley wasted no time following up on their next lead. It took nearly five minutes to make the long trek down The Hall of Doorways.

"Close your eyes," Hayley said as she stopped and grabbed Ethan by the hand. "You are about to enter the Caretaker city of Zen."

Ethan closed his eyes while Hayley opened the door and slowly guided him inside. She closed the door, and they took several steps forward. Ethan listened to the sounds of a city vaguely reminding him of home—without the car horns and sirens.

"Okay, open your eyes."

Ethan squinted as his eyes adjusted to the morning brightness, but they grew wider and wider as he slowly took in the sights of the wondrous Caretaker city. The scene reminded him of a sci-fi movie: there were no cars, but large transparent bubbles floated all about the skyline with people inside. They were standing at the end of a vast street, running straight down the middle of the city. Giant cylindrical skyscrapers lined the sides of the road and stretched skyward as far as the eye could see. Ethan furrowed his brow as he witnessed several bubbles hit and melt into the sides of the buildings.

"Elevation pods," Ethan said. "I rode in one at the Drone Wars."

"Yep, and we are going to take one right up there," She pointed almost straight up in the direction of the nearest building.

Ethan's eyes gazed down the street where hundreds of people in Caretaker robes walked about tending to their daily business. Lines of people waited in front of small telephone booth-like structures. They entered one by one only and disappeared in a bright beam of light that strobed skyward from the top.

"Those are part of our teleport network into the human world," Hayley said.

"I thought the portal plane was your way into the human world."

"The portal plane gives us access to anywhere, which requires special privileges most Caretakers don't have. So they hardwired the teleport network to specific locations throughout the world. Most Caretakers use them to travel to work daily, but others choose to live amongst the humans."

Ethan's gaze wandered from place to place as he took in the sights of the fantastic Caretaker city. Hayley grabbed his hand to guide him toward their destination. They angled down the street and approached the nearest building on the left. She stopped at the end of a queue of Caretakers at the base of the building. They stood for several minutes, but the line moved fast.

"We're next," Hayley said as she gently tugged at Ethan's arm and guided him to the center of the bubble machine.

"Name and destination please?" a young Caretaker asked from the platform's edge.

"Hayley Ravenwood and Ethan Fox to visit Vanessa Ravenwood."

Ethan stood in awe as the bubble formed around them, and they slowly floated into the sky. He felt nearly weightless inside the bubble and could not sense any motion even as it picked up speed and changed course to circle the building.

"We must be a thousand feet up," Ethan said as he gazed down. "The people look like tiny Caretaker ants."

The bubble slowed to a crawl and turned towards the skyscraper. Light shined from a small hole that appeared on the side of the building where the bubble touched. The circle of light grew larger and larger as the bubble melted into the condo unit. Ethan and Hayley stood on a tiled floor at the edge of a plush carpeted living room. The tall viewing windows behind them curved around the outer edge of the living area like a luxurious Manhattan high-rise.

"Kinda reminds me of home," Ethan said as he and Hayley slowly scanned their surroundings. His gaze stopped at a prominent symbol embossed on the wall in front of them.

"That symbol—Hayley, do you know what that symbol is?"

"I've seen it somewhere before, but I don't remember anything about it."

"That symbol—"

"Oh, come now, my dear," a raspy yet feminine voice said from behind them. "You don't recognize your family crest when you see it. I must have a word with your mother."

Ethan and Hayley spun around in unison to find out where the voice came from. A tall woman with a thin slightly wrinkled face stood in the room's foyer, studying Ethan and Hayley with her deep blue eyes. She had long flowing half-black half-white hair and wore a black robe with a golden Ravenwood crest on the lapel. And finally, a shimmering golden chain and pendant dangled from her neck. It was the same swirly eye-shaped necklace the Shadow Princess wore.

"Grandmother," Hayley said as her eyes widened. "I—I—my memories are still quite scattered. I don't remember everything—yet."

"Don't worry yourself, my dear. It's my fault for not visiting more often. I lost a husband and a son at The Residence. This place brings me dark memories, so I choose to live elsewhere."

Hayley's grandmother strode across the room and knelt in front of her.

"I know that's no excuse, I will visit more often in the future. Please forgive me."

"Of course, I forgive you, gramma," Hayley said as she gently embraced her grandmother.

After the warm reunion, Vanessa stood and turned to Ethan.

"And you must be the boy causing such a stir."

"His name is Ethan and he's my friend," Hayley said.

"Vanessa Ravenwood. Pleased to make your acquaintance, Ethan Fox," she said and extended her hand.

"Nice to meet you," Ethan said and shook Vanessa's hand.

"Mother said you haven't lived here since grandfather died. How did you know we were coming?"

"How I learned of your visit is unimportant. What is important is the reason for your visit. So, child, what answers do you seek today?"

"Well—" Hayley said.

"That necklace you are wearing," Ethan interrupted. "What can you tell us about it, and what do you know about the Shadow Princess?"

"Very direct. Now I understand why my granddaughter fancies you."

Ethan and Hayley blushed.

"Very well," she said. "I suppose you've both earned an explanation. But first, let us move this conversation to a more suitable location. Would either of you like a refreshment?"

"No thank you," Hayley said.

"We just had breakfast for dinner," Ethan replied.

Vanessa led them into the living room with a huge comfortable couch and two cozy recliners. Ethan and Hayley sat side by side on the sofa. But Vanessa stood facing them, she touched her chin with one hand while resting the other on her hip, and then she let out a deep sigh.

"You ask about my necklace because you've seen it elsewhere, I suppose."

"Yes, it's the same one the Shadow Princess wears," Ethan said. "But how did you get one just like it?"

"I had this one made because the original captivated me from the first moment I saw it," Vanessa replied. "I'd recently received the gift of second sight, so it seemed fitting. I suppose that's what attracted me to it in the first place."

"Where did you see the original?" Ethan asked.

"The same place you did," she answered. "She came to me in one of my first visions. It foretold the return of a shadow spirit whose return would set off a chain of events that would shape the future."

"She's not a shadow spirit," Hayley said. "She is the Shadow Princess and her name is Adara."

Vanessa gasped. Her face grew pale, and she wobbled back and forth.

"Are you okay?" Ethan and Hayley asked in unison. They stood, dashed to her side, and each grabbed an arm to escort her to the nearest seat.

"Gramma, what's wrong?" Hayley asked.

"Oh, nothing, my dear," she replied. "Just the teetering of an old woman. I was probably just standing too long."

"Are you sure?" Ethan asked as he shot Hayley a questioning glance.

"Yes, of course. Now, where were we?"

"You told us about your necklace," Ethan said. "And your vision of the Shadow Princess. Is there anything else you can tell us about that?"

"Not much more to tell," Vanessa said. "My visions don't often contain much context; they leave a lot to interpretation."

"Do you know anything about a desert fortress?" Hayley asked.

Vanessa sat quietly and appeared to be gathering her thoughts. She looked from Ethan to Hayley and let out another deep sigh.

"Possibly," she said. "It reminds me of something that happened long before Odin was headmaster – but it's quite a long story."

"We have the time," Ethan said and looked at Hayley.

"Yes, please tell us the story," said Hayley.

"It all started with a surprise visit from Creator Stravis," Vanessa began. "It was the first time he confided in Odin and me, and at the time, it was unheard of for a Creator to call upon any Caretaker other than the headmaster. So naturally, his visit surprised us and caused us to wonder why he chose us?"

Vanessa paused to catch her breath while Ethan and Hayley hung on her every word.

"We learned Stravis distrusted the other Creators, especially Zamalador. He insisted Gaylord Trabblemore was under Zamalador's thumb. So, he sought out a high-ranking Caretaker he could trust—one with an impeccable reputation and who shared his elemental origins."

"They had to be from Zephyr," Ethan said, "that's what led Stravis to you and Odin."

"Correct on both counts."

"What did he want from you and grandfather?"

"He told us of a powerful righteous presence he encountered in the desert."

"The Seers," Ethan said.

"Correct again. At first, he experienced visions of eyes peering at him from beneath the sand."

"I have the same visions," Ethan said.

"Not surprising. You are the Hybrid Child – so your connection to Stravis and the Seers is strong."

Ethan and Hayley exchanged glances.

"They found a way to communicate with Stravis. He said they warned him of a fortress in the desert under construction for evil purposes."

Wisps of golden whimsy wafted from Ethan's pocket. He retrieved his pocket tote, pulled out the awakened poem book, and held it in his open hands. The pages flipped to a torn-out page that was growing back. When it finished, another poem had arrived. The passage read:

The Fortress of Fate

North of where the sun will shine, they labor night and day.
Enslaving meek and innocent, to ensure the gracious pay.

Three edges on each side, and four that touch the ground.
A fortress built for wicked plans, to be lost and later found.

Creator from a chosen world, you must find the desert site.
Then enlist the help of others, to assist you with this plight.

The fortress will be hidden, by fate and sleight of hand.
Its secrets devoured forever, till the Hybrid makes a stand.

"It appears Jasper's paid you a visit," Vanessa said as they gathered around to read the poem.

"This must be what they communicated to Stravis," Hayley said.

"Yes, but there was more to it. Stravis showed me this book and read me this very passage – and he explained that the words bore deeper meaning. When he read the Seer's words, he felt their true intent."

"How can that be?" Ethan asked. "The last line is about me, I am sure – but that was before I was even born."

"Stravis said not all the words were for him to understand. It appears they have finally found their intended audience."

"How is that possible?" Hayley asked.

"The Seers are multi-dimensional beings. They view all of time in an instant," Vanessa said. "They understand all possible outcomes of all possible actions and reactions. So it's not hard to imagine they were writing to both of you—even though you exist in different timeframes."

Ethan and Hayley stood in silence, pondering what they had learned.

"So what did Stravis ask of you and Odin?" Ethan asked.

"He gave us the location and asked Odin to investigate what was happening there. So Odin visited the site and witnessed the atrocities they committed. They had evolved ants into three foot giants and used them to assemble huge stones into pyramids. What he witnessed incensed him – so he spoke to the Caretaker in charge."

"What did he say?" Ethan asked.

"He insisted he was under orders from Headmaster Trabblemore and gave a cockamamie story. He said the headmaster needed a fortress to hide from something he feared."

"Did Odin tell you the man's name?" Ethan asked.

"Yes. I'll never forget the man's name—Jason Crowley."

"Why?" Hayley asked. "What makes that name so unforgettable?"

"Not so much his name," Vanessa said. "It's what happened after."

"What?" Ethan and Hayley asked.

"Someone left his corpse on our doorstep. The sight was ghastly, like all his life's energy was drained from his body."

Hayley gasped.

"It happened shortly after Odin visited the pyramids. We were living in an old-town villa at the time. The story made headline news—even on the elemental worlds."

"What happened after that?" Hayley asked.

"These events led to Odin uncovering Gaylord's crimes and exposing him. Gaylord denied any knowledge of the pyramids or fear of anything. But when Odin pressed him about fearing a boogieman, he said he saw the fear of Hades in Gaylord's eyes."

"Anything else?"

"Not much else to tell. Once he became headmaster, Odin sent a team to the site of the desert fortress – but everything had vanished. There was not a trace of anything ever having been there. The disappearance bothered him for years. He never understood how a giant fortress in the desert could up and walk away. After that, he kept everything hush-hush, said he didn't want to put me in harm's way."

"You said this was the first time Stravis came to you," Ethan said. "What about the other times?"

"That is a question not ready for answers," said Vanessa. "Stay the course – and the answers will come when you are ready."

"Why won't you answer?" Hayley asked.

"Oh—but I have, my dear," Vanessa said.

She stood, approached Hayley, and grabbed her by the hand. Then she enveloped Hayley's hand in her own and whispered into her ear.

"And as for you, my dear boy," Vanessa said and turned to Ethan. "That book of yours is a very powerful gift. Pay attention to what it tells you. It may lead you in unusual directions – but the Seers' path is true."

"I—I think I understand," Ethan said.

"And with that, I bid you adieu." Vanessa twirled her hand, spun around, and disappeared in a puff of smoke.

"But wait—" Ethan said—but was too late.

"She always makes a flashy exit," Hayley said.

"I wanted to ask her what Hybrid Child means. If she knew Stravis, she might know something."

PANDORA'S BOX

Ethan and Hayley arranged to meet Tinx for breakfast in the dining hall the following morning. There, Tinx told them about all the places she searched for Gruggins, including the secret wishing well. But she had no luck. He obviously did not want to be found right now. Then they decided it was probably a good time to check in with Damien—to make good on their side of the bargain and keep the headmistress off their back.

After breakfast, Hayley led them to where she was sure her brother would be. They followed her to the front room, where Hayley made a quick detour to check if Gruggins was in his box.

"I thought you were taking us to your brother," Ethan said.

"I am," said Hayley, "he's in the basement."

"The creepy place where we found the grimtailed dread?"

"Damien has repurposed Daavic's secret room," Hayley said. "He's remodeling from top to bottom."

"Doesn't take much to improve upon dark, damp, and dingy," Ethan said.

Hayley knocked at the door to the basement, and the sound of Damien's muffled voice echoed up the stairwell.

"Come in, and I'll be right with you."

They opened the door and their faces bathed in the bright white light shining up the stairwell. Ethan's jaw dropped when he reached the base of the stairs and entered a vast white room lit by the glowing floor and ceiling. Damien stood at a tall white lab bench at the center of the near-empty room. He was hovering over something and tinkering with it under a giant magnifying glass mounted to the end of the extended bench.

"Wow, I love what you've done to the place," Ethan said.

"Thank you. I have turned Daavic's dingy basement into a laboratory with room to grow."

"What are you working on?" Hayley asked as they approached.

"I found Daavic's ELMO in the top drawer of the study. I'm trying to unlock it to peek at what he was doing. I may find clues as to why he joined Victor Qruefeldt."

"That's impossible—from what I've read," Hayley said.

"Difficult, yes; impossible, no. It may take a couple of years, but I will crack the code and unlock it."

Ethan and Hayley stood at Damien's side as he fiddled with the insides of Daavic's ELMO. Tinx fluttered off Hayley's shoulder, landed on the bench, and walked into his field of view. Damien stopped what he was doing and glanced from Tinx to Hayley to Ethan.

"To what do I owe the pleasure?"

"We're just checking in," Hayley said. "To abide by our part of the bargain we struck with mother."

"Well? Anything to report?" Damien asked.

"Not really," Hayley replied. "We're trying to learn more about the Shadow Princess – but so far, nothing earth-shattering."

"Well, didn't you say you are the only one who can understand her? Maybe if you draw her out again, you can ask her."

"That sounds like a great idea," Hayley said and then fell silent.

"I'm still trying to figure out what we missed at Stravis' bunker," Damien said. "I was sure there would be more for us to find."

"Me too," Ethan said. "Instead, it was a total bust – and Azron almost—"

"Ethan, your pocket tote," Hayley said and pointed at the golden wisps of whimsy wafting from his pocket tote.

Ethan quickly retrieved the poem book, the pages flipped open, and a new poem wrote itself up the page. When it finished, they stared at the passage in silence and read:

Pandora's Box

Unearthed by human raiders, a trapdoor in the sand.

Leading to a bunker, with treasures small and grand.

They tried to find the secrets, buried deep inside.
Searching very recklessly, until the girl died.

She stumbled upon a token, that concealed a hidden room.
But instead of finding answers, it led her to her doom.

Pandora's Box was opened, she took a peek inside.
And found unearthly treasures, that left her petrified.

But before that fateful ending, she found the hidden key.
Entombed in wood and waiting, a Creator's gift to thee.

"Entombed in wood and waiting," Hayley repeated. "Pandora—whatever she found must still be with her petrified body."

"Fascinating," Damien said. "It appears we may have been right after all."

Tinx rode on Hayley's shoulder as she, Damien, and Ethan dashed down The Hall of Doorways. They hurried by the trembling nomads, through the tunnel of foliage, and past the skyclimber vine.

Hayley took out her ELMO as they approached the fenced-off petrified Pandora. They stopped at the white picket fence, and Damien watched with a smirk as Ethan and Hayley jumped into action. She tapped at her ELMO screen as she held it up and a green beam of laser light scanned up and down Pandora's body.

"There's something in her left front jacket pocket," Hayley said.

"We'll need something to pry it out," Ethan said as he fished through his pocket tote to retrieve the jeweled dagger.

He hopped the short white fence and pried at the partially rotted wooden pocket. It didn't take much effort to force Pandora's jacket pocket to pop off and fall to the ground. Ethan picked up the petrified piece of wood and turned it over to chip at the embedded object with the dagger.

"Whatever this is, it's embedded in the wood snuggly," he said and continued to chip tiny pieces of wood away from the object.

Damien, Hayley, and Tinx stood silently as Ethan pried the object away and rubbed it against his pant leg to wipe the dirt away. Then he reattached Pandora's pocket so it was hardly noticeable and would not raise Mrs. Moongarden's suspicion. He held the hand-sized metallic object up to show them when he finished.

"Is that an emblem or crest of some kind?" Tinx asked.

"She found the hidden key," Hayley said, quoting the poem.

"Huh?" Ethan asked.

"That's not a crest," Damien said. "It's the missing piece to the puzzle."

"We were right," Ethan said. "There was more to Stravis' bunker than meets the eye."

They returned to the basement lab where Damien could examine it in more detail. He studied the object closely from front to back underneath his magnifier light. He sat in silence, rubbing his chin and pondering something.

"It has to be the hidden key the poem spoke of," Hayley said.

"I understand what it is," Damien said. "I'm trying to figure out our next move."

"We have to take this to Stravis' bunker," Ethan said.

"Yes," said Hayley, "it matches the engraving on the back wall."

"I realize that, but things are not so simple. After our previous venture to the bunker, mother took measures to ensure we would not return. She's locked away the book to *Sand Miser Dunes* – and the only other way I know would take us too close to the great vanishing dune. Sand harpies would attack us for sure."

"Why can't we just use a portal beacon?" Ethan asked.

"We could, if one were there to transport to," Damien replied. "Under normal circumstances, we use portal beacons to return from a protected realm. We don't normally leave them behind for just anybody to find."

"Can't we go around the dune?" Hayley asked.

"No, the whole area is inside one of the protected realms. Venture too far off course, and you end up in the middle of a human desert with no way back."

"Too bad we can't commandeer an elevation pod from a floater port," Ethan said. "Then we could float over the dune and the sand harpies."

Damien gazed at Ethan, furrowed his brow, and turned to his sister.

"That might just work. All I would need is samples of the bubble solution, and I can fabricate one here large enough for all of us."

"But they program elevation pods to hone in on their destination," Hayley said. "How will we steer the bubble to our destination?"

"True—but they are also immune to wind resistance, so the slightest energy will push or pull it wherever we desire. If I can design a way to 'lasso' the bubble, we can attach a tether, and Tinx can tow us to the bunker."

Damien spent the next few days working tireless hours in his lab to finally figure out how to 'lasso' an elevation pod. Ethan, Hayley, and Tinx checked in daily to help and deliver more bubble solution they borrowed from the Drone Wars floater ports.

"I think I've finally figured this out," Damien said on day three. "Actually, it's quite simple. All I must do is add iron to the bubble solution and apply a magnetic field to pull the bubble along."

"Sounds too simple," Tinx replied.

"Well, the idea is sound, but I did over-simplify. I can't use just any iron. The compound must be colorless and very strongly magnetic so a small magnetic field will attract the bubble."

"So, you haven't solved the problem yet," said Hayley.

"No, but I am ready to test the prototype. I've shaved down a small slab of strong-iron from Ceres and removed its pigments."

CHAPTER EIGHT

Damien held up a small jar of colorless crystals as he explained.

"First, I dissolve this into the bubble solution. Then, all I need to do is create the bubble and apply a magnetic field."

Damien poured a beaker of the mixed solution onto a metallic plate sitting alone on the floor. He tapped at his ELMO, and a bubble appeared on the plate's curved surface and grew to the size of a basketball before detaching and floating straight up where it came to rest against the ceiling.

"And now for our moment of truth," he said and pointed a horseshoe-shaped magnet at the bubble. But nothing happened.

"You still have a few kinks to work out, I guess," Tinx said.

"Hold on. This magnet creates a minimal magnetic field. I may need to be a little closer for it to engage."

Damien took a couple of steps towards the bubble, and it swiftly drifted towards him. He walked from one end of the room to the other, and everywhere Damien went, the bubble was sure to go.

"It works. You've done it," Hayley exclaimed.

"Yeah, I've done it all right. All we need now is a portable fabricator, more bubble solution, and a way to strap this magnet to Tinx."

They agreed to tackle Damien's list as a team. Ethan and Hayley would procure more bubble solution, while Tinx would enlist Irvin's help to modify a harness she already had from her job delivering drinks at the Deadwood Saloon.

Meanwhile, Damien would get to work on a portable bubble fabricator.

It took nearly a week to get everything together. Ethan and Hayley helped by painstakingly grinding down a giant slab of strong-iron into crystals small enough to be de-pigmented and dissolved. When they finished, they needed to agree upon the best time to leave The Residence and make their journey. Ethan, Hayley, and Tinx were flexible – so Damien's busy schedule would dictate the best time to not raise the Headmistress' suspicion.

The day had finally arrived, and they all met in the study, where they knew Jordanna would not be during her weekly meeting with Fin Drenchler. Damien arrived toting a huge duffle bag with Tinx riding on top. She wore a harness strapped to her underbelly to hold the magnet in place— making it difficult for her to walk.

"You've brought everything we need?" Hayley asked.

"Everything we need once we arrive," said Damien.

"Where exactly are we starting from?" Ethan asked.

"Yes, Damien, tell them," Tinx said. "Tell them what you've told me, and don't leave out the added dangers you've forgotten to mention till now."

"What is Tinx talking about?" Hayley asked as her eyes bore holes into Damien's.

Damien put down the duffle bag and walked to the shelf of brown books. He pulled one from the shelf and gazed at its golden lettering.

The Glass Pillars of Nym

"We start here. We book-travel to *The Glass Pillars of Nym* – and yes, we will face a few added dangers. But nothing Tinx can't handle."

"Easy for you to say," Tinx said. "If I make one wrong move, I will have to live knowing I caused your deaths."

"What is Tinx talking about?" Ethan asked.

"I think navigating a giant bubble through a forest of towering, jagged glass pillars with us inside is what worries her," Hayley said and peered at her brother.

"Is that true?"

"Yes, but I've triple-checked the calculations. We will have ten feet of clearance on each side—if we take the proper route."

Ethan and Hayley agreed with Damien, the mission was too important to stop now, and they all understood the risks when they signed up. But it still took another five minutes to reassure Tinx and calm her nerves.

Damien handed Hayley the brown book and shouldered the duffle bag Tinx was still standing on. They all joined hands as Hayley slowly opened the book, bright beams of light radiated from its pages, and they were gone in a flash.

When they awoke from the short slumber that usually followed book-travel, they were on a hard patch of sandy ground. Ethan stood and stretched, and as he yawned, his eyes opened. He scanned his surroundings and saw a forest of massive crystalline trunks forming the base of the pillars.

They stretched skyward like giant arms trying to reach up and grasp the clouds. Ethan spun around and saw the pillars surrounding them in all directions as far as his eyes could see.

Damien wandered the area, scanning the ground, and pillars with his ELMO. He needed to double-check his calculations and find a clearing suitable for his portable bubble fabricator.

"This place is amazing," Ethan said. "I've never seen anything like it."

"Nor will you ever again," Damien replied. "This place is an anomaly created by a hyperhole event. The unusually powerful electromagnetic fields caused by the event pulled the desert sands skyward and crystalized them into the towering pillars surrounding us."

"What is a hyperhole event?" Ethan asked.

"They are anomalous high energy vortex events that have appeared randomly throughout Earth's existence," Hayley said.

"They are quite rare," said Damien.

"What causes them?"

"We are not sure, but as my brother pointed out, they are rare. Only a handful have occurred that we are aware of."

"Yeah, and I'm the lucky guy who got to experience one firsthand," Damien said.

"You saw one?" Ethan, Hayley, and Tinx asked in unison.

"So I'm told, I don't remember anything from that day – but the experience left me with this dashing moon-shaped pupil."

Everyone got quiet as Damien set up the bubble fabricator in the clearing he picked out. When he was done, he checked his ELMO to see if it had finished performing the navigation calculation.

"This can't be right," he said as he stared at the screen. "I triple-checked my calculations."

"What's wrong?" Tinx asked.

"The pillars appear to have grown since we last mapped them," he replied. "The clearances are much tighter than I calculated."

"Oh great," Tinx said. "Now, I will kill you all for sure."

"Maybe we should scrub the mission," Ethan said. "We'll find another way."

"Hold on—I may have a solution," Damien said as he tapped away at his ELMO.

"Let us know when you figure it out," Hayley said.

"Well, I have a solution – but I don't like it," Damien said.

"What?" Hayley asked.

"If I stay behind and recalibrate the fabricator to create a smaller bubble for just the two of you—that should give us back the clearance we lost."

"That sounds like a good plan," Ethan said.

"It is – but I don't feel good about sending you three off alone on such a dangerous mission."

"We can do this," Hayley said. "We've come too far to turn back now."

Damien pondered the situation, but then reluctantly agreed to let them go. He explained the new plan. First, he would teach Hayley how to navigate to the bunker and open the hatch. Then, after they launched, he would monitor their trajectory from the ground and relay directional commands to Tinx with his ELMO—just as they had practiced. The only difference was he would no longer be inside the bubble. In addition, he would maintain direct contact with Hayley's ELMO as well. Once they were all comfortable with the new plan, he gave them a few minutes to ready themselves. Then he rummaged through his duffle bag, retrieved the bottle of bubble solution, and gave the bag to Hayley.

"Okay, is everyone ready?"

Ethan and Hayley stood on the shallow round fabricator dish as Damien poured the solution at their feet. The liquid spread out and quickly ran to the outer edges of the fabricator as walls of a giant bubble slowly grew to form around them. Within minutes the bubble entirely enveloped them and slowly rose into the air.

"That's odd," Damien said. "The bubble appears larger than my calculations would suggest. Ten ounces of solution should not have grown to that size."

Ethan and Hayley looked at each other as they realized their mistake.

"We gave you twelve ounces," Hayley admitted.

"We thought you might need extra," Ethan said. "In case you needed to run more tests."

Damien quickly tapped at his ELMO as the bubble rose higher and higher.

"Well, that will make things tighter."

"How much tighter?" Tinx asked.

"How do you feel about five feet of clearance on each side?"

"Horrible—but it's too late to turn back now," Tinx said with a deep sigh.

Ethan gazed up and saw a sizeable, jagged branch protruding out from the side of the nearest pillar, and they were minutes from running into it. He glanced down and saw they were already at a dangerous height.

"Well, Tinx better start steering," Ethan said. "Or we are going to run into that."

He pointed up, and Tinx and Hayley followed his gaze to the jagged crystal branch.

"Well, that's not ideal," Damien's voice said from Hayley's ELMO.

"What's not?" Tinx asked.

"The navigation map I plotted earlier is gone, and my ELMO is going haywire."

"Mine is, too," Hayley said as her ELMO screen went blank.

"The hyperhole event occurred here fairly recently," Damien shouted. "Its lasting electromagnetic activity is off the charts and causing our ELMOs to malfunction."

"So, what do I do now?" Tinx asked.

"Steer us away from the jagged branch, for starters," Ethan said and pointed up. "After that, you'll have to go it alone."

Tinx darted up and hovered by the bubble as the magnet strapped to her underbelly engaged and quickly pulled the bubble towards her.

"Take things slowly, and we will have to try and guide you by eye," Ethan said.

"That's not going to be easy," Hayley said as she scanned the area. "Most of the jagged branches are nearly invisible till you are right up next to them."

"I don't think I can do this," Tinx said. "I didn't feel good about this even with Damien's guidance."

Ethan's palms started to tingle, so he opened his hands to witness the glowing yellow symbols spinning around. They stopped suddenly, both pointing to 2:00 on a clock face.

"How would you feel about guidance from Stravis himself?" Ethan asked.

"Tickled to death," Tinx said. She glanced over her shoulder enough to spy Ethan and Hayley's faces bathed in the yellow glow.

"Veer right," Ethan said. "Perfect, now continue straight ahead slowly."

Tinx followed his directions, and they proceeded slowly as the giant bubble rose higher and higher into the sky.

"We should be at a safe altitude soon," Hayley said, "the pillars taper off the higher we go."

Tinx continued executing Ethan's every command to perfection, and within minutes they glided along the tops of the pillars where she could navigate by eye. As soon as they were out of danger, Ethan's palm symbols returned to their normal position and shimmering white color.

They continued zig-zagging eastward between the tips of the giant pillars for another half-hour before reaching the edge of the desert proper. The sky was clear, and the temperature quickly grew warmer when they floated past the last of the towering shards of glass. Once clear of the danger, Tinx picked up the pace, and they quickly sailed along. Their next hurdle soon became visible as they gazed ahead at the enormous mountain of sand they were speeding directly towards.

"There it is, the great vanishing dune," Hayley said. "We'll fly directly over the top, approaching from the opposite direction we saw it from before."

The height of the expansive dune amazed Ethan. He continued watching the sand quickly climb towards them as they neared the peak of the giant dune.

"It didn't vanish," Hayley said.

"That's not what I expected either," Ethan said. "Which makes me wonder if anyone has ever flown over it before?"

"Exactly what I was thinking," Hayley said. "I bet someone is cloaking it whenever anyone on the ground gets too close."

"I agree—and they are probably inside that building," Ethan said and pointed straight down to the ground below them.

They were clearing the top of the peak, and floating over the other side, when a tall stone building became visible— half-buried by the base of the dune. But the structure was tall and wide enough that the entrance was still visible on the side opposite the sand.

"Could be," Hayley said. "I don't recall reading about any buildings near the vanishing dune. I wonder what's inside?"

"Looks like some kind of a shrine," Ethan said. "It's probably hidden by the horizon when the dune is visible but disappears with the dune when anyone comes near."

"Sounds reasonable," Hayley said.

"I wonder," Ethan said. "If the harpies are down there right now."

Hayley rummaged through Damien's duffle bag, pulled out a small black cube, and tossed it through the bubble wall at the building. The cube disappeared from view before hitting the ground somewhere near the building's entrance. Seconds later, the sand around the building's entrance churned with sand harpies looking for something to attack.

"Well, that answers my question," Ethan said. "But how did you know that wouldn't pop our bubble?"

"I used a portal beacon," Hayley said. "Elevation pods are designed for planetary survey and passing portal beacons is part of that design."

Ethan looked at Hayley with a concerned expression.

"Don't worry, I took inventory before we left," she said. "Damien always packs extra portal beacons."

Ethan's gaze moved back and forth from the harpies to the dark entrance, barely visible from their altitude. A glimmer of light twinkled at the center of the opening, and something flashed into his mind. He was no longer looking down at the building. He was inside. It was dark all around, and glowing yellow eyes slowly moved toward him. The

Shadow Princess was motioning and speaking to him, but her words were unintelligible.

"Ethan, are you okay?" Hayley asked, and her voice snapped him out of it.

"Y-Yes, I just saw her in a daydream," he replied.

"Saw who?"

"The Shadow Princess," Ethan said. "We were inside that structure. It was dark, and she was trying to tell me something."

They continued to glide for another twenty minutes, and the great vanishing dune was a bump on the horizon when Hayley took out her ELMO and tapped its screen.

"It is working fine now that we're away from the anomaly."

She directed Tinx to veer a little bit to the left and slow to a stop as quickly as possible. They halted as Tinx hovered like a hummingbird, and Hayley stared at her ELMO.

"Okay, I think that should do it, Tinx. Now head straight down."

Tinx slowed the pace of her beating wings and began slowly falling towards the ground—pulling them along as she did. Hayley waited until they fell to a hundred feet off the ground and tapped at her ELMO.

"The hatch should appear soon," she said as the pole once again popped up to reveal the hatch buried beneath the sand.

"There it is," Hayley said and pointed.

Tinx beelined straight for the hatch and slowed as she neared. They landed on the desert floor next to the bunker's entrance. The bubble burst as soon as they touched down on the hot sand, leaving them standing next to the opening. Hayley wasted no time; she attached a mechanical gizmo to the hatch as Damien instructed and it swiftly swung open. They quickly descended the staircase to escape the desert heat and the swarm of harpies that soon arrived.

"Seems like they were expecting us," Ethan said.

"They probably were," Tinx said.

"Where is the key?" Hayley asked as she paced back and forth by the wall at the back of the bunker.

"I've got it right here," Ethan said and handed the key to her. "You do the honors."

"Wait one second," she said as she rifled through Damien's duffle bag to find another portal beacon. "In case we need to make a hasty exit."

Hayley approached the engraving in the stone wall and slowly placed the metal key inside. It fit perfectly and made a satisfying clanking sound as the rock appeared to suck the key into place. At first, nothing happened, but then part of the rock wall melted away, exposing a yellow door with Stravis' symbol embossed on it. Ethan and Hayley glanced at one another as they recalled seeing something similar while spying on Blair.

"I'll take it from here," Ethan said as he stepped forward and placed his hand against the symbol that quickly disappeared along with the door.

"OMG," Ethan said.

"Wow, look at all that," Hayley said. "I think we just furnished Damien's laboratory."

"And then some," Tinx said.

Tinx fluttered over and landed on Hayley's shoulder as she entered Stravis' secret room. Ethan followed as bright lights clicked on one at a time until they illuminated the entire room. It was nearly identical to Damien's basement laboratory in size and shape, except this one was yellow and fully stocked. One long row of laboratory benches ran down the room's center, arranged back-to-back in pairs to double the allowable working area. To each side of the line of benches stood rows of shelves stocked floor to ceiling with supplies, equipment, specimens, and samples.

"Cool arrangement," Hayley said, "I bet Damien will want to duplicate this room entirely when we move it to The Residence."

"How are you planning on doing that?" Tinx asked. "Your mother will find out for sure."

"We'll cross that bridge when we get there," Hayley said. "That's my brother's problem anyway."

Ethan walked to the other side of the row of benches and stopped cold.

"Hayley, come here. You must see this."

Hayley followed him and stopped in her tracks as she turned the corner and saw what Ethan was talking about. Sitting atop the adjacent lab bench was an extensive collection of swirly eye-shaped medallions like the one hanging from the Shadow Princess' necklace, only smaller.

They were spread out and ordered in rows as if Stravis had been cataloging them.

"I count sixteen," Ethan said.

"Me too," Hayley said. "This is definitely related to the Shadow Princess."

"I agree," Ethan said. "I think we should take them and keep them between us for now. At least until we know what it means."

"I was going to suggest the same thing," Hayley said as she gathered the necklaces. "Here, put these in your pocket tote."

Ethan and Hayley agreed to stash their find away—for now, and return to it once they returned to The Residence. Until then, they would continue their current mission and keep their eyes open for more clues.

Hayley turned down one of the aisles to peruse the fully stocked shelves.

"I've never seen so many samples of animals, vegetables, and minerals from the elemental worlds as well as Earth."

"You might want to come check this out," Ethan shouted from across the room.

Hayley and Tinx followed the sound of Ethan's voice to an aisle at the back of the room, where he stood next to a shelf full of yellow notebooks.

"Stravis kept a lot of journals," he said as they joined him.

"Holy moly," Hayley said. "This is a huge find. We can't tell anybody about this."

"This discovery will please Master Damien," Tinx added.

"Yeah—and it might even prove to your mother the importance of what we've found," Ethan said.

"I'm sure it will," Hayley said. "Maybe that's how we convince her to move it all back to The Residence."

"Good point," Ethan said. "But I agree, we must keep this secret. Victor has already infiltrated The Residence, so we must not speak of this till we meet with your mother and brother."

They spent another hour scanning every aisle with their ELMOs. They needed to document everything for their return. That way, they would have something concrete to show Damien and the Headmistress.

A GRIM NEW START

Upon their return to The Residence, Damien greeted them at the front room door to the portal plane. It surprised them to learn nobody found out about their journey, especially Jordanna, who was none the wiser. Damien eagerly led them to his near-empty laboratory, so they could brief him on their findings.

Hayley told her brother about every detail of their journey and showed him the footage from her ELMO's proximity encoder. His jaw nearly hit the floor as he watched the footage they had taken. Then he copied it to his own ELMO for further scrutiny.

They agreed that Damien would study it more and create a presentation for Jordanna. She needed to know about such a significant find, so they could convince her of the importance of moving it all to The Residence.

The following day, they decided to take a break from the chaos. Ethan helped Hayley study for the placement exam required for her first-year of Caretaker training. They were in the study sitting on the couch by the fireplace when the door barged open, and a voice filled the room.

"Oh, here you are, my d-dears," Bella Wentworth said. "You've b-been summoned to an impromptu CAGE m-meeting."

She shuffled through a small stack of envelopes with two hands while her other arms held tissues up to her face and dabbed at her cheeks and eyes.

"I, I'm t-t-told it is of u-utmost importance," she said and broke out balling.

"Why are you crying?" Ethan asked as he ran to her side to calm her.

"You're such a n-nice b-boy," she said between sobs.

Hayley hurried over to help, and Bella handed her two envelopes. She opened one up and scanned it, but she and Ethan knew what the meeting was about.

"Mother is convening a meeting. We are to join them in the CAGE meeting room."

"It's the eleventh door on the right, in The Hall of Doorways," Bella whimpered.

It took several minutes for Ethan to get Bella to stop crying. She was upset about not being invited to the exclusive CAGE meeting—but Ethan and Hayley understood why. The need-to-know nature of today's subject meant no Bella. The last thing the Caretakers needed was for her to blab about their find to everyone who would listen.

Ethan and Hayley were the last to arrive. They entered and parted the dark curtains separating the foyer from the meeting room proper. The room was square with a giant round table and a tall ceiling to accommodate Azron's height. Jordanna sat at the far side of the table with Damien to her right and an empty seat to her left where Alexander usually sat. Nicholas, Brianna, Azron, Ethan, and Hayley took up the remaining seats clockwise from Damien's right. Tinx sat curled up on a small pillow on the table next to Hayley. A glass of water stood on the table before each meeting participant.

"Some of you are already aware of what the rest of you are about to learn," Jordanna said as her gaze wandered from Ethan to Hayley to Tinx. "Let me start by saying, I cannot stress enough how important secrecy is with this information. It is strictly need-to-know, and in my assessment, only those in this room need to know."

Jordanna paused, took a drink of water, and let out a deep sigh.

"Well—that was quite the buildup," Nicholas said.

"My thoughts exactly," Brianna said between lashes of her black serpent tongue. "We know the drill. S-spill it already."

Jordanna tapped at her ELMO, and a holographic screen popped up from the table's center. The screen was plus-shaped by design to divide the table into quadrants and create the illusion they were all watching from the same angle.

"Damien will walk you through what they found," she said as the presentation started.

"My sister took this video inside Stravis' bunker."

"How is this possible?" Nicholas asked. "I've been there myself. Stravis' bunker consists of no more than a dry sandy cavern."

"I've s-seen it too," Brianna said. "And nothing was there."

"Stravis cleverly crafted a secret room behind the back wall of the cavern," Damien said. "Even our most sophisticated instruments did not detect its presence."

"How were you able to find this?" Brianna asked.

"It was brought to my attention by—"

"Let me guess," Nicholas said, turned to Ethan, and flashed a toothy smile. "A little divine intervention."

"Yeah, I guess you could say that."

"Tell them what we are looking at," Jordanna said.

"Best I can tell, Stravis was studying something. What you are seeing is the best-equipped research laboratory I've ever run across. He appears to have taken detailed notes – so I should be able to recreate everything he did."

"But that could take yearsss," Brianna said.

"I agree," Nicholas said and glanced at Jordanna. "We have legions of scholars. Why not send a team of them to recreate Stravis' experiments and learn what he was up to."

"We cannot do that," Damien said and tapped at his ELMO to speed through the footage. "We cannot because of this."

The room fell silent as the scene changed to the shelves full of Stravis journals. The feed slowly scanned from left to right and shelf to shelf and panned back for effect.

"Now, I hope you all understand the urgency of this matter," Jordanna said and stood. "Victor Qruefeldt found a single journal from Creator Stravis important enough to enlist Daavic's help to steal. What do you think he'd be willing to do for shelves full of them."

Deep sighs filled the air, and the room remained quiet as they absorbed Damien's presentation.

"What are you suggesting?" Nicholas asked Damien.

"I suggest we rehouse Stravis' laboratory here at The Residence."

"That will be tricky if we are to keep it a s-secret," Brianna said.

"Tricky, but not impossible," Nicholas said. "But where do we move it to?"

"I've already figured that out. I've been retrofitting my brother's basement hideout into a lab of my own. It's mostly empty now, but with a little expansion, I think we can accommodate everything."

The room fell silent again as Nicholas and the others thought Damien's idea over.

"Well, what do you think?" Jordanna asked.

"Logistically speaking, the basement is perfect," Nicholas said. "You will have to restrict access to the front room and the study for a week. That will allow us to bring everything in through the portal plane."

"But how do we travel to the bunker without raising suspicion?" Brianna asked.

"Got that one covered, too," Damien said. "Hayley wisely left a portal beacon so we can use the portal plane and travel directly to the bunker."

"But that—"

"I know," Jordanna said and glared at Damien. "It is strictly against protocol – but I'm willing to overlook it in this case—if you all agree."

"Agree," Nicholas said.

"Agree," Brianna said.

"Gree," Azron said.

"Great, I know the rest of the guilty party agrees, and I have Alexander's proxy – so let's get on with it."

Jordanna excused Ethan, Hayley, and Tinx from the rest of the meeting while the others stayed behind to map out the details.

Four days had passed since the CAGE meeting, and Ethan and Hayley had not heard a peep out of Damien. They met Tinx bright and early every morning for breakfast before heading to the study to peruse its books for references to a desert fortress or anything that might refer to a princess named Adara.

Ethan and Hayley entered the dining hall and like clockwork, Tinx was sitting atop the table in the corner by the piano, patiently awaiting their arrival. They chose both the table and the time because nobody came early or sat anywhere nearby, so they could speak openly in private if they whispered.

"Good morning, you two," Tinx said as they approached.

"Morning, Tinx," Ethan and Hayley said.

Tinx scanned the dining hall and paused before she spoke.

"I think they've finished. Yesterday was our first normal CAGE meeting since the move started. Everybody showed up on time, and the Headmistress lifted the restrictions on the front room and study."

"Sounds like they've finished the move," Ethan said.

"Yes," Hayley said. "But I wonder why Damien didn't tell us himself."

"You saw how obsessed he was with the laboratory," Tinx said. "I'd bet he is so engrossed that the thought never crossed his mind."

"Yeah, you're probably right."

They didn't want to raise suspicion, so they sat together and enjoyed their morning breakfast as they had every day this week. After breakfast, they hurried to the front room and gathered around the basement door in anticipation.

"Come on in," Damien's voice said from a small speaker barely visible above the door.

He didn't need to tell them twice; Hayley swung the door open, and they scrambled down the stairs to witness what Damien was up to. They stopped at the base of the stairs and scanned the room to see what had changed.

"Wow, I love what you've done with the place," Hayley said.

The now full room was more extensive than before and nearly identical to Stravis' laboratory, minus the yellow walls. The main difference was the white floor and ceiling lit up from within, giving the lab a clean, sterile appearance. Damien was standing at the nearest lab bench, pouring over one of Stravis' yellow journals. Ethan, Hayley, and Tinx stopped at the bench to witness him set miniature furniture up inside a brown box with the top and one side removed. It looked like he was creating a tiny living room.

"So, you are playing with dollhouses now," Tinx said, causing Ethan and Hayley to chuckle.

"I've skimmed through several of Stravis' journals. He has them numbered, which will make my life much easier. I'm starting with the first journal and have read through it several times. Stravis had an interesting style of notetaking. Many passages are his thoughts of the moment, like diary entries. Then we have detailed notes on his experiments and some encoded entries I have yet to decipher."

"Have you learned anything important yet?" Hayley asked.

"Nothing concrete—only that Stravis did not trust the other Creators, especially Zamalador."

Ethan and Hayley exchanged glances as they both remembered Vanessa telling them the same.

"Anything else?"

"Yes, the purpose of this lab," Damien said and stopped what he was doing to look at them. "He built this lab to research peculiar interactions between elemental and earthly matter. What I find odd, though, is I skimmed through several journals and have only come across references to Atlantis, Ceres, and Hades. Thus far, I've not seen any mention of Zephyr."

Damien scratched his head and went back to what he was doing.

"So, what are you working on here?" Ethan asked.

"This one caught my attention. Stravis called it a habitat absorbing reflection trap."

"What does it do?" Tinx asked.

"Stick around, and you might find out."

He finished setting up the tiny room mock-up and attached an empty picture frame to the missing side of the box. Next, he slid a rectangular piece of glass into the frame and spray-painted the outer side black.

"You're making a mirror," Ethan said.

"Maybe, maybe not. The glass and paint are earthly, but the paint is gray, so I mixed powdered lava rock from Hades to create the black hue."

Damien shined an intense light on the wet paint for at least a minute as they watched silently.

"Should dry quickly; I think it's ready now."

Ethan spotted the reflection of the scene in the box on the surface of the glass.

"As I said, you are creating a mirror."

"Am I?" Damien detached the framed glass from the box and spun it around to face them. The image of the mini dollhouse remained on the surface like a three-dimensional picture.

"The glass captured the image," Hayley said.

"No, the glass absorbed the reflection and created a perfect copy of the environment," Damien said. "But I think something is missing, don't you?"

Damien plucked a small figurine of a person off his lab bench. Then he reached his hand into the image, and it passed right through as if the glass were not there. He set the figure down in the middle of the room and pulled his hand out.

"Much better, don't you think?"

Ethan's jaw dropped as he stared into the image that now included a tiny person in the middle of the room. He slowly moved his hand towards the picture, but the glass barrier stopped it.

"How did you do that? Is this a magic trick?"

"The first one's free," Damien said as a broad grin crossed his lips. "But I'm not finished."

He moved to the next lab bench and set the framed image down flat. Then he picked up a wood plank and laid it on top, covering the glass entirely within the frame's borders. Next, he grabbed a rubber mallet and hammered away at the plank. Ethan heard the muffled sounds of glass shattering underneath. When he finished, Damien lifted the frame and left the board and shattered glass on the bench. He held up the empty frame and turned it towards Ethan, Hayley, and Tinx to show them the image was still there.

"Now reach inside," Damien said.

Ethan slowly moved his hand towards the image, and this time it continued into the scene. He felt around and was able to grab everything inside. He grabbed a tiny chair, removed it from the picture and handed it to Hayley, who studied it carefully.

"And look, two for the price of one," Damien said and flipped the image over. The same image reflected on both sides of the glassless frame, surprising Ethan.

"Here, see for yourself," Damien said and handed the frame to Hayley.

She set it down flat and reached her hand inside to put the tiny chair back. It appeared to Ethan the lab bench was swallowing her arm. She flipped the frame over to check if the chair was back in place and reached inside to touch and feel everything on that side too.

"This is amazing. Both sides are windows into the same environment."

"Yes, and this is only the beginning," Damien said. "I can't begin to imagine what else we can learn from Stravis' research. I'm excited to continue, but between this and my CAGE duties, I don't know where I will find the time."

Ethan and Hayley took Damien's excitement as their queue to let him get back to his work. Tinx offered to stick around and help, and Damien accepted without a thought. It excited him to have her help. She'd learn where everything was and could dart about the lab to retrieve samples as he needed them. Sure, Tinx's size would cause some limitations, but any help was better than none.

Ethan and Hayley met in the Moongarden the following day to help Mildred with the skyclimber harvest. An infrequent event that only occurs once every two hundred years, according to an excited Mrs. Moongarden. But first, they would meet Irvin at Market Square to help him procure and transport specialized containers to house the seedlings once they were found.

"Today sounds like a scavenger hunt," Ethan said as he and Hayley entered the door to Market Square.

"Yeah, it should be fun," said Hayley.

"Shnickyrooners and things like that," Irvin said. He was waiting for them at the edge of the yellow brick road that led to Market Square. "It's a shiny moose tail that catches the slimy green mountain poodle in the afternoon trailer sewage."

"I always wondered about those green mountain poodles." Ethan's reply brought a glow to Irvin, and a giant ear to ear smile washed over his face.

"Hi, Irvin," Hayley said. "I hope we aren't late."

"Oh—no—Miss Hayley, you are not late. Irvin is just eager to get started. Mrs. Moongarden is blossoming with joy."

Red and yellow flowers sprouted from Irvin's head to illustrate Mildred's mood.

"Well then, let's get going," said Hayley.

Ethan, Hayley, and Irvin strolled along the yellow brick path into town. Market Square was teeming with people when they arrived. Rows of tents stood at its center, where patrons bartered with vendors for their goods. The tables lining the outer edges of the town were packed with people eating and drinking the fare from the various food merchants.

"I believe the vendor we are looking for is right down that aisle," Irvin said and pointed.

Ethan and Hayley followed Irvin as he pushed through the bustling crowd. A mixture of Caretakers, humanoids, and other elemental creatures patiently waited their turn to barter with their vendor of choice. Irvin stopped and turned to check if Ethan and Hayley were still following.

"We are almost there."

Ethan lunged forward and crashed into Irvin's chest, but Irvin reacted quickly and caught him before he could fall. Ethan regained his footing and turned around to find out who had pushed him. Hayley was already busy giving Blair and Caden a piece of her mind. Ethan stepped in front of her to confront Caden directly.

"Look, Blair, the mutant child is going to blame me for his clumsiness," Caden said with a devilish grin.

Ethan clenched his fists together and stepped toward Caden, but the bigger boy stood his ground. Irvin gently placed his hand on Ethan's shoulder and pulled him back.

"Ethan Fox is Irvin's friend," he said as he stepped between the two boys and stared into Caden's eyes. "Irvin will not permit you to bully his friend."

"Oh no, the Ravenwood butler-servant has come to their rescue," Blair said.

"You don't scare me," Caden said to Irvin.

"Bad idea to piss off a mimic," Hayley said to Ethan.

"Oh, it's not me you need to worry about," Irvin said calmly. "The big bad wolf is who you need to worry about!"

Irvin's face and body instantly morphed into a tall grey werewolf towering over Caden. Long sharp canines protruded from his snout and dripped with blood as he raised his dagger-like claws above Caden's head. Caden jumped back in shock as the crowd backed away from the commotion.

"This, this i-isn't over," a shaken Caden said to Ethan. "You won't always have someone around to save you."

"Let's go, Caden," Blair said as she stood by Caden's side. "We have a job to do. Daddy is expecting us."

The crowd returned to normal as Blair and Caden turned and pushed through. Ethan stood on his tippy toes to watch them closely. They moved to the opposite side of the lane and stopped at a merchant's tent. The letters on the sign read:

Ceresian elderwood for sale.

"Let's go. Those bullies won't mess with Irvin's friends again."

They followed Irvin to the container merchant to purchase seven containers. Irvin bartered with the merchant and was proud to have gotten all seven for only two sacks of mimicking melons. Irvin carried three containers for the trip back while Ethan and Hayley each carried two. They passed the sister cafes at the edge of town when something caused Ethan to turn around. He instantly spotted Blair sitting at a table sipping on a hot drink while Caden impatiently stood nearby holding up an enormous wooden plank.

"What's keeping you, Master Ethan," Irvin said from the yellow brick road where he and Hayley waited.

Upon returning to the Moongarden, they headed straight for the base of the skyclimber. Mrs. Moongarden was waiting patiently with her assistant Rosebud while Grubner and his brothers paced around like a small herd of cattle. Mildred wasted no time asking everyone to gather around, so she could explain today's mission.

"Whip-dilly-doodles," said Mildred. "Many of you have met her already – but for those of you who haven't, I'd like for you to meet Lois."

Mrs. Moongarden motioned to the massive trunk of vines weaving their way into the clouds.

"Seems like Lois dropped her last batch of seedlings only yesterday," she continued. "Yet here we are, waiting for the same precious moment two hundred years later."

Mildred paused to wipe a tear from her cheek.

"Lois will drop exactly seven seeds, no more, no less. She will eject them randomly into the sky in all directions. Small parachutes will sprout to guide them to the ground safely. They may land anywhere – but you can identify them by Lois' markings. They will be visible on the seed and parachute."

Ethan gazed up at one of the giant leaves protruding from Lois' side and stared at the unique swirling pattern that vaguely reminded him of something. He turned his head to look at it sideways, and his mind jumped back to meeting Vanessa Ravenwood. Then another memory flashed into his head; he and Hayley pressed their hands against the embossed symbols, and it zapped them. Then his mind returned to when his hand pressed against Stravis' symbol, and he opened the secret laboratory.

"Ethan, are you okay?" Hayley said softly into his ear and awoke him from his thoughts.

"Yeah — but I remembered something important. Something I meant to tell you earlier — but something distracted me."

"That's understandable. A lot has happened to distract us lately. You can tell me as soon as this scavenger hunt begins, and we are alone."

"Look there. I think I see one," Grubner shouted, causing his brothers to gaze skyward.

"Oh yes, and there is another," Mrs. Moongarden said. "Okay, everybody, the skyclimber harvest has begun. A dozen candied foxtails to anyone who finds a seed."

Grubner and his brothers split into two groups and ran off zig-zagging through the Moongarden in a feeble attempt to follow the parachutes as they fell. Rosebud and Mrs. Moongarden patiently waited for the next seed to eject but were pleasantly surprised when three shot out in succession, followed by the other two a minute later.

"Oh my," said Mildred, "Lois wanted to get it over with quickly this time."

Rosebud counted, traced, and plotted the courses of the five newest ejectees.

"Our chances appear best if we head in that direction," she said to Mildred.

Ethan and Hayley stayed behind to talk as Rosebud and Mildred headed off to search for skyclimber seeds.

"Okay, so what did you mean to tell me," Hayley said.

"When we broke into that room upstairs to spy on Blair. I counted six doors – but only two had symbols etched onto them."

"Yeah, I remember, and they zapped us when we touched them."

"Yeah—but did you look at the door that zapped me?"

"No, I was too focused on getting Blair's opened."

"Well, I did, and I saw the same symbol again on the wall of your grandparents' condo."

"My family crest," Hayley said. "Those rooms must be the headmasters chambers."

"What is that?"

"Special quarters given to each headmaster. Headmasters use them to do with as they please. I've heard talk that they existed but never knew where they were."

"Well, we do now, and the Ravenwood chamber may hold clues about the desert fortress," Ethan said. "Or even the Shadow Princess. I have a feeling your grandmother didn't tell us all she knew about her."

"Me too. She nearly fainted when I mentioned the name Adara," Hayley said. "But how are we going to get inside? My mother won't allow us to go poking around in there."

"You're forgetting something. If I was able to open Stravis' lab, and Blair was able to open the Trabblemore chamber—"

"I should be able to open the Ravenwood chamber," Hayley said as a deep grin grew across her lips.

Ethan and Hayley agreed to check out the Ravenwood chamber as soon as they finished helping Mrs. Moongarden find her precious seeds. There was a slight chill in the air, and the hunt went very slowly.

"I wish they would tell us where they landed," Ethan said and rubbed his hands together.

"Yeah, this is a slow and frustrating scavenger hunt, all right."

A white glow emanated from Ethan's palms as his symbols came to life and pointed out a direction. It took only fifteen minutes to find four seeds before Ethan's symbols returned to normal.

"They must be all accounted for," Hayley said as she and Ethan headed for the skyclimber.

Grubner and his brothers were standing at Lois' base when they arrived. They had found the other three seeds and were bickering about who would receive the prized candied foxtails. Ethan and Hayley broke up the quarrel by giving them their seeds so they could all receive a prize. Mrs. Moongarden and Rosebud returned empty-handed minutes later. Mildred heaped praise on Grubner and his brothers and awarded them each for finding the seeds. But she gave Ethan and Hayley a wink to tell them she knew the truth.

Upon leaving the Moongarden, Ethan and Hayley headed straight for the third floor headmasters chambers. Hayley approached the door slowly, moved her palm up, and gently pressed it against her family crest. A soft yellow glow emanated beneath her hand as a keypad materialized on the door.

"What now?" Hayley asked.

"I don't know. There was no keypad when I opened Stravis'."

"Wait, I may already have the combo," she said.

Hayley reached into her pocket, pulled out a piece of paper, and unfolded it.

"Where did you get that?" Ethan asked.

"Do you remember before my grandmother's exit?"

"Yeah, when she whispered something to you."

"She said we would come upon an obstacle we would not know how to overcome. She gave me this and told me not to open it until then. I think that time is now."

Hayley glanced down at the paper and held it up to show Ethan the numbers. She punched them into the keypad, and the door swung open. The room was dark inside until they were far enough in to set off the automatic lights. The chamber was like the study but much smaller. Ethan and Hayley wandered the room and poked around.

Ethan approached a large desk at the end of the room and opened the top drawer. He shuffled around inside and found a folded-up piece of paper. He unfolded it and studied the handwritten list for a minute.

"Hayley, come check this out," he said.

Hayley walked over and studied the note with Ethan. It read:

The Four Cohorts

1. Drake Evans
2. Lindrew Scragmort
3. Jason Crowley
4. Heldrik Vonn Grim

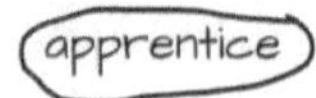

Ethan and Hayley studied the list in silence.

"Jason Crowley," Hayley said. "That's the name of the man my grandmother said was building the pyramids in the desert."

"Yeah, that's what caught my eye, too," Ethan said. "Heldrik is the only other one that sounds familiar to me."

"Me too—but I wonder what apprentice means and why it's circled."

"I have an idea what that means," Ethan said. "I meant to tell you, but I learned about it on the night of the Drone Wars."

"What does it mean?"

"Heldrik Vonn Grim had an apprentice, and his name is Dakota Drakelan. I read about it in an old *Daily Star* article by Boris Wentworth."

"That must be what Boris was referring to when he said he uncovered dark dealings from Dakota's past."

"Yeah, that's what I was thinking too."

"Tuck that away in your pocket tote," Hayley said. "We'll investigate it more later. We should keep digging around, there is bound to be more in this big room, but it could take weeks to—"

"Shhh," Ethan said and put his finger to his lips. "I hear someone."

They tip-toed to the door and placed their ears against it to listen. Blair and Caden talked as they entered the Trabblemore chamber.

"Daddy will be here soon," Blair said. "He will be overjoyed with the work you've done."

"Do you think he will let me come along?"

"He might," Blair said. "He will likely want to proceed with the plan as soon as he arrives."

The sound of a door opening and closing interrupted their eavesdropping.

"Did you hear that?" Hayley said. "Whatever their plan is, they are about to put it in motion."

"Yeah, I heard. We need to tell someone."

Hayley was hesitant to tell her mother anything, so they would discuss the matter with Damien first. They quietly slipped out the door and ran to the basement laboratory as fast as possible, but nobody answered the locked door.

"He must not be here," Hayley said as she pulled out her ELMO and tapped at its screen. "He's in the CAGE meeting room."

They dashed as fast as their light beetle could run. Ethan opened the door, and Hayley stormed through and swiped the dark curtain aside, disturbing the CAGE meeting.

"What is the meaning of this?"

Hayley froze at the sound of her mother's voice. Ethan entered the room and stood by her side.

"It's the Trabblemores," he said. "They're planning something, and we have reason to believe whatever they are planning is about to happen."

"We are well aware of the Trabblemores intentions," Nicholas said. "They've been trying to undermine Ravenwood leaders since Gaylord's downfall."

"Nothing the Trabblemores do could be more important than CAGE business," Jordanna said.

"But Mother—"

"We will listen to what you have to say after our meeting."

Ethan and Hayley sat quietly at the table as the CAGE meeting continued. Nearly forty minutes passed, and Ethan's patience was waning. He looked at Hayley, who was staring daggers at her mother. But then something happened to interrupt the meeting for good.

Wisps of golden whimsy wafted from beneath the table grabbing everyone's attention. Ethan quickly retrieved the awakened poem book. It flipped open, and a new poem slowly appeared. Ethan and Hayley read the poem as Damien and Jordanna hurried around the table to read the passage over Ethan's shoulder. It read:

Mirror Mirror

Mirror mirror on the wall, its secret started with a ball.

Bouncing on the checkered plane, to end the curse that caused refrain.

Unknown to those who live inside, created by the one who died.

Useless standing where it stood, till shattered under elderwood.
The Grim rejoice a brand new start, made from shards of a
broken hart.

The four of them stood in silence, pondering the meaning of the latest Seer communication.

"I think this refers to when Ethan unlocked the portals," Hayley said.

"Yes," said Jordanna. "But they spelled 'heart' wrong. Have they ever made such a mistake before?"

"They didn't spell anything wrong," Ethan said as he spun around to face them.

"Damien, when you showed us the experiment in your lab, what was the wooden plank made from?"

"That was the secret sauce," Damien said proudly. "Ceresian elderwood treated with Hadean tanzanite."

Ethan's eyes widened as he realized his theory was correct.

"The Seers don't make mistakes," he said. "Hart stands for habitat absorbing reflection trap. And if I'm right, we must hurry to the front room immediately."

Ethan stood and bolted out the door, followed by Hayley and the CAGE members. When they arrived in the front room, it confirmed Ethan's worst nightmare. Shards of broken glass covered the floor by the wall opposite the front door, and the giant mirror normally reflecting the portal plane was gone.

"I don't understand," Jordanna said. "Why would anyone want to break the mirror and steal an empty frame?"

"This wasn't just anyone," Ethan said. "Victor Qruefeldt did this and we have reason to believe the Trabblemores helped him."

"And that wasn't an empty frame they stole," said Damien. "It was a working replica of the portal plane."

"If what you say is true," Jordanna said. "The Grimleavers now have complete and total access to the human and elemental worlds."

"Yes, this is horrible news," Damien said. "This changes the game completely."

THE

NIBBLEWARTS

After allowing somebody to steal a copy of the portal plane, The Residence was on high alert, and the Caretakers did everything they could to ready themselves for what was to come. Ethan and Hayley felt partially to blame since they learned of the Trabblemores' plan before anything happened. And because Jordanna had failed to listen to their warnings, the divide between mother and daughter was widening. Damien and Tinx wanted to smooth things over, but now was not the time to try with tensions on the rise around The Residence. Besides, Jordanna spent every waking hour in the Map Room or CAGE meetings while Hayley was spending all her time with Ethan, and they were mostly out of sight lately.

To be precise, Ethan and Hayley were secretly staking out the headmasters chambers. They felt defeated after seeing the shattered mess on the front room floor nearly a week earlier. The feeling did not sit well with either of them; and they were determined to do something about it. But for now, Hayley insisted they stake out the Ravenwood chamber. She hoped to accomplish two things by doing so. For one, they would continue to search Odin's chamber for any other valuable information. They had a lot to sort through; so for now, they would focus on anything related to Jason Crowley and the secret pyramid fortress in the desert. In addition, they would keep an ear to the wall and listen for any word out of the Trabblemores they might overhear.

Thus far, there was no peep out of the Trabblemores. The only part of Hayley's plan bearing fruit was something Ethan found rummaging through Odin's bookshelves. He found a couple of folders stuffed between two books. They contained pages of notes and pictures. One folder contained photos of the four men believed to be "The Four Cohorts" and accompanying notes Hayley recognized as her grandfather's handwriting. The other folder had a picture of a young Victor Qruefeldt, with handwritten scribbles on the back that were unintelligible.

Up until now, the only thing they learned was Hayley's grandmother was not as forthcoming as she seemed. According to Odin's notes, she was way more involved than she led them to believe.

Ethan sat at Odin's desk with the medallions they found at Stravis' bunker laid out in front of him. Hayley had organized them into rows and fastened them to a large piece of felt for safe keeping. After studying each one carefully, the only thing he learned was they were all identical. Ethan was at the end of his rope with all this waiting around, and he was ready for action. All he had to do now was convince Hayley.

Ethan's hair blew back as hot grains of sand pelted his forehead, and he struggled to see what was in front of him. He held his arms up to shield his face as he leaned into the strong wind to make his way through the desert. He did not know where he was going, but the importance of what he was striving toward drove him forward. The wind stopped abruptly, and everything fell silent as Ethan wiped the sand boogers from the corners of his eyes to see the man in a yellow robe.

Stravis approached a tall woman in a hooded black-and-yellow Caretaker robe. Her back faced Ethan, so he could not tell who she was as Stravis spoke to her and motioned his arm at the surrounding desert. The woman turned her head from Stravis to focus on the desert as she knelt to place her hands on the warm sand. She bowed her head and chanted something unintelligible. At first, nothing happened, but then the sand churned in front of her as something arose from beneath the desert floor.

Stravis walked towards the disturbance, his arms filled with white fabric clothing. Then, one by one, bare humanoids with enormous oversized blue eyes emerged from the desert sand and accepted Stravis' offering. They were bald and totally naked except for a golden swirly eye-shaped medallion embedded in each of their chests. It continued for several moments until fifteen to twenty of them were visible, but it was hard to tell because they circled another woman that Ethan could not see well in the crowd. The big-eyed humanoids looked at one another and embraced as they passed, like at a family reunion. The scene was strange, but the happiness in their generous eyes brought calm to Ethan and made him smile.

The festive scene changed into a dark, dreary one in the blink of an eye. Black clouds hung in the sky over the rain-soaked desert. The big-eyed people lay chained to one another on the ground. They had hair now and sat in a half-circle around a woman chained to a post. Her blonde locks fell past her shoulders and framed her beautiful face and golden swirly eye-shaped pendant necklace. But she had regular-sized blue eyes, and they glared at the man standing before her.

He was a young man wearing a half-black half-white Caretaker robe and holding a small black box in the palm of his opened hand. Ethan recognized the man as a young Victor Qruefeldt as the woman shook her head at him in defiance. He reached his arm towards her, spoke some words, and the box came to life. Light emanated from the box as its lid flipped open, and wiry black strands shot out and enveloped the woman. A purplish glow surged within the strands, and the color drained from the woman's face and body as the life force slowly drained from her.

The chained survivors cried out to mourn their fallen leader, who stood pitch black and motionless before them. But something happened—she opened her eyes, and a bright yellow light glowed from within as a sheen flowed over her prune-wrinkled black skin, making her smooth again. The black apparition of the woman floated free of her restraints and moved slowly towards her captor. Shock erased the evil grin from Victor's face as he held the box out and shouted. The apparition vaporized into a thick black cloud of smoke that was quickly sucked into the box. The lid clamped shut, and the woman was gone.

Then, the scene changed again in a flash, and Ethan was standing under a calm night sky. He was still in the middle of the desert, but now tiny creatures moved all around him. They were three to five inches tall and looked like little cavemen with long ropy braids of hair that hung to the ground and covered their faces and most of their bodies. Their little arms and legs were only visible when they moved about, and their braids moved from side to side.

A yellow flash of light caught the attention of the little critters as the apparition of the woman in black appeared from out of nowhere. She stood alone in the sand and smiled down at the puny beings. Storm clouds formed overhead, and lightning bolts danced across the sky. A vortex opened behind the woman as she turned to the creatures and motioned for them to follow. She ushered them into the open vortex Ethan could now see into. He peered into the maelstrom and saw giant three foot tall ants standing upright and welcoming the new arrivals. Then, all at once, the clouds, the vortex, and the woman disappeared—leaving Ethan alone under the calm night sky.

Something glistened in the sand under the light of the silvery moon. Ethan walked over to investigate and knelt to see what it was. He found a golden medallion half buried in the sand. It was swirly and eye-shaped like the ones embedded in the chests of the big-eyed people. A strong gust of wind crawled across the desert's surface and peeled a layer of sand away as it passed. It exposed several more pendants scattered around the area and glistening under the night sky.

The sound of Ethan's ELMO awakened him from the life-like dream. He had fallen asleep at the table while thumbing through some of Odin's library books. He tapped at the screen, and Hayley's voice filled his room.

"Ethan, meet me in the study."

"But what about our stakeout?"

"Almost a week has passed. We need to regroup and start making things happen."

"You don't have to tell me twice," Ethan said as a full grin enveloped his face. "Be right with you."

He folded up the medallions, put them away, and bolted out the door. Then, he ran down the stairs so fast that Hayley had barely set her ELMO down when he entered the study. She was sitting at the reading table with a newspaper in front of her. Wordly stood on the table next to her and a stack of more newspapers.

"Wow, you got here fast."

"Your call sounded important. What have you—"

The sound of Tinx entering the room cut Ethan short. She darted over and landed on the table next to Wordly.

"Good, you're all here," she said. "Where have you two been hiding out lately?"

"Well, we've been—"

"Never mind, forget I asked. If you tell me, I'll want to tag along, and I am far too busy helping Damien with his lab research. On top of that, the Headmistress even sends me on some CAGE-related missions now. Ever since the portal theft, it's all hands on deck for CAGE."

"Okay, what can we do for you?" Hayley asked.

"I've come to cordially invite you to the unveiling of my family memorial. We will be holding the service at The Grimleaver Atrocities Memorial in a few days."

"We would love to be there for you," Hayley said.

"Great, I will ELMO you the details."

Tinx turned her attention to Wordly.

"Of course – you are more than welcome, too, Wordly. But I have other business to discuss with you as well."

"What can I do for you?"

"Well, let me start by saying this is sensitive CAGE business," Tinx said. "But I have the okay to bring you into the inner circle."

"Sounds intriguing. I'm in."

"But you don't even know what I am asking yet."

"You had me at CAGE. Tell me what you want me to do."

"A secret CAGE mission recently recovered a treasure trove of vital information. Damien has set up a laboratory in the basement, and I've been helping him organize things. I had an idea I think you would be perfect for."

"Books are my expertise – but I am not well versed in laboratory procedures."

"Exactly, I'm getting to that part," Tinx said. "A crucial component of what we recovered includes hundreds of journals written by Creator Stravis himself."

"Oh, now that sounds intriguing," Wordly said and rubbed his tiny hands together.

"Yes—and that is where my idea comes in. We would like you to go through the journals. Read them and re-read as many times as you need to catalog them for us."

"I'm a bookworm. It will take no more than one read through each journal for me to have a complete recall of the entire set."

"I don't want to burst your bubble," Hayley said. "But many journal entries are encoded or written in Creator Stravis' sloppy shorthand."

"Well, that's a different story. I may require several reads through. As for the encoded entries, until we crack the code, I won't understand the meaning, only the location of certain segments."

"Perfect, what you describe is light years from where we are now," Tinx said. "Damien will be pleased."

"When do I start?"

"Damien's CAGE duties consume him lately," Tinx said. "But he promised to find some time tomorrow if you agreed to help."

"That works for me, and will give me time to finish my daily duties here in the study, if Miss Hayley does not require more of my time."

"I think we are okay," Hayley said.

Tinx exited the study to continue her work in the laboratory. Wordly estimated it would take a few days to sift through Stravis' notes, and he was eager to start. So he book taxied his way back to the study bookshelves and disappeared.

"So, what's all this?" Ethan asked as Hayley went through the stack of newspapers on the table.

"These are old *Residential Daily Stars*. I asked Wordly to pull all stories referencing anything about my grandfather cross-referenced with pyramids or Jason Crowley. He didn't recall anything involving Odin and pyramids, but these all contain articles about Jason Crowley's dead body showing up on my grandparents doorstep."

"Have you learned anything?"

"Not a lot," she replied and pointed at the stack of newspapers. "Those are all follow-up articles by various reporters. They are mostly speculation and innuendo, but there's not much substance. But this is the original article covering the crime, written by your pal Boris Wentworth."

Ethan peered over Hayley's shoulder and read the title of the article: *Up and Coming Caretaker Couple Make a Grisly Discovery*. He continued scanning through the article but didn't find any new information.

"So, Jason Crowley was one of Gaylord Trabblemore's right hand men. But we already knew that from the notes in your grandfather's office."

"Yeah, I know, this seems like a dead end."

Hayley's words were lost on Ethan as his eyes moved to another article halfway down the page titled: *Magnetic Maelstrom*, and he began reading.

"Earth's magnetic field has always been of keen interest in the human world. But now, the new world's latest surprise development has stumped Caretakers and elemental scholars. A magnetic maelstrom of sorts has confounded experts who have no idea how or even when Earth's magnetic poles abruptly shifted."

"Ethan, are you daydreaming again?" Hayley asked, causing Ethan to stop reading.

"No, just distracted. But now that you mentioned it—I did have a strange dream earlier."

Ethan told Hayley about the vivid three-part dream that flashed from scene to scene like a slide show in his head.

"Parts of it sound like what my grandmother described."

"Yeah, I saw giant humanoid ants – but I didn't see any pyramids – and I don't remember Vanessa mentioning tiny caveman creatures."

"Excuse me," Wordly said as he popped out from between two books on a nearby shelf. "I wasn't eavesdropping, but what I did hear sounds like something I think you need to view."

"What would that be?" Hayley asked. "We welcome any help you might give."

"Have you heard of the Alcove of Enigma?"

"No, the name doesn't ring any bells," Hayley said.

"The Alcove of Enigma is a specialized room in the Gallery. What makes the alcove so unique is all paintings in that room have one thing in common. They were all determined to be significant by the Fates, yet we still have no idea what they mean or represent."

"And why would we need to view that?" Ethan asked.

"Because one of those paintings is similar to what you described."

Ethan's eyes widened as he turned to Hayley and saw her mouth gaped open.

"Yeah," she said and paused, "we need to see that."

"Thank you, Wordly, you've been a great help," Ethan said.

He grabbed Hayley's hand and ushered her out the study door. They ran the rest of the way and stopped to catch their breath before entering the enormous canvas room. Dorkin Drumbles immediately took notice of his visitor's arrival and hurried over to greet them.

"Wonderful day it is," Dorkin said in his usual Yoda'ish tone. "Happy, Dorkin is, to help Miss Hayley and Ethan Fox. Now how can Dorkin help?"

"We would like you to take us to the Alcove of Enigma," Hayley said.

Dorkin's head jumped back, and his glasses slid down his long, sloped nose.

"Is something wrong?" Ethan asked.

"Wrong—oh no—nothing is wrong. It's just, Dorkin does not get many requests for that."

They followed Dorkin as he walked towards the far side of the room, to the corner opposite the viewing hall. At first, they were walking straight at a blank wall, but when they got close enough, the outline of a door appeared against the white canvas.

"The Alcove of Enigma is in there," Dorkin said.

"Aren't you going to show us in?" Ethan asked.

"Oh no—Dorkin does not go in there. That room is a den of inequity if you ask Dorkin's opinion."

Ethan and Hayley opened the white door as Dorkin scurried away as fast as his little legs would carry him. They stepped into the well-lit white room filled with dozens of canvas paintings. Rows of them stood on easels and were covered in sheets at the room's center.

"I get the feeling Dorkin is afraid of this room," Ethan said.

"Ya think?" Hayley said and giggled as they approached the rows of covered easels.

"If we split up, we'll find it faster," Hayley said as she hurried past Ethan to search a different row.

"That sounds like a—"

"Ethan, we don't need to search for anything," Hayley said cutting him off mid-sentence. "I'm pretty sure I've found it."

Ethan hustled toward Hayley and when he rounded the corner, he immediately saw what she was talking about. Standing on an easel at the row's center was a canvas covered in a yellow sheet with a black swirly eye-shaped emblem stamped on it. They wasted no time uncovering the canvas to see what secrets it held.

"*The Pyramids of Never*," Hayley said, reading the title.

The two of them stood side by side and stared in silence. The painting depicted the building of a complex of pyramids off in the distance. One enormous pyramid stood in the middle with two smaller ones on each side. Near the build site, a much smaller temple-like structure was already complete.

In the foreground, a mountainous boulder crawled with tiny cavemen-like creatures with long braids of hair tied behind their tall heads. Their long faces were nearly twice the size of their bodies and mainly consisted of huge blue eyes and even bigger chomping teeth. Enormous three foot tall ants hauled giant rectangular stones to the build site. Two by two, the ants hoisted stones over their heads and walked them in a long single-file line stretching to the distant build site.

"The little cavemen creatures are eating the boulder," Hayley said.

"Yeah, they appear to be cutting that mountain of rock into giant stone bricks for the construction."

Ethan's gaze followed the trail of ants to the build site, and a tiny sparkle appeared on the central pyramid. His mind raced, and in a flash, he was inside the enormous pyramid watching as the Shadow Princess slowly floated towards him.

"Ethan, are you with me?"

"Huh," Ethan said and shook his head.

"Are you okay? You've been acting strange lately."

"I, I saw her again, the Shadow Princess."

"Are you talking about your dream again?"

"No, she came to me in a vision just now. And it's not the first time that has happened."

"She's trying to tell you something," said Hayley. "If only I could get inside your head and translate."

"Yeah, I wish you could."

They returned to the painting and studied the scene in silence.

"Interesting," Hayley said as she moved closer to gaze at the tiny cavemen creatures.

"What?"

"Well, I can think of a valid explanation for the giant ants. Any Caretaker could evolve one to grow that large and even walk upright. But I have no earthly idea where the little rock-eaters came from."

Something Hayley said jogged Ethan's memory.

"I wonder," he said.

"Wonder what?"

"Gruggins called them rock-eating roaches. Could they be Nibblewarts?"

"Well, I've never seen one myself – but now that you mentioned it, they fit the descriptions."

No sooner had the words slipped from Hayley's lips than Ethan's pocket tote erupted with golden wisps of whimsy. He pulled out the poem book as the pages turned to a blank one and wrote a new poem. The passage read:

The Nibblewarts

Bestowed with Seer spirit, they came to save the day.
The Sayers were awakened, with the gift of what we say.

But evil spied their presence, and tried to learn their truth.
By imprisoning Adara, a princess in her youth.

She gave her life to save them, and sacrificed her soul.
Disabling his weapon, to thwart his evil goal.

Attempts to kill them failed, and the Nibblewarts were born.
They fled indentured servitude, when a rift in time was torn.

But if you want to find them, make haste and leave right now.
For they are standing at the altar, of green grump with
furrowed brow.

"Nibblewarts," Ethan said. "They are Nibblewarts, and we need to get to Gruggins' box now!"

They quickly exited the alcove and ran past Dorkin towards the Gallery's exit. Halfway down the dark curved hallway, they heard Gruggins shouting.

"This is the last time you lousy gravel eaters will disrupt my nap," Gruggins screamed. "If I have to tell you again, I'm gonna—"

Gruggins stopped his rant when Ethan and Hayley entered the room. He gazed at Hayley, and his demeanor changed too.

"Well, hello, Miss Hayley—and err, Master Ethan. I was discussing the importance of proper sleep with my friends here."

The caravan of Nibblewarts was on their hands and knees, mumbling at the foot of the small table Gruggins' box sat on. All at once, they stood up, turned around, and stared up at Ethan and Hayley. The long hair braids fell to the sides of their faces exposing big blue eyes and fat buck teeth. One carried a miniature golden staff and raised it over his head as he spoke to the others in a low-pitched, unintelligible grumble. The others gathered their things, walked to their miniature wagons and wheelbarrows, and headed for The Hall of Doorways in single file.

"Wait, we need to speak with you," Hayley said. "Ethan, they are leaving."

Hayley frowned, but the Nibblewarts continued slowly towards the door.

"Don't bother," Gruggins said. "They never listen."

Ethan's eyes followed the caravan from front to back, and that's when he spotted the three inch tall blue bunny rabbit with yellow spots walking backward, waving at him. Ethan shook his head and wiped his eyes to ensure he wasn't seeing things – but then he heard a cartoonish voice.

"Don't miss out on all the fun Ethan Fox," tiny Jasper said. "But come prepared. They don't speak to giants."

"Ethan, are you having another vision?"

"No, I'm looking at a mini-Jasper. He's following the caravan, and I think he wants us to follow them too."

The caravan stopped to allow the door to swing open. Ethan and Hayley moved slowly so as not to spook them. The Nibblewarts entered the dark hallway and turned right instead of left as expected.

"They're going the wrong way," Hayley said. "The negative doorways lead to the past, and our rules forbid their use without proper authorization."

Ethan and Hayley followed the caravan into the hallway and turned right. They slowed their pace to stay at the trailing edge of their light beetle's light field. The procession stopped, and a door magically opened. The Nibblewarts entered, and Ethan nearly followed, but Hayley grabbed his arm to stop him.

"We can't follow them, Ethan."

"But we have to."

"Even if we wanted to, we can't go now. We wouldn't have a way back to the present."

"But Jasper followed them, and he might show us the way."

"Jasper. Really?"

"But I—"

"Is that a chance you are willing to take?"

"Yeah, your right, I guess."

"I know I'm right," she said as a broad grin spread across her lips. "If we do this, we will make a plan first."

THE PYRAMIDS OF NEVER

The door closed as the last of the Nibblewarts disappeared. Ethan tilted his head to watch as Hayley stood silently with her hands on her hips. The determination on her face was the only signal he needed to keep his mouth shut and wait for it.

"If we do this, the first thing we need is a tether port."

"Dakota has one," Ethan said. "The one he took from George."

"Yeah, I remember – but convincing him to give it to us might not be so easy."

"Never know till we try. But there is one more thing, something Jasper said to me."

"What did Jasper say?"

"He told me to come prepared because they don't talk to giants. I think he was speaking of the Nibblewarts."

"They did appear to be intimidated when they saw us," Hayley said.

"Yeah, to them, we are giants. But even if we could approach without scaring them, we can't understand a word they are saying."

"No, we don't – but my ELMO does, and it can translate."

"Great, then we are back to, they don't speak to giants."

"I think I've got that one covered, too," said Hayley. "Grubner Trowel oversees the Moongarden's supply of dwindle-berries, and he owes me a favor. Four each would be enough to shrink us down to Nibblewart size. Of course, we will need four more to return us to size – so that's sixteen total."

"Dwindle-berries?"

"Yes, each one we eat will roughly halve our size. By my calculations, four each will reduce us to three or four inches. But don't worry, they're delicious."

"Oh—right—you tell me you will shrink me down to three inches, but don't worry about a thing."

"The way I see it, our biggest challenge will be talking Dakota Drakelan into letting us use his tether port without telling my mother."

"Then maybe we don't talk him into anything. We could borrow the tether port for a few hours. I mean, we will return it."

After discussing the matter, they talked themselves into the more morally corrupt option. Ethan would distract

Dakota while Hayley located the tether port and retrieved it with her copycat.

The long walk down The Hall of Doorways gave Ethan time to think about what he would say to Dakota. They entered the twelfth door on the right and nervously inched their way up the trail to Dakota's shack on the hill. It was late afternoon, and the sky was pinkish orange as they stepped onto the creaky front porch. The door slowly squealed itself open, allowing the remnants of the day's light to fill the dimly-lit cabin. Ethan and Hayley paused at the entrance as their eyes adjusted.

"Well, are ya goin' ta come in 'ere or not," said Dakota's gruff voice.

"Your place is quite dark," Hayley said.

"Pardon me," Dakota said and snapped his fingers, causing lights to flip on around the room. "I fergot my manners. Not used ta gettin' so many visits from light lovers."

As Ethan and Hayley entered, Dakota stood up from his reclining chair.

"What can I do fer ya?"

"I, I h-have a few questions," said Ethan as he moved closer.

"Well, spit it out," Dakota said and chuckled.

Hayley casually scanned the room as Dakota and Ethan spoke. She stroked her Tabby Cat hidden away inside her robe.

"I've discovered your secret," Ethan said.

"And what, pray tell, would that be?"

"You were Heldrik Vonn Grim's apprentice."

"Not much of a secret, Boris Wentworth made sure a that."

"I'm not talking about the article. I'm talking about this." He waved the note they found in Odin's office at Dakota, who took it from his hand and studied it.

"Yeah, so?" Dakota said and handed the note back to Ethan. "Why do ya think he circled the word 'apprentice'? It's circled because Odin knew I served as Heldrik's apprentice. It's why he hired me. He was skeptical of me at first, but he was a fair man and decided ta give me a chance."

"Then why do you hate Boris so much? Because of the article?"

"Because 'es a scoundrel, and when that article came out, it caused Odin a lotta grief. Didn't hurt me none, but Odin was new ta bein' headmaster and didn't need the added strife."

"So you've seen this list before," Ethan said.

"Odin showed it ta me before hirin' me. An I'll tell you the same thing I told 'im. The only thing I know 'bout them names is they're all associates a' Gaylord Trabblemore."

"And that's all you told him?"

"No, I also told him Heldrik wasn't the monster everyone made 'im out ta be. Sure, he had 'is demons, but he was a decent man."

"Anything else?"

"I've said ma peace. If I didn't know any better, I'd think ya'd gone ta work fer Boris and 'is rag of a newspaper."

Ethan pressed Dakota more to give Hayley time, but he was running out of things to say.

"Let's go, Ethan. I think we've worn out our welcome here," said Hayley.

She grabbed him by the arm and pulled him towards the exit when Dakota sat back in his chair.

"Little lady, I trust yer goin' ta bring that back when yer done goin' wherever yer goin.'"

"W-what are you talking about?"

"The tether port ya pilfered."

"B—but how did you know?"

"I wasn't born yesterday," said Dakota as a broad smile appeared beneath his mustache. "Ethan Fox comes ta my house with a strong-minded Ravenwood woman, and she stands by silently as he asks all the questions. You'd have ta be a darn fool ta not be suspicious a that."

"He's got a point," Ethan said and chuckled.

"Yes, I will return it to you, I promise."

They left the creepy house perplexed. Ethan was sure Dakota knew more about the names on the list. But he'd let them take the tether port. Dakota seemed to have ulterior motives. But for now, they had bigger fish to fry.

Hayley woke bright and early the following morning to help Grubner with his chores in the Moongarden. Sixteen dwindle-berries was a tall ask, even if he did owe her a favor. So she would butter him up before broaching the subject. Noon was approaching when she met Ethan in the front room.

"Mission accomplished," she said and showed him a pouch full of colorful purple berries.

"So you have everything we need?"

"Tether port, check. Dwindle-berries, check. ELMO, check."

"Let's get a move on."

They entered The Hall of Doorways, looked around to check for spying eyes, turned right, and hurried to the door the Nibblewarts had used.

"Well, here goes nothing," Hayley said as she pulled the door open, grabbed Ethan's hand, and pulled him inside. Ethan felt dizzy as purple sparks flashed in his eyes, and everything grew dark.

When he came to, they were at the edge of a vast desert under the calm night sky. Behind them, an enormous spherical rock stood partially buried in the sand. The flicker of flames was barely visible at the base of the distant boulder.

"That rock is huge," Ethan said. "Nearly the size of a small town."

"Yeah, it's gigantic, alright."

"Where on Earth did they find that?" Ethan wondered aloud.

"I don't think they found it on Earth."

Bright lights beamed from the desert floor not far from them, lighting the sides of gigantic pyramid structures under construction. Ethan and Hayley instantly recognized this place from the painting in the Alcove of Enigma. They moved stealthily towards the construction site to avoid being seen by the Caretakers guarding the area. When they got close enough, they crept on their bellies to hug the ground. A Caretaker in a half-black half-red robe emerged from the small temple near the build site. He spoke to the guards, which, thankfully, gave Ethan and Hayley the cover they needed to run and duck behind a row of enormous, stacked bricks.

"Yes, sir, we understand, sir," one of the guards said.

"Of course, Mr. Crowley, we take turns circling the site every hour as you have ordered," the second guard said.

The guards sounded frightened by the man, so Ethan peeked out from behind the rock wall. He recognized the man from the pictures in Odin's folder, but he witnessed something else that shocked him to his core. He ducked back behind the rock wall and took several deep breaths to maintain composure.

"What did you see?"

"You're not going to believe it! Jason Crowley is here — and he's holding a Heldrik Vonn Grim puzzle box."

"Let me see."

Hayley switched places with Ethan and took a peek for herself, and when she turned back to him, her eyes were as wide as saucers.

"But—how is that possible? We are thousands of years before your birth."

"Yeah—and I thought Heldrik created it for Victor Qruefeldt."

They sat behind the rock wall, quietly pondering their discovery. Jason Crowley bid the guards farewell, then one of them left for their scheduled hourly rounds. Ethan and Hayley took that as the perfect time to run away before being spotted at the build site.

"We should head for the giant boulder," Ethan said. "That's where we are most likely to find the Nibblewarts."

"Great idea, and even if we don't find them, we can use the rock for shelter. Deserts can become very cold at night."

They spent the better part of an hour covering the distance to the base of the giant rock. From closer up, the flames from many torches were visible around the area where they quarried the rock. A small team of the giant ants were moving enormous stone bricks and stacking them into a long, tall row, partially blocking their view of the area.

The giant ants ignored Ethan and Hayley as they slowly crept around the wall of stacked rock. A massive bonfire burned at the area's center to warm the tiny caveman creatures that were now visible to Ethan and Hayley. The Nibblewarts worked in small teams to eat straight lines into the rock and cut perfect blocks away from the giant boulder. When one group filled their bellies, they would go to the back of the long line to rest while another team took their place to carve out the next brick.

"Well, I haven't seen any guards here," Ethan said. "Let's go in for a closer look."

"Ethan, you are forgetting what Jasper said."

"I'm not forgetting anything. But Jasper giggles after nearly everything he says, which doesn't exactly inspire my confidence. So before I shrink myself into an itty-bitty, I will be darn sure he is speaking the truth."

Ethan stepped out from behind the rock wall and into the bonfire light. Hayley followed as he slowly strode towards the long line of Nibblewarts gathered on a flat surface carved into the giant rock. Several tiny creatures spotted them and pointed as the others turned and a low pitch grumble filled the air. Then, all at once, the perfect line of Nibblewarts turned to chaos as the creatures hopped to the desert floor and scurried in random directions like confused ants. But the confusion was short-lived and quickly turned into an orderly evacuation as they beelined left and right around the base of the boulder. Ethan followed the escaping Nibblewarts to a series of small tunnels burrowed into hardened sand beneath the boulder. He turned to Hayley, who stood behind him with her arms folded.

"Got any more bright ideas?"

"No—but I had to be sure."

"Okay, now that that's settled, we must follow them."

Hayley pointed at the holes at the base of the giant rock, pulled out the pouch, and handed Ethan four dwindle-berries. He was still staring at them in the palm of his hand when Hayley quickly shrunk down to half barbie doll sized. He barely heard her tiny voice as Hayley shouted up at him.

"Come on. They're getting away."

Ethan popped the dwindle-berries into his mouth and swallowed. His head grew fuzzy, and his vision blurred. Everything around him appeared to be in slow motion and grew larger and larger. Twenty long seconds passed while Ethan shrank to Hayley's size. His head was still wobbly, and he was losing his balance, so Hayley put her arm around him to steady him.

"You didn't chew," she said. "It goes much faster if you chew. Dwindle-berries are delicious."

Once he regained his composure, Ethan scanned his new, much larger surroundings. It amazed him how different everything appeared from a puny perspective. The previously small holes burrowing underneath the giant rock were now large tunnels.

"Let's get moving," Hayley said.

Ethan followed her into the nearest tunnel, and she quickly turned on her ELMO flashlight. But the light from the shrunken ELMO was feeble and barely lit their way, so Ethan asked her to turn it off.

"Everything is pitch black in here," Hayley said. "We need light."

"No, we don't. Remember, in the Trabblemore chamber, I could see perfectly while you barely saw a thing. My eyes will adjust to the darkness."

Hayley switched off her ELMO light, and they waited a minute for Ethan's eyes to adjust – but once they did, his vision was like watching a fuzzy black and white television.

"Grab onto my shoulders and walk behind me."

Hayley pawed around in the darkness, trying to find Ethan's shoulders and scooted her way behind him.

"Tell me if I'm going too fast," he said as he headed into the deep dark cave.

The tunnel descended deeper beneath the desert sand and joined with other tunnels leading to unknown destinations. They continued down the remaining tunnel that made a U-turn and leveled off before turning perfectly straight and circular.

"Our path seems to have straightened," Hayley said.

"Yeah, we appear to be inside a long pipe or something."

"You can go faster now," she said. "As long as we are on a straightaway."

They continued down the long straight corridor for another half hour before reaching a flickering light at the end of the tunnel.

"I can see," Hayley said. "Burning flames up ahead from the looks of it."

She moved to Ethan's side, and they continued towards the flickering orange light dancing across the wall at the end of the tunnel. They slowed to a crawl as they reached the entrance to an expansive chamber and peeked around the corner. The Nibblewarts gathered around a bonfire burning at the center of the room. They were aware of Ethan and Hayley's presence and turned to look at them but were not scared.

Hayley fished her ELMO from her Caretaker robe and turned it on as she slowly entered the chamber. Ethan followed her lead and stayed by her side as she inched towards the Nibblewarts.

"We mean you no harm," Hayley spoke into her ELMO.

She tapped at the screen and held her ELMO up into the air. An unintelligible low-pitched grumble erupted from the ELMO and filled the cavern. The Nibblewarts remained quiet at first but then all burst out in laughter.

"Great, they think you are telling them jokes."

"We only want to speak with you," Hayley said into her ELMO and held it up again.

This time the grumbling sound did not garner any reaction. The Nibblewarts sat quietly by their fire and stared at Ethan and Hayley. The uncomfortable silence ended when the one with the golden staff stood and approached them. He seemed to be their leader, stepping forward to speak for his tribe. Hayley tapped her ELMO to record the low-pitched grumbling from the Nibblewart leader. When he finished speaking, she tapped again for translation.

"Nibblewart high priest recognize shrunken giants. Nibblewarts no afraid and no listen to lies of shrunken giants."

He turned and started back towards his people.

"As Gruggins said, they don't listen," Hayley said.

But something she said struck a chord, and Ethan's mind drifted back to their return from Stravis' bunker. Gruggins was in a tirade, shouting at the 'rock-eating roaches' that had just left the room. He fast-forwarded through the scene in his mind and tried to remember what Gruggins had said.

"Wait a minute," Ethan said to Hayley. "Gruggins said, they always speak of the Shadow Princess."

"Yeah."

"And he said something else," he continued, his feet tapping on the ground. "I was the only one listening, but there was something else they speak of. The um—er—the— that's it—the Nibblewart prophecies."

"Wait," Hayley shouted and tapped at her ELMO to speak into it.

"We want to learn about the Shadow Princess and the Nibblewart prophecies."

This time, the ELMO's grumbles caused the Nibblewart high priest to stop and turn around.

"Show him a picture of Gruggins," Ethan said.

Hayley tapped at her ELMO, and a holographic Gruggins appeared on her shoulder. The Nibblewart high priest fell to his knees and bowed before them. The others turned away from the fire and fell to their knees as the room filled with low-pitch chants.

"That got their attention. I'm turning the translator to persistent mode. It will allow us to speak freely to them but won't pick up our whispers if we need to speak to one another."

She tapped her ELMO, and Gruggins' holograph disappeared. The Nibblewart high priest stood and walked towards them.

"Master Gruggins asked us to come," she said. "He sent us to learn more about the Nibblewart prophecies and the Shadow Princess."

"Shadow Princess, save Nibblewarts from evil giant," said the high priest. "Shadow Princess disappear long time."

"What do you know of Adara?" Ethan asked.

"Adara become Shadow Princess. Shadow Princess save Nibblewart people. Adara save Nibblewart people."

"I think he's talking about what I saw in my dream," Ethan said to Hayley. "The woman chained to the post must have been Adara. Victor Qruefeldt transformed her into the Shadow Princess, and then she saved the Nibblewarts."

"That sounds like a reasonable explanation," Hayley agreed.

"What does the Shadow Princess want with me?" Ethan asked the high priest.

"Shadow Princess, return. Shadow Princess lead chosen one to Nibblewart prophecies."

"But what are the Nibblewart prophecies?" Hayley asked.

"What was, what is, and what shall be," the priest said.

"Great, he is telling us 'it is what it is,'" Ethan quipped.

Hayley rolled her eyes at Ethan. The Nibblewart high priest stood silently, staring at them as if pondering something. Then he turned around, waved, and spoke.

"Come."

They followed him into another corridor, this one filled with bright purplish light; and as soon as they entered, they understood why. This short corridor ended at a swirling vortex with no path around it.

"He's leading us into that vortex," Ethan said. "I hope he knows where he is going."

Hayley glanced behind them and saw the whole tribe of Nibblewarts was following too.

"I doubt he would lead his whole tribe into a death vortex."

When they reached the mouth of the ominous-looking vortex, the Nibblewart leader did not hesitate and walked through like it was an open door. Ethan and Hayley took a leap of faith and followed. Purple sparks flashed in Ethan's eyes, like when they walked through the negative doorway. When they shook off their dizziness, they found themselves standing in a vast room lit by torches attached to the walls.

"That vortex," said Hayley as she stared at her ELMO. "It was a time portal; we are back to our present time."

In front of them, a vast wall column rose to a very high ceiling. On each side, a stone staircase ascended into the darkness of what was above. On each side of the staircases, more stone flooring led to tall walls on each side of the room. And beyond the wall column, the room stretched into more darkness where no torches were lit.

"Where are we?" Hayley asked.

But the high priest did not answer. Instead, he walked forward towards the tall wall column. He stopped and pointed up at the wall with both of his hands, and he turned towards them.

"Shadow Princess, come here; Nibblewart prophecies, come here."

Ethan peered at the tall empty wall where the high priest was pointing. His gaze continued up the wall towards the ceiling, and that's when he spotted them out of the corner of his eyes. Stealthily creeping down the walls on both sides were vicious black dragons with blue swirls and gleaming green eyes.

"Pixie-devils," Ethan said as he pointed at the walls above.

"Pixie, they look more like real dragons at this size," Hayley said.

Ethan scanned the room and saw glowing green eyes emerging from the darkness behind the column wall. He quickly spun around and spotted the bright light of an exit at the front of the room.

"There's an exit over there," Ethan said to Hayley. "If we make it outside, we may be able to return to size. At least then, we'll have a fighting chance."

A dragon leaped from the wall and landed between Ethan and Hayley and the Nibblewart high priest. The creature inched towards the priest, but his tribe was quick to defend their leader. Four sprang to action and jumped between the beast and their chief. They stabbed at it with spears while others from the tribe shot arrows at the other prowling devils. Ethan grabbed Hayley's hand as she spun around and glanced at him.

"Let's run," Hayley said.

They ran towards the exit as more Nibblewarts leaped into action to fight the attacking pixie-devils. They reached the entrance and continued through, leading them into a giant-sized room. This room was dark too, but they continued running towards the light source, which was the exit.

"We have plenty of space now," Ethan said and stopped running.

Hayley quickly fished out the pouch of dwindle-berries and poured them into her hand. They each grabbed four and gobbled them down. Ethan chewed them to a fine mush before swallowing, and he grew back to size quickly.

Ethan glanced down to where they had just been. A miniature replica of the pyramid site sat on the ground at their feet, and they had emerged from the largest pyramid at its center.

"We were in a model," Hayley said.

The Pyramids of Never

Ethan scanned the rest of the room that was darker towards the back as the only light came from the tall spacious entrance. They were in a huge rectangular room with towering columns rising to the ceiling in the darkness above. One wide aisle split the room down the center from the front entrance to the blackness in the back. The rest of the room consisted of square and rectangular enclosed structures scattered randomly about, dividing it into a maze.

"We are in a mausoleum or something," Hayley said.

"The Nibblewarts won't be able to hold off those pixie-devils forever," Ethan said and motioned for the exit.

A creepy hissing noise echoed from the blackness of the room's depths.

"Let's get out of here," Hayley said.

She grabbed Ethan's hand, and they hurried towards the light and charged through the entrance. Their eyes took a minute to adjust to the bright desert sun. They found themselves on a veranda outside the front of the building. Enormous stone columns rose to support the heavy rooftop of the gothic structure. A massive dune of sand covered the stone floor on the left half of the veranda and blocked most of their view in that direction. Ethan stepped off the stone floor and walked into the desert to scan the horizon to the right.

"You see anything?" Hayley asked from the shade of the veranda.

Suddenly, his feet began to vibrate as a disturbance several hundred feet away churned the sand like ocean waves.

"Harpies," Ethan shouted. "We can't leave this way."

"Get back here," Hayley said.

Ethan hesitated as something caught his attention. A small black shiny object rode the vibrations, floated to the surface, and peeked out from beneath the sand.

"What are you waiting for," Hayley shouted. "They are moving fast."

Ethan turned and ran back to Hayley. They stood watching the harpies from the stone floor of the veranda but retreated inside when they reached jumping distance. Their eyes took another minute to adjust to the darkness inside.

They tiptoed deeper into the building, passed the tiny replica on the floor, and stopped between two of the many structures that divvied up the room.

"We need to keep our eyes open," Ethan whispered.

"But it's so dark in here. I can barely see anything."

"Right, I will keep my eyes open."

They stood quietly, trying to gather their thoughts and find a way out of their predicament.

"I saw something green flash," Hayley said. "Over in that direction."

Ethan looked to where Hayley pointed but saw nothing. He turned to her and spotted a set of green eyes glaring at them from the floor behind her. He shoved Hayley into a dark hallway, dove, rolled away, then jumped to his feet and ran behind one of the structures as a yellow energy beam burst from the pixie-devil's mouth.

"Take cover," he said. "They shoot energy beams from their mouths."

"Where are you?"

"I'm a couple of structures over," he said. "Hang tight, and I will find you."

"When you first encountered the pixie-devils, how did the Shadow Princess save you from them?" Hayley asked.

"She jumped between us and shielded me from them."

"Ahh, that gives me an idea."

Hayley reached into her robe pocket, pulled out her copycat, and whispered as she stroked it. The cat figurine flattened out and widened into a circular shield with a mirrored chrome-like finish. Hayley stood and held the shield up in front of her and stepped out into the center aisle. She could barely see in the darkness, but several glowing green eyes glared back at her, so she advanced toward them. Their little mouths gaped open as yellow light radiated between their sharp teeth. Hayley bent low to the ground as she continued forward and kept her eyes on the pixie-devils about to blast her. She crept into Ethan's view, and he saw what she was doing.

"Where did you find Captain America's shield?" he whispered.

Hayley glanced to her left and spotted Ethan bathed in yellow light reflecting from her shield. He took cover between two of the room's many structures. Then, all at once, the pixie-devils let loose with their energy blasts. All of them hit their mark, striking the shield dead center and showering out in all directions like a fireworks display. Hayley's shield withstood the devil's wrath without a scratch. The room lit up for several seconds as if someone had tossed a yellow road flare in, but the brightness subsided, and the darkness returned.

Ethan's eyes adjusted quickly to the darkness. He glanced at Hayley and noticed something moving in the reflection of her mirrored shield. He peeked around the corner and saw a small battalion of pixie-devils backing away and staring up at something. Their movement stopped in an instant as they quickly turned to stone. The creepy hissing noise returned as Ethan's gaze moved away from the stone devils to where they were looking. At first, he saw another structure, but then a tall snake-like figure moved into view. His veins chilled as the creature slithered towards the still pixie-devils, and the nest of red-eyed serpents swayed back and forth atop her head.

Ethan recalled the first time he saw a likeness of Medusa. Hayley had taken him to The Grimleaver Atrocities Memorial. They met Brianna, mourning in front of her sister Medusa's exhibit. Even the distant memory sent a chill up his spine. Later, he learned more about Medusa while helping Hayley study for Caretaker training. If you look Medusa in the eyes, you'll turn to stone, he repeated in his head.

"Ethan, what's that?"

Medusa spun around, spotted Hayley, and slithered slowly towards her next victim.

"Our worst nightmare," he shouted.

Medusa stopped in her tracks and turned towards Ethan.

"Run!" he shouted.

Hayley bolted for the exit.

Ethan ducked into the nearest hallway and ran deeper into the building, screaming to ensure the serpent followed. He circled around and returned to the wide center aisle he knew would lead to Hayley. But when he stepped into the corridor, Medusa was there blocking his way, so he ducked back into hiding unnoticed by the lurking creature.

"I need something to distract her," Ethan thought as he scanned the floor for rock or debris. He crept down the hall and spotted a damaged wall with a hole blasted through, so he pried some stones free and put them in his pocket. He tiptoed back to the center aisle and peeked around the corner. Medusa was still there, scanning the area and staying as still as possible to listen for any nearby disturbance.

Ethan stepped into the wide aisleway to throw a rock and distract her. But his palm symbols suddenly came to life, bathing him in a white glow as they spun around to point at the back of the room. Medusa saw him and quickly slithered towards her prey at top speed. Ethan clasped his hands together as he bolted across the aisle and down another corridor between two crypt structures. He ducked behind the structure on his right as he tossed a couple of rocks over the adjacent structure. Medusa was right on his tail but did not see his maneuver, so she followed the sound of the rocks when they hit.

Ethan sprang from behind the structure and backtracked to the center path and towards the exit as fast as he could run. Medusa detected his footsteps and followed in hot pursuit. But she stopped and retreated when he reached the bright light at the building's entrance. Hayley stood on the door's threshold, staring into the darkness as Ethan emerged.

"I wasn't sure if you were going to make it," she said.

"I wasn't either. That was close," he replied.

His mind poured over their seemingly meager options. What would be a better way to die—getting buried by sand harpies or turned to stone by Medusa?

"I'd give anything for a portal beacon about now," he said.

Hayley gazed up at him and the glimmer in her eyes told Ethan all he needed to know—she had an idea.

"Ethan, you're a genius."

"I—I am?"

"I don't know why I didn't think of this before. The tether port connects two points in time and space. We've already moved back to the present time, but the tether port is still connected to its location in space."

"Then, if I understand you correctly, it should transport us to my dad's place in Manhattan."

"Yes, unless Dakota reprogrammed it, then who knows when or where we might end up."

"Well, wherever that is, it can't be worse than where we are now."

THE SAYERS

The tether port transported them to someplace very dark. Ethan stood and helped Hayley to her feet. His eyes were still adjusting, so he only saw what was right in front of him. But he heard something stir, and a loud clapping noise rang out. Candles lit up in succession around the small room they were in. Ethan recognized the small stick creatures with their hands and arms burning in apparent agony.

"Thought ya'd be gone more'n a day," Dakota said from his corner chair. "Are the two a' ya okay?"

"We're fine," Hayley said.

"Did ya learn anything from yer little adventure?"

"Nothing we're going to tell you," Hayley said.

"I'm thinkin' you'n me got off on a wrong foot, little lady."

"I do have one question I have to ask you," Ethan said. "Jason Crowley was there, and he was holding a Heldrik Vonn Grim puzzle box."

"Well, don't that beat all."

"How is that even possible?" Hayley asked. "We were thousands of years in the past. Long before Ethan was ever born, and long before Victor Qruefeldt commissioned the puzzle box."

"Victor Qruefeldt," Dakota said. "He didn't commission Heldrik ta build the box. What gave ya that idea?"

"That's what his plaque says in The Grimleaver Atrocities Memorial."

"Never been ta see it," Dakota said. "Sounds like someone's tryin' ta bury somethin' in the past."

"How can you be so sure?"

"I was 'is apprentice, remember," Dakota said. "Someone commissioned the box long before anyone'd ever heard a Victor Qruefeldt. I remember, plain as day, Heldrik worked day an' night tryin' ta figure out how to power the darn thing. He was stumped. Then, one day, he received a strange letter an 'is problems were solved."

"What did the letter say?" Ethan asked.

"Dunno, I didn't see it – but Heldrik described it to me. Wasn't till years later I realized what he was describin' was a leap-letter."

The room fell silent as Ethan and Hayley absorbed what Dakota had told them. Ethan remembered when they witnessed Daavic send a leap-letter. He didn't even know what one was, but Hayley explained they were telegrams sent backward in time.

"Well, we better be going, Hayley said to break the silence. But first, this is for you."

She handed the tether port to Dakota.

"Thank you for letting us use this," she said. "You won't tell my mother—will you?"

A huge smile appeared below Dakota's thick mustache.

"Heavens no, little lady. I think we may 'ave just regained our footin'. This'll be our little secret."

They left Dakota's shack and were near The Hall of Doorways when Hayley stopped abruptly.

"What?"

"Leap-letters," Hayley said. "Daavic sent one to Victor to relay information from the future. Now, we learn a leap-letter helped Heldrik complete the most dangerous weapon ever created."

"Yeah—but where are you going with this?"

"I'm wondering how often they've used leap-letters and if there's anything we can do to stop them."

"Good question," said Ethan. "All I know is, anything to do with time travel boggles my mind."

The sound of Hayley's ELMO ringing interrupted their conversation. Tinx was calling to tell them she would not be available for breakfast. They scheduled her family's unveiling for first thing in the morning, which lasted till noon. Hayley assured Tinx, they'd miss her company but would visit her immediately afterward, and asked if they could bring her something from the dining hall. Tinx was grateful and sounded relieved her two friends would be by her side.

They arrived at The Grimleaver Atrocities Memorial promptly after breakfast. Hayley brought Tinx a small plate of cricket toast so she would have something in her belly. They stopped at the golden plaque inside the entrance. Ethan glanced down a corridor to their left and spotted Brianna coiled up in front of her sister's memorial where they first met. Her head, full of green tube-like worms, smiled and glistened as Brianna turned to flash him a smile.

"I think our destination is over there to the right," Hayley said. "That's where we mourn the smaller victims."

Ethan turned to where Hayley was pointing.

"Yeah, kinda hard to miss with Azron standing there."

They walked over to join Azron and Tinx in front of the display, which was exceptionally bright due to the two extra light beetles assigned for this special day. The display sat upon a sizeable golden pedestal and depicted Tinx's cousin in her original form on the left side. On the right stood a black and blue pixie-devil that Ethan and Hayley were all too familiar with.

"Hey Tinx. Hey Azron," Ethan and Hayley said as they arrived.

Azron nodded to them and attempted to wink by wrinkling his forehead and closing his only eye. Hayley's thoughtfulness pleased Tinx, and she made quick work of the cricket toast.

"Boy, you must have been hungry," Hayley said.

"Yeah, I'm not used to skipping breakfast."

"Has anyone else been by?" Ethan asked.

"Brianna stopped by earlier," Tinx said. "And Azron has been here all morning."

Ethan glanced down the aisle, and Brianna still looked at him, her worm hairs moving back and forth as if waving at him.

"I'm sure the others will stop by, too," said Hayley.

"No, they won't. The Headmistress already informed me it's all hands on deck. Everybody is too busy thwarting Grimleavers' plans. I'm going to cut this short today. I'm not serving anybody by standing around here when I can be helping elsewhere."

"Makes sense, I guess," Ethan said. "I'm surprised Azron and Brianna were able to come."

"Azron, no look human," Azron said. "Brianna, no look human. No look normal for human world."

They stuck around for another fifteen minutes making small talk, then agreed to meet Tinx in Damien's laboratory later in the day when he'd be available. Hayley gave Tinx a wink when Azron wasn't looking to let her know they had some juicy news to share. Hayley noticed Brianna's apparent interest in them on their way out, so they made a quick detour.

"Hi Brianna," Hayley said as they stopped by her sister's display.

Ethan's skin tingled when he peered at Medusa's hideous figure and recalled their close encounter the day before.

"I came here today," Brianna said. "Sss-seeking you out."

"How can we help?" Ethan asked.

She turned to Hayley.

"What have you learned of my species?"

"I know you are serpeneze," Hayley said, "but I haven't learned much about your species yet."

"Serpeneze sss-sisters share a powerful bond. When Medusa and I were young, we barely needed to speak to know how one another felt."

"Yeah," said Hayley, "sounds like telepathy."

"When they took her from me," Brianna turned away from them as she continued. "I wondered if our bond would change, and if so, how."

"And did it?"

"In our case, it did change. I no longer feel what she feels," she said and spun around to face them. "But I do often see through my sister's eyes. I've seen nearly every corner of the dark mausoleum she wanders."

Ethan and Hayley glanced at the shock on one another's faces as Brianna spoke.

"Sss-so imagine my surprise when I watched through my sister's eyes as she chased after and nearly killed you both."

"We—we can explain," said Ethan.

"Promise you won't tell my mother," Hayley said.

"I've been looking for her for so long. Tell me where she is, right now, and I won't tell a soul."

"We can't tell you exactly where she is because we don't fully know ourselves," Hayley answered.

"What nonsense is this? I saw her chasing after the both of you."

"Please give us a chance to explain Brianna," Ethan said, "we are meeting with Tinx and Damien this afternoon in his laboratory. Join us, and we will explain everything."

Afternoon arrived fast, and Damien was the last to arrive.

"I love what you've done with the place," Brianna said as she reached the foot of the stairs.

"Brianna, what a lovely surprise," he said and glanced at Ethan and Hayley.

"I didn't mean to crash your little party," she said to Damien. "But these two know the whereabouts of my sister."

"Not exactly," Hayley said.

"Out with it," Damien said. "I've only got an hour – so tell us what this is all about."

"It all started with the Nibblewarts," Ethan said.

He opened the poem book and set it down on the nearest lab bench for them to read.

"Wordly told us about a painting in the Alcove of Enigma," said Hayley. "So we went to see for ourselves."

"We wondered about the little hippy caveman creatures," Ethan said. "And the poem appeared."

"Interesting," Damien said.

"We ran to Gruggins' box, and that's when we saw them," Hayley said.

"They left as soon as we arrived," Ethan said. "But I saw a mini-Jasper following them, and he motioned for us to follow too."

"We followed them into The Hall of Doorways," Hayley said. "They turned right, and we followed them to a negative door."

"They used the forbidden doors," Brianna said. "Why would they be traveling into the past?"

"I've been wondering the same thing," said Hayley. "Gruggins says they pass through often – so I think they travel back and forth a lot."

"They must have a reason for doing so," Damien said.

"All we saw them do was eat rocks," Ethan said.

"Yeah, until we scared them away."

"They may have specific dietary needs," said Damien. "If only we had a sample of that rock, we might learn something."

"Here, I grabbed these to distract Medusa," Ethan said as he reached into his pocket and pulled out a hand full of rocks. "These aren't the exact ones they were eating, but they look and feel the same."

Damien held his ELMO over the rocks – and a beam of light scanned across them.

"Very interesting. These rocks are from a Ceresian bloating stone."

"Aren't those prohibited on Earth?" Brianna asked. "I've never heard of such a thing."

"Wait a minute," Ethan said. "What is a Ceresian bloating stone?"

"A form of rock found on Ceres," Hayley said. "When exposed to water, they expand, almost limitlessly depending on the size of the water source."

"Which is why we outlawed bringing them to Earth," Brianna said. "If exposed to Earth's oceans, who knows what havoc might ensue."

"What's even more interesting," Damien said, "is that these rocks were not grown using earthly water. According to my ELMO, Atlantian water hydrated them."

"But why go to all that trouble?" Brianna asked.

"Good question," Damien said.

"We can discuss that later," Hayley said. "Let us continue with what happened."

"Agreed," Brianna said. "And most importantly, where my sister is."

"But that's what we are trying to tell you," Hayley said. "We don't know where your sister is. Not exactly."

"Explain," Brianna said.

"We scared the Nibblewarts away. So we took some dwindle-berries and followed them into a series of small tunnels. We spoke with them and talked them into trusting us. They led us through another time portal into the present time, but we have no idea where we were."

"How did you return to The Residence if you didn't know where you were?" Damien asked.

"We used the tether port we took for the trip back from the past," Hayley said.

"Great thinking," Damien said. "But if you'd have used a portal beacon, we'd be able to trace the location."

"We didn't think we'd need one," Hayley admitted, "so we didn't take a portal beacon."

Damien looked at his sister and furrowed his brows.

"I know, I know," she said. "I should never leave The Residence without a few portal beacons—"

"So, I'm no closer to finding my sister," Brianna interrupted with a deep sigh.

"It doesn't look like it," Ethan said.

"What did the Nibblewarts say?" Damien asked. "Maybe there are clues."

"They told us about the Shadow Princess," Hayley said. "They said she will lead the chosen one to the Nibblewart prophecies."

"The Nibblewarts are a mush-mouthed little species who have spewed gibberish for centuries," Brianna said. "Nibblewart prophecies would be of interest to absolutely nobody."

"True," Damien said. "Nobody regards what they say with esteem, and they won't likely start now."

"But they speak the truth," Ethan said. "The Shadow Princess has come to me, and I have visions of her trying to tell me something."

"I saw her once myself," Hayley added. "And I was able to speak to her."

"You've got my attention," Damien said.

"You've got mine too," Brianna said.

"This poem, The Nibblewarts," Ethan said. "It has something to do with a dream I had. I saw Victor Qruefeldt use the puzzle box on Princess Adara and try to kill her. I think she was one of the Sayers, but something went wrong, and the puzzle box didn't kill her. It shocked him at first, but he used the box again, and it sucked her inside."

"Do you know anything about these Sayers?" Brianna asked.

"No, only that they have giant blue eyes," Ethan said. "I'm mostly reading between the lines and making connections that may or may not be right."

"You're doing great. Keep going," said Hayley.

"Well, I-I think the Sayers and Seers are somehow related, but I'm not sure how."

"What became of them?" Damien asked.

"I don't know what happened to them after Adara disappeared. But a Caretaker woman was present when they rose from the desert sand. If we find out who she was, she might be able to tell us something."

"You may find your answer," Damien said. "Your Seer friends have more to say."

Wisps of golden whimsy wafted from the poem book as the pages turned to the next blank page, and a passage wrote itself backward. When it finished, the passage read:

The Shadow Princess

She appeared from out of nowhere, with piercing yellow eyes.
Pointing out the dangers, that crept down from the skies.

She tries to speak but is not heard, it's an unfamiliar sound.
Understood by the one and only, whom together she was bound.

Devolved from Seer spirit, as a favor for a friend.
For reasons that will become known, in the messages we send.

Seek out the friend of Stravis, the oracle of her day.

And behold the Shadow Princess, as she strives to lead the
way.

"Your grandmother—I thought she was holding
something back."

"Me too," Hayley said. "Her reaction when I said the
Shadow Princess' name was Adara was suspicious. She
knows more about what's happening than she told us."

"Well then," said Damien, "it's time to visit dear
Grandma. But first, I must tell our mother something
important has come up."

Damien pulled out his ELMO, tapped the screen, and
stepped away to speak with the Headmistress.

"I'm glad you called," Jordanna's voice echoed from the
ELMO. "Have you seen Brianna? I need you both in the Map
Room."

"She's with me, but you'll have to do without us.
Something important has come up. I will explain later."

"Does this have anything to do with our other thing?"

"Yes," Damien said, "and I believe it is about to bear
fruit."

"Okay, we will make do for now. But give me an update
as soon as you learn more."

Damien tucked his ELMO into his robe and turned to
face his sister as she stared at him with her hands on her hips.

"What was she talking about?" Hayley asked. "Our other
thing is Ethan and me. Isn't it?"

"Yes."

"But I trusted you. How could you betray my trust?"

"How did you think this little arrangement happened?" Damien asked. "I spoke to her on your behalf, and she agreed to stop being overly protective. But only under the condition that I gain your trust and keep a close eye on you."

"We have been able to come and go as we please," said Ethan.

"True, I guess," Hayley said. "But he's been telling her everything we've been up to."

"You haven't exactly been giving me regular updates — and I've been much looser than our mother is comfortable with."

Hayley conceded her brother was looking out for her best interests and trying to maintain the peace between her and Jordanna. Besides, they had bigger Ravenwood fish to fry.

"So, how do we find our grandmother's creepy castle?"

"Follow me," Damien said.

He led the others up the stairs in the front room, where he proceeded up its never-ending staircase. They continued their ascent to the thirteenth floor and turned right on the landing, which led them to a dark hallway where two torches burned at its entryway. Damien grabbed one for himself and handed the other to Brianna.

"I'll take the lead, and you bring up the rear."

They entered the narrow hallway and followed Damien for several minutes before reaching a thick wooden door framed in iron. Damien slowly pulled the creaky door open and side-stepped through it. The others followed and found themselves at a clearing at the foot of a small mountain.

"How much farther?" Hayley asked.

"The castle is at the top of this hill," Damien said and pointed to the black silhouette of a castle.

The night was dark, windy, and raining as they started up a steep path winding its way to the mountain's top. The torches barely lit their way as they fought to stay burning – but the constant flash of lightning helped them on their way. Surprisingly, the journey took only twenty minutes to reach the top, where they found themselves at the entrance to a giant castle.

"I think we've found Count Dracula's house," Ethan said.

They made their way over the stone steps leading to an enormous front door. Damien raised his fist to knock, but the door slowly creaked open. Light from inside showered through the door as a tall, white faced butler appeared. He wore a pinstriped tuxedo with a red rose corsage pinned to the lapel, and he looked like a department store dummy had come to life.

"Irvin, what are you doing here?" Ethan asked.

"Irvin—" the butler said in a flat, monotone voice. "You must have me confused with my goofball of a brother. My name is Melvin McGillicutty, and the madam is awaiting your arrival."

"Thank you, Melvin," Damien said. "She is expecting us?"

"Yes, they are waiting in the sitting room," Melvin said, "right this way."

"I know the way," Damien said as he entered and beelined past Melvin.

They followed Damien through an expansive foyer, past a double staircase, and into a large room. A fire burned in an enormous fireplace that reminded Ethan of the study at The Residence. Vanessa and Dakota Drakelan stood to greet them as they entered.

"Greetings," Vanessa said.

She nodded at Brianna, Damien, and Tinx as she strode by them to face Ethan and Hayley.

"So, your journey has led you here," she said. "The questions you seek answers to are finally ready for answers."

"Show her the passage," Hayley said to Ethan.

He fished out the poem book, turned to the correct page, and handed it to Vanessa.

"What can you tell us about this?"

Vanessa read the Seers' new passage and paused.

"This refers to the second visit Stravis paid Odin and me. He came to ask me for a favor."

"You? Why you and not grampa Odin?"

"Because Odin was now the Caretaker headmaster. Stravis wanted him protected from any fallout if anyone exposed us."

"Sounds ominous," said Damien. "What was he asking you to do?"

Vanessa sighed.

"The Seers required certain skills only Caretakers possess. But to accomplish what they were asking, I had to break our most sacred rule."

"What rule? What did you do?" Damien asked.

"She created the Sayers," said Ethan.

Vanessa nodded and stared at the floor. Ethan gazed at her, and a light turned on in his head as the picture became clear.

"How? Caretakers do not have powers of creation," Hayley said.

"She didn't create anything," Ethan said.

Vanessa nodded.

"What Ethan says is true. The Seers are a very evolved lifeform. The only way to create a humanoid from them is to devolve them."

"Oh, so that's the rule you broke," Hayley said.

"Yes—and in return, the Seers gifted me with second sight. Though I often wonder if their gift is not a curse cast down upon me for breaking the most sacred of our oaths."

"But if you devolved the Seers," said Hayley. "Who is communicating with Ethan?"

"I didn't devolve them all, only a select few who volunteered for the mission."

"What mission?"

"The Sayers' mission was to bring the word of the Seers to the Caretakers. They were to deliver the portal prophecies described in the Book of Creators."

"I think I'm beginning to understand," Ethan said. "I witnessed part of it in my dream. Victor Qruefeldt had them all chained together. He used the puzzle box to turn Princess Adara into the Shadow Princess. But I don't know what became of the rest of them."

"Because your dream was incomplete," Vanessa said. "Let me show you what your dream did not."

She approached Ethan slowly, reached up, and pressed her left hand against his temple. Ethan's eyes shut. And when they opened, his eyes were white, and he was in a trance.

"What are you doing to him?" Hayley asked.

"Filling in the blanks," said Vanessa.

Ethan's head shook, and his eyes returned to normal. His brows furrowed, and his eyes widened as his head moved from Hayley to Damien and back to Hayley.

"The answers have been staring me in the face this whole time."

"What answers?"

"The poem even spells them out: Attempts to kill them failed, and the Nibblewarts were born."

"What are you saying?"

"Don't you see? Victor couldn't kill the Sayers with the puzzle box – so he devolved them into Nibblewarts."

"Yes," said Vanessa, "I had a vision long ago and witnessed some of the horrors – but I lacked context. As time passed, it became clear the Seers left me with a piece of a puzzle – but it would be up to others to solve. I didn't know the shadow spirit was Adara, until Hayley told me. But then I had an epiphany, the two of you are the ones. You are meant to find the fortress and uncover the truth."

The room fell silent as they absorbed Ethan and Vanessa's words.

"The Nibblewart prophecies," Damien said. "If what you say is true, the portal prophecies and the Nibblewart prophecies are one and the same."

"Yes—and the Nibblewart high priest showed us where they would appear," Hayley said. "In *The Pyramids of Never.*"

Ethan froze as his mind drifted, and past scenes replayed in his head. He skipped through them like flashcards. He was on the back of a sand slug watching his palm symbols follow the vanishing dune across the horizon. Then he was in a bubble looking down at a structure half-buried in the giant dune. In a flash, he stood inside the building with the Shadow Princess. Next, he was in the Alcove of Enigma, looking at a painting of a pyramid construction site. Then, in a flash, he was inside the central pyramid with the Shadow Princess.

"All this time, she was trying to tell me something," Ethan whispered to himself.

His mind raced, and now he stood in the sand staring at a small black shiny object as a legion of desert harpies approached.

"But how is that even possible," he whispered.

The scene flashed again, and he was in the library with Hayley, and she was talking as his gaze wandered to an article called *Magnetic Maelstrom.*

"Ethan, did you hear me?" Hayley asked. "Snap out of it."

He shook his head and looked at the others with a broad smile perched upon his lips.

"Yes, you said *The Pyramids of Never,* and I just figured out where they've been hiding all this time."

MEDUSA

Ethan told the others he was sure of his theory, but he wanted to show them rather than tell them. To do so required the Map Room, where Jordanna was meeting with other CAGE members. But that worked out perfectly because they would report any critical news to her anyway. They entered the Map Room and headed for the crow's nest, where they heard Jordanna and Nicholas speaking.

"The Grimleavers have increased their attacks since acquiring their own portal plane," she said.

"We expected that," Nicholas said. "Thus far, we've been able to keep things under control."

"Great—and have we learned anything from implementing Damien's idea?"

"Yes, I am told the algorithms are beginning to bear fruit. The Grimleaver attacks are not as random as they might appear."

The group reached the top of the stairs and stepped onto the crow's nest platform. Jordanna and Nicholas spun around in their chairs and appeared surprised.

"You've brought an entourage," Jordanna said. "What brings you all?"

"Important news, Mother," said Damien.

"Ethan knows where they hid *The Pyramids of Never*," Hayley said.

"*The Pyramids of Never*," Jordanna said. "What are you talking about?"

"The pyramids themselves are not important," Damien said. "But what's inside will interest you. If what they tell me is correct, the central pyramid holds the portal prophecies foretold by the Book of Creators."

Jordanna stood, approached Ethan, and peered into his eyes.

"You've found the prophecies? Please, tell us what you know."

"I-I can't be sure, but with the help of the Map Room, I was hoping to prove my theory."

"The floor is yours," Jordanna said. "Tell her what you need."

"Hi, Map Room," Ethan said awkwardly.

"Hello, Ethan Fox," a soft feminine voice said. She reminded him of George's Alexa back home. "How may I assist you today?"

"Headmaster Odin Ravenwood reported visiting a construction site in the desert. Do you have any records of that?"

"Scanning archive," the voice said. "Yes, I have located several references."

"Great! Could you please show us the location on a map?"

The spherical room's walls lit up, and a giant globe of Earth surrounded them. The globe spun around and shrunk smaller as it did until a large holographic globe of Earth hung in the air. A black dot appeared over a desert in northern Africa.

"This is where Odin reported the site," the voice said. "And where he later sent a Caretaker survey team."

"Okay, keep showing that, but also show us the location of the great vanishing dune."

"The vanishing dune is in one of the protected realms," the voice said. "And not accessible from the human world."

"If the protected realm was part of the human world, can you show us where it would be physically located?"

"Affirmative, plotting now."

Another black dot appeared on the map halfway across the continent.

"You can't be suggesting these two locations are somehow related," Nicholas said. "They are deserts apart."

"How do Caretakers determine location?" Ethan asked.

"It's quite embarrassing, actually," Damien said. "These days, we use human GPS satellites."

"But in Odin's day, human GPS did not yet exist. So, how did you do it then?"

"The same way everybody used to," Hayley said. "We used Earth's magnetic field."

"That's what I thought," Ethan said. "Computer, can you reference articles from *The Residential Daily Star*?"

"If you are referring to me, the answer is yes. But I am an artificial intelligence and do not appreciate being called a computer."

"Please accept my apology. Can you find an article titled *Magnetic Maelstrom*?"

"Yes, the article details an abrupt shift in Earth's magnetic field," the voice said.

"Great. Now, using a different color, plot where Odin's reported location would have fallen before the shift."

"Re-plotting."

A green dot appeared on the map at the same spot as the vanishing dune.

"They used an old magician's trick," Damien said.

"Sleight of hand," Ethan said.

"The pyramids have been hidden beneath the vanishing dune all along," said Hayley.

"Yes, and Brianna's sister is there too," Ethan said. "She's inside the structure we flew over that was half-buried in the dune."

"Sss-she is protecting something. She patrols the dark depths of that mausoleum like it's her life's mission."

"We've already determined something is cloaking the dune whenever anyone gets close," Ethan said. "I believe we will find whatever is doing that inside the structure."

"We must dispatch a team immediately," Damien said.

"How do you propose we get past the desert harpies?" Nicholas asked. "The desert is their domain, and we have no chance of defeating them."

"I'm afraid the point is moot anyway," said Jordanna. "After we cleaned out Stravis' bunker, I had the *Sand Miser Dune* portal destroyed."

"Why would you—"

"We don't need it," Ethan said. "Hayley dropped a portal beacon when we floated over the dune. I didn't realize it was a portal beacon at the time, but when we followed the Nibblewarts there, I saw a shiny black object in the sand near the entrance."

"You mean when desert harpies almost overran you," Hayley said.

"Yes—but the beacon is not far from the entrance. If we distract the harpies, that will buy us the time to run to the entrance."

"That's a fantastic idea," Damien said. "I'll rig up a small sounding device to mimic approaching nomads. If we transport Tinx first, she can drop it in the desert, far enough away to buy us all the time we need."

"Great, we have a plan for getting there," said Jordanna. "But we still need a plan for defeating Medusa."

"I will handle my sister. I sss-see through her eyes and feel through her skin, which will give me an advantage."

Ethan and Hayley glanced at one another. They knew Brianna was fibbing and wanted a chance to save her sister.

"Even if I believed you could defeat your sister," Jordanna said. "I would not—"

"What about Dakota Drakelan?" Hayley interrupted. "He's a dark master. He might be able to defeat Medusa with a little help from his friends."

Ethan's eyes widened at Hayley's sudden fondness for Dakota.

"He's retired. Sleep is about all that old codger does anymore," Jordanna said. "But I will consider it."

"Well, I'd hate to throw another wrench into the mix, but what about the dune itself," Nicholas said. "How do we move a mountain of sand so vast?"

"I've been pondering that question," Damien said. "The winds should have dispersed a dune that enormous long ago."

"If that's true," Ethan said. "I'd bet the answers to that also lie inside the structure."

"Very well. I will speak with Dakota Drakelan. Brianna, Damien, Ethan, Hayley, and Tinx will accompany us to the site. Nicholas, you will stay behind to lead our operations while I am gone."

"You—you're going to let me go along," Hayley said to her mother.

"You've earned it, my dear. And I'm fully aware you've already lived through many dangerous encounters since Ethan's return."

Hayley smiled, approached her mother, and they embraced.

"Thank you, Mom, for believing in me."

"But don't expect me not to worry. I am your mother, after all."

CHAPTER THIRTEEN

Nicholas was not happy with Jordanna's decision to leave he and Azron behind, but he followed her orders as he always did. Damien would need some time to craft the miniature sounding device while Jordanna made the rest of the arrangements. But the team would be ready to leave at sunrise—vanishing dune time.

Tinx was the first to arrive, as planned. She book-traveled to *The Glass Pillars of Nym* and flew the rest of the way to be safe. They couldn't risk her losing consciousness and being swallowed up by the harpies before the mission started.

"Wooo-hooo," she roared to herself. She darted over the vanishing dune and started her descent at full speed. Tinx was ecstatic about finally going on a real mission fully sanctioned by the Headmistress.

Damien estimated the harpies traveled through the sand at about twenty miles per hour. So she continued two miles past the structure as he instructed. That would be close enough to attract the harpies but not trigger the cloak, which made the trip roughly a six minute one-way journey. Tinx stopped suddenly and hovered midair as she climbed to approximately one hundred feet above the desert floor. She dropped the device and let it plunge to the ground. The fall from that height would awaken the device and alert Damien's ELMO that it was time to move.

The team stood on the black-and-white checkered plane, waiting single file next to a beacon of light rising skyward from one of the squares.

"Where is Dakota Drakelan?" Hayley asked.

"He promised he would be there," Jordanna said. "But he hates portal beacons, so he said he would find his own way."

Damien's ELMO signaled the activation of the sounding device.

"Okay, now we wait until they are five minutes from the structure," Damien said. "That should give us plenty of time if the beacon is as close as Ethan described."

Five minutes later, the team walked single file into the light and disappeared from the checkerboard plane. After nearly a minute, they regained their balance and shook off the effects. Ethan spun on his feet and spotted the temple entrance. But it was much farther away than he remembered, and they were in a broad depression in the sand, so the trek would be uphill.

"The entrance was much closer before," he said. "They must have moved the beacon."

"This is going to be a close call," Damien said. "But if we run, we should all make it."

The team took off running – but it was a slow trod uphill through the thick sand. Brianna slithered like a sidewinder, so the trip only took her a couple of minutes. She waited on the veranda and watched the harpies turning up the sand in the distance.

"Hurry, they're getting close," Brianna said a couple of minutes later.

The team was still a hundred feet away, and the harpies were closing the distance fast. Tinx darted past them and quickly saw their dilemma. She stopped in front of Brianna's face and hovered.

"Did you bring your ELMO?"

"Yes," Brianna said.

"Tune it to a human radio station, turn the volume as high as possible, and put it in my claws."

Brianna quickly did what Tinx asked. The miniature dragon darted straight up into the sky, past the approaching harpies, and dropped the ELMO. It plunged to the ground and landed a few hundred feet behind the school of harpies. They instantly stopped, turned around, and swirled into attack formation. They surrounded the ELMO and churned the sand into a whirlpool that slowly swallowed the device to the tune of Eddie Van Halen's *Eruption*.

The team made it to the safety of the veranda and stopped to catch their breaths as the attacking harpies calmed to a quiet stir.

"That was a close call," Jordanna said.

"You would not have made it," Brianna said, "if not for Tinx's quick thinking."

"Yes, it appears my daughter is not the only one I've underestimated."

They entered the dark temple cautiously. Brianna's head worms glowed green to help light their way while the others held up their ELMOs to see where they were going.

"Medusa must be sleeping," Brianna whispered. "I'm unable to see through her eyes."

"Over here is the tiny scale model of the whole complex," whispered Ethan as he motioned the others to follow.

They approached the small model on the floor and stopped when they spotted something on the ground moving towards them. The tiny object grew larger with each step closer until finally, they could recognize Dakota Drakelan returning to size.

"You followed the Nibblewarts," Hayley said to Dakota.

"Ain't gonna let you an Ethan have all the fun."

"I don't want to know," Jordanna said as her eyes moved back and forth from Dakota to Hayley.

"Medusa has awakened," Brianna said. "She is moving quickly towards our light."

No sooner had she said the words than the serpent slithered from the shadows and let out a piercing hiss that echoed through the building like a screeching owl. Dakota backed away as she crept between him and the rest of the group. Everyone else backed away except for Brianna, who inched her way closer to her sister.

"Remember, don't look into her eyes," Jordanna said.

Brianna closed her eyes and continued forward. The green tube worms on her head danced from side to side and glowed brighter as if trying to hypnotize Medusa. But that angered the nest of vipers on Medusa's head. Their eyes burned with laser-like intensity as their black bodies lunged at Brianna like a team of snapping turtles.

Dakota quietly knelt and set down three small creatures on the ground. Balder, Gilly, and Skronk scurried away and disappeared into the darkness.

"Please, sister, let us help you," Brianna said. "The Hybrid Child is here, and he may be able to—"

The girth of Medusa's lower body swiftly whipped around like a catapult and slammed into Brianna's side. The impact launched Brianna at the others like a cannonball. Ethan tackled Hayley to the ground just as Brianna sailed over their heads and slammed into Damien and Jordanna, sending them to the ground. Ethan struggled to his feet as Medusa beelined towards them. Hayley jumped to her feet, stepped in front of Ethan, and held her shield in front of their faces. Medusa was nearly on top of them but backed away from the sight of her own reflection.

Balder, Gilly, and Skronk emerged from the shadows from different directions. They were now gigantic versions of themselves and ready for a fight. Balder grabbed Medusa from behind, ensnaring her head and upper torso in his hooked tentacles. Skronk wrapped his long arms around the circumference of her lower torso, while Gilly caught her tail in his mouth to stop her stabbing attacks. Medusa's head vipers closed their eyes, and she gradually stopped struggling. Hayley lowered her shield as the others rose to their feet, and Brianna approached her entangled sister.

But it was all a ruse, and the viper's piercing red eyes opened. Half of them snapped at Balder's tentacles while the other half spit acid at Gilly. Medusa's body writhed fiercely, so Skronk tightened his grip on her lower torso. But one of the acid spurts hit Gilly in his right antenna eye, causing the mouth at the end of his tail to lose its grip. The dagger-like tip of Medusa's tail darted forward and hovered in front of Ethan and Hayley, who froze in place. The tail danced slowly from side to side as if deciding which one to kill. Medusa's tail thrust at Ethan but hit the shield Brianna swatted from Hayley's hands to block the strike. Ethan jumped back as the shield fell to the ground. Medusa's tail lurched back, readying for another strike, but this time at Hayley.

"No!!!" Ethan shouted.

Everything around him slowed as he watched Medusa's tail lurch forward. He jumped into action and ran towards Hayley, hoping to push her out of the way. But then, he froze as if a giant invisible hand had suddenly grabbed hold of him. Something moving at normal speed caught his attention. He turned and saw Dakota Drakelan approaching with his hand raised, and he was speaking unintelligibly.

Medusa's tail swiftly thrust forward as everything returned to normal speed. At first, it appeared to disappear into Hayley's chest but then reflected out. It continued its path forward, burying itself in Medusa's own chest and impaling her. Medusa curled up and writhed in pain as her hair-vipers' eyes grew faint.

"Release her now," Brianna shouted.

Balder and Skronk released their grip, and Medusa's body fell to the floor. Brianna rushed to her sister's side and began to weep.

"Ethan, your palms," Hayley said.

Ethan raised his hands, and when he saw them glowing green, he somehow understood what to do. He ran to Brianna's side and held his palms against her dying sister. The color of Medusa's skin changed beneath his hands, and a new pigment quickly swam over her entire body bringing back her natural shade of greenish blue. The black nest of vipers transformed, too, returning to the same green tube-like worms on her sister's head.

"B-Brianna, I thought we'd never find each other again," Medusa said in a barely audible whisper.

"I'm so sorry," Brianna cried. "I came here to save you."

"It'sss not your fault. I left you no choice. You've always made the right choices, and even though you're my baby sister, I've always looked up to you."

Tears streamed down Brianna's cheeks as the life slowly drained from her sister.

"Please, promise me one thing," Medusa said.

"Anything."

"Don't waste time mourning over me. Get on with your life," she said as her eyes closed and her body went limp for one final time.

Brianna buried her face in her sister's chest and wept uncontrollably while the others stood by quietly and let her mourn.

THE NIBBLEWART PROPHECIES

Brianna grieved for several moments, and when she finished, her lower body coiled as she rose and turned to Ethan.

"That was a very precious gift," she said.

"But—I didn't save her."

"No—but you allowed us one final moment together. And for that, I will be forever in your debt."

Brianna turned to Jordanna with a determined look in her face.

"Let's get on with it," she said. "Let's find out what they enslaved my sister to protect."

Dakota Drakelan stepped out into the open and clapped his hands together.

"Well, if yer lookin' ta see in this crypt of a place, I'll start by removin' the darkness."

He waved his hands in a circle over his head and whispered unintelligible words. The building's interior slowly grew brighter as the darkness in the room condensed into ever-shrinking clouds. The smaller they shrank, the lighter the room got. And when they finished, black baseball-sized orbs hovered overhead all around the room. There were no apparent light sources around, yet everything was visible from one end of the room to the other.

"She sss-spent most of her time in the back," Brianna said and pointed. "That's where we will find what she was protecting."

"That's where my palm symbols pointed," Ethan whispered to Hayley. "When I was hiding from Medusa the first time that we were here."

They followed Brianna down the center aisle into the room's previously pitch-dark back half. The end of the corridor led to a clearing where two odd contraptions stood. Each half of the clearing housed a device, and a short wall of stones divided the two.

"Well, there's the cloaking device," Damien said.

He walked to the left and stood by the tall device. The bottom part was a shiny black metallic cylinder, tapering from top to bottom, and was taller than Damien. The top consisted of an enormous flattened-out transparent glass sphere that reminded Ethan of a giant skipping stone.

"Yeah, I've seen those in my Caretaker studies," Hayley said. "But I want to find out what this is. I haven't seen one of these."

Hayley stood next to the sizable flat black cube sitting at the center of the right side of the clearing. She bent down to inspect the ribbed ridges covering the cube's surface.

"Be careful little lady. Ya don't wanna be touchin' that till I see what's inside."

"You know what that is?"

"Looks like a giant HVG puzzle box," said Ethan.

"Astute observation – but if yer lookin' ta win a prize, I'm fresh out."

"What are you talking about?" Jordanna asked. "What is it?"

"Don't know exactly. Seen a lotta different contraptions that looked similar. Heldrik had a thing 'bout black boxes. Said they were his signature."

"So Heldrik Vonn Grim created that," Damien said as he hopped the stone wall and dashed over.

"Yep, but yer all gonna have ta stand back while I peek inside. Could be any sorta danger inside."

Everyone backed away.

"Or—could be a bowl of fruit," Dakota said with a chuckle. "Heldrik was an odd sort."

The others looked on as Dakota rubbed his hands together and placed them on each side of the box. He hunched down to put his ear against the lid. He repeated the process from each side of the cube.

"Stand back a little more," Dakota said as he stood and walked to the front of the box. "I'm a fixin' ta open 'er up."

They backed away and watched as Dakota rubbed his hands together again. He bent down and held them out over the top of the box and whispered unintelligible words. Bright beams of red light radiated up and showered his face as the lid slowly slid open and disappeared. Dakota studied the insides of the box for several quiet moments.

"Can I have a look?" Damien asked.

"Sure! If yer keen ta havin' another moon-shaped pupil, come take a peek."

Damien took Dakota's warning to heart and stayed back while the old master studied his mentor's handy work. Then he stood tall, snapped his fingers, and the lid slid back in place.

"Well?" Jordanna asked.

"I'm familiar with it," Dakota said, "an if I recall correctly, I helped build the prototype. But this one's far more complex than the one I remember."

"Are you going to tell us what it is?" Tinx asked.

"Gimme a minute," said Dakota. "First, I need more information. Tell me, have ya run inta any sorta infestation in these parts?"

"We encountered pixie-devils our first time here," Ethan said.

"Nah, them are of Grimleaver origin. I'm talkin' more like rodents or any kinda vermin with a hive-like behavior."

"The desert harpies," Hayley said. "They protect the whole outside area around this place."

"Very good little lady," Dakota said and smiled. "If I did have a prize, it'd go ta you."

"What are you getting at?" Tinx asked.

"Can one of ya lemme borrow yer little ELMO gizmo?"

Hayley stepped forward and handed Dakota her ELMO. He held it up and tapped the screen as he headed towards the building's entrance. The others quietly followed him onto the veranda but stopped when he walked out into the desert. In no time, the harpies were churning up the sand and headed towards him. Dakota stood calmly, stared at the ELMO screen, and scanned the harpies as they drew closer. He turned towards the vanishing dune, scanned from its base to its peak, and returned to the veranda just as the harpies arrived.

"Interestin'. No wonder this one's so complicated."

Jordanna and the others followed Dakota inside and down the center aisle to the black box.

"Well," Jordanna said as she placed her hands on her hips. "What is it?"

"Better question might be, who're they?"

"They're desert harpies," Hayley said. "Everyone knows that."

"That's what this device has scattered em inta. But desert harpies don't exist, really. They're merely part of a bigger whole, and most 'a that bigger whole's body lies dormant outside coverin' up this complex."

"I'm not sure I follow," Jordanna said.

"I'll tell ya a simpler way. Me an Heldrik tested the prototype device on a colossal mud worm. Scattered the creature inta thousands of tiny vermin. We called 'em mud-stingers—nasty little creatures. But they took orders nicely and worked together as a collective."

"Hive mentality," Brianna repeated. "So Heldrik discovered a way to create new lifeforms from existing ones."

"Not exactly. This device scatters a lifeform inta smaller ones, but the whole of the original lifeform is still intact. That's where the hive mind comes from."

"So, those desert harpies are pieces of a larger lifeform?" Jordanna asked.

"Yeah—but only a small part. Mosta its body is the vanishin' dune itself."

"Do you have any idea what that lifeform might be?" Damien asked.

"I scanned the dune, and it's mostly made o' Zephyrian dust with some earthly sand mixed in. So yer probably lookin' at a Zephyrian dust goliath."

Jordanna and Brianna gasped at Dakota's admission, but Damien grew more excited.

"Of course," Damien said. "The specific gravity is far too great, which would explain why the winds haven't disturbed the dune."

"What kind of creature is a dust goliath?" Ethan asked.

"They're from the elemental world of Zephyr," Hayley said. "Like a Hell-Giant, only much bigger and made from wind and dust instead of fire."

"So let me get this straight," Ethan said. "If we were to destroy that device, the harpies and the vanishing dune would reconstruct themselves back into a dust goliath?"

"That's about the size of it," Dakota said.

"But we can't even consider doing that," Brianna said. "We have no way of wrangling a dust goliath."

"There's got to be a way," Ethan said.

"Water," Hayley said. "When harpies attacked us, you fought them with the water pistol Irvin gave you."

"Yeah—and I didn't even have it set to full power," Ethan said. "But if the dust goliath is as enormous as you describe, even on full power, I doubt if that will be enough to kill the creature."

"Your right," Hayley said. "But if we each had hydrosphere ejectors as well, we could blast it from all directions."

"That might work," Ethan said, "but if you remember correctly, my water pistol didn't kill the harpies. It only repelled them."

"Yeah," Hayley said, "we need a way to solidify the creature, and I doubt it's just going to sit around and let us do that."

"No – but if we weakened it enough," said Ethan. "RGB could lasso it like they did with the Hell-Giant."

Jordanna listened to Hayley and Ethan, wide-eyed, her hands folded up in front of her chin. She lowered her hands, exposing a hint of a smile on her lips and a glimmer in her eyes.

"Ethan, do you still have the water pistol Irvin gifted you?" She asked.

"Yes."

"Good," Jordanna said. Her smile widened as she pulled out her ELMO and tapped the screen.

"What can I do for you, Headmistress?" Nicholas asked.

"I need you, Azron, and RGB to join us at the site."

"RGB? What have you gotten yourselves into?"

"Nothing we can't handle. But I also need you to gather a few supplies and bring them."

"What do we need to bring?"

"Hydrosphere ejectors, gravity shoes, and sand-peepers for all of us. Have the ejectors modified to switch between earthly and Atlantian water sources."

"Got it," Nicholas said. "That's a strange request. Might I ask why?"

"I will explain to everyone when you arrive."

"Anything else?"

"Yes, we'll also need energy coils for you and Azron."

Jordanna finished her conversation and put her ELMO away.

"What was that all about?" Hayley asked.

"I'm just getting you and Ethan what you need. I'll explain when they arrive."

Nicholas wasted no time contacting the Caretaker technicians and putting them to work building the hydrosphere ejectors. He tracked down RGB in the Arts and Literature archive. They attempted to capture Wordly again, but he got the best of them as usual. He met Azron on the checkered plane two hours later, and they were ready to join the others.

Jordanna and Tinx stayed to scout every square inch of the mausoleum while the rest of the team waited for the others in the shade of the veranda. Dakota noticed Ethan staring at him, so he walked over and sat next to Hayley, who sat alone with her back against a tall column.

"I'm seein' some not-so-friendly looks from yer boyfriend," he whispered to Hayley. "Did I do somthin' ta anger him?"

"It's not anything you've done," Hayley said. "It's what you—"

"You been lying to me," Ethan said loudly across the veranda. "Fin told me he saw you and Stravis meeting with Odin."

"I told ya I'd met him," Dakota said.

"Yeah—but you held back important details," Ethan said. "You didn't tell me I was there as an infant. Which means you know about my past."

"I don't know as much as ya might figure. Sure, I've been keepin' an eye on ya for Vanessa, and I helped 'em look after ya back when George was around. I even helped Alexander out with your ma after ya disappeared."

"What do you know about my mother?" Ethan asked. His jaw dropped, and his eyes widened as he waited for Dakota to speak.

"Well—I—um," Dakota said and paused. "She was in bad shape after ya disappeared. Stayed in a catatonic state fer quite some time."

"What happened to her? Where is she now?" Ethan asked.

"Can't say fer sure," Dakota answered. "When she came to, she began havin' episodes—visions of evil, courtesy of Victor Qruefeldt. Best we could figure, when the Seers intervened ta rescue ya, it left Tiffany's mind somehow connected ta his. She was there, after all. After a time, it nearly drove 'er mad."

"Where is she now?" Hayley asked.

"Not sure. We all agreed she had ta be moved. If she could see through Victor's eyes, he could likely see through hers. So Alexander took 'er someplace safe, and only he knows where that is."

"So she is alive," Ethan said.

"Yeah, she's alive," Dakota said. "Alexander visits her occasionally, but he says she's not his Tiffany anymore. Somethin' happened ta change 'er."

"What happened to her?" Ethan asked.

"Don't know. Alexander wouldn't say, said it'd give away her whereabouts."

Ethan grew quiet as a wave of emotions flooded his mind. This was the first solid piece of information he had learned about his birth mother, and it came from a reliable source.

Jordanna joined the others on the veranda, and her presence quickly broke up the silence.

"It's time," Jordanna said.

She laid down a fresh portal beacon so Azron and Nicholas could transport directly to the veranda and not suffer the same close call with the harpies. A flash of light radiated from the beacon. Azron and Nicholas appeared on the veranda, each carrying a leather saddlebag. Jordanna led the team inside to the scale model on the floor so they could map out a plan.

"That was fast," she said. "I thought the ejector modifications might take longer."

"Having me watch over their shoulder may have sped up the process."

"And RGB?"

Nicholas zipped open one side of his saddlebag.

"You can come out now," he said.

Three colored balls, one red, one green, and one blue, shot out and unraveled midair. The three mischievous pyrodevlins flew overhead and darted around the room, performing aerial stunts.

"Yippee," Albert shouted.

"Woohoo," Linus screamed.

"Yeehaw," Newton cheered.

"Behave yourselves," Jordanna said. "I've asked you here for an important mission."

RGB beelined for the Headmistress, landed by her side, and stood at attention. Tinx arrived shortly after and landed on Damien's shoulder. She had stayed inside to continue mapping out the interior while Jordanna gathered the others. The team gathered around the Headmistress as Nicholas and Azron emptied the contents of their saddlebags onto the stone floor.

"Tinx, did you find any other exits?" Jordanna asked.

"I think so. There are two stone walls at the back corners of the structure. They're framed like doorways and appear to be exits – but they're beneath the dune for now."

"Perfect. I asked Nicholas to bring you all a pair of gravity shoes, sand-peepers, and a hydrosphere ejector."

Nicholas handed them each a pair of silver glasses with horizontal slits for lenses.

"These are sand-peepers," Nicholas said to Ethan. "They will enable us to see in the sandstorm."

He handed them each a pair of black foot-shaped flats that looked like shoe inserts.

"Gravity shoes will keep you from getting sucked off the ground by the creature."

Hayley tossed hers to the ground and stepped on them. Metallic fibers sprouted from beneath her feet and grew over her existing shoes like a shrub enveloping a house. He followed her lead and did the same.

"Last but not least," Nicholas said as he picked up a hydrosphere ejector. "I had these modified to switch between earthly and elemental water sources. They are preset to earthly, but you can use this selector switch to change that."

"Why do we need two water sources?" Ethan asked. "Normal water worked fine before."

"Yes—but you said it yourself," Jordanna said. "Earthly water only served to repel the harpies."

"We're making pottery," Damien said.

"I'm lost," Ethan said.

"Artisans on the elemental worlds," Damien said. "They craft durable goods using a mixture of Zephyrian dust and Atlantian water. That creature is made of Zephyrian dust."

"Exactly," Jordanna said. "We use earthly water to repel the beast, then switch to Atlantian water to solidify it – or turn it to pottery, as Damien pointed out."

"I see," Ethan said, "but what are those for?" He pointed at two glowing energy coils that reminded him of Wonder Woman's rope. One was much larger than the other and obviously met for Azron.

"Those are energy coils," Brianna said. "They're used to restrain deplorables."

"Remember when RGB lassoed the Hell-Giant," Hayley said. "Energy coils enable Caretakers to do the same."

"Okay," Jordanna said and looked from Ethan to Hayley. "I've provided you with everything you two discussed. So what's the plan?"

Ethan and Hayley looked at one another in disbelief. Was the Headmistress really going to let them plan out the most essential details of the mission?

"We can do this," Ethan whispered to Hayley.

"I know we can," she replied.

Ethan grabbed Hayley by the hand and led her around the scale model of the complex. They faced the others, and Ethan began to speak.

"Okay—so here's the plan," Ethan said. "Dakota will destroy Heldrik's device, which will cause the harpies to merge into a dust goliath."

"Dust goliath," Nicholas said and looked at Jordanna. "You're going to purposely unleash a dust goliath."

"Yes, we are," Jordanna said. "Please, continue."

Ethan looked at Hayley and nodded.

"Once the harpies fully merge with the body," Hayley said. "The vanishing dune will lift off the complex and allow

Azron to open one of the rear exits. We will exit out the back when he does, which should let us out here."

She tiptoed around the model, knelt, and pointed to the back of the temple structure they were in.

"Given what Dakota has described," she continued, "the monster should be somewhere around here."

Jordanna watched with a proud smile as Hayley pointed to the largest pyramid at the center of the complex.

"Ethan, you'll be the only one without a hydrosphere ejector. You start the barrage with your water pistol set to full power. We will join in with our ejectors using earthly water, which will back the creature away. Azron, Brianna, and Nicholas take the far side of the center pyramid, while Mother, Dakota, Ethan, and I take the near side. RGB, stick by Nicholas' side until he gives the order. We won't hear one another in the windstorm the creature will unleash. So, Tinx will remain with Ethan and me to relay information to all of you."

She pointed to the front of the complex.

"Once we've advanced that far, switch to Atlantian water. That will solidify the creature enough for RGB's energy lassos. Azron and Nicholas will help RGB wrangle the beast with energy coils. They will pull the creature away while we switch back to earthly water to repel it. Eventually, the monster will tire, the winds will subside, and it will solidify."

"That's one heck of a plan," Dakota said.

"Yes, it is," Jordanna agreed.

"But will it work?" Brianna asked.

"Well, it should," Damien said. "In theory."

"Does anyone else have a better plan?" Ethan asked.

Nobody had a better plan, so the team discussed the details for another hour until they were all comfortable with their roles. Because they had never seen a dust goliath, Ethan and Hayley stood by the entrance to watch the harpies re-merge into the monster. When most of the creature's body mass lifted itself off the complex, they'd run back to the others and inform them it was go time. They stood at the entrance waiting with bated breath—and then it happened.

"Are ya ready boys 'n' girls?" Dakota shouted from the back of the temple. "Let's rustle us up a behemoth."

Flashes of bluish-white light strobed from the back of the temple, and everything fell silent.

"The calm before the storm," Hayley whispered.

They gazed out at the churning desert sands stretching across the horizon and growing taller as they moved closer rapidly. Only a minute went by before the wall of leaping harpies became visible, but this time they were not coming straight at them.

"They're heading for the dune," Ethan said.

"Yeah—and there are a lot more of them," Hayley said.

They continued watching as the harpies leapt one after another at the giant mountain of sand and disappeared inside. As the onslaught continued, ripples of sand moved on the mountain's surface as strong winds gusted around the dune in a circular motion.

"The dune," Ethan said, "is beginning to break apart."

An enormous harpie jumped out from the dune and exploded into a cloud of dust that the growing winds instantly swept away. Another giant harpie leapt out, followed by another, and another, and another. The winds grew stronger and louder as they circled in tighter swirls and sucked the giant harpies into the developing tornado.

"I think I'm ready for the sand-peepers. I can hardly see anything," Hayley shouted.

Ethan followed her lead and fumbled around to put his on too, and when he finally got them on, he saw the monster. Several hundred feet from them, growing up from the center of the tornado, an enormous creature was forming before their eyes. It had no legs; its bottom half was the tornado that glided the monster effortlessly over the desert sand like a giant genie.

"I can see the pyramids now," Ethan shouted.

"Me too. Let's warn the others," Hayley yelled back.

They bolted inside, pulled up their peepers, and ran towards the others as fast as possible.

"It's time," Hayley shouted to her mother.

"Do it," Jordanna said.

Azron's giant hands slammed against the stone slab like a pair of sledgehammers, sending rock slabs crashing into the open desert and unblocking the exit.

Azron, Brianna, RGB, and Nicholas dashed out into the swirling winds first and headed for the far side of the center pyramid. The rest of the team followed Ethan and Hayley as they made a U-turn and headed down the broad clearing between the temple and center pyramid. They spread out and walked side by side towards the creature, now fully formed beside the pyramid. The beast looked like a tornado, with the upper half of a devilish sand monster growing from its center. It reminded Ethan of a pissed-off giant sandman with ram horns. The dust mass making up the creature's shape flowed like liquid through its body. The tornado sucked in any particles falling to the ground and replenished its form.

Ethan was the first to open fire and start the barrage, but he braced himself first. Then, he flipped the switch to full power, aimed up at the creature's torso, and pulled the trigger. The stream from the toy pistol expanded as water gushed from the tiny pinhole and blasted the beast like a military-grade water cannon. The monster winced and backed away from the barrage of water. The others opened fire with hydrospheres and backed the monster up farther.

They continued their slow advance for several minutes and finally reached the front corner of the pyramid. Ethan gazed down the front edge of the giant fortress and saw Azron and the others advancing in the distance. He continued dousing the creature as the rest of the team stopped to switch over to Atlantian water. The behemoth used the lull to his advantage and swiftly glided towards them, closing half the distance. Ethan continued moving towards the creature to buy the others more time. But when the barrage of Atlantian water started, he instantly knew something was wrong. The giant water balls dissipated and blew away as soon as they neared the swirling winds around the creature's torso.

Without the others to worry about, the monster turned its focus to its biggest threat, Ethan. The beast extended its massive arm and waved its four long fingers at him. Then, with a quick flick of its wrist, the fingers launched at him like a salvo of missiles. But Ethan was alert. He ran to his right and dove away as they crashed into the sand.

He jumped to his feet and blasted them with his water cannon. The fingers split apart into wet clods of dust. They rolled across the sand, and the tornado sucked them up. The monster winced and backed off again, which gave Ethan an idea. He ran over to Hayley and stopped by her side as he continued to douse the beast that was advancing on them.

"The Atlantian water is acting unexpectedly," she shouted to Ethan.

"I know. It can't break through the swirling winds – but if you aim your shots at the tornado's base, the suction will suck them in."

"Great idea, Tinx. Tell the others," Hayley ordered.

Tinx darted through the wind like a bullet relaying Ethan's idea and was back in a flash. The team quickly retargeted their shots at the creature's base, and the results were immediate. Within minutes, the monster writhed and slowly backed away as its color and consistency became visibly darker.

"Tinx, tell Nicholas to unleash RGB."

Tinx darted off to relay the orders, and in no time, RGB were in the sky buzzing around the creature's head like flies. Azron and Nicholas dropped their ejectors and ran around to flank the beast. Bright, colorful glows, one red, one green, and one blue, radiated from RGB's bodies as they circled the monster. Then, all at once, they stopped midair, hovered, and blasted the beast with their energy lassos. Albert's red lasso wrapped around the creature's neck, while Linus' green one wrapped around its left horn, and Newton's blue one found the right horn.

The monster recoiled, but RGB were swift and agile in the air and quickly adjusted to counter its every move. Right on time, Azron and Nicholas' energy coils wrapped several times around the monster's upper midsection. The five of them pulled and tugged while the rest continued blasting away with earthly water. Several minutes passed, and the demon did not appear to be weakening.

"Something is wrong," Hayley shouted. "The creature should be weakening by now and hardening."

Ethan's mind raced, and in a flash, he was back at home with his mother Betsy. She was smiling and holding up a red ceramic pot. He snapped out of the trance and turned to Hayley.

"I think I have an idea," he shouted and ran towards Dakota.

"Dakota, I need to know something about your powers," he said when he reached him. "Do you have the ability to create heat or fire?"

"Can't make somthin' from nothin'," Dakota said. "But I could summon a Hell-Giant if yer lookin' ta roast marshmallows."

Ethan shook his head and did a double-take but stopped to peer into Dakota's eyes.

"Can you summon two?"

Dakota stopped what he was doing and stared back at Ethan.

"Whatcha wantin' me ta do?"

Ethan whispered in Dakota's ear and waved his hand towards the monster as he explained. He backed away from Dakota, ran back to Hayley, and whispered in her ear. She glanced at him and paused – but then said something to Tinx, who darted about relaying the message.

Moments later, Ethan watched Dakota Drakelan approach the beast as he rubbed his hands together. Hayley turned in time to see him raise his hands and summon two Hell-Giants. The fire creatures appeared out of thin air halfway between Dakota and the dust goliath. They were enormous, but the dust behemoth towered over them at nearly thrice their height. Dakota stood to witness from close up as the two fire giants strode across the desert sand to battle the larger beast. At first sight, the match-up didn't appear to be a fair fight.

"If this doesn't work, we're in big trouble," said Hayley.

"It will," Ethan said. "Just keep your eyes opened."

Azron and Nicholas' energy coils disappeared, followed by RGB's. The dust goliath lunged forward and started towards the approaching Hell-Giants. The gigantic fire creatures stopped and turned to one another as if communicating. The dust beast continued towards them and bent down to swipe at them with both arms. But that was a mistake, and the Hell-Giants quickly took advantage by leaping over the whipping appendages and wrapping their arms around them as they flew by. The dust goliath rose in agony and waved its burning arms skywards. The Hell-Giants slowly climbed to the beast's upper arms and cuddled them like a child hugging mommy. The scene reminded Ethan of his first time watching a firelyte melt into a log.

"The goliath is tiring," Hayley said as she flashed Ethan a smile.

The others joined them and witnessed the winds subside as the dust goliath made its final movements. Minutes later, a statue of an enormous beast stood half-buried in the sand.

"Hell-Giants," Nicholas said. "I don't recall them being part of the plan."

"The plan wasn't working as expected," Hayley said. "So Ethan devised a new plan, and we improvised."

"Dust goliath no like Ethan Fox. Har, harr, harrr!" Azron roared.

"What gave you such a crazy idea?" Hayley asked Ethan.

"I remembered Damien saying something about making pottery. Then I had a flashback to Betsy telling me about baking her pottery in an oven."

"Darn near almost restrained ya when ya asked me ta summon the hellions – but I saw it in yer eyes."

Once the pleasantries were over, they turned their attention to the mission at hand, the pyramid. The massive structure made the nearby temple pale in comparison. They entered through the tall, dark entryway at the front of the fortress. The room inside was dark, but Dakota performed his darkness banishing trick so they could see.

"You're gonna have to teach me that one," Ethan said.

"Sure enuf, soon as ya teach me a few o' yers."

They entered a massive square room, and torches lit up in sequence on the surrounding walls as they moved farther inside. A rectangular pond, embedded at the room's center, had a bottom so black that the water reflected like a mirror. Ethan winked at Hayley as they peeked over the side to see if anything was swimming around.

"Reminds me of a coy pond," Ethan said.

"I don't think anything's been swimming in there for a while," Hayley said.

Beyond the pond stood a tall wide column rising into the darkness high overhead. To each side of the column, a staircase rose into more darkness. Ethan and Hayley gazed at one another as the feeling of deja vu overcame them.

"We've been here before," Ethan said.

"Yes, except for the pond, this room is exactly like the miniature in every detail," Hayley said.

"Which means the Nibblewart prophecies should appear on that wall."

Ethan pointed at the tall wall column as he made his way around the pond, but the others stood quiet right where they were. He stopped and turned to the others, but they were all staring across the pond at something in his path. When he turned back around, Ethan was face to face with the Shadow Princess. Adara had come to fulfill her destiny. He peered into her beaming yellow eyes, and a smile flowed across her face as golden wisps of light escaped from between her lips.

"Hayley," Ethan said. "I think you better get over here to translate."

Hayley hurried around the pond and stood at Ethan's side to help him greet Princess Adara.

"Hello, Adara," Hayley said. "It's so good to see you again."

Adara's eyes widened, bathing Hayley's face in a shower of yellow rays. Her smile widened as she turned to gaze at Ethan, and then Jordanna and the others.

"Adara wants me to tell you," Hayley said, "she is the daughter of Seer Hippocrates and princess of the Sayers."

"Tell her I am pleased to make her acquaintance," Jordanna said.

Hayley relayed the information, and the Shadow Princess continued.

"She wants to know if Ethan is the Hybrid One," Hayley said.

"Well, I—"

"Tell her we need her to lead us to the prophecies," Jordanna interrupted.

Adara glanced from Ethan to Jordanna and back to Ethan.

"She says the Hybrid One connects to the Seers," Hayley said. "They require his presence to reveal the prophecies."

"Tell her I am the Hybrid Child," Ethan said.

"She said she's witnessed you from afar and felt your strength. She believes you are the hybrid but requires proof."

Ethan moved closer to the Shadow Princess and held up his hands. The symbols on his palms flashed white twice as if blinking hello to her. Adara's smile widened further as she turned back to Jordanna.

"She asked if you are the Caretaker leader," Hayley said to her mother.

"Yes," Jordanna said and slowly approached.

The Shadow Princess spoke directly to Jordanna.

"What did she say?" Jordanna asked.

"The Nibblewart prophecies as foretold in the Book of Creators," Hayley translated, "they are yours now to protect."

"But—where are they?" Jordanna asked.

Adara waved her arms towards the wall, and ripples of golden whimsy wafted through the air showering the wide blank wall. They stood watching in silence as writing etched itself into the stone. When the etching finished, the words read:

The Nibblewart Prophecies

I.   The Hybrid Child Returns

II. A Hell-Giant Breaches the Silent Forest

III. Grim Times Enter the Human World

IV. The Hidden Fortress is Unearthed

"Four of them have already occurred," Damien said.

"Adara says as more come to pass, they will appear as foretold."

"But—how many prophecies are there?" Jordanna asked. "How will we know when to perform the ritual?"

"She says the Hybrid One will know. Protect him from the Grimlord, and his journey will lead us to the answers we seek."

Adara spun around and slowly floated towards the wall column. Ethan turned his head to Hayley, who was rubbing her infinity ring.

"Wait," Hayley said. "Where are you going?"

Adara stopped, turned around, and peered at Hayley.

"I have fulfilled my destiny, but before I leave, I owe you thanks."

"Thanks? Why?" Hayley asked.

"Because you saved me. I bound my soul to the rift-key to save my people from the evil one. When you recovered it from the puzzle box, you freed my soul from eternal damnation."

"That's why you're so familiar to me," Hayley said. "You were the voice who spoke to me through my ring. You helped us, and I should be thanking you."

"And I led you to the Hybrid One. We are familiar because of the time we shared, bound to the same prison."

"Will I see you again?"

"My soul is free now. Whether our paths cross again is in fate's hands."

She turned away, floated towards the wall, and disappeared below the prophecies she had delivered. Ethan turned to face Hayley, who was still rubbing her ring. But the smile on her face told him this was not the last they'd see of the Shadow Princess.

A GRISLY

DISCOVERY

The following morning Ethan and Hayley met Tinx in the dining hall for breakfast as usual. They liked returning to a routine, so at least things seemed normal again. But the Headmistress told them they were to meet her in the study at 9:00 AM sharp. So they took their time, and all had seconds while they made small talk to bide their time.

Nine AM came quickly, and they entered the study right on time. Jordanna, Nicholas, and Irvin were already present. Irvin was busy dusting the bookshelves while Jordanna and Nicholas quietly discussed things.

"The others should be along shortly," Jordanna said. "But Dakota Drakelan has declined."

No sooner had she spoken the words, then Azron and Brianna entered the room, followed by Damien and Tinx.

"I've called you all here for a quick informal meeting. Mostly as a debrief of yesterday's events, but also to update you on current events. Nicholas, the floor is yours."

"We've searched the entire pyramid complex and found nothing else of interest. But now that we have discovered the prophecies, the responsibility falls upon us to keep them protected. The Headmistress and I have discussed various strategies and decided on our best course of action."

"What's to decide," Brianna said. "Send in a platoon of armed Careguards and call it a day."

"That is precisely what we've decided not to do," Nicholas said. "We are all aware that Jordanna's reign as headmistress has its detractors. We cannot afford to call attention to the fact, we are protecting something. To that end, the existence of the complex and the prophecies, must remain a secret."

"The secret is safe with those in this room," Damien said. "But what about Dakota Drakelan? I notice he isn't present."

"While I agree Dakota is a wildcard, I discussed the matter with Alexander, and he vouched for the old coot."

"So you've also let Alexander in on the secret," Brianna said.

"Yes—but we've all put our lives in his hands on numerous occasions. Alexander is beyond reproach."

"Agreed," said Brianna, "But what about Irvin? He's in this room and knows our little secret now."

"Irvin could never become a leak," Damien said. "He's been a part of the Ravenwood family for eons, and he would no more betray us than you would."

"So—what is the plan?" Tinx asked. "We still need to hide and protect this secret. How do we achieve that?"

"I updated the cloaking device," Nicholas said. "It is now a projector as well as a cloak. It projects a copy of the vanishing dune that is only seen from a distance, and at the same time, it cloaks the complex from those who pass by."

"Okay, that solves part of the problem," Brianna said. "But what about the indigenous lifeforms living in the protected realm? What if they wander straight into the complex and learn of its existence?"

"That is a good point," Damien said. "Many are thieves and nomads who have found ways into and out of the human world."

"I also placed proximity detectors around the perimeter. If anything approaches by land or air, they will alert us. A gnat couldn't get to within a mile of the complex without us knowing."

Out of the corner of his eye, Ethan saw Hayley fiddling with her ring.

"What about the portal plane," he said. "You mentioned detractors. If they were to find out, they could teleport directly to the complex."

"That's where the Careguards come in," Jordanna said. "I've ordered two armed soldiers to guard the portal plane at all times. They will strictly monitor its usage from here on out."

"Yes—but the Grimleavers have a portal plane, too," Hayley said. "You can't police theirs."

"We don't need to," Damien said. "Theirs is a copy of our portal plane, the same in every way – but they are separate entities. A beacon tuned to ours will not work from theirs; they would need to place their own portal beacon."

"Sss-sounds like you've covered all the bases."

"Yes—but there is one more fly in the ointment," Jordanna said. "I have spoken with the Council of Elders, and as required, I briefed them on the matter."

"Wonderful," Damien said. "I guess the question is, who doesn't know about our secret?"

"The situation is not as bad as it seems. I only told them we'd recovered the prophecies. They know nothing of the complex."

"Several council members pressed us for more information," Nicholas said. "But we insisted where and how we protect the prophecies must remain our secret for security reasons."

"How did they react?" Damien asked.

"In the end, they agreed to trust us," Jordanna said. "But that does bring up another related matter. My sources on the council tell me Roman Trabblemore has been busy on the elemental worlds. He is rallying my detractors to further undermine my authority within the council itself."

"Thus far, he has only been moderately successful," Nicholas added. "Their numbers are small but growing, so we must keep an ear to the ground and monitor the situation."

The room fell silent as they mulled over the news.

"Moving on, I would like to update you on other matters. At Damien's urging, I asked a team of scholars to scour all available data on Grimleaver activity in the human world. They created algorithms to scan through gazillions of data points and search for patterns of any kind. Nicholas will update you on what they found."

"After painstakingly sifting through mountains of data from all over the human world. Our scholars determined the Grimleavers are attacking random cities across the globe to cover up what is happening in a select few. Atlanta, Boston, Chicago, and Washington DC, these are the cities—"

"Atlanta, Boston, Chicago, and DC," Irvin interrupted. "ABC news investigates is trying to learn—"

"Irvin, this is not the time for your babbling," Nicholas said. "Where was I? Oh yes, the cities I mentioned have all experienced museum break-ins coinciding precisely with the Grimleaver attacks. We believe the Grimleavers are searching for something in these museums."

"Duh, even the humans have figured that out."

"Irvin!" Nicholas shouted.

"Wait, I think Irvin is trying to tell us something," Ethan said. "He views a lot of human television channels. I believe he is mimicking something he's seen in the news."

"Irvin, you may continue," Jordanna said.

Irvin straightened up and morphed into a human anchorman to aid his presentation of the human news story.

"ABC news investigates is trying to learn what the break-ins have in common. But the list is growing, as sources confirm others are occurring across the pond, in Berlin, London, and Rome. And it gets more chilling as our crack team of researchers has discovered one common denominator. Each of the galleries in question exhibits artifacts shared from the same mystery collection. While neither the owner of the collection nor its origins are known at this time. Sources confirm pieces from the mystery collection have gone missing due to these break-ins."

The room fell silent as they all took in Irvin's revelation.

"So much for our crack team of scholars," Jordanna said. "Next time, we should monitor the human TV networks."

"It makes sense the humans found out first," Damien said. "They react to what happens in their world, but our scholars were searching for a needle in a universe of haystacks. I'd give them kudos for learning what they did."

"At any rate," Jordanna said. "We must send investigators to each of those cities. They must learn about this mystery exhibit and find out what they stole."

"I will get on that right away," Nicholas said.

The team debated the pros and cons of what they had learned for another hour. But Hayley asked her mother to excuse her and Ethan, and the Headmistress obliged. They exited the study, and Ethan instinctively headed towards The Hall of Doorways, but Hayley had other ideas.

"Follow me," she said.

"What are you up to?"

But she did not answer, so he followed her up the stairs and into her grandfather's chamber.

"Last night, I did some digging," she said as she shuffled through papers on Odin's desk. "I think we've missed something."

"Is this you talking? Or are you getting a little help from your friend?"

He pointed to her infinity ring. Hayley's eyes widened, and her lips pursed as she stood looking into his eyes.

"She wanted me to keep it a secret, but I should have known better. You read me like a book."

"Listen, you don't have to tell me anything," Ethan said.

"No, it's okay. She says I can tell you anything, but she wants this to stay between us."

"You speak as if she's here right now," Ethan said. "Is she back inside your ring or something?"

"No, it's more like telepathy, I guess. She doesn't have to be here physically for us to hear each other's thoughts. Adara thinks our connection is stronger because her soul is free now, and she's fulfilled her destiny."

"Okay, so what have we missed?"

"Let me back up a little," Hayley said. "I was lying in bed thinking about everything that has happened. I remembered Dakota Drakelan saying all the names on Odin's list were Gaylord's associates. So I dug into the other names, and here's what I found. Drake Evans was a long-time friend of Gaylord's. When Gaylord became headmaster, Drake was his number one and consulted on his every decision."

"Yeah, that doesn't sound so ominous," Ethan said.

"No, it doesn't, not until he went missing and Gaylord started to act irrationally. Then there's Lindrew Scragmort, the portal master during the Trabblemore administration. He oversaw the four portals during the Great Exodus and became Gaylord's number one after Drake Evans' disappearance. He, too, later went missing."

"An interesting pattern is emerging," Ethan said. "We already learned of Jason Crowley's fate. You could argue he went missing too."

"Exactly, until someone tried to make a point by leaving his body on my grandparents' doorstep."

"What about Heldrik? Do we know what became of him?"

"I haven't discovered a word about him. Like he's disappeared from existence with no record."

"Dakota Drakelan might be able to tell us something," Ethan said.

"Again, my thoughts exactly, but I don't think he'll tell us anything. He shares a bond with Heldrik and gets nervous at the mere mention of their past together."

"Yeah, you're probably right, but he's sure taken a shine to you."

Hayley blushed at Ethan's observation.

"Oh, I almost forgot," she said. "I was also wondering about the pixie-devils."

"What about them?"

"I find it bizarre we encountered them at the pyramid complex. How could they have possibly found us? But Damien just confirmed my suspicions."

"That's right," Ethan said. "Grimleavers cannot teleport to the complex, so they couldn't have found us. They had to have followed us."

"Yes, which means they were in The Residence, and someone is helping them."

"I think we all know who that is," Ethan said.

"Maybe, maybe not."

"Adara told you herself, remember, she was afraid she had put me in danger because he was after the hidden fortress too."

"That's right, I almost forgot about that," Hayley said. "But I'm sure the pixie-devils didn't learn anything. Medusa killed them all."

"You and Adara sure burned the midnight oil. Did you sleep at all last night?"

"A little—but there's one more thing."

"What?"

"Adara and I have a funny feeling about the pyramid complex. Too many things don't make sense."

"Like what?"

"Why did they build it for one. They sure didn't build it so the Nibblewarts would have a place to put the prophecies. The Nibblewarts stumbled upon it after being transported into the past by the hyperhole event. They only stayed to help, and continue to return, because the rock is their only viable food source."

"Good point," Ethan said. "I assumed Victor Qruefeldt was after it to ensure we didn't find the prophecies. But if it serves a different purpose, he might have a different reason altogether. Come to think of it, the poem clearly says, 'A fortress built for wicked plans.'"

"So the question is, what could they use a structure that big for?"

"I don't know, but I think you two are on to something," Ethan said. "We've missed something in those pyramids just like we did at Stravis' bunker."

They continued brainstorming for several more hours and decided to take a break. A leisurely stroll through the Moongarden would be the perfect remedy for brain fatigue. But along the way, they changed their minds and chose to visit Damien's laboratory instead. Damien and Tinx were hard at work on another experiment when they entered.

"Tinx, fetch me the jar of wobble stones, please," Damien said as he hovered over his lab bench.

Ethan and Hayley moved close enough to watch but still be out of their way.

"You're just in time," Damien said. "I'm about to detonate my next blast."

"What—are you making bombs?" Ethan asked.

"In a word, yes," Damien said and smiled. "Stravis' findings reveal a strange alchemy between certain earthly and elemental combinations."

"A strange alchemy indeed," Tinx said as she landed on the lab bench with a jar of quivering green rocks.

Damien removed one of the tiny rocks and dropped it into the left side of a glass box divided in the center by a glass divider. The rock wobbled inside the container and reminded Ethan of a Mexican jumping bean. Damien opened a small pouch, tweezed out a pea-sized gold nugget, and dropped it into the other side of the glass partition.

"Here, put these on," Damien said as he handed them a set of dark glasses.

"Ready for the blast when they touch," he said. "And you might want to cover your ears too."

"How big of a blast are we talking about?" Ethan asked.

"Approximately the equivalent of a ten-kiloton nuclear explosion."

Ethan's eyes widened, and his jaw dropped open.

"Nothing to worry about," Damien said. "This enclosure has a one hundred megaton rating."

Ethan and Hayley held their hands over their ears as Damien touched the screen of his ELMO. The glass partition disappeared as the two rock samples slowly floated towards the center of the glass cube. But when they met in the middle and touched, nothing happened.

"Wow—that blew my socks off, brother," Hayley said.

"I'm sorry, my mistake," Damien said. "I used normal gold when the recipe calls for once-cloaked leprechaun gold."

Damien reset the enclosure, separated the samples, and set the experiment up again using once-cloaked gold.

"Okay, I guarantee I will knock your socks off this time."

Ethan and Hayley cupped their hands over their ears as Damien touched his ELMO screen. The samples floated towards one another, and this time when they touched, a bright white flash of light enveloped the room and a sonic boom shook the ground. Even with his ears covered, the sound made Ethan's ears ring.

"Wow—" Ethan said, "that was amazing!"

"That was nothing," said Tinx. "One of his earlier blasts cracked the enclosure, so we had to get a new one."

"Thus far, my results are confirming Stravis' findings. Minerals from Ceres react when they encounter once-cloaked leprechaun gold. What I find interesting is the effects are not consistent. Some minerals create a much more powerful blast than others."

"What cracked the enclosure?" Hayley asked.

"A Ceresian bloating stone hydrated with earthly water. Which leads me to another oddity Stravis uncovered. The same stone, hydrated with Atlantian water, does not react."

"That must be why they used Atlantian water to hydrate the stone used to build the pyramid complex," Hayley said.

"If that's true, Jason Crowley must have known something about these reactions," Ethan said.

"Excellent observation," Damien said. "That must be why they went to all that trouble."

Ethan and Hayley witnessed Damien detonate a few more samples of various Ceresian minerals, but none equaled the yield of the bloating stone. Learning the new information fatigued their brains more, so again they decided to take a walk in the Moongarden. But along the way, Hayley stopped to ponder something.

"What's wrong?"

"Something my brother said is bothering me. Why did they go to all that trouble? I can think of only one reason. They knew the structure would encounter leprechaun gold."

"Could be."

"Which brings me back to something I asked you earlier. What purpose does such a giant structure serve?"

"I see where you are going with this. They could store things in a giant structure like that."

"Store many things, and I suspect that is what we missed."

After Hayley's epiphany, they strolled quietly through the Moongarden and spent some time skipping stones in the pond next to the Moon Orchard. After that, they settled on an early dinner and decided to call it a day.

The following morning, Ethan woke up to find a note from Hayley slid underneath his door. It read:

Dear Ethan,

I got an early start and came up with a few new ideas. I'm going to skip breakfast this morning to follow up on another possible lead. I have no idea how long it will take so I will meet you at noon in the cafeteria, we can discuss what I found then.

With love, Hayley

Ethan met Tinx for breakfast, she was waiting in their usual spot. He read Hayley's note to her and filled Tinx in on some of their latest thoughts about the pyramid complex. After that, they made small talk as they ate. Ethan had a light breakfast because he was meeting Hayley later for lunch.

When they finished, Ethan accompanied Tinx to the laboratory on his way to Odin's chamber. Tinx disappeared down the basement stairs. Ethan stood silently as the door creaked closed.

"Well, well, well," Gruggins said as he popped out of his box and stood at the table's edge. "Not often I see you without Miss Hayley. Did you finally piss her off?"

"No, it's not like that. She hasn't slept well lately and didn't want to wake me – so she left to run an errand on her own."

"I wouldn't exactly call visiting the Wentworths an errand," Gruggins said. "Sounds more like torture to me. Bella is like fingernails on a chalkboard."

"She is meeting with the Wentworths?"

"She passed through here a few hours ago and stopped by to say hello. Told me she was off to Zen city to visit the Wentworths."

"Did she say why?"

"Didn't ask why. I'm not nosey."

"Okay, thanks for cheering me up, Gruggins," Ethan said. He turned and started towards the stairs.

"I'm sorry. Did I say something wrong? No offense, you're still my favorite Hybrid."

"I'm the only Hybrid you know."

"Well, there is that."

"Anyway, no offense taken. Thanks, Gruggins. I'll see you later."

Hayley had made Ethan a copy of her hand so he could enter her grandfather's chamber without her. He mulled around for several hours, looking for any clue as to why she might want to speak with the Wentworths. But he found nothing by noon, and it was time to meet Hayley for lunch.

He sat at their usual table again and waited. Ten minutes went by, but Hayley did not arrive. He sat for another twenty minutes, checking the time every two minutes. It was not like Hayley to not show up like this, which worried Ethan. So he thumbed his way around his ELMO and found the app she used to find Wordly Pagemore. But when he saw her name, only dashes appeared where her location should be.

"Gruggins said she was going to the Wentworths," Ethan thought.

He pulled up the Caretaker condo's directory to find out where they lived and sprinted into The Hall of Doorways. He ran down the hallway to the 99th door on the right and entered the Caretaker city of Zen. It didn't take long to run down the crowded street to Tower number three. But twenty minutes went by while he waited in line for an elevation pod.

"Name and destination?" the young Caretaker asked.

"Ethan Fox, to visit the Wentworths."

Ethan grew more worried by the second, making the three minute ride seem like an eternity. But his bubble finally arrived and melted into the Wentworth condo, dropping him off in a dark, quiet room.

"Hello, is anybody here?" Ethan called out.

Nobody answered, but Ethan's palm symbols quickly turned on and showered the darkroom with a soft white glow. He gazed down at them, and they spun around in his palms to point to his left, so he followed their direction. The sound of rustling came from around the corner where his symbols pointed.

"Is anybody here? Who is that?" Ethan asked as he turned the corner to see a sizeable spider-like shadow rising from the ground. But the lights came on, and he quickly recognized the shadow was not a spider at all. It was Bella Wentworth using all four of her arms to pick herself up off the floor. Ethan quickly ran to her side to help her.

"What happened? Are you okay?"

"I—I don't recall," Bella said. "But you are such a dear to come to my rescue."

"You don't remember what happened? Hayley came to visit. Do you remember seeing her?"

"Oh yes, I remember now. She came to see my Boris, but he was out. So the dear girl stayed to comfort me."

"Why did she comfort you?"

"M-M-My B-Boris," Bella said and started sobbing.

"What about Boris? What happened? Why are you crying?"

"He's not himself lately. He comes and goes all hours of the night. And his temper, he's not my Boris since his return."

"What about Hayley?"

"The girl was such a dear to listen to all my troubles."

"What happened to Hayley?" Ethan said louder.

"I—I don't know. I was telling her something when the lights went out. The next thing I remember is you helping me off the floor."

"What were you telling her?"

"I—I don't remember," Bella said and cried uncontrollably.

Ethan tried to calm Bella and ask her more questions, but quickly decided it was a waste of time. So he scrambled from Zen city to find help, and Damien's basement laboratory was his first stop. He ran down the stairs into the bright white room, but only Tinx was present.

"I need to find Damien now."

"The Headmistress called him away," Tinx said. "They are out in the field on CAGE business."

"Great, now what will I do."

"Maybe I can help."

"No offense—but I doubt there is anything you can do."

"What's wrong?"

"It's Hayley, I can't find her anywhere. And I'm worried."

"I saw her about an hour ago. She wasn't very talkative, and they seemed to be in a hurry."

"They? Who was she with, and where were they going?"

"She was with Boris Wentworth, and they went upstairs somewhere."

"They must have gone to the headmasters chambers."

He turned and ran towards the stairs.

"Now you've got me worried," Tinx said. "I'm coming with you"

Tinx followed Ethan up the stairs to the third floor headmasters chambers. He fished out the replica of Hayley's hand and used it to enter the chamber. Nobody was there, but Ethan slowly walked around the room and scanned every inch.

"Well, somebody's been here. Odin's desk was different when I was here a few hours ago."

He dashed over to study the desk and noticed a piece of paper on the floor beneath it. So, he picked it up to examine and instantly recognized Hayley's handwriting.

> Where's Heldrik?
>   * Dakota Drakelan
>   * Boris Wentworth
>
> Bella Wentworth
>   * Boris not himself
>   * Bad Temper
>   * Bella saw someth—

"Based on this, I think she went to ask Boris about Heldrik Vonn Grim. We were going to speak with Dakota together. But Boris wrote articles about Dakota's past with Heldrik. So she must have figured Boris knows something about what became of Heldrik."

"Makes sense."

A loud knock on the door interrupted their discussion.

Tinx fluttered over and landed on Ethan's shoulder as he pulled the door open. But something fell into the room and thudded to the floor at Ethan's feet. He and Tinx looked down, and what they saw shocked them both to the core. Lying on the ground in front of them was a shriveled grey corpse.

The body appeared to be that of a short man based on his clothing, but he was lying face down on the stone floor. Ethan knelt to flip him over, and when he did, a chill crept down his spine as he grew cold and began to shiver.

"What is it? What's wrong?"

Ethan studied the man's clothing and the monocle in his right eye to ensure he wasn't seeing things. The wrinkled grey skin on the terrified face gave the appearance something had drained the life from his body while he watched in horror.

"This body," Ethan said as he stood up. "It, it's Boris Wentworth."

THE DAY OF RECKONING

Ethan stood expressionless, staring down at Boris' shriveled limp body. Tinx stared down from his shoulder with an equally perplexed expression.

"Well, if that's Boris," said Tinx. "Who did I see Hayley with?"

"I don't know, but there's something tucked behind his lapel."

He knelt to retrieve a piece of paper crudely pinned to the chest of Boris' corpse. He unfolded it and read its words:

Dear Ethan Fox,

    The Residence blocks the conscious connection we share, so it is left to my imagination to show me how delightfully terrified you must be

right now. Your dear Miss Hayley is
safe for now, but I will leave you to
your imagination to wonder what horrors
might fall upon her if you do not heed
my words exactly. You have three hours
to join us in the central pyramid. Come
alone. If you fail to make it, the
desert fortress will become her tomb.

Best wishes, Victor Qruefeldt

Ethan's hands shook as he finished reading the note and stood pondering his next step.

"How can we possibly make it there in three hours?" Tinx asked. "The Headmistress has posted guards on the portal plane, and nobody can access it without her approval."

"There is no us. Didn't you read the message? I must go alone."

Ethan's fists clenched as he concentrated on saving Hayley, and slowly but surely, a plan was forming in his head.

"Yeah, I understand," Tinx said. "I don't want to endanger Miss Hayley. I only want to help."

"Well, maybe there's a way you still can."

It took an hour to find Gruggins and Wordly, tell them about Hayley's predicament, and get them up to speed on Ethan's plan. Tinx and Wordly would make necessary arrangements while Gruggins went with Ethan to the Moongarden. They found Grubner tending to the trembling nomads. Ethan didn't even need Gruggins' help talking him into eight dwindle-berries. Grubner was happy to help the Hybrid Child with anything his heart desired.

Afterward, Ethan sprinted down The Hall of Doorways to the door the Nibblewarts used to venture into the past. He opened the door and ran through without hesitation. It was daytime in the desert, so the terrain appeared quite different, but the long line of giant ants walking enormous bricks towards the build site led him to the right place. He spent the next hour backtracking through the maze of tunnels to find the long straightaway to the chamber where he and Hayley had met the Nibblewarts. But eventually, his palm symbols woke up to show him the way.

Even during the day, everything beneath the sand appeared the same; so, once he found the straightaway, he quickly found the portal back to the future. He emerged from the tiny replica, chomped down four dwindle-berries, and promptly returned to size inside the temple structure. The trek through the sand to the center pyramid only took another few minutes, but he still worked up a sweat under the hot desert sun. He checked the time as he walked through the tall entrance.

"Twenty minutes to spare," he thought to himself.

The room was dark and quiet when he entered, but there was not a soul around. Ethan's night vision struggled to adjust as he ventured deeper into the dark. But he triggered the torches, which lit themselves around the room's perimeter. His vision worked perfectly under the flickering flames that barely lit the room. The pond in front of him looked like a pool of black oil as he approached.

He stopped and peered down at his reflection, but something moving caught his attention. The gecko on his shirt crawled towards his head like a cartoon on the fabric's surface. The garment frill popped out of his shirt and morphed into a live gecko that climbed onto his shoulder. The color drained from the gecko as it transformed into a tiny metallic humanoid that reminded him of the Silver Surfer. The small shape of a man sprang up, dove off his shoulder, and landed on the stone floor. The trinket landed splat on the ground and flattened out into a pancake. But the transformation was not over, as an object slowly grew from the circular pancake shape, Ethan's eyes widened as he slowly came to recognize the object before him and the realization of what it meant. A portal beacon stood before Ethan. Victor Qruefeldt had just tricked him into giving him access to *The Pyramids of Never.*

A bright flash of light strobed inside the room, and two figures appeared from nowhere. It was Hayley, and Boris had his right hand wrapped around the back of her neck.

"Ethan," Hayley cried out. "He's not Boris!"

"I know who he is," Ethan said as he glared into fake Boris' eyes.

Devilish laughter filled the room as Boris grew taller, his face contorted, and his clothes morphed into a tattered black robe. Victor Qruefeldt's piercing red eyes bore through Ethan's as a broad grin stretched across his face revealing sharp pointed teeth that reminded him of Pennywise, the evil clown. The brainy ridges covering his scalp pulsated between the enormous ears that protruded over his head like devilish horns. His guttural laughter grew louder and louder.

"Let her go," Ethan shouted. "Your quarrel is with me."

Victor threw Hayley to the ground at his feet as he stepped closer to Ethan and glared down at him. The dank odor of death filled Ethan's lungs as he breathed in Victor's unforgettable scent.

"My quarrel is with the whole lot of you," Victor screamed. "You and anyone else who stands in my way."

"Like my mother stood in your way," Ethan said. "She didn't do anything to deserve what you did to her."

"Oh—so you've learned of our little tryst," Victor said. "I kept it to myself at first. Thought I'd use our connection to eavesdrop and be the first to know when the Hybrid Child returned. But I quickly grew tired of listening to the thoughts of her feeble human mind."

"You drove her mad," Ethan said.

"That was the fun part," Victor replied. "After months of listening to the cacophony of worries in her head. Between that and the love she felt towards you, it nearly drove me mad. So I gave her a little peek into my mind. Showed her some wonderfully horrid ways I could dispose of her beloved child."

"You'll pay for what you've done," Ethan said. "I promise, I will make you pay for what you did to my mother, and for what you did to Adara."

"Adara—" Victor repeated. "So the shadow spirit—is Princess Adara. Interesting, I hadn't made the connection. But when she kept coming to you in your dreams, I knew there was a reason. That's why I planned the attack, to draw her out."

"I'm surprised you came here alone," Ethan prodded, "without your minions to protect you."

"He's not alone," Hayley said. "He has a whole army of Grimleavers coming."

No sooner had she said the words than the room lit up like a disco ball. One flash after another signaled the arrival of vampires, trolls, ogres, and other dark creatures.

"Norell, you've made it. I wondered if my confidant failed to inform you of my plans."

A tall vampire woman with long black hair stepped forward and bowed to Victor.

"All hail the Grimlord," she said.

"All hail the Grimlord," a chorus of voices echoed around the room.

"Whatever you're planning is destined to fail," Hayley said as she rose. "Caretakers will come, and we will defeat you."

Norell's arm whipped around like a club and pummeled Hayley's back to the ground. Ethan lunged at Norell, but Victor froze him cold with a swipe of his long, wicked hand. A cold wave of chills washed over his body as he struggled to move. But the harder he fought, the more frozen he became.

"What are our orders?" Norell asked.

"We must not underestimate Mr. Fox again. I must assume he has made contingency plans, and the Caretakers will arrive shortly. How fast can your army remove the cargo?"

"I've brought hundreds, and they are all equipped with sticky beacons. They will teleport the larger containers using those, and the rest will be hand-carried by the trolls and ogres."

"What about the other structures?"

"I've already sent teams to the other pyramids. They are awaiting word. I estimate twenty minutes once I've given the order."

"Give the order and tend to the cargo while I play with our guests," Victor said with a wicked scowl.

Hayley rose to her feet and stood next to Ethan, still frozen in place.

"Calm yourself," Hayley whispered to Ethan. "Adara says calmness will free you."

Ethan closed his eyes and thought of when he first met Hayley on the beach. He remembered her grabbing hold of his hands and the butterflies he felt. A warm rush of energy swept through his body; and suddenly, he could move again.

"You've learned to defeat my freezing hex," Victor said with a wide smile. "Not surprising, curses are so amateur. I hesitate to use them."

Norell moved across the room to the gigantic wall rising into the darkness above them. She ordered four of the enormous ogres to follow her. They looked like dirty, dumb, and mean versions of Shrek; only much bigger, and they carried small trees like clubs.

"Two of you take this one," she said and pointed at the wall. "And two of you take that one."

She pointed to an identical wall across the room. The ogres stood looking at one another like four stooges. One scratched its head, while two of the others picked at their noses.

"Dumb, stupid creatures," Norell said under her breath. "You and you, take down this wall while you and you take down that one."

She pointed at the ogres as she spoke, and they finally followed her instructions. Two giant oafs began slamming their trees against the wall like battering rams, while the other two slowly strode across the room to do the same.

"What are you going to do with us?" Hayley asked.

"You, my dear, still have something that belongs to me," Victor said. He held his right arm out towards Hayley and waved. Her hand involuntarily opened as the rift-key unwrapped from her finger and flew into his ghastly hand. Victor held out the black puzzle box with his left hand, and the top slowly slid open and disappeared. He dropped the rift-key in, and the lid slid back into place like a trap door.

"There will be no tricks this time," Victor said.

He cupped the puzzle box between his hands and held it in front of his face.

"Bind him," he said.

Ethan's arms moved behind his back as if the invisible man were restraining him. Something wrapped around his wrists like a coiling snake and tightened until he barely felt his fingers.

"What are you doing to him? STOP THIS!" Hayley screamed.

The loud noise from the smashing rock wall distracted Victor. He turned and took a few steps towards the commotion to watch the ogres break through the barrier to a secret cargo hold. Walls of sizable, stacked containers filled the room. Several vampires took flight to slap small devices onto the sides of the boxes, causing them to disappear in a flash of light. The legion of trolls took care of the ground-based containers as soon as the vampires freed them.

"Some of the leprechaun gold has been de-cloaked," Norell said to Victor. "But the extraction seems to be moving along faster than I expected. I will leave you now to check on the other structures."

"Leave this complex as soon as the last of the cargo has been teleported," Victor said.

"All hail the Grimlord," Norell said and was gone with a flash.

"Now, now, where was I," Victor said as he turned his attention back to Ethan and Hayley.

"You were about to let us go," Ethan said.

"Oh yes, there will be no tricks," Victor continued as he moved his hand over the puzzle box and pet it. "Fetch me the copycat."

A small metallic figurine of a cat appeared on the floor at his feet. Hayley glanced at Ethan as Victor bent down to pick it up and toss it over his shoulder.

"How did he know about my copycat?" She whispered to Ethan.

"I—I may have mentioned something to Boris."

"Give that back to me," Hayley said as she stepped toward Victor.

"That would not be a wise choice," Victor said.

A loud noise erupted from the other side of the room, where the other two ogres broke through the wall. The vampires and trolls finished clearing out the other hold, so they charged across the room to start on the new one. Victor turned to watch.

"It's time," Ethan whispered.

"What?" Hayley whispered back. But he did not answer. She turned away from Victor to see Ethan and glanced something green out of the corner of her eye. Gruggins was clinging to Ethan's back and climbing down towards his invisibly bound hands. He hopped off, landed between Ethan's wrists, rubbed his hands together, and touched the invisible binds. A coil of black rope instantly became visible around Ethan's wrists. Gruggins wasted no time. He pulled out a serrated knife and carefully hacked away. Ethan's hands were free within a minute, but he kept them behind his back to maintain the illusion.

Victor turned back to Ethan and Hayley, stroked his puzzle box, and grinned a wide tooth-bearing smile.

"Sadly, our time together is coming to an end," he said and stepped towards them.

The expression on one of their faces must have betrayed Ethan's intentions.

"You are up to something," Victor said to Ethan. "I feel it in my bones."

"He's not up to anything," Hayley shouted to draw his attention away from Ethan. "He's only here to rescue me from you. Now give me back my Tabby Cat."

She took several steps toward him – but Victor reacted quickly.

"Repel her."

Hayley flew across the room and landed nearly twenty feet behind Ethan. But she shook it off and quickly jumped to her feet.

"Tabby Cat, Tabby Cat, Tabby Cat," Hayley said. With each utterance, she took a step closer.

Victor stared Ethan in the eyes and gave him the most demonic look possible. Hayley's copycat apparated in her outstretched hands. Victor turned towards Hayley and started walking in her direction.

"You, my dear, have become a nuisance I will no longer tolerate."

He continued towards her, raised the puzzle box, and stroked it. A tingle started at Ethan's feet and slowly crawled up his legs and over his body as he felt what Victor was about to do. A loud diabolical laugh erupted from his lips as he opened his mouth.

"End her, now," Victor said as he stretched his arms out in Hayley's direction. A tiny purplish-black vortex appeared before his extended hands and swirled faster and faster as the room grew silent. Then, the vortex abruptly rocketed towards Hayley like a missile.

Everything in the room slowed down as Ethan burst into action. He swiftly sprinted in a feeble attempt to move between Hayley and the vortex. But he quickly realized he was moving too slow, so he launched his body into the air and zipped into the path of the menacing whirlwind. The vortex struck him dead center in the chest and instantly changed his direction, sending him volleying across the room like a bowling pin.

The blast from the collision threw Hayley to the ground as well. Gruggins fluttered over and landed on her chest to see if she was okay.

"You pitiful boy," Victor said. "Heroic till the very end, and I had such plans for you."

Hayley peered across the room at Ethan. He was on the ground gasping for breath and writhing in pain.

"What have you done to him!" she screamed.

"Reaped his soul, I'm afraid," Victor said. "But in my defense, it was meant for you. Sadly, there is nothing you can do to save him."

Victor's sinister laugh echoed throughout the room as strobes of light bounced off the walls. The vampires, trolls, and ogres had finished their task and were teleporting away.

"What am I going to do with you? It would be such a waste to kill you now that your life is about to be filled with sorrow. But I suppose I must."

Victor took another step toward Hayley, but Gruggins acted quickly. He rubbed his hands together, raised them into the air, and moved them in a circular motion. Hayley and Gruggins instantly disappeared, hidden from harm by a Grumpling's cloak.

"I must remember to exterminate all grumplings," said Victor.

He let out a deep sigh, turned, and headed for the portal beacon. But he stopped and turned to watch the life slowly drain from Ethan's body.

"So much for their Hybrid Child."

His laughs echoed through the room, but he quickly stopped when Jordanna and the rest of CAGE hurried through the entrance accompanied by an armed battalion of Careguards.

"I guess that's my cue," Victor said. He turned, grabbed hold of the portal beacon, and vanished.

Gruggins and Hayley reappeared, and she was kneeling at Ethan's side, sobbing uncontrollably. Jordanna and the others rushed over to them.

"It's Ethan," she cried. "He needs your help."

"What happened to him?" Jordanna asked.

"A soul reaping vortex," Gruggins said. "He threw himself in its path to save Miss Hayley."

"We have to save him!" Hayley screamed as tears streamed down her cheeks.

"I'm afraid there is nothing we can do," Jordanna said in a quivering tone.

"But you can do something," she cried to her brother. "All of Stravis' journals . . . the answer must be there somewhere."

"I'm sorry," Damien said. "If the answer does lie within Stravis' journals, there's no time. He'll be gone before we can find it. Even with our vast knowledge of the universe, there is no cure for this."

Ethan's face turned grey. His breaths grew shorter as his life continued to drain away. A bright yellow flash strobed across the room, drawing everybody's attention. It was the Shadow Princess swiftly gliding over the black pond to where Ethan lay dying.

"You have to help him, please!" Hayley pleaded to Adara.

Everyone moved out of her way as the Shadow Princess floated to Ethan's side and knelt beside him. She reached her arms down and held his head in her hands. Then moved one hand over his head to feel his cold forehead. She gazed up at Hayley and calmly shook her head back and forth.

"YOU CAN SAVE HIM! I KNOW YOU CAN!" Hayley cried louder.

Ethan's body quivered, and he slowly reached his hand up at Hayley. She knelt at his side opposite Adara and gently grabbed his hand as more tears flowed from her eyes. The Shadow Princess lightly forced her arms underneath Ethan's upper torso, lifted him, and cradled him in her bosom.

"What is she doing?" Tinx asked.

But nobody spoke a word. They stood by quietly as Ethan turned as black as the Shadow Princess. Then, Adara and Ethan dimmed without warning until the stone floor was visible through them both. They continued fading, becoming more and more translucent until, finally, they were gone.

Two Weeks Later

A KRAKEN'S FURY

Two weeks went by with nary a peep out of Hayley. She was not taking the loss of Ethan well and was deep in mourning, spending most of her time behind door number 6L in The Hall of Doorways. Staying in Ethan's room made her feel closer to him and safe in some strange way. But with Caretaker training looming on the horizon, she needed to find a way to summon the strength and learn how to live without him.

She pulled herself out of the pillowy cloud bed in Ethan's room and stretched. Today was the first day of the rest of her life, and from here on out, she would take it day by day. Her plan for today was to return to her room, take a shower, brush her teeth and hair and dress.

"So far, so good," Hayley thought to herself. She stood in front of a full-length mirror and stared at herself in her Caretaker robe, pondering whether or not she could do it. But a rustling sound distracted her, and she spun around as a green blob appeared on her dresser and Gruggins popped out.

"My dear girl," he said. "I know you miss him. I miss him myself—but life goes on."

Tears streamed down Hayley's cheeks, so Gruggins fluttered over and landed on her shoulder to comfort her.

"Ethan Fox would not want you to mourn him. He would want you to celebrate his life by living yours to the fullest. He'd want you to be happy."

Gruggins sat down, scooted closer, and rested his head against her neck. Hayley wiped her tears away and calmly stood as Gruggins cuddled her neck.

Jordanna sat behind the study desk, discussing current events with Damien, Nicholas, and Tinx. Tinx perched on Damien's lap while he and Nicholas sat in chairs across the desk from the Headmistress. Hayley entered, and the room fell silent.

"I—I came to study a little," she said.

"That is quite all right," Jordanna said. "We will move to the CAGE briefing room."

"No, please don't," Hayley said. "I want everything at least to seem normal again. Pretend like I'm not here and return to your conversation."

Jordanna looked at the others and nodded.

"Well then, where were we? Bring me up to speed on our findings on the museum break-ins."

"I received the full report this morning," Nicholas said. "It appears they took similar items from each of the museums. They were thoroughly ransacked, which leads me to believe they were looking for something specific."

"So they must have found what they were looking for," said Jordanna. "What did they take?"

"All the museums they hit had exhibits with items pilfered from Stravis' bunker during the Pandora fiasco," Nicholas said.

"And?"

"And, according to gallery workers, the only things missing were small rock collections."

"Rock collections," Damien said. "What kind of rocks? Did you order a molecular scan of the exhibit?"

"Yes, it took some doing, but I had a clandestine team slip in and perform the scan under cover of night."

"And—what did they find?"

"Various elemental minerals were present. I have the list right here."

Nicholas handed a piece of paper to Damien. His eyes moved down the list and stopped as his mouth gaped open.

"What is it?" Jordanna asked.

"This could be a problem," he said. "I believe they were looking for this, a Ceresian bloating stone."

"And why is that a problem?"

"Because of what I've learned from Stravis' research. He studied peculiar alchemy between earthly items when they come in contact with certain elementals."

"And a Ceresian bloating stone is one of those elementals," said Jordanna.

"Yes, one of the worst. At least as far as I've learned thus far."

"How dangerous?" Nicholas asked.

"Well, my experiment used a tiny pebble from an earthly hydrated bloating stone and an equivalent nugget of de-cloaked leprechaun gold. The resulting blast cracked a containment cube rated at one hundred megatons."

Jordanna and Nicholas gasped in unison, and Hayley stood up from the study table.

"Did you say leprechaun gold?"

"Yes. Why do you ask?"

"The cargo holds in the pyramids, that was part of the cargo the Grimleavers took. I heard the female vampire named Norell, and she told Victor some of their leprechaun gold was de-cloaked."

"Then it's a safe bet the Grimleavers also know about the alchemy you describe," Nicholas said.

"Therein lies our problem," Damien said. "Victor Qruefeldt now has all the material he needs to blow up a vast portion of the known universe."

"I agree we have a problem," Jordanna said. "But mutual self-destruction or martyrdom is not Victor's style. No, he has definitive plans for his new weapon of mass destruction."

Hayley pulled up a chair and joined their conversation as they debated dealing with this new revelation and the other issues they faced. But Dorkin Drumbles scrambled into the study and interrupted their talk. He hurried to Jordanna's side, whispered in her ear, and ran out. Jordanna stood up and looked around the room before she spoke.

"Dorkin has informed me of an important new painting in the Gallery. You are all welcome to come along."

Damien and Nicholas followed her to the study door, Tinx rode along on Damien's shoulder, but Hayley went back to studying. Jordanna opened the door, stopped, and turned to her daughter.

"Hayley dear, you will want to see this. Dorkin was adamant."

Hayley reluctantly agreed and followed them to the Gallery. Dorkin was waiting by the entrance when they arrived and wasted no time escorting them down the long hall of significant works of art.

"It took no time, no time at all," Dorkin said. "The Fates were unanimous in record time, and they even gave this one a name."

"That's odd," Jordanna said. "They don't normally name them for us."

"Very odd indeed," Dorkin said. "This is the first time they have named one."

Dorkin stopped at the last painting in the hall that was still on the easel and covered with a white sheet.

"What did they name it?" Tinx asked.

"A Kraken's Fury."

He pulled the cover off, and they all stood and studied the painting. The scene was a dark cavern lit by a green glow and yellow highlights where a giant beast perched majestically upon a raised platform. The creature was dark green, with three dragon heads up top. Its bottom consisted of long tentacles and a sharp tail. Massive arms hung to the ground below the dragon heads, and it used them to lean on. At the monster's midsection, between its arms, a mouth with rows of sharp teeth gaped open. Above that, several randomly placed eyes peered out.

"The creature is a full-grown earthly Kraken," Damien said.

In front of the beast, lying to its left at the platform's base, sat a perfectly round black orb, cracked at the top where yellow rays of light beamed up at the Kraken.

"Who cares about the monster," Hayley said. "Who is that?"

She rubbed her eyes and stepped closer to the painting, and the others backed away to give her space. She focused her eyes on the lower middle left portion of the scene where the body of a boy lay on the ground. Upon first glance, he appeared to be unconscious or dead. His back was to the platform, and his face flat against the floor. Hayley turned her head sideways to view the boy's face, but then she turned her attention to his hands. His right arm tucked in and hugged his chest, but his left arm lay flat on the ground, palm up, and the symbol in its center gave off a dim yellow glow. Hayley perked up and spun around to face the others.

"That's Ethan," she said with a tearful smile. "He is alive, and he needs our help!"

BOOK

WORDLY PAGEMORE'S

EARLY WORM ACTIVITIES & GAMES:
THE SHADOW PRINCESS EDITION

E. L. SEER

GREET ETHAN FOX

Ethan starts out the Ethan Fox Books original series as a thirteen year old boy in book #1, Ethan Fox and the Eyes of the Desert Sand. In book #2, Ethan Fox and the Shadow Princess, Ethan is fourteen years old. Ethan had kept his promise and told nobody, not even his parents George and Betsy (his adoptive partents) of his adventures. But things could never truly return to normal now that he knew he was the Hybrid Child and connected to the hidden Caretaker universe.

Victor Qruefeldt was the master and creator of the Grimleavers and the archnemesis to Ethan's Caretaker friends at The Residence. During their previous encounter, Ethan had outsmarted the Grimleaver leader, making him look foolish. And that left Victor with a particularly strong disdain for young Ethan Fox.

ADVENTURES

BIG APPLE

BIRTHDAY

CARETAKER CITY

CREATOR LANGUAGE

DAYDREAMING

DESTINY

ETHAN FOX

FRIENDS

FOURTEEN

HEART THUMPED

HYBRID CHILD

JASPER

MEMORIES

NEW YORK

PALMS GLOW

PARENTS

PERUSED

PHANTOM

SANDSTORM

SHOELACE

SPOKE IN TONGUES

TELEPATHY

TRANCE

Ethan Fox

```
S D N E I R F K R O Y W E N C
E A R D G B I G A P P L E R A
U Y D E P M U H T T R A E H R
G D E S I B I R T H D A Y M E
N R S T R O W R W V T P F R T
O E U I I P A O E O E A O O A
T A R N A N L N R X M R U T K
N M E Y C G T L O E O E R S E
I I P E S U A F M R T N T D R
E N S M R N N O E L N T E N C
K G L E G A R P T T A S E A I
O A S U H I S P I P H S N S T
P O A T E A T E L E P A T H Y
S G E S J H T E C A L E O H S
E D L I H C D I R B Y H R F A
```

ETHAN FOX AND THE
SHADOW PRINCESS EXCERPT

"What happened after that?" Ethan asked.

"We sent in a team. Alexander Sturgis cleaned up the mess and ensured no humans would discover it again."

"Alexander Sturgis—" Ethan repeated the name of his birth father.

"Yes," Jordanna said. "Your mother was present as well. Alexander took Tiffany on that mission, and you were born."

Ethan's face felt flush, and he grew antsy. He had tried to avoid thinking about it for George and Betsy's sake. But the mere mention of his birth parents caused a flood of emotions to rush through his mind.

"They might have missed something," Ethan said. "We should go to the bunker and have a look."

"Alexander is the best we have," Jordanna said. "He missed nothing."

GREET GEORGE FOX

George Fox was not only Ethan's dad, he was a prankster to boot—he called it the "crack Ethan up game." He'd fumble around in his coat pocket with one hand and pluck two cucumber slices out of the water glass with the other. A wide grin swept across his face as he ducked under the table. Moments later, a loud wallowing noise rumbled from under the table.

"I am Charlie, the Walrus man of Wiltor. I am here to speak with Ethan Fox!" A loud voice growled as George emerged from beneath the table. Ethan erupted with laughter at the sight of George's face. A rubber walrus nose with whiskers and tusks covered the bottom half of his face, and cucumber slices stuck to his eye sockets to look like enormous green eyes—George was a Walrus man indeed!

ABDUCTED

APPRENTICE

BABY BROTHER

BELLY

BELT-LOOSENING

BETSY

CHAIR

CHARLIE

CLOCKWORK

DEEP SIGH

DESK

DESSERT

GEORGE FOX

GRASP

GRIMLEAVERS

MANHATTAN

PEPPER

RESCUED

SANTA CRUZ

STRUGGLING

TALETADDLER

TATTOOS

TETHER PORT

WALRUS MAN

George Fox

```
H I G S R E V A E L M I R G T
G N T T E X O F E G R O E G A
I Z U R C A T N A S M D N N L
S R V U B E T S E Y E I S S E
P E Y G Y L L E B S N C D M T
E H S G L T N H S E H L E A A
E T A L I S I E S A K O U N D
D O B I T S R O I S T C C H D
E R D N A T O R E T S K S A L
I B U G T L Z D S F V W E T E
L Y C O T E T H E R P O R T R
R B T L O I P E P P E R D A H
A A E F O R P S A R G K I N T
H B D A S E C I T N E R P P A
C W A L R U S M A N R N S P M
```

ETHAN FOX AND THE
SHADOW PRINCESS EXCERPT

Ethan opened the door as George stood up from behind his desk and gave him a wide-eyed stare.

"George Fox," Dakota Drakelan said as he entered the room and stepped in front of Ethan. "How long's it been? Seems like a hundred years."

George glanced at Dakota, then at Ethan, then back at Dakota.

"Ur all grown up since ur days at The Residence. Up and out from the looksa it." Dakota pointed at George's belly and laughed.

George turned back to Ethan, let out a deep sigh, and sat back in his chair.

"I guess an explanation is long overdue."

"Ya think," Ethan said and held up his open palms. "Are you going to tell me these aren't tattoos from an evil cult?"

"How long have you known?" George asked.

GREET BETSY FOX

Betsy Fox always made it a priority to share the New York lights lifestyle with her two men, George and Ethan. Together, they'd often go out on the town for a Broadway show, followed by dinner. Their routine was to eat a late dinner after the show and discuss their opinions about the performance.

In route, Betsy always asked the taxi driver to drop them off several blocks from their dinner destination. She was a stickler for making sure George got at least a short walk in before what would become a belt-loosening feast followed by at least one dessert.

Betsy and George agreed to take Ethan in as an infant to hide him from the Grimleavers—and it worked almost.

Ethan has fond memories of Betsy smiling and holding up a red ceramic pot. Holding the pot, she'd explain the process of baking pottery in an oven.

BETSY FOX

BROADWAY SHOW

BUILDING

CENTRAL PARK

DESTINATION

DISAPPEARED

ELEVATOR

EMBARRASSMENT

ENVISION

ETHAN

FAMILY

FOYER

GAME ROOM

GEORGE'S STUDY

PENTHOUSE

POTTERY OVEN

RED CERAMIC POT

RESTAURANT

SCENARIO

SHRIEK

TAXI DRIVER

UPSTAIRS

WALK

WORRIED

Betsy Fox

R E V I R D I X A T T T N A B
B E T S Y F O X K E I R H S R
Y S D E R A E P P A S I D W O
D U L C E N T R A L P A R K A
U O E L E V A T O R E S E D D
T H G C E R F D E F K C S E W
S T N M U N A O E T L E T S A
S N I O P A V M Y D A N A T Y
E E D O S H Y I I E W A U I S
G P L R T T L R S C R R R N H
R M I E A E I H I I P I A A O
O O U M I O M A M O O O N T W
E M B A R R A S S M E N T I T
G A E G S E F M D E I R R O W
O F M P O T T E R Y O V E N T

ETHAN FOX AND THE SHADOW PRINCESS EXCERPT

"Cat got ur tongue, George? Don't remember ya being the speechless sort."

"I—I've spent years trying to prepare myself for this. Betsy and I tried to envision every scenario."

"Betsy," Ethan said. "Where is she? Is she okay?"

"She is safe. After the attack, Alexander paid us a visit. We decided Betsy would be safer if he took her to stay with family."

"Alexander," Ethan said.

"Yes, Alexander Sturgis, your real father," George said. "I'll explain, but let me start at the beginning."

"Please do."

"When I was a young boy, a taletaddler named Pepper visited me," George said and smiled as he remembered. "We quickly became the best of friends. He would visit me every day like clockwork. But then one day—"

GREET HAYLEY RAVENWOOD

Hayley Ravenwood has learned that she has an extensive family, including twin brothers (Daavic and Damien), parents (Ryvias and Jordanna), and grandparents (Odin and Vanessa). The Ravenwoods are the headmasters of the Caretakers. Previously, the Trabblemores were the headmasters of the Caretakers.

Hayley now has her own apartment in the Caretaker city of Zen. Her grandmother, Vanessa, has an apartment in the city as well. However, Vanessa decided to move outside of the Caretaker realm into a castle elsewhere. Nevertheless, there are still plenty of family reunions.

At the beginning of the book, when Ethan reunites with Hayley, she is wearing the same white sundress with yellow flowers, which Ethan remembered from seeing her the first time on the Santa Cruz Beach Boardwalk.

ANOMALY

BABYSITTER

BOOK-TRAVEL

CARETAKER

CITY OF ZEN

CONVERSATION

COPYCAT

GIDDY

HAYLEY

HISTORY

INFINITY RING

INSUBORDINATE

LEARN

PARALLEL WORLD

PORTAL BOOKS

REBELLIOUS

RESEARCH

RIVETED

SESSION

STRATEGIZING

TABBY CAT

TEENAGER

TINKERED

TRAINING

Hayley Ravenwood

```
C O P Y C A T Y B B A T Y T L
O B O A R H B L A N N I T S E
N A R R R E A R I C O N T R V
V B T Y E A S Y A L M K I R A
E Y A R R B L E L A A E D E R
R S L O A C E L A E L R E G T
S I B T A I I L E R Y E T A K
A T O S T R N T L L C D E N O
T T O I N Y O I Y I W H V E O
I E K H L E A R N O O O I E B
O R S E S S I O N G F U R T Y
N G R E K A T E R A C Z S L D
S T R A T E G I Z I N G E A D
M E M G N I R Y T I N I F N I
E E T A N I D R O B U S N I G
```

ETHAN FOX AND THE
SHADOW PRINCESS EXCERPT

"Well, you don't have to be rude," Hayley said. "Ethan was only being polite."

"You've got your mother's spirit," Dakota said. . . .

"You're hurting them!" Hayley shouted at the top of her lungs.

"An yer grandmother's," Dakota said.

"Stop it, put them out now!" Hayley insisted.

"Alright, alright, calm down, was only for effect anyway."

Dakota smiled, snapped his fingers, and the burning candle creatures vanished. Various antique lamps around the room flickered on to replace the candlelight.

"Definitely a Ravenwood woman," Dakota said.

"Where did they go?" Hayley asked.

"Back to where I summoned 'em from," Dakota said. "And for your information, those little liars were not'n pain. Their fakin grief to feed off ur sympathy."

REMEMBER DAAVIC RAVENWOOD

In the case of Daavic and Damien being twins, there was definitely a good son and a bad son. In book #1, Ethan Fox and the Eyes of the Desert Sand, we learned that Damien was never the bad son; it was Daavic all along.

At the end of book #1, Victor Qruefeldt and his pet grimtailed dread, Poe, tended to Daavic's demise. Daavic begged for his life, "I CAN STILL BE OF SERVICE MASTER!" But Victor was done with him, and the dread dove at Daavic and whizzed by his face leaving a small black vortex behind—this was a death vortex. A ray of light shot out from the center of the vortex and scanned the length of Daavic's body. Daavic slowly turned transparent—he was dematerialized. The vortex was gone. Daavic was gone—Daavic was dead.

BASEMENT
BLACK PUZZLE BOX
BORIS WENTWORTH
CURSE
DAMP
DARK
DECLOAKED
DEMONIC
DIABOLICAL
FREEZING HEX
GRIMTAILED DREAD
GUESTS
HELDRIK
LEAP-LETTER
LEPRECHAUN GOLD
NUISANCE
POE
REAP
RIFT-KEY
SINISTER
SOUL
TIME TRAVEL
VICTOR
WHIRLWIND

Daavic Ravenwood

```
D A E R D D E L I A T M I R G
I R C D E C L O A K E D R B D
A R N E N C B O P M A D O L L
B R A A G U A A R R K R V A O
O E S F L R S Y K T I I X C G
L T I D R S E R K S R F T K N
I T U V N E M A W E D T I P U
C E N R I L E E P P L K M U A
A L R L E C N Z N O E E E Z H
L P E A U T T O I E H Y T Z C
L A E S W T S O E N R A R L E
U E U O I N K I R O G T A E R
O L R H D E M O N I C H V B P
S T S E U G L O P I D B E O E
H W H I R L W I N D S A L X L
```

ETHAN FOX AND THE
SHADOW PRINCESS EXCERPT

"What's to learn from a heap of old stone ruins?" Ethan asked.

"Lots of things," Hayley replied. "What were they before? Who built them? Who destroyed them, and why?"

"But why does any of that matter now?"

"Because whoever built them also built the spin dial Daavic showed us."

"Good point. What have you learned?"

"I haven't been able to find much information on them. It's like somebody erased their past. There are the rumors they're haunted, but that is all anybody seems to know."

"Have you asked Wordly for help?"

"Not yet. So far, it's been my secret. But I may ask him for help at some point."

GREET DAMIEN RAVENWOOD

Damien has repurposed Daavic's secret room into a lab; he's remodeled from top to bottom.

The out-door is missing, and Damien has a theory. It disappeared after Ethan unlocked the door to the portals in book #1, Ethan Fox and the Eyes of the Desert Sand. His theory; the idea is the lock on the portal plane was causing the duality, and when unlocked, the door reverted to normal.

In book #2, Ethan Fox and the Shadow Princess, Damien is obsessed with Stravis' bunker and the findings inside. So much so, he talks his mother, Jordanna, into letting him transfer Stravis' secret room of research and journals to his new laboratory. Subsequently, he has brought Tink on board—The Residence's newest CAGE member.

BENCH
CATALOG
COMPROMISE
CRITICAL
DAMIEN
DESERT BUNKER
DUALITY
ELMO
ENCODED ENTRIES
HYPERHOLE EVENT
INFILTRATED
JUDGEMENT
LABORATORY
LAPSE
MAGNIFYING GLASS
MOON-SHAPED PUPIL
OVERSEE
PATTERN
PORTAL PLANE
PROPHECIES
ROOM
SECRET
TINX
TREASURES

Damien Ravenwood

```
M R E K N U B T R E S E D G C
A O J U D G E M E N T R T N O
G S O D A M I E N O E O N I M
N E L N E K C A C G S O E D P
I I A C S H T B O H P M V E R
F C B R P H R L D C O Z E T O
Y E O I A Z A E E N R T E A M
I H R T L T L P D E T R L R I
N P A I A M L U E B A E O T S
G O T C O D A V N D L A H L E
G R O A L L E D T R P S R I C
L P R L I F I R R J L U E F R
A S Y T I N X E I C A R P N E
S Q Y O V E R S E E N E Y I T
S N R E T T A P S S E S H L L
```

ETHAN FOX AND THE SHADOW PRINCESS EXCERPT

"How about this," said Damien. "Tinx will accompany them, but I will remain in close contact and oversee everything they do."

Jordanna's gaze moved from Ethan to Hayley and then Damien as she contemplated his compromise.

"Fine," she said and let out another deep sigh. "I will agree to Damien's compromise only because we are already spread so thin – but I feel like you've all sold me a bill of goods."

"I suggest you track down Tinx," Damien said to Hayley. "You can inform her of her new assignment, and I will be in touch."

"Will do," Hayley said and smiled.

It seemed rehearsed to Ethan. He felt like it was all for show, and Jordanna was right about being hoodwinked by her two children.

GREET VICTOR QRUEFELDT

Victor Qruefeldt's latest victims were devolved from Tinx's relatives; he is using pixie-devils.

CAGE was short for Caretaker Anti-Grimleaver Enforcement. A special group of Caretakers focused on fighting against Victor Qruefeldt and his army of evil Grimleavers. As a result, the newest member due to the atrocities committed against her family, Tinx too is now a CAGE member.

In book #2, Ethan Fox and the Shadow Princess, Victor causes much havoc in the United States and abroad—museum break-ins; taking similar items from each of the museums. Each had exhibits with items pilfered from Creator Stravis' bunker during the Pandora fiasco. And so, Victor now has all the material he needs to blow up a vast portion of the known universe.

ARCH NEMESIS

ARMY BOOTS

ATROCITIES

BATTALION

BLACK ROBE

COLD

COMMITTED

DARK CREATURES

EVOLVED

GARGOYLE

GRAVEYARD

GRIMLEAVERS

HAND

KAMIKAZE-STYLE

OGRES

PUZZLE BOX

PYRAMIDS

QUARREL

REANIMATE

SHADOW SPIRIT

STONE STATUES

TROLLS

VAMPIRES

ZOMBIES

Victor Qruefeldt

```
S A S E U T A T S E N O T S D
E B V B A T T A L I O N L K D
I T G L R P R S E D N L A V A
T D D A M Y O E E O O M A X R
I G A C Y R C R A R I M G O K
R R L K B A I G T K P A E B C
I A E R O M T O A I R V T E R
P V R O O I I Z R G O D A L E
S E R B T D E E O L M N M Z A
W Y A E S S S Y V M E A I Z T
O A U D T X L E N T B H N U U
D R Q Y U E D L O C T I A P R
A D L K E C O M M I T T E D E
H E W G R I M L E A V E R S S
S I S E M E N H C R A M M E P
```

ETHAN FOX AND THE
SHADOW PRINCESS EXCERPT

"Poe is here," Norell said, "our master has arrived."

The dread swiftly broke into a dive towards the rooftop and pulled up into a quick loop maneuver causing a small swirling vortex to open near the vampires. The whirling disturbance grew darker and fuller as bright jolts of electricity danced out from its center. A black army boot poked out as Victor Qruefeldt stepped through the vortex to join his Grimleaver army. . . .

"All hail the Grimlord," Norell said.

"All hail the Grimlord," the vampires echoed from the rooftops.

"Master, you've arrived just in time," Norell said. "The target is on the move."

"Has the devil's swarm arrived?" Victor asked.

"We've seen no sign of them."

"They'll arrive shortly," Victor said with a grin. "Their tiny wings slow them down . . ."

GREET JORDANNA RAVENWOOD

Jordanna Ravenwood became headmistress over the Caretakers after her husband, Ryvias was murdered. As headmistress, she spends much of her time in the Map Room within The Residence, strategizing, collecting intel, and in CAGE meetings. However, her position does not go without controversy. She is well aware that her reign as headmistress has its detractors.

As a result, the Trabblemores, more specifically, Roman Trabblemore is gunning for the return of his family's position. Roman's father, Gaylord was headmaster before he lost his position to the Ravenwoods. Along with the position, the family assigned to "headmaster" or "headmistress" is granted a family chamber. For example, the Trabblemore chamber; the Ravenwood chamber.

APOLOGY

CAREGUARDS

CARETAKERS

COMMONERS

COUNCIL OF ELDERS

CROW'S NEST

DANGEROUS

DETRACTORS

EARTH

FRIGHTEN

HEADMISTRESS

HENCHMEN

HOODWINKED

MAP ROOM

PARENT

POLICE

PROTECTIVE

ROGUE

RYVIAS

SMIRKED

SUMMONED

TARGET

THREATEN

TOLERATE

Jordanna Ravenwood

```
D E K R I M S R E N O M M O C
P R O T E C T I V E A M I O A
P O M N A H C T A P N C U H R
H P A N R N O O O E H N B T E
E N P E T L G L M D C D R D G
A E R T H I O H E I R E I E U
D T O A A G C T L G C N M K A
M H O E Y N R O T I E O M N R
I G M R E A F E L A N M P I D
S I V H C E G O S A V M A W S
T R N T L R P C A P E U R D A
R F O D A N G E R O U S E O I
E R E T S E N S W O R C N O V
S R R K L E T A R E L O T H Y
S R E K A T E R A C E U G O R
```

ETHAN FOX AND THE
SHADOW PRINCESS EXCERPT

"But that's my point, Damien. We do not have any idea where to look. So we will focus on what is real—the Grimleavers have infiltrated the human world and are attacking humans."

"I won't drop this, Mother. We thought it crazy for Victor to have wanted the portals open—yet he did. The whole notion is crazy unless he had help on the other side. And if I'm right, we will need all the help we can get."

"You are stubborn like your father," Jordanna said as a proud smile slipped onto her lips. "Alright, I will indulge you this once—what have you learned?"

"Stravis wanted to protect this information; he encoded some of his entries, and I think I've cracked the code on some of these markings. I believe they are timestamps, and some of them are dated after the Creators locked the portals."

REMEMBER ODIN RAVENWOOD

Odin Ravenwood, Jordanna's father-in-law, endured much debate during his reign as well—when he was alive. Boris Wentworth wrote an article, damning Odin: "Thumbing his nose at popular opinion, new Headmaster Odin Ravenwood has decided against abolishing the Master of Dark Studies position. Created during predecessor Gaylord Trabblemore's tumultuous reign, the position has come under intense scrutiny as calls for its banishment have reached a crescendo. Opponents insist Gaylord's downfall was a direct consequence of him creating the position for his questionable appointee, Heldrik Vonn Grim . . ."

The article continued: "As if the groundswell of negativity were not troubling enough, the position is already filled . . . sources confirm Dakota Drakelan . . ."

APPOINTEE

APPRENTICE

BANISHMENT

CAPTIVATED

CONTROVERSY

CRESCENDO

DARK STUDIES

DOWNFALL

ENCOUNTERED

FIRST

GAYLORD

GRAMPA

HAPPENED

HEADMASTER

HELDRIK

OPINIONS

OPPONENTS

PREDECESSOR

QUESTIONABLE

REIGN

SITE

TRABBLEMORE

TUMULTUOUS

VISIT

Odin Ravenwood

```
S R E L B A N O I T S E U Q C
I N T T P R E D E C E S S O R
T C S U D O W N F A L L N P E
E A E M A H I H E D D T O P S
D R I U P E R A R B R R I O C
E T D L M A L P A O I A N N E
R N U T A D E P V I K B I E N
E E T U R M S E V N T B P N D
T M S O G A R N T S I L O T O
N H K U A S N E R N S E O S N
U S R S Y T H D R E I M V S G
O I A R L E W Q O M V O E L I
C N D O O R F I R S T R P A E
N A P P R E N T I C E E A P R
E B T I D E T A V I T P A C A
```

ETHAN FOX AND THE
SHADOW PRINCESS EXCERPT

. . . Hayley led him to the third level and stopped to whisper to her copycat that transformed into an ELMO device in Hayley's hands. She stared at the directions on the screen, and they guided her into a hallway . . .

"I overheard a conversation between Blair and Caden some time ago. They were talking about her father's trip to Hades and how if everything went as planned, the Trabblemores would be returning to power. They hate my family and are up to something, so I've been spying on them to find out what."

"I had a run-in with Blair and Caden last night," Ethan said. "Did you ever find out why they hate the Ravenwoods so much?"

"They hate us because my grandfather, Odin Ravenwood, exposed Gaylord Trabblemore for his crimes against humanity. He was our first headmaster, and his crimes disgraced his entire family."

MEET VANESSA RAVENWOOD

Vanessa Ravenwood still maintains her apartment in the Caretaker city of Zen; however, she had moved outside the realm of The Residence, into another realm, upstairs, on the thirteenth floor—her home looked more like a castle and it reminded Ethan of *Count Dracula's* house. Inside, her butler was Irvin McGillicutty's brother, Melvin McGillicutty.

While her husband, Odin Ravenwood was the Caretaker headmaster, Stravis came to Vanessa to ask her a favor—leaving Odin out of the loop. Since Odin was now the Caretaker headmaster, Stravis wanted him protected from any fallout if anyone exposed them. The Seers required certain skills only Caretakers possessed. Vanessa complied, and in return she was given second sight—she is an oracle; she can foretell the future.

ADARA

ANSWER

CASTLE

CITY OF ZEN

DISAPPEARED

FAMILY

FORETOLD

FUTURE

GOLDEN CREST

GRANDMOTHER

HUSH-HUSH

INTERPRETATION

JASON CROWLEY

JORDANNA

MELVIN

NECKLACE

ODIN

ORACLE

READ

SECOND SIGHT

SEERS

SHADOW PRINCESS

TEETERING

VISIONS

Vanessa Ravenwood

```
I S S E C N I R P W O D A H S
A N S W E R A E R B N I D O E
N O T F F A M I L Y I S A A C
N I S E O V E L G H V A R W O
A S E C R N I K N O L P A R N
D I R A E P O M I W E P O C D
R V C L T E R R R B M E N I S
O F N K O L S E E R S A E T I
J U E C L T J A T A A R L Y G
N T D E D S U D T A G E C O H
O U L N N A O W E I T D A F T
S R O C U C L K T N G I R Z T
A E G H U S H H U S H E O E Y
J G R A N D M O T H E R F N U
Y E L W O R C N O S A J A D B
```

ETHAN FOX AND THE
SHADOW PRINCESS EXCERPT

"The Headmistress suspected as much," Nicholas said.

"Not surprisin'," Dakota replied. "Ya may as well tell 'er, the arrival of that shadow spirit is a sign. Things've been set in motion, things Vanessa foretold long ago."

"Vanessa—are you talking about my grandmother?" Hayley asked; but they ignored her inquiry.

"If she knows more about the Grimleavers plans, she must tell the Headmistress immediately."

"If there's anything ta report, we'll be 'n touch," Dakota said.

"Why are you here anyway?" Nicholas asked.

"The boy wants ta visit his folks," Dakota replied and winked at Ethan. "Return to The Residence and tell Jordanna I'll guarantee their safety an escort them from here."

"Will do," Nicholas said. "Though, I'm not sure how comforting that news will be to her."

GREET BLAIR TRABBLEMORE

Blair Trabblemore, daughter to Roman and Silvia Trabblemore, granddaughter to Gaylord Trabblemore, was still the official mean girl. And rarely do you find her separated from her boyfriend, Caden Stanley and his brutehound Malik.

Her father was up to no good, and he had enlisted his daughter and her boyfriend to be part of his evil plan.

Blair has access to the Trabblemore chamber, which dawned on Ethan and Hayley that the Ravenwoods would also have a Ravenwood chamber. Blair also has a smart mouth; and Hayley had overheard her and Caden talking about her father's trip to Hades, and how if everything went as planned, the Trabblemores would be returning to power.

ARRIVES
CACOPHONY
CADEN
CHEERED
CORRUPT
ENCOUNTER
FATHER
HURRIED
INTENTIONS
MEMORIES
OVERJOYED
PLAN
PREDICTION
PROCEED
PROTECTION
RESCUE
RESIDENT BULLIES
ROMAN
RUN-INS
SHADOW
STAIRS
UNPLEASANT
WHEREABOUTS
WONDERING

Blair Trabblemore

```
M E M O R I E S T P U R R O C
F N O D E P N P R O C E E D A
A C E C S A O T D E R E E H C
T O F U I E R U E T E D E U O
H U N N D O C B S N I N U R P
E N O P E L V A S H T M R O H
R T I L N M G E D E E I E M O
E E T E T H K N R E V H O A N
S R C A B U H S I J N I N N Y
C I E S U R E N R R O P R N S
U F T A L R D A A I E Y O R H
E N O N L I D L N T A D E O A
U U R T I E C P N I S T N D D
R G P R E D I C T I O N S O O
G R U P S T U O B A E R E H W
```

ETHAN FOX AND THE
SHADOW PRINCESS EXCERPT

The thundering sound of a gong rang out over the arena, causing Ethan to flinch. Caden and Blair roared with laughter.

"Mutant boy is afraid of loud noises."

"He's probably afraid of his own shadow," Blair said as they continued to laugh.

"That's enough," Boris said from behind Blair and Caden. "Ethan Fox is my guest here – and you will treat him respectfully."

"We were leaving anyway," Blair said as she tugged at Caden's arm to lead him away.

"I said you will treat him with respect," Boris said louder. "Do you understand me?"

"Yes, sir," Caden and Blair said.

"Very well, return to your father. He is wondering as to your whereabouts."

The two troublemakers turned and hurried away . . .

GREET CADEN STANLEY

Caden Stanley, Blair Trabblemore's boyfriend, was all too happy to assist Blair's father, Roman Trabblemore with his dirty work. Eager to please Roman, Caden repeatedly asks Roman, "Is there any more we can do to help, sir?" "How else can we serve the cause."

Caden has put himself smack down in the middle of the Trabblemores evil plans. But it sounds like even the Trabblemores are working for someone else.

As the plot thickens, the dynamic duo are even so bold that they unwittingly brag to Ethan and Hayley, "We have a job to do. Daddy is expecting us." This slip of the tongue caused Ethan to watch where they were going. They were going towards a sign that read: Ceresian elderwood for sale. A clue has been given away; a clue in which Roman Trabblemore would not be pleased with.

AFRAID

ATTEMPTS

BEHIND

BLAIR

CAUSE

CLENCHED

CLUMSINESS

COWERED

DESK

FRAME

KICKED

LAUGHTER

MALIK

MATCH

MEASUREMENTS

MUTANT CHILD

READY

RECLINED

ROARED

SERVE

SMACKED BEHIND

STENCH

TROUBLEMAKERS

WAITING

Caden Stanley

H I R G N N O C O W E R E D M
C D M U T A N T C H I L D E E
N R T K F E D R O V I C T N A
E L N R S E S O A B R N P I S
T T A R K E S U L E E G D L U
S M A C K E D B E H I N D C R
E L I L O S E L E I U I S E E
R K E U H U H E L N O T A R M
E K S M O A C M F D W I B R E
T I M S Y C N A D N S A L O N
H L A I D O E K T I A W A A T
G A T N A C L E P P A D I R S
U M C E E F C R E F I R R E B
A I H S R E G S E R V E F D O
L R L S T P M E T T A L L A A

ETHAN FOX AND THE SHADOW PRINCESS EXCERPT

"Daddy will be along shortly," Blair said as she, Caden, and Malik entered. "I didn't speak with him last night due to all the interruptions. It's been good to have him back these last few weeks—he was away on business for so long."

"What does he want us to do now?" Caden said as he sat down, reclined, and kicked his feet onto the desk.

"I don't know, but it will surely be the end of you if he finds you sitting at his desk like that."

Caden quickly returned to his feet just as the door swung open again – and someone else entered the room. Ethan and Hayley peeked around the box and down the aisle as Blair approached the tall man with long black hair. He wore a half-black-half-red robe split diagonally lengthwise.

"Hello, Daddy," Blair said as she reached up to hug the man. "I'm so glad your back."

MEET ROMAN TRABBLEMORE

Roman Trabblemore and the Trabblemore family are from the elemental world of Hades. Sources tell us that he has been busy on the elemental worlds—Hades, Ceres, Atlantis, and Zephyr. He is also the source of who is rallying Headmistress Jordanna Ravenwood detractors to further undermine her authority within the Council – the Council of Elders – itself.

He has enlisted his daughter, Blair, and her boyfriend Caden to help with his devious plan.

Roman is arrogant that his plan will work. He even goes as far as to say, "And when it does, it will shock everyone at The Residence to their core."

BUSINESS

CORE

DEPLOYED

DIAGONALLY

EFFORT

EXPECTED

HADEAN TANZANITE

HADES

HALF-BLACK

HALF-RED

INTERRUPTIONS

LEGACY

LENGTHWISE

ORDERS

PLAN

POUCH

PROCURED

ROBE

ROMAN

SHOCK

SHORTLY

SILVIA

THE RESIDENCE

TRIP SUPPLIER

Roman Trabblemore

```
H E L P O U C H A D E S G D G
I F S I L V I A E D R R R I M
I F E S D I B D V E O L K A Q
N O C B H H E E A M E C M G R
T R N U P O A A A N O P T O E
E T E S L R R N G H Z W A N I
R K D I A V Q T S C D J I A L
R C I N N N H A L W E S D L P
U A S E H W R N R Y R R E L P
P L E S I E C Z O D U E Y Y U
T B R S T H G A B F C D O C S
I F E R O C E N E A O R L A P
O L H C I R C I E D R O P G I
N A T L U D E T C E P X E E R
S H H A L F R E D J T L D L T
```

ETHAN FOX AND THE SHADOW PRINCESS EXCERPT

A cacophony of corrupt laughter filled the room as Caden and Blair cheered her father's prediction. Caden made several more failed attempts to kiss up to him . . .

"Blair's father was there last night," Ethan said. "Boris left to speak with him about something."

"His name is Roman Trabblemore," Hayley said. "He blames the Ravenwoods for killing the Trabblemore legacy. But I wonder what Boris would need to discuss with him."

"Boris is a reporter," Ethan said. "Maybe he's working on a story."

"Maybe," Hayley replied. "It sounds like Roman is working for someone. He didn't name any names – but when Caden asked if he could serve the cause, a chill crept up my spine."

"Me too," Ethan said. "I'd bet anything it's Victor Qruefeldt."

REMEMBER GAYLORD TRABBLEMORE

Gaylord Trabblemore was the first headmaster of the Caretakers, from the elemental world of Hades. He lost his position, when he was charged and convicted of crimes against humanity. Odin Ravenwood was next chosen, as the second headmaster of the Caretakers. The Ravenwoods are from the elemental world of Zephyr.

After Odin was murdered, his son, Ryvias Ravenwood took over. After that, Ryvias was also murdered; and so, his wife, Jordanna Ravenwood continues the Ravenwood legacy as headmistress of the Caretakers. Who murdered Odin and Ryvias was covered in book #1, Ethan Fox and the Eyes of the Desert Sand. But the Trabblemores have been trying to undermine Ravenwood leaders ever since Gaylord's downfall.

ACTIVITY
BLASTED
COMBINATION
CRIMES
DISGRACED
EMBOSSED SYMBOL
EXPOSED
FAMILY
FEAR
FIRST HEADMASTER
GAYLORD
GRANDFATHER
GRINDLE
HADES
HUMANITY
IRON DOOR
JASON CROWLEY
ODIN RAVENWOOD
PLANNED
POWER
RED GLOW
RETURNING
SUSPICIOUS
ZAMALADOR

Gaylord Trabblemore

```
F L O B M Y S D E S S O B M E
I A I P L A N N E D A G E N Y
R J Z R B A R A E G R O W O D
S T A U O A S X D I P P I I O
T L M S E N P T N E G M S T O
H W A F O O D D E R T G E A W
E O L I S N L O A D R A A N N
A L A E H E C N O A E Y C I E
D G D I E R D R C R W L T B V
M D O N I F W E O A O O I M A
A E R M A A D J L W P R V O R
S R E T Y L I M A F L D I C N
T S H U M A N I T Y E E T F I
E E S U O I C I P S U S Y H D
R E T U R N I N G S E D A H O
```

ETHAN FOX AND THE
SHADOW PRINCESS EXCERPT

"We learned Stravis distrusted the other Creators, especially Zamalador. He insisted Gaylord Trabblemore was under Zamalador's thumb. So, he sought out a high-ranking Caretaker he could trust—one with an impeccable reputation and who shared his elemental origins." Said Vanessa.

"They had to be from Zephyr," Ethan said, "that's what led Stravis to you and Odin."

"Correct on both counts."

"What did he want from you and grandfather?"

"He told us of a powerful righteous presence he encountered in the desert."

"The Seers," Ethan said.

"Correct again. At first, he experienced visions of eyes peering at him from beneath the sand."

"I have the same visions," Ethan said.

"Not surprising. You are the Hybrid Child . . ."

MEET JASON CROWLEY

Jason Crowley was one of Gaylord Trabblemore's right hand men. When Ethan and Hayley go back in time, to the pyramids, they witness Jason Crowley holding a Heldrik Vonn Grim puzzle box—hundreds of years before Ethan was born. As they watched, they saw Jason Crowley bid the guards farewell, then one of guards left for their scheduled hourly rounds. Fast-forward to present time, Heldrik Vonn Grim has claimed the invention of the puzzle box.

The Residential Daily Star – The Residence's local newspaper – archives contain articles about Jason Crowley's dead body showing up on Hayley's grandparents' doorstep. The main article is titled: *Up and Coming Caretaker Couple Make a Grisly Discovery*. But other than that, the record is silent.

COCKAMAMIE

CORPSE

CRIMES

DOORSTEP

DRAINED

ELEMENTAL WORLDS

EXPOSING

FORTRESS

GAYLORD

GHASTLY

GUARDS

HEADLINES

HEADMASTER

HELDRIK VONN GRIM

JASON CROWLEY

LIFE'S ENERGY

NEWS

ODIN RAVENWOOD

ORDERS

PUZZLE BOX

PYRAMIDS

STORY

TRABBLEMORE

VISITED

Jason Crowley

```
M L L P T R A B B L E M O R E
I I D B U C D E T I S I V I L
R F I O D Z C O R P S E M J E
G E P D R N Z M O D N A F A M
N S E I A E P L R H M I O S E
N E T N I W R A E A D S R O N
O N S R N S U A K B D E T N T
V E R A E G D C S I O A R C A
K R O V D L O R M N H X E R L
I G O E I C E A I S N E S O W
R Y D N R D R C R I M E S W O
D N E W R Y D R O L Y A G L R
L S D O P L G N I S O P X E L
E S T O R Y I G H A S T L Y D
H E A D M A S T E R S I U Q S
```

ETHAN FOX AND THE SHADOW PRINCESS EXCERPT

"Did Odin tell you the man's name?" Ethan asked.

"Yes. I'll never forget the man's name—Jason Crowley."

"Why?" Hayley asked. "What makes that name so unforgettable?"

"Not so much his name," Vanessa said. "It's what happened after."

"What?" Ethan and Hayley asked.

"Somone left his corpse on our doorstep. The sight was ghastly, like all his life's energy was drained from his body."

Hayley gasped.

"It happened shortly after Odin visited the pyramids. We were living in an old-town villa at the time. The story made headline news—even on the elemental worlds."

"What happened after that?" Hayley asked.

"These events led to Odin uncovering Gaylord's . . ."

MEET HELDRIK VONN GRIM

Heldrik Vonn Grim was one of "the four cohorts." He, Drake Evans, Lindrew Scragmort, and Jason Crowley, were listed on a note found inside the Ravenwood headmasters's chamber desk drawer. In the note, Heldrik Vonn Grim was listed fourth, and under his name the word "apprentice" was circled.

Heldrik Vonn Grim had an apprentice, and his name is Dakota Drakelan. Dakota believed that he wasn't the monster everyone made him out to be. According to Dakota, he said, "Sure, he had 'is demons, but he was a decent man."

Someone commissioned him to build a puzzle box; but he could never figure out how to power it. Then one day, he received a strange letter—the problems were solved.

APPRENTICE

ARTICLE

BACKWARD IN TIME

BLACK BOX

BORIS

BUILD

COMMISSIONED

CHANCE

CREATED

DAKOTA

DANGEROUS

DECENT

GAYLORD

HELDRIK

LEAP-LETTER

POWER

PUZZLE BOX

SIGNATURE

SKEPTICAL

STRANGE

STUMPED

TELEGRAM

WEAPON

WORKED

Heldrik Vonn Grim

```
D L I U B C S X O B K C A L B
E E V V X O B E L Z Z U P A O
P N V A A M S E C N A H C P R
M D E R N M S T E T B K R P I
U I G T A I K L R G W S E R S
T R N I T S E R E A G E A E I
S E A C O S P R R Y P B T N G
U T R L K I T D D L O G E T N
O T T E A O I E U O W K D I A
R E S U D N C S O R E I A C T
E L R D T E A P W D R R N E U
G P O I N D L J U W Y D Z S R
N A M T O A I B R P T L R N E
A E N O P A E W O R K E D O I
D L T E L E G R A M Q H D M T
```

ETHAN FOX AND THE
SHADOW PRINCESS EXCERPT

"You were Heldrik Vonn Grim's apprentice."

"Not much of a secret, Boris Wentworth made sure of that."

"I'm not talking about the article. I'm talking about this." He waved the note they found in Odin's office at Dakota, who took it from his hand and studied it.

"Yeah, so?" Dakota said and handed the note back to Ethan. "Why do ya think he circled the word 'apprentice'? It's circled because Odin knew I served as Heldrik's apprentice. It's why he hired me. He was skeptical of me at first, but he was a fair man and decided ta give me a chance."

"Then why do you hate Boris so much because of the article?"

"Because 'es a scoundrel, and when that article came out, it caused Odin a lotta grief. Didn't hurt me none, but Odin was new ta being' headmaster and . . ."

GREET JASPER

Nearly a year had passed since Jasper lured Ethan and Hayley to The Residence and introduced them to the strange Caretaker world. Things had almost gotten back to normal since Ethan returned home – but that didn't stop him from thinking about his time with the Caretakers and all the friends he had made.

Jasper is a three foot tall blue bunny-like creature with yellow polka dots, who'd periodically come to Ethan.

Jasper is a taletaddler, Ethan Fox's imaginary friend. As a taletaddler, Jasper is not visible to anyone other than his chosen child; in this case, Ethan Fox, the Hybrid Child. In book #2, Ethan Fox and the Shadow Princess, Jasper returns to Ethan to give him back his poem book. In book #1, Ethan Fox and the Eyes of the Desert Sand, Ethan used the poem book to unlock the portals.

CARETAKER WORLD
CIRCLED
DESERT
FINISHED
FLIPPED
GIGGLES
GOLDEN WISPS
HYBRID CHILD
JOURNEY
LURED
MINI-JASPER
OPEN
PAGES
PASSAGE
POEM BOOK
READ
SEERS
STAIRCASE
STRAVIS' BUNKER
THE RESIDENCE
VISITOR
WAFTING
WAVING
WHIMSY

Jasper

C I R C L E D M E T R E S E D
A B R O T I S I V H P N E L Y
R L U R E D N N Y E O E L A E
E G E N B L A I E R E P G B R
T Y E N R U O J S E M O G G D
A E S A C R I A T S B E I O L
K U O D A E R S S I O G G L I
E G N I V A W P E D O A E D H
R H E H R V T E E E K S T E C
W A F T I N G R R N O S I N D
O W H I M S Y E S C S A N W I
R F P I P A G E S E G P G I R
L A E L R E D E P P I L F S B
D E H S I N I F N G I I I P Y
S T R A V I S B U N K E R S H

ETHAN FOX AND THE SHADOW PRINCESS EXCERPT

Ethan reached the top of the stairs and followed Jasper right past Azron, sitting in the sand. Azron's eye followed Ethan as he continued into the desert, but then he stood and followed quietly to ensure the Hybrid Child's safety.

Jasper continued into the desert for several hundred feet but then stopped and turned to face Ethan.

"They want you to have it back, Ethan Fox," Jasper said in a cartoonish voice. "The Hybrid Child's journey has only just begun."

Ethan was suddenly walking in the middle of a cold, fierce sandstorm. He squinted his eyes as he struggled to move forward but felt compelled to continue . . .

"Ethan Fox feel okay?" Azron asked.

"That sandstorm, you didn't experience it?"

"Azron, no see phantom storm."

"And Jasper? I suppose Jasper wasn't here either."

GREET ALBERT

Albert is the red pyrodevlin from Hades. Pyrodevlins are creatures that can transform into balls or ball up. Each, no more than two feet tall, have tiny slits for noses and yellow catlike eyes. Their small devilish horns are accented by rows of spikes that flow down the center of their backs to the end of their forked tails. They have long arms with folds of skin underneath that attach to their bodies like flying squirrels. The smooth skin on their bellies is surrounded by colorful gold speckled feathers that cover the rest of their bodies.

Hades is the red elemental world. The spheres on the checkerboard plane just outside of The Residence front room are portals to the elemental worlds of the Chrysalis. Atlantis, Ceres, Hades, and Zephyr—the Caretakers home worlds. In other words, the elemental worlds are a coalition of planets united under the Chyrsalis.

AGILE

AZRON

BALLS

BOOKS

DARTED

ENERGY LASSOS

FIERY

FLAMES SKYWARD

GAYLORD

HADES

HELLISH

MARBLES

MIDAIR

MISCHIEVOUS

NAIVE

PORTAL SPHERES

RED PLANET

SHOUTED

SNATCH

TRABBLEMORES

WORDLY PAGEMORE

WRANGLE

YIPPEE

ZAMALADOR

Albert

```
W R A N G L E N A S E D A H M
P O R T A L S P H E R E S D I
H H R L E D D E T U O H S C S
U H E D W O R D T T D G D M C
M C D L L A E L I G A N A I H
A T P R L Y L G A Y L O R D I
B A L L S I P Y I R A T T A E
S N A V A D S A C A M R E I V
E S N A I V E H G P A A D R O
L T E A N C I H T E Z V D E U
B R T T R A B B L E M O R E S
R A R E D N A X A Z R O N D L
A F L A M E S S K Y W A R D A
M A Y E F I E R Y I P P E E N
B N N E N E R G Y L A S S O S
```

ETHAN FOX AND THE SHADOW PRINCESS EXCERPT

Nicholas zipped open one side of his saddlebag.

"You can come out now," he said.

Three colored balls, one red, one green, and one blue, shot out and unraveled midair. The three mischievous pyrodevlins flew overhead and darted around the room, performing aerial stunts.

"Yippee," Albert shouted.

"Woohoo," Linus screamed.

"Yeehaw," Newton cheered.

"Behave yourselves," Jordanna said. "I've asked you here for an important mission."

RGB beelined for the Headmistress, landed by her side, and stood at attention. Tinx arrived shortly after and landed on Damien's shoulder. She had stayed inside to continue mapping out the interior while Jordanna gathered the others. The team gathered around the Headmistress as Nicholas and Azron . . .

GREET LINUS

Linus is the green pyrodevlin from Ceres. Pyrodevlins are creatures that can transform into balls or ball up. Each, no more than two feet tall, have tiny slits for noses and yellow catlike eyes. Their small devilish horns are accented by rows of spikes that flow down the center of their backs to the end of their forked tails. They have long arms with folds of skin underneath that attach to their bodies like flying squirrels. The smooth skin on their bellies is surrounded by colorful gold speckled feathers that cover the rest of their bodies.

Ceres is the green elemental world within the Chrysalis. The Chrysalis is the energy that surrounds the elemental worlds and shields them and any planet under the Caretakers protection. Earth is currently under such protection from The Destroyer—evil's ultimate.

AERIAL STUNTS

BEAST

BLOATING STONE

CERES

CERESIAN

DRIFTED

ELDERWOOD

ELEMENTAL WORLD

FIRELYTES

GRASSY MEADOW

GREEN PLANET

HOVERED

IRON SLAB

LUNGED

MINERALS

PORTAL PLANE

PYRODEVLINS

SCREAMED

SHOT OUT

SPACE

SWIFT

TRICK

VRAITOR

WOOHOO

Linus

```
F X H E L C E R E S I A N D A
L E B E W E F I R E L Y T E S
W S L E D R C E S O S E R R L
O N O E A E T L W A N I I E B
D I A S M S H L R A A T C V O
A L T W T E T E L L U P K O G
E V I I E E N P S O R S B H E
M E N F G I L T T Y P U A S L
Y D G T M A U O A A N O L D D
S O S L T N H T C L E O S E E
S R T R T S N E I C W H N G R
A Y O S L A R E N I M O O N W
R P N I L E V R A I T O R U O
G R E E N P L A N E T W I L O
V S C R E A M E D E T F I R D
```

ETHAN FOX AND THE SHADOW PRINCESS EXCERPT

"Tinx, tell Nicholas to unleash RGB."

Tinx darted off to relay the orders, and in no time, RGB were in the sky buzzing around the creature's head like flies. Azron and Nicholas dropped their ejectors and ran around to flank the beast. bright, colorful glows, one red, one green, and one blue, radiated from RGB's bodies as they circled the monster. Then, all at once, they stopped midair, hovered, and blasted the beast with their energy lassos. Albert's red lasso wrapped around the creature's neck. While Linus' green one wrapped around its left horn and Newton's blue one found the right horn.

The monster recoiled, but RGB were swift and agile in the air and quickly adjusted to counter its ever move. Right on time, Azron and Nicholas' energy coils wrapped several times around the monster's upper midsection. The five of them pulled and tugged while the rest . . .

GREET NEWTON

Newton is the blue pyrodevlin from Atlantis. Pyrodevlins are creatures that can transform into balls or ball up. Each, no more than two feet tall, have tiny slits for noses and yellow catlike eyes. Their small devilish horns are accented by rows of spikes that flow down the center of their backs to the end of their forked tails. They have long arms with folds of skin underneath that attach to their bodies like flying squirrels . . .

Atlantis is the blue elemental world. When The Designer finished his greatest design, he needed a world to house them. So, he called upon the Caretakers Council of Elders to select four Creators. Each elemental world chose one—Driveous, Vraitor, Zamalador, and Stravis. The emblem on their robes – the candelabrum – the red, green, blue, and yellow, all are representative of the four elemental worlds of the Chrysalis.

AQUATIC LIFE
ATLANTIAN WATER
ATLANTIS
BLASTED
BLUE WORLD
BRIANNA
BRIGHT
CATCH
CHECKERBOARD
CHEERED
CIRCLED
DRIVEOUS
ENVIRONMENT
GLASSY WATER
IGNITE
MIDAIR
MONSTER
PLANE
RADIATED
RECOILED
SWIMMING
TURQUOISE
UNRAVELED
YEEHAW

Newton

```
S B E N E S I O U Q R U T C R
R D R A O B R E K C E H C D S
E R R E C O I L E D N G L E R
T I A E H P U N R A V E L E D
A V D C E G D A E T I N G I L
W E I R E N E P N L R R P I R
N O A D R I L W I A O I L W O
A U T E E M C A R N N A A S W
I S E T D M R H E T M D N A E
T C D S S I I E W I E I E N U
N A C A K W C E O S N M A N L
A T G L A S S Y W A T E R A B
L C S B A M O N S T E R I I T
T H N E L N R O N T H G I R B
A Q U A T I C L I F E E G B F
```

ETHAN FOX AND THE SHADOW PRINCESS EXCERPT

Ethan quietly entered the study to investigate and immediately stopped in his tracks to witness the scene. The fact that RGB were up to no good did not surprise him. . . . This time, they were at the base of the bookshelf wall that ran the room's length. RGB were looking up at three books hovering over their heads. They were frantically lunging at the books, trying to snatch them from the air.

"I almost got mine," Albert shouted.

"No, you didn't," Linus rebutted.

"I'll catch mine first," Newton insisted.

RGB's antics reminded Ethan of old videos he'd seen of *The Three Stooges*. He stood quietly as one book floated down teasingly close to Albert's head while the other two rose higher. Linus and Newton turned their attention towards Albert as he lurched up at the book above his head. But the object of Albert's desires . . .

REMEMBER KEPLER

Kepler is the yellow pyrodevlin from Zephyr. Pyrodevlins are creatures that can transform into balls or ball up. Each, no more than two feet tall, have tiny slits for noses and yellow catlike eyes. Their small devilish horns are accented by rows of spikes that flow down the center of their backs to the end of their forked tails. They have long arms with folds of skin underneath that attach to their bodies like flying squirrels. The smooth skin on their bellies is surrounded by . . .

Zephyr is the yellow elemental world. Sadly, Kepler from Zephyr was abducted by the Grimleavers and has not been heard from since.

The portals are created as a side effect when the Caretakers pull a finished planet into the Chrysalis – they serve to transport the Caretakers to and from the elemental worlds.

BEACH

BUNKER

CREATORS

DESERT STORM

DUST GOLIATH

GOLDEN SAND

HATCH

KAAFOO

KEPLER

JASPER

JOURNALS

MISSING

NOMAD

PANDORA'S BOX

PHANTOM

RAVENWOODS

SAND SLUG

SEERS

STRAVIS

TIMESTAMPS

WRITINGS

YELLOW PLANET

ZEPHYR

ZEPHYRIAN

Kepler

```
D U S T G O L I A T H N O C R
E P G J I M K A A F O O D E A
S H A O U R E G R E K N U B V
E A S N N P P P W T N D E E
R N T N D Q L K R I E G N A N
T T R U I O E W M O N N A C W
S O A S T R R E Y S A I S H O
T M V D E I S A L G L S N A O
O R I P T T N A S R P S E T D
R F S I A R N D Z B W I D C S
M A N M Y R A R I P O M L H E
J G P H U M O S D N L X O A E
S S P O O S A N D S L U G T R
L E J N E S R O T A E R C N S
Z Z E P H Y R I A N Y E Y L W
```

ETHAN FOX AND THE
EYES OF THE DESERT SAND EXCERPT

"Pyrodevlins," Hayley said.

"Indeed," Daavic said. "Those little troublemakers are pyrodevlins. Albert, Linus, and Newton referred to collectively as RGB for obvious reasons, and because they normally find mischief together. There was a fourth that kept them in line, but Kepler's gone missing."

"Daavic, you will take care of RGB. Keep them balled up until you need them. Unleash them on Nicholas' command. Gruggins, you'll ride along with Hayley. Azron, protect our guests and make sure they return unharmed."

"Mrs. Jordanna?" Linus asked.

"Yes, Linus."

"Do we have to stay balled up? We need to keep our eyes out for Kepler."

"Very well – but remain balled up until you . . .

GREET IRVIN MCGILLICUTTY

Irvin McGillicutty is the butler of The Residence – but his duties don't end there. He is also the chef, tailor, handyman, and assistant to the Caretaker headmistress. Irvin is a mimic, a species with limited shape-shifting abilities that he uses to maximum effect. His appearance reminded Ethan of a living department store dummy wearing a black pinstriped tuxedo with a red rose corsage.

Since Ethan's last visit, Irvin has become quite the student of human behavior. He monitors their television channels and follows the news, TV shows, reality shows, and cartoons. But his favorites are what he calls "the mini shows" played during the breaks. And he remembers most of them. He is also thinking of producing his own version of the Real Housewives at The Residence—The Real Caretakers of Zen City.

ANCHORMAN
ASSISTANT
BUTLER
CAFETERIA
CHEER
CHEF
COMMERCIALS
DINING HALL
FLOBBYKNOCKER
HANDYMAN
HUMAN BEHAVIOR
HYDRO-GENERATOR
ILLUSTRATE
IMPRESSIONS
MERCHANT
MIMIC
PINSTRIPED
ROSE CORSAGE
SHNICKYROONERS
SMILE
STUDENT
TAILOR
TELEVISION
TUXEDO

Irvin McGillicutty

```
H U M A N B E H A V I O R U R
Y L E N O I S I V E L E T S E
D L R C E F S T A I L O R I K
R L C H E E R O M N E E M L C
O A H O I H H I A G N P A L O
G H A R S C M M A O R I S U N
E G N M T I Y S O E R N S S K
N N T A C D R R S E E S I T Y
E I R N N O Y S T O L T S R B
R N O A C K I E D E T R T A B
A I H E C O F E L M U I A T O
T D S I N A X I A L B P N E L
O O N S C U M N G H T E T H F
R H U B T S S O S T U D E N T
S L A I C R E M M O C U C O S
```

ETHAN FOX AND THE SHADOW PRINCESS EXCERPT

"Shnickyrooners and things like that," Ethan said as his light beetle merged with Irvin's, and they came face to face.

"Ethan Fox, Irvin is happy to talk to his bestie on such a lovely day"

"Nice to see you too, Irvin. You're in great spirits today."

"Oh yes, Irvin is going to view some of his favorite new shows on TV. The Real Housewives always make Irvin laugh. Would Ethan Fox like to join Irvin this evening?"

"I'm sorry, Irvin, I've got plans. I'm going to the Drone Wars with Boris Wentworth tonight."

"Bahhh, Drone Wars are a kiddie show compared to the Housewives. Irvin is thinking of producing his own version here at The Residence—The Real Caretakers of Zen City."

MEET MELVIN MCGILLICUTTY

Melvin McGillicutty is Irvin McGillicutty's brother. He works for Vanessa Ravenwood outside of The Residence's realm and The Hall of Doorways. Vanessa lives in another Caretaker realm, upstairs, on the thirteenth floor in what looks like a castle. Like, Irvin, Melvin is also the butler of Vanessa's home.

And so, it is not surprising that Ethan thinks Melvin is Irvin during their first encounter. In fact, Melvin dresses in the same uniform that Irvin does—a pinstriped tuxedo with a red rose corsage pinned to his lapel. And Melvin, too, looks like a department store dummy that had come to life.

ARRIVAL
AWAITING
BEELINED
BROTHER
BUTLER
CONFUSED
EXPECTING
FIREPLACE
FOYER
GOOFBALL
GREETINGS
IRVIN
JOURNEY
LAPEL
MADAM
MELVIN
MIMIC
MONOTONE
NODDED
RAVENWOOD
SITTING ROOM
STAIRCASE
VANESSA
VOICE

Melvin McGillicutty

```
G  S  B  L  S  R  O  T  B  R  O  T  H  E  R
R  D  U  E  E  C  I  O  V  A  N  E  S  S  A
F  O  T  P  D  B  N  I  V  L  E  M  H  M  V
F  Z  L  A  M  L  L  A  B  F  O  O  G  A  E
B  E  E  L  I  N  E  D  O  O  F  N  U  D  N
A  S  R  B  M  F  R  Y  R  A  I  O  R  A  W
W  A  B  U  I  Y  E  G  O  T  R  T  A  M  O
A  C  W  H  C  R  N  R  C  F  E  O  R  L  O
I  R  R  J  M  I  F  E  O  N  P  N  R  Y  D
T  I  A  D  T  S  P  E  N  C  L  E  I  E  E
I  A  P  T  R  X  M  T  F  H  A  T  V  N  T
N  T  I  R  E  O  M  I  U  E  C  C  A  R  S
G  S  E  I  F  A  B  N  S  C  E  A  L  U  N
A  E  I  R  V  I  N  G  E  P  E  D  F  O  O
N  O  D  D  E  D  W  S  D  A  C  E  D  J  M
```

ETHAN FOX AND THE SHADOW PRINCESS EXCERPT

"I think we've found *Count Dracula's* house," Ethan said.

They made their way over the stone steps leading to an enormous front door. Damien raised his fist to knock, but the door slowly creaked open. Light from inside showered through the door as a tall white-faced . . .

"Irvin, what are you doing here?" Ethan asked.

"Irvin—" the butler said in a flat, monotone voice. "You must have me confused with my goofball of a brother. My name is Melvin McGillicutty, and the madam is awaiting your arrival."

"Thank you, Melvin," Damien said. "She is expecting us?"

"Yes, they are waiting in the sitting room," Melvin said, "right this way."

"I know the way," Damien said as he entered and beelined past Melvin.

GREET GRUGGINS MCGHEE

Gruggins McGhee is the grumpling of the house at The Residence. In book #1, Ethan Fox and the Eyes of the Desert Sand, he lived in a little green box, which when tapped three times, the lid opened. However, in book #1, his green box was found smashed and the thought was that Gruggins was kidnapped—but really, he went willingly. Thus, in book #2, Ethan Fox and the Shadow Princess, Gruggins has a new box—a tiny brown box that still sits on the table near the study door.

In the first chapter in book #2, Gruggins appears to Ethan on a restroom mirror as a small green blob. Like a wad of gum, he pops off and lands on the sink in front of Ethan. Gruggins' fuzzy green face looks like a grumpy old man with tall blue Tweety Bird eyes. He has come to escort Ethan back to The Residence.

ADMIRATION

CARAVANS

CHANT

CLOAKED

CRYSTAL BALL

DRONING

ENCHANTMENT

ESCORT

FIST

GOODWILL

GRAVEL EATERS

GREEN BLOB

GRUMPLING

GURGLING

MUFFLED

NAPPING

NIBBLEWARTS

NOISES

PARAMOUNT

PORTAL BEACON

PROPHECIES

ROACHES

ROCK-EATING

WISHING WELL

Gruggins McGhee

```
P C W S R E T A E L E V A R G
R A D T N A P P I N G E O R R
O R R R D E K A O L C A U S E
P A O A R I X K T H C M H S E
H V N W M C L N M H P U R L N
E A I E A O A T E L T F O L B
C N N L I H U S I K S F C A L
I S G B C A S N N C I L K B O
E Y G B I M G A T I F E E L B
S N O I T A R I M D A D A A T
E U E N C H A N T M E N T T R
S Y O Z G N I L G R U G I S O
I H O G O O D W I L L Q N Y C
O W I S H I N G W E L L G R S
N N O C A E B L A T R O P C E
```

ETHAN FOX AND THE SHADOW PRINCESS EXCERPT

. . . They entered the front room of The Residence, and the sound of Gruggins' angry voice greeted them.

"Come back here, you rock-eating roaches," Gruggins shouted as he shook his fist in the air. He was standing at the edge of his table, looking at the ground, but nothing was there.

"What's wrong, Gruggins?" Hayley asked and ran to his side.

Gruggins gazed up at Hayley and the grumpy scowl on his face melted into a smile.

"Those dastardly Nibblewarts are interrupting my nap for the millionth time. They've been on the move lately, coming through in caravans, and they always stop to chant below my table."

"Nibblewarts believe grumplings symbolize good luck," Tinx said from her perch on Damien's shoulder. "Their chanting is a gesture of admiration and goodwill."

MEET WORDLY PAGEMORE

Wordly Pagemore is a bookworm who manages the Caretaker Arts & Literature archive at The Residence. He is brilliant and loves to read so much that he has read every book in the archive over 100 times. His knowledge of the Caretaker universe makes him a valuable source of information. He is also often consulted by Headmistress Jordanna Ravenwood and called upon to join CAGE meetings as a resource. He also has a vast knowledge of the Caretaker art archive, where non-significant pieces are stored away after being rejected by the Fates.

Appearance-wise, he is a four inch bookworm with round nerdy glasses over his baby blue eyes. He is bluish on top, fading to green in the middle, and yellow at the bottom. Oval red rings with yellow centers line his sides.

ARCHIVE

ARTS

BOOK TAXIED

BOOKSHELF

BOOKWORM

CATERPILLAR

CREATURE

DAILY DUTIES

DRAWN

EAVESDROPPING

EXPERTISE

FLOATING

HOVERING

LITERATURE

NERDY GLASSES

PAINTED

PRIVILEGE

PUPPETEER

READING LAMP

SIGNIFICANT

STUDY

TRICK

WORM-CLIENT

WRITTEN

Wordly Pagemore

A R T S W O R M C L I E N T P

E E L I C A T E R P I L L A R

R A I G N S G A E G H M N R I

D D T N W E D V A N O R T D V

L I E I A T D E T I V O R A I

D N R F R S E S U T E W I I L

E G A I D T T D R A R K C L E

I L T C D U N R E O I O K Y G

X A U A N D I O A L N O P D E

A M R N G Y A P U F G B P U V

T P E T P U P P E T E E R T I

K E X P E R T I S E A E L I H

O W R I T T E N U B E S O E C

O P N E R D Y G L A S S E S R

B O O K S H E L F T T I L P A

ETHAN FOX AND THE SHADOW PRINCESS EXCERPT

Ethan witnessed the process cycle several times, and RGB fell for the same trick every time. Then something caught his eye. A small green caterpillar stood atop the bookshelves directly above RGB. Its tiny arms moved like a puppeteer's controlling the books. Ethan smiled as the little creature waved his arms gracefully like a maestro conducting a symphony. He laughed and caught the creature's attention.

The books hovering over the pyrodevlins slowly drifted lower and changed shape as they fell. Then, all at once, RGB lunged up and grabbed their prizes. . . .

"Wordly Pagemore, at your service, Master Ethan," he said and extended one of his many tiny arms.

"You know my name," Ethan said as he shook his puny hand.

"Everyone at The Residence has heard of Ethan Fox. I was away on business during your last visit."

GREET DORKIN DRUMBLES

Dorkin Drumbles is the curator of the Gallery of Memories. The Gallery is a magical room where paintings paint themselves onto a vast canvas wall. Finished works are cut away from the self-healing wall and brought in front of three hags—the Fates. The Fates determine if a piece is of significance to the Caretakers in their battle to save humanity from the Grimleavers.

Most of the gallery workers are forest elves, uniquely adapted for hanging in trees. "Help out we do," Dorkin had a quirky voice that reminded Ethan of Yoda. "Monitor the artwork, collect and mount for display, a crucial task it is." As the elves cut finished pieces from the walls and collect them, the cutaway canvas magically grows back like a healing wound.

ALCOVE OF ENIGMA
ARRIVAL
CANVAS
DEN
DETERMINED
EASLES
ENORMOUS
FATES
GALLERY
GLASSES
HAPPY
INEQUITY
OPINION
PAINTINGS
REPRESENT
REQUESTS
ROOM
ROWS
SCURRIED
SHEETS
SIGNIFICANT
VIEWING HALL
VISITORS
WONDERFUL

Dorkin Drumbles

```
A  R  R  I  V  A  L  E  T  E  A  S  L  E  S
N  L  E  E  I  G  A  Y  P  P  A  H  S  F  I
I  W  C  P  Q  R  Y  O  R  T  D  B  S  O  G
T  O  V  O  R  U  O  T  R  E  B  L  A  R  N
E  N  I  H  V  E  E  W  I  N  L  A  V  E  I
D  D  S  D  I  E  S  S  U  F  L  N  V  F
E  E  I  E  E  N  O  E  T  L  Q  N  A  S  I
N  R  T  I  W  O  S  F  N  S  A  E  C  G  C
I  F  O  R  I  R  E  A  E  T  S  M  N  N  A
M  U  R  R  N  M  T  R  S  N  D  E  N  I  N
R  L  S  U  G  O  A  U  A  Y  I  L  Y  T  T
E  O  N  C  H  U  F  M  O  O  R  G  D  N  T
T  N  B  S  A  S  H  E  E  T  S  H  M  I  R
E  S  E  G  L  A  S  S  E  S  W  Z  C  A  O
D  S  X  P  L  M  B  L  N  O  I  N  I  P  O
```

ETHAN FOX AND THE
SHADOW PRINCESS EXCERPT

"Wonderful day it is," Dorkin said in his usual Yoda'ish tone. "Happy, Dorkin is, to help Miss Hayley and Ethan Fox. Now how can Dorkin help?"

"We would like you take us to the Alcove of Enigma," Hayley said.

Dorkin's head jumped back, and his glasses slid down his long, sloped nose.

"Is something wrong?" Ethan asked.

"Wrong, oh no, nothing is wrong. It's just, Dorkin does not get many requests for that."

They followed Dorkin as he walked towards the far side of the room, to the corner opposite the viewing hall. At first, they were walking straight at a blank wall, but when they got close enough, the outline of a door appeared against the white canvas.

"The Alcove of Enigma is in there," Dorkin said.

"Aren't you going to show us in?" Ethan asked.

GREET TINX

Tinx is a winged pixie-dragon about four inches tall and six inches long. Her lizard-like skin is peach colored with white swirls. On missions, she darts around like a playful hummingbird searching for nectar.

Tinx moonlights at the Deadwood Saloon. After her shifts, she enjoys sipping from a tiny mug of dragon's breath. As she watches the thick fog waft from her mug, a glowing purple liquid bubbles beneath the layer of fog; she says it gives her clarity.

But most recently, she has become a CAGE member. CAGE is short for Caretaker Anti-Grimleaver Enforcement. A special group of Caretakers focused on fighting against Victor Qruefeldt and his army of evil Grimleavers.

ETHAN FOX BOOKS

ASSIGNMENT
BOOK-TRAVELED
BREAKFAST
BROWN BOOK
BUBBLE SOLUTION
CAGE
CREST
DARTS
DEADWOOD SALOON
DEVOLVED
DISCIPLINE
DRAGON'S BREATH
EMBLEM
ESCORT
FIELDWORK
GLASS PILLARS NYM
HARNESS
INDISCRETION
PIXIE-DEVILS
SEARCHED
SHOULDER
SUGAR-PICKLE SODA
TOW
UNDERBELLY

Tinx

```
D R A G O N S B R E A T H S S
E B E L S H O U L D E R P W U
A R G A S E M B L E M S R I G
D E A S U Z N B O D H T K D A
W A C S U W O L P E A R O E R
O T D P N K I E I H R A O L P
O S I I D R T S X C N D B E I
D A S L E O E O I R E E N V C
S F C L R W R L E A S V W A K
A K I A B D C U D E S L O R L
L A P R E L S T E S C O R T E
O E L S L E I I V S R V B K S
O R I N L I D O I T E E T O O
N B N Y Y F N N L O S D O O D
T N E M N G I S S A T U W B A
```

ETHAN FOX AND THE
SHADOW PRINCESS EXCERPT

Ethan scanned the room and saw nothing, but then a tiny, winged dragon fluttered down from atop the bookshelf above their heads. She carried a brown book in her claws and set it down gently on the reading table at the other end of the room.

"Planning a trip, are we?" she asked.

"Tinx, what are you doing here?" Hayley asked.

"Rebelling against an over-protective Headmistress," said Tinx. "Does that ring a bell?" . . .

"I remember you," Ethan said. "From the Deadwood Saloon, you served us sugar-pickle soda."

"Likewise," Tinx said as she smiled and bowed to Ethan.

"I don't understand," Hayley said. "You're a CAGE member now. Why would you rebel?" . . .

"Yeah, the newest CAGE member due to the atrocities committed against my family. But . . .

MEET PIXIE-DEVILS

Although "pixie-devil" may very well be a misnomer. They look more like real dragons at the size of them. Black and blue in color, pixie-devils, when attacking, blast yellow energy beam bursts from their mouths. More often than not, pixie-devils are grouped as a small battalion, whenever on assignment. In fact, when Ethan first encountered the pixie-devils, it was the Shadow Princess that saved him from them.

Pixie-devils work for Norell, and Norell works for Victor Qruefeldt. And pixie-devils are Victor's latest victims, who were devolved from Tinx's relatives. Also see Victor and Norell's character word search puzzles.

ATTACKING

BATTALION

BEAST

BLACK DRAGONS

BLASTS

BLUE SWIRLS

CHIEF

CREEPING

ENCOUNTERED

ENERGY BEAMS

FIREWORKS

GLEAMING

MOUTH

PIXIE-DEVILS

PROWLING

PYRAMIDS

SHIELD

SHOOT

SPEARS

STABBED

STEALTHILY

STONE

VICIOUS

WRATH

Pixie-devils

```
B P Y L I H H T L A E T S E C
A L T P S D G N I M A E L G N
T R A H Y E E L B T J B I V G
T O A C E R D B T T L L V I I
A L O M K L A A B U E A E C S
L M S H E D C M E A P S D I M
I I P I S K R S I P T T E O A
O R H T I S W A R D E S I U E
N S O N A I R O G R S B X S B
F N G L R L W E E O O E I P Y
E M T L D L D T R U N A P E G
I O S F I R E W O R K S E A R
H U A N A T O W W R A T H R E
C T G N I P E E R C E N D S N
T H N A D E R E T N U O C N E
```

ETHAN FOX AND THE
SHADOW PRINCESS EXCERPT

Her mouth moved like she was trying to speak to Ethan, but he did not understand the unusual sounds she made.

"I'm sorry, I don't understand what you are trying to say."

She raised her arm and pointed up at the wall behind him. He turned to look at what she pointed to and jumped back at the sight. A horde of small dragon-like creatures clung to the wall glaring at Ethan with piercing green eyes. Swarms of them swooped down from the darkness and hovered in front of the others. They were pitch black like the woman but had blue swirl patterns covering their bodies. Ethan backed away as the tiny dragons slowly advanced toward him. Then, all at once, the creatures stopped moving and opened their mouths. The dim yellow glow inside slowly grew brighter and brighter.

GREET AZRON

Azron is a one-eyed giant that stands at least twelve feet tall, a member of the soleyed dwarf-giant species. However, size can have its fall backs.

After being attacked by the desert harpies and their exploding shards of glassy sand into his arms and neck, sadly his fingers were much too big to pick out all the glass from his body; he was in agony, groaning "Arrrrrr." Without hesitation, Tinx came to his rescue, "Stop your whining," she said as she flew over and gently landed on his shoulder. "Your giant sausage fingers aren't going to help."

Azron grew up on Hades and is well adapted for traversing the desert. He calls himself "hell-walker," as he thumps his chest. He says the desert is cold like ice compared to the red planet Hades.

He is also a member of CAGE.

BUNKER DOOR
BURIED
COLD
DESERT HARPIES
DWARF-GIANT
EJECTOR
GLASSY SAND
GROANED
HADES
HANDLE
HEAVY IRON HATCH
HOT
HULK-LEAPED
HYDROSPHERE
ROBBERS
SADDLEBAG
SAND CREATURES
SHELTER
SLEDGEHAMMERS
SWATTED
VANISHING DUNE
VERANDA
WATER CANNON
WRANGLE

Azron

E N U D G N I H S I N A V H E
R G L A S S Y S A N D E E D J
W S A D D L E B A G R A E S E
E A V B U R I E D A V S R D C
R G T G N I H E N Y E E O T T
E S R E D E T D I R M S O N O
H H O O R T A R T M E R D A R
P E J B A C O H A L F E R I S
S L S W M N A H G S L B E G E
O T S A H R E N U D D B K F D
R E Q A P G A D N L V O N R A
D R T I D R H A O O T R U A H
Y C E E W W H C L E N R B W O
H S L O H U L K L E A P E D T
T S A N D C R E A T U R E S H

ETHAN FOX AND THE
SHADOW PRINCESS EXCERPT

Damien made sure Ethan and Hayley were adequately seated before seating himself. The sand slug jolted into motion and sailed along the surface of the sand like a jet boat. Tinx darted around like a playful hummingbird searching for nectar. Azron stood in place to let the rest of the party get a head start.

"What's he doing?" Ethan asked, staring back at Azron as he disappeared into the distance.

"He'll be along shotly," Damien said with a grin.

Azron squatted down and launched skyward like the Hulk. He flew several hundred feet into the sky before falling and landing gently back on the desert surface. Azron continued Hulk-vaulting his way across the desert landscape and caught up with them quickly.

"Look," Hayley said and pointed up at the horizon to an enormous dune.

"What is that?"

GREET NICHOLAS KNIGHT

Nicholas Knight is from the vampril species. He is the last vampril to remain with the Caretakers after the others fled. (See book #1, Ethan Fox and the Eyes of the Desert Sand for the story.)

He is a muscular man with a tanned golden complexion. He wears a long white robe with gold trim on the shoulders and collar. He sports expansive angelic wings on full display, protruding from under his white robe.

Nicholas is a member of CAGE. His wife, Nicole was abducted by the Grimleavers and thought to be dead— book #1, Ethan Fox and the Eyes of the Dsert Sand. In book #2, Ethan Fox and the Shadow Princess, we learn that Victor Qruefeldt had devolved her into Earth's first vampire; and she is now a member of the Grimleavers.

ANGELIC WINGS
ANNOYANCES
CANINES
CHATTER
CREATURES
DISTRACT
DISTURBANCE
FLAPPED
GLOBE
GRAVITY SHOES
GRIMLEAVERS
LASSOED
NICOLE
NORELL
OTHERWORLDLY
REPORTS
SAND-PEEPERS
SCHOLARS
SHED
SOARED
SWOOPED
VAMPIRES
VAMPRIL
ZOMBIES

Nicholas Knight

```
S E R I P M A V A M P R I L J
S E O H S Y T I V A R G N A J
U F F T C C A N I N E S I S D
O H L C H E A I L G G O C S S
S D A A A E N S A N S A O O S
E I P R T D R S I C O R L E R
C S P T T N Z W H S T E E D E
N T E S E R C O O E H D E R P
A U D I R I L O M R E E S S E
Y R A D L A L P E B L C D T E
O B R E R M T E R B I D I R P
N A G S H T M D D S O E Y O D
N N O R E L L U T I O L S P N
A C R E A T U R E S P L G E A
T E E R G R I M L E A V E R S
```

ETHAN FOX AND THE
SHADOW PRINCESS EXCERPT

Loud screeching sounds flooded down from above. Ethan and Hayley followed Nicholas' gaze up the sides of the surrounding buildings. Dozens of black figures clung to the brick walls and were inching their way down while others swooped in from both ends of the alley. Two groups of vampires landed in the alleyway, blocking them from both sides. Nicholas started towards the group nearest them but stopped cold when he got close enough to recognize their faces.

"Nicole—but you're—dead," Nicholas said. "I was told he killed you to create—them."

"I no longer answer to that name," said Norell. "And as you can see, I'm not dead—I merely serve a different master, one with a higher purpose."

"But there may be something we can do, Nicole. Please, come back to us. We will figure this out together at The Residence."

MEET NORELL

Norell was Nicole Knight, Nicholas Knight's wife before being abducted by Victor Qruefeldt. As Nicole, she was a vampril like her husband. Vamprils are not vampires, but a blood sucker just the same. Vampril canines peek out as they smile. They are for piercing the fruit of a blood turnip. After Nicole's abduction by the Grimleavers, Victor devolved her into Earth's first vampire. As Norell, her loyalty is to Victor.

Norell can often be heard proclaiming her allegiance to Victor, "All hail the Grimlord." She has a small army of vampires that await her orders—orders from Victor; and her vampires repeat after her, "All hail the Grimlord."

She has massive batwings growing from beneath the back of her robe. This is in stark contrast from Nicholas' white angelic wings. When taking to the sky, she lets out an unforgettable ear-piercing screech.

BATWINGS

BLACK ROBE

BOWED

CARGO

CLUB

COMPANIONS

CONTAINERS

GRIMLEAVERS

GRIMLORD

HAIL

NICHOLAS

NICOLE

OGRES

ORDERS

PUMMELED

PYRAMIDS

RETREATING

STICK BEACONS

TELEPORT

TROLLS

VAMPIRE

VICTOR

WHIPPED

WOMAN

Norell

```
C P C B A T W I N G S A R T E
O W H D R E T R E A T I N G O
M H G E N I L S N A I D H R R
P I R W R H N B O O C E I I D
A P I O G H I P D E K L A M E
N P M B L A C K R O B E W L R
I E L A K I O P E R E M C O S
O D E P W L L W I N A M L R D
N Q A P O O E N I W C U E D I
S S V A M O N S T E O P R C M
L C E S A L O H C I N E I L A
L A R E N I F I F Q S I P U R
O R S R E N I A T N O C M B Y
R G D G T E L E P O R T A A P
T O N O E L C R O T C I V D E
```

ETHAN FOX AND THE SHADOW PRINCESS EXCERPT

"Go, Norell, take our new children and join the others," the dark figure said in a low gnarled tone.

"Will you be joining in on the fun?"

"I wouldn't dream of missing out," the master said. "But our party is not yet complete. I have a graveyard or two to visit before the festivities begin. Join the others and await my arrival."

Norell edged forward as massive batwings grew from beneath the back of her robe. The newborn gargoyle jumped from the side of the building and joined the others behind Norell. She stretched her wings out, and the small battalion of gargoyles did the same.

"All hail the Grimlord," she said and then ran to the edge of the building and jumped off, followed by her gargoyle companions.

MEET ALEXANDER STURGIS

Alexander Sturgis, though a bit older, Alexander looks human. He is tall, dark, and handsome. His dark brown hair and eyes perfectly accent his tan complexion. He wears the same style white and black robe as Damien and Jordanna. He is a man of confidence.

He is a member of CAGE. In book #1, Ethan Fox and the Eyes of the Desert Sand, Alexander was away on a secret mission. In book #2, Ethan Fox and the Shadow Princess, he is once again unavailable.

He was married to a human woman, Tiffany Sturgis. They had just had a male child together when the infant was abducted. Later, her despair drove her mad; Alexander took her away to some place that only he knows where.

Alexander is Ethan's birth father.

ALEXANDER
ALIVE
ATTENTION
BEYOND REPROACH
BIRTH FATHER
COURSE OF ACTION
DAKOTA
DEBRIEFING
ETHAN
MATTER
MISSION
OLD COOT
PRECISELY
PROPHECIES
PROTECTED
REIGN
RESPONSIBILITY
SECRET
SOMEPLACE SAFE
STRATEGIES
TIFFANY
VISITS
VOUCHED
WILDCARD

Alexander Sturgis

```
N C X Y L E S I C E R P Y N A
E B I R T H F A T H E R G O T
F D E T C E T O R P I O V I T
A E T Y N N L P B T L P J T E
S B H N O D G P O D A H R C N
E R A A I N T I C I T E E A T
C I N F S O D O E H O C D F I
A E A F S N O R E R K I N O O
L F L I I T S R E E A E A E N
P I I T M T S H E P D S X S G
E N V F I U Z E S T R E E R R
M G E S E C R E T H T O L U A
O E I D R A C D L I W A A O H
S V O U C H E D H C U O M C C
R E S P O N S I B I L I T Y H
```

ETHAN FOX AND THE SHADOW PRINCESS EXCERPT

"What happened after that?" Ethan asked.

"We sent in a team. Alexander Sturgis cleaned up the mess and ensured no humans would discover it again."

"Alexander Sturgis—" Ethan repeated the name of his birth father.

"Yes," Jordanna said. "Your mother was present as well. Alexander took Tiffany on that mission, and you were born."

Ethan's face felt flush, and he grew antsy. He had tried to avoid thinking about it for George and Betsy's sake. But the mere mention of his birth parents caused a flood of emotions to rush through his mind.

"They might have missed something," Ethan said. "We should go to the bunker and have a look."

"Alexander is the best we have," Jordanna said. "He missed nothing."

MEET TIFFANY STURGIS

Tiffany Sturgis is the wife of Alexander Sturgis. Tiffany and Alexander are Ethan's birth parents. George and Betsy Fox are Ethan's adoptive parents.

Tiffany was a human woman. Her and Alexander had just had a male child together when the infant was abducted. Many years later she went mad in her despair; so with the help of Dakota Drakelan, Alexander had taken her to a safe place.

At The Residence, in book #1, Ethan Fox and the Eyes of the Desert Sand, there is a portrait of Tiffany in the front room. The portrait depicts an angelic woman hovering midair in a frosty ice wonderland; she wore a flowing white gown bathed in crystals.

AGED
ANGELIC WOMAN
BAD SHAPE
BATHED
BEAUTIFUL
BIRTH MOTHER
CATATONIC STATE
CRYSTALS
DISAPPEARED
DROVE
EPISODES
FRONT ROOM
FROSTY ICE
HOVERING
MIND
MOVE
PAINTING
PORTRAIT
SEERS
THE RESIDENCE
VISIONS OF EVIL
WHITE GOWN
WONDERLAND
WORRIES

Tiffany Sturgis

```
V V D M O O R T N O R F D R N
T B I R T H M O T H E R C C E
T E S S D E H T A B G G A R T
T A A E I H S R B N F T E Y N
H U P I O O J U I R A P O E A
E T P R D N N T O T I D S P M
R I E R E E N S O S N R G A O
E F A O G I T N O A T N D H W
S U R W A Y I D L F I M N S C
I L E P I C E R G R E O I D I
D S D C S S E E E I N V M A L
E U E T N D E V O R D E I B E
N R A E N P O R T R A I T L G
C T F O R H W H I T E G O W N
E F W O R S S L A T S Y R C A
```

ETHAN FOX AND THE
SHADOW PRINCESS EXCERPT

"Where is she now?" Hayley asked.

"Not sure. We all agreed she had ta be moved. If she could see through Victor's eyes, he could likely see through hers. So Alexander took 'er someplace safe, and only he knows where that is."

"So she is alive," Ethan said.

"Yeah, she's alive," Dakota said. "Alexander visits her occasionally, but he says she's not his Tiffany anymore. Somethin' happened ta change 'er."

"What happened to her?" Ethan asked.

"Don't know. Alexander wouldn't say, said it'd give away her whereabouts."

Ethan grew quiet as a wave of emotions flooded his mind. This was the first solid piece of information he had learned about his birth mother, and it came from a reliable source.

GREET BRIANNA TANGLEWOOD

Brianna is a member of the serpeneze species from the elemental world of Atlantis. She's blue-skinned with a snake's body and bright green hair that was alive. When she speaks, she speaks between lashes of her black serpent tongue.

She often visits The Grimleaver Atrocities Memorial, mourning her sister Medusa. Ethan reflects back to the first time he met Brianna in book #1, Ethan Fox and the Eyes of the Desert Sand, at the Memorial; she was coiled up in front of her sister's memorial. In book #2, Ethan Fox and the Shadow Princess; again, he glances down the aisle, and finds Brianna looking at him, her worm hairs moving back and forth as if waving at him.

Brianna is a member of CAGE.

BOND
BRIANNA
CHASED
COILED
DRILL
FORBIDDEN DOORS
LASHES
MEDUSA
MEMORIAL
POWERFUL
SECRET
SERPENEZE
SERPENT TONGUE
SIDEWINDER
SISTER
SLITHERED
SNAKE
SPECIES
SURPRISE
TELEPATHY
TRICKY
WATCHED
WEPT
WHEREABOUTS

Brianna Tanglewood

```
F S I S T E R S E H S A L U B
C O T K S P E C I E S N A R O
S W R E D N I W E D I S I A N
U A I B S N A K E L N A R W D
P T C T I T O L V T N S O H R
E C K P P D I O D N U U M E I
Z H Y E O O D E A S S D E R L
E E W G C W R E S Y D E M E L
N D R N L E E E N E S M S A D
E A I I H T S R S D C O R B E
P T N T X I Q A F D O R T O D
R E I R R N H B O U D O E U H
E L L P S C N R Y R L O R T T
S E U G N O T T N E P R E S S
F S T E L E P A T H Y C W S L
```

ETHAN FOX AND THE
SHADOW PRINCESS EXCERPT

"Serpeneze sss-sisters share a powerful bond. When Medusa and I were young, we barely needed to speak to know how one another felt."

"Yeah," said Hayley, "sounds like telepathy."

"When they took her from me," Brianna turned away from them as she continued. "I wondered if our bond would change, and if so, how."

"And did it?"

"In our case, it did change. I no longer feel what she feels," she said and spun around to face them. "But I do often see through my sister's eyes. I've seen nearly every corner of the dark mausoleum she wanders."

Ethan and Hayley glanced at the shock on one another's faces as Brianna spoke.

"Sss-so imagine my surprise when I watched through my sister's eyes as she chased after and nearly killed you both."

MEET MEDUSA

Medusa is Brianna's long lost sister. She too was a serpeneze. Medusa was taken by the Grimleavers and transformed into a hideous creature with an enormous serpent's body—her lower body girth is used to swiftly whip around like a catapult to slam her enemies down. In her transformation, her vibrant green hues of blue had drained away to a lifeless grayish-green. And if one looks into her eyes, they turn into stone.

A nest of black vipers with piercing red eyes grow from her head. The black vipers are a defense mechanism. Their eyes burn with laser-like intensity as their black bodies lung like a team of snapping turtles.

She's enslaved protecting something. She patrols the dark depths of a mausoleum like it's her life's mission.

ATROCITIES

AWAKENED

BRIANNA

CLOAKING

DARK TEMPLE

ENSLAVED

EXHIBIT

GRIMLEAVERS

HISS

MAUSOLEUM

MEDUSA

MEMORIAL

MISSION

MOURNING

NEST OF VIPERS

PATROL

SERPENT

SISTERS

SLEEPING

SLITHERED

SNAKE-LIKE

SNAPPING TURTLES

STRUCTURE

WANDERS

Medusa

```
P P Q E S N A K E L I K E T H
A A M M N I E R U T C U R T S
N T O E A S S R E D N A W L Z
O R U D P U L T C P T K I N G
I O R U P H S A E I R T O D R
T L N S I T A O V R H A A E I
B R I A N N A T L E S R T N M
L C N M G E D H R E K E R E L
A L G I T P D E I T U N O K E
I O E S U R D S E S L M C A A
R A L S R E R M T I S O I W V
O K O I T S P K I N G C T A E
M I S O L L R E X H I B I T R
E N L N E S T O F V I P E R S
M G O L S G N I P E E L S E W
```

ETHAN FOX AND THE
SHADOW PRINCESS EXCERPT

"Release her now," Brianna shouted.

Balder and Skronk released their grip, and Medusa's body fell to the floor. Brianna rushed to her sister's side and began to weep.

"Ethan, your palms," Hayley said.

Ethan raised his hands, and when he saw them glowing green, he somehow understood what to do. He ran to Brianna's side and held his palms against her dying sister. The color of Medusa's skin changed beneath his hands, and a new pigment quickly swam over her entire body bringing back her natural shade of greenish blue. The black nest of vipers transformed too, returning to the same green tube-like worms on her sister's head.

"B-Brianna, I thought we'd never find each other again," Medusa said in a barely audible whisper.

"I'm so sorry," Brianna cried. "I came here to save you."

GREET BELLA WENTWORTH

Bella is from the quadroll species. She is a middle-aged woman of medium build. Except for her four arms, she almost looks human. She has red hair that stands up on top of her head in a beehive hairdo. Other than that, she has average looking human features.

She is yappy in nature and has a tendency to talk too much. She is noted to be a "chatty Cathy" among the Caretakers, and can often be quite abrasive.

Bella is married to Boris Wentworth, who had gone missing in book #1, Ethan Fox and the Eyes of the Desert Sand. In book #2, Ethan Fox and the Shadow Princess, Boris has returned. Their daughter is Blakelyn Wentworth.

Bella is the CAGE secretary.

BARGED

BALLING

BLAKELYN

BORIS

CAGE

CARETAKERS

CHALKBOARD

CHEEKS

DABBED

ENVELOPES

EVERYONE

EXCLUSIVE

IMPORTANCE

IMPROMPTU

MEETING

NATURE

NEED-TO-KNOW

SHUFFLED

STACK

SUMMONED

TISSUES

UTMOST

WHIMPERED

ZEN CITY

Bella Wentworth

```
S A I V Y S R E K A T E R A C
E B A L L I N G T U N S T H H
G V L S E R N P M U I H E R A
A X E F F I R A T R S E A O L
C G T R T A R P O E K N N M K
E F R E Y N M B V S C S Y Y B
N E E D T O K N O W A E L T O
V M C F R N N E O H T U E I A
E L E P I V D E Y I S S K C R
L P M N A T U R E M D S A N D
O I E C N A T R O P M I L E E
P S H U F F L E D E M T B Z G
E Y F U T M O S T R P B R N R
S E V I S U L C X E A B S U A
M O S U M M O N E D G D E Y B
```

ETHAN FOX AND THE SHADOW PRINCESS EXCERPT

"Is anybody here? Who is that?" Ethan asked as he turned the corner to see a sizeable spider-like shadow rising from the ground. But the lights came on, and he quickly recognized the shadow was not a spider at all. It was Bella Wentworth using all four of her arms to pick herself up off the floor. Ethan quickly ran to her side to help her.

"What happened? Are you okay?"

"I—I don't recall," Bella said. "But you are such a dear to come to my rescue."

"You don't remember what happened? Hayley came to visit. Do you remember seeing her?"

"Oh yes, I remember now. She came to see my Boris, but he was out. So the dear girl stayed to comfort me."

"Why did she comfort you?"

"M—M—My B—Boris," Bella said and started sobbing.

"What about Boris? What happened? Why . . ."

MEET BORIS WENTWORTH

Boris Wentworth is a pudgy man that wears black formal attire, with a pocket watch chained to his vest. He is shorter than his wife Bella, and has grey flattop hair, long sideburns, and a monocle over one of his brown eyes. A fat droopy nose sits in the center of his round face, and a thick bushy mustache covers his upper lip. Boris and his family are members of the four-armed quadroll species. Boris and Bella's daughter is Blakelyn Wentworth.

Boris is a reporter at *The Residential Daily Star*. In book #1, Ethan Fox and the Eyes of the Desert Sand, Boris had gone missing. So, his daughter Blakelyn has been working at *The Residential Daily Star* as a reporter on his behalf. In book #2, Ethan Fox and the Shadow Princess, it appears Boris is back.

Boris Wentworth

```
N E W Y O R K C I T Y S Y R C
U A R A T S Y L I A D E H T H
A C M P B B A T T L E V G P A
D F S O A S R A W E N O R D R
E I E C W J S F L B Y L I O M
H G A K W T L R U B E U D T D
S U R E A T A I F A N T N S I
I R E T R O P E R R O I N E S
R I C W E B E N O B F O T I T
U N O A H I L D L A R N R M R
O E V T O R W S O R I E O E I
N S E C U D W S C I L E P N C
L Y R H S A R T I C L E S E T
A P Y E E D L R O W N A M U H
M E A T P A C K I N G G Z G E
```

ETHAN FOX AND THE
SHADOW PRINCESS EXCERPT

Boris took out his pocket watch and glanced at the time.

"Oh my, I must have lost track of time. I've somewhere to be, so I must be off."

"It was nice meeting you," Ethan said.

"The pleasure was all mine," Boris said and paused. "Tell me, my boy, are you a fan of the Drone Wars?"

"Drone Wars?"

"Well, if you've never experienced them, you simply must join me for tomorrow night's match. I've access to a VIP seating box, and there is plenty of room for the both of you."

"No, thank you," Hayley said and pursed her lips.

"What are Drone Wars?"

"The sport of Caretakers," Boris said. "A head-to-head battle of evolutioneer ability and wits. The Drone Wars are as much a game of chess as a show of raw . . ."

GREET
MRS. MOONGARDEN

Mildred Moongarden is the Caretaker chief botanist and creator of the wonderous Moongarden. She can grow anything and is the original 'Green Thumb." She is responsible for creating many plant species, including trembling nomads, squid blossoms, dancing angels, and butterfly shrubs, just to name a few.

Mrs. Moongarden is an excited woman, when it comes to her Moongarden, especially during harvest time. She blossoms with joy when flowers sprout. She also has a flare with words, "whip-dilly-doodles." She calls herself Moonshoes; Bella calls her "Old Moonshoes." And Irvin calls her "Moonflowers."

Her assistant is Rosebud. Her helpers are Grubner and his six brothers.

BEANSTALK

CLOUDS

COURTYARD

DAFFODILS

DWINDLE-BERRIES

EVERGREEN

FOLIAGE

FOUNTAIN

GRUBNER

MOON ORCHARD

MOONGARDEN

MOONSHOES

OPERATION

ROPE

ROSEBUD

SCAVENGER HUNT

SKYCLIMBER

SPIN DIAL

STONE RUINS

STUCK

TREMBLING NOMADS

UPROOTING

VINE

WITHERING-FROO

Mrs. Moongarden

```
D O O R F G N I R E H T I W T
R W N D U P R O O T I N G O R
A N I L A I D N I P S E C L E
H O A N R F S E O H S N O O M
C I T I D F F T R L W I U R B
R T N N T L O O K O Y V R E L
O A U G A I E L D V P R T B I
N R O R R N A B I I U E Y M N
O E F U U T F Z E A L M A I G
O P S B S T U C K R G S R L N
M O O N G A R D E N R E D C O
R S A E R O S E B U D I W Y M
N E E R G R E V E M B L E K A
B T N U H R E G N E V A C S D
C L O U D S N I U R E N O T S
```

ETHAN FOX AND THE SHADOW PRINCESS EXCERPT

Upon returning to the Moongarden, they headed straight for the base of the skyclimber, where Mrs. Moongarden was waiting patiently with her assistant Rosebud, while Grubner and his brothers paced around like a small heard of cattle. Mildred wasted no time asking everyone to gather around – so she could explain today's mission.

"Whip-dilly-doodles," said Mildred. "Many of you have met her already, but for those of you who haven't, I'd like for you to meet Lois."

Mrs. Moongarden motioned to the massive trunk of vines weaving their way into the clouds.

"Seems like Lois dropped her last batch of seedlings only yesterday," she continued. "Yet here we are, waiting for the same precious moment two hundred years later."

Mildred paused to wipe a tear from her cheek.

MEET GRUBNER AND THE TROWEL BROTHERS

Grubner is a dwarf who works in the Moongarden. He's become Mrs. Moongarden's right hand man. And his greatest desire is to gain more responsibility and earn the respect of his mentor, Mildred Moongarden.

He has six brothers—Grabner, Gribner, Grobner, Gripner, Gropner, and Daryl. They remind Ethan of Snow White's little friends. Even so, Grubner's brothers hated when Grubner made Snow White jokes; but knew his ribbing was all in fun, and they would do anything for their brother Doc.

The Ethan Fox Books original series, loves Mrs. Moongarden and the Trowel brothers so much that a Chapter Book has been spun off, titled: Mayhem in the Moongarden.

The Trowel Brothers

```
Z I G Z A G G I N G M R T S C
S P A R A C H U T E S R M R I
N R S D A M A G E D O O E E N
O S R F M D E R B W O E T H F
I U A I D I E L E N P P H T E
T R V D A R R L G I T D I O S
C R I G H T H A N D M A N R T
U O S E Y O R G T E D R K B A
D U H T E D T N H I R K R I T
O N E I E A A C E R O V A F I
R D R N N L A U N O C N W L O
T E S G P D J N O M A D P E N
N D L E A M S N O W W H I T E
I E R E W O O D B E R R I E S
R S H P S F R A W D N E V E S
```

ETHAN FOX AND THE SHADOW PRINCESS EXCERPT

"Look there. I think I see one," Grubner shouted, causing his brothers to gaze skyward.

"Oh yes, and there is another," Mrs. Moongarden said. "Okay, everybody, the skyclimber harvest has begun. A dozen candied foxtails to anyone who finds a seed."

Grubner and his brothers split into two groups and ran off zig-zagging through the Moongarden in a feeble attempt to follow the parachutes as they fell. Rosebud and Mrs. Moongarden patiently waited for the next seed to eject but were pleasantly surprised when three shot out in succession, followed by the other two a minute later.

"Oh my," said Mildred, "Lois wanted to get it over with quickly this time."

Rosebud counted, traced, and plotted the courses of the five newest ejectees.

GREET DAKOTA DRAKELAN

Dakota Drakelan is a retired Caretaker dark master. As an orphaned child, young Dakota was captivated by dark and gloomy things. As he grew older, the subject of dark studies absorbed most of his time. Then one day, he encountered a man named Heldrik Vonn Grim. Dakota's dreary demeanor and thirst for darkness attracted Vonn Grim. And so, Heldrik took him under his wing as his apprentice. He would become Headmaster Odin Ravenwood's first appointee.

Dakota is an older man with long gray hair, a goatee, and a bushy mustache. He wears a long duster-style overcoat, a worn leather vest, and a beat-up brown cowboy hat. When he speaks, he talks in slang.

He lives in the scary old house on the hill outside Deadwood. He has a reputation for being creepy.

ETHAN FOX BOOKS

APPRENTICE
ATTACK
CANDLE
COWBOY HAT
CREATURES
CURTAIN
DARK MASTER
DARK REALM
DARK STUDIES
DEADWOOD
ESCORT
FRIENDS
GIBBERISH
HELDRIK VONN GRIM
HILL
MONSTERS
ODIN RAVENWOOD
OLD HOUSE
OLD-TIMER
RETIREMENT
SAFETY
UNINTELLIGIBLE
VESTED INTEREST
WINDOW

Dakota Drakelan

```
U  G  I  B  B  E  R  I  S  H  M  R  O  V  H
N  D  O  O  W  D  A  E  D  G  S  D  O  E  S
I  R  T  A  H  Y  O  B  W  O  C  A  L  S  A
N  E  E  M  L  A  E  R  K  R  A  D  D  T  F
T  L  S  T  D  I  E  L  E  S  R  A  H  E  E
E  D  E  R  I  R  N  A  D  I  W  R  O  D  T
L  N  I  O  R  R  T  N  K  D  I  K  U  I  Y
L  A  D  C  Y  U  E  V  H  H  N  M  S  N  R
I  C  U  S  R  I  O  M  I  G  D  A  E  T  E
G  U  T  E  R  N  R  L  E  A  O  S  A  E  M
I  R  S  F  N  I  L  T  N  N  W  T  W  R  I
B  T  K  G  K  C  A  T  T  A  T  E  U  E  T
L  A  R  N  D  M  O  N  S  T  E  R  S  S  D
E  I  A  P  P  R  E  N  T  I  C  E  A  T  L
M  N  D  O  O  W  N  E  V  A  R  N  I  D  O
```

ETHAN FOX AND THE SHADOW PRINCESS EXCERPT

Dakota snapped his fingers, and three tiny creatures crept out from beneath a couch, miniature versions of the ones stalking Ethan. They grew as they crawled across the room, growing to about eight inches tall.

"Are they shape-shifters?" Hayley asked.

"Not exactly. I've taught 'em various dark techniques to help 'em help me."

The tiny critters stopped at Dakota's feet and turned to face Ethan and Hayley.

"Balder, Gilly, and Skronk," Dakota said as he pointed to them. "Meet Ethan and Hayley."

Ethan and Hayley waved and said hello, and the creatures smiled and curtsied to acknowledge them.

"Are they from the Dark Realm?" Ethan asked.

"These ur the ones I rescued. But their kin are still in that god-forsaken place."

"What is the Dark Realm?" Hayley asked.

MEET KAAFOO

KaaFoo is a one-armed desert nomad who wears a patch over his eye. We don't yet know a lot about KaaFoo. What we do know is that in order to travel to Stravis' bunker, one must seek out KaaFoo first. Then, and only then, will he decide if the traveler is worthy of continuing the path.

Hayley and Ethan had received the above instructions on how to get to Stravis' bunker by Wordly Pagemore.

KaaFoo holds the key to the sand slug; the transportation used to get to Stravis' bunker. Not an ordinary key, but a small disc-shaped object. The key is used to throw onto the desert floor to summon the sand slug, which resides in the distant desert.

BEWARE
BOOK-TRAVEL
BROWN TENT
CIVILIZATION
CONTINUING
CRIMINALS
DAILY STAR
DECISION MAKER
DESERT
DISC-SHAPED
EMERGED
EYE PATCH
HIDE
KAAFOO
NOMAD
ONE-ARMED
PATH
SAND SLUG
SEEK
SHANTYTOWN
STRAVIS' BUNKER
THIEVES
TRAVELER
WORTHY

KaaFoo

```
S A G D R A T S Y L I A D L S
E T F E E P P H C T A P E Y E
R R R P L D E S E R T V C E P
A T O A E T E R H T A P I M N
W S N H V I N L T R O M S E O
E B E S A I N O T P K W I R I
B G A C R N S K M A P B O G T
G C R S T O O B A A R Z N E A
U R M I E O W F U O D S M D Z
L I E D B A O T W N I E A T I
S M D I H O R N N O K V K L L
D N W O T Y T N A H S E E K I
N A I N D E H N S B L I R F V
A L D K N U Y E E D I H A N I
S S D T S G N I U N I T N O C
```

ETHAN FOX AND THE
SHADOW PRINCESS EXCERPT

"Well," Damien said with a smirk, "since you two were so foolish to make the trip, I had to come after you. But who's to say you didn't make the journey to Stravis' bunker before we could stop you."

"Who's to say," Hayley agreed and smiled at her brother. "We need to find KaaFoo."

"Follow me," Damien said.

He led them to a brown tent near the end of town and disappeared inside. He emerged with a one-armed man with an eye patch several minutes later. The man handed Damien a small disc-shaped object and pointed behind his tent.

Damien walked into the desert and waved for them to follow. He continued for several hundred feet, stopped, and threw the disc onto the desert sand.

"Our ride will be along shortly," he said.

Moments later, the ground trembled, and . . .

MEET BALDER, GILLY, AND SKRONK

Balder, Gilly, and Skronk are scary creatures but they are not monsters. Unfortunately, we categorize many of the world's creatures as monsters based on appearance alone. It is all a matter of perception.

Balder, Gilly, and Skronk are Dakota's friends. They grow as they crawl forward to about eight inches tall. They are three tiny creatures, miniature versions of the ones stalking Ethan.

They've been stalking Ethan because he is in danger. Fact is, they have been protecting Ethan since he first arrived back at The Residence. That's how they caught all the death scarabs. Someone is out to get Ethan.

AQUARIUM
BALDER
CIRCUMFERENCE
CRAWL
CREATURES
CREEP
CRITTER
DAKOTA
DARK REALM
DARKNESS
DEATH SCARAB
DISAPPEARED
ENSNARING
GIGANTIC
GILLY
SCURRIED
SECRETS
SKRONK
SLITHER
STABBING
TENTACLES
TRIANGULAR HEAD
VAMPIRES
WHIPPING

Balder, Gilly, and Skronk

```
S A G D S E L C A T N E T G S
E D E C N E R E F M U C R I C
C D E G I I E R R E H T I L S
R A H A T M U I R A U Q A L M
E R S T T I E L T R O M N Y E
T K E W A H N D D A C I G D N
S R S H C S S D E I R R U C S
G E S I Y R S C T S A E L S N
N A E P E L E N A K W D A E A
I L N P P A A E N R L L R R R
B M K I H G L T P O A A H I I
B M R N I T J I E N O B E P N
A A A G D M A D A K O T A M G
T V D E R A E P P A S I D A T
S C R E A T U R E S V O S V E
```

ETHAN FOX AND THE SHADOW PRINCESS EXCERPT

Let's even up the odds a little," Dakota Drakelan said.

He knelt and set three tiny creatures free on the concrete alley floor. Skronk and Gilly scurried past the vampires and stopped at Ethan's feet, while Balder slowly approached the vampires and grew a foot taller with each step. He was nearly seven feet tall by the time he reached them. The vampires fearlessly attacked Balder — but their offensive was futile. Balder countered their attacks by whipping at them with his hooked tentacles. He tore holes in their clothing and ripped pieces of flesh from their bodies with his lashing hooks. One unlucky vampire took flight to flank Balder but was quickly ensnared and slammed to the ground for his trouble.

"Skronk, Gilly, tend to the others," Dakota said and pointed at the unattended vampires. They followed his order and grew larger with each step towards Norell and her companions.

GREET FIN DRENCHLER

Fin Drenchler looks like a colorful amphibious humanoid. His deep navy-blue color glistens with yellow highlights, and his oversized orange eyes bulge from his frogish face. Fish-lips and scaly fin-lke ears protrude from his head. He has long webbed hands, and his smooth, shiny skin appears wet.

Fin is from the hydromorph speices. Hydromorphs are the shape-shifters of the sea; they most commonly take the form of porpoises so as not to be recognized by humans. Hydromorphs are the Seakeepers—Caretakers of the Ocean. He reports to Headmistress Jordanna Ravenwood.

Fin is married to Lyn Drenchler. Their son, Gil, looks like a mini-Fin. And Gil has a crush on Hayley (read more in book #1, Ethan Fox and the Eyes of the Desert Sand).

AQUATIC

BENCHES

BRIEFING

CAPSULE

CAVERN

FISH TANK

GHOST OF STRAVIS

HOMEBASE

HUMANOID

HYDRATION

HYDROMORPHS

MEETING

MYSTERY

OCEANS

ODIN

POCKET TOTE

PORPOISE

POSEIDON

RECRUITED

SEAKEEPER

STAIRCASE

SYMBOLS

WATER

WHEREABOUTS

Fin Drenchler

```
O A G D R E C R U I T E D T G
D C F L A P D I O N A M U H O
I M E E T I N G S O S A O O C
N W H A N S Y M B O L S H M E
R H S L P O C K E T T O T E A
S E A K E E P E R O T K O B N
T R Q C R M I T F D N C I A S
A E U R A O Y S H A O A P S G
I A A W E P T S T G I V O E N
R B T T A R S H T A T E S T I
C O I I A T S U N E A R E L F
A U C V E I E I L E R N I A E
S T I N F M A R S E D Y D F I
E S H P R O M O R D Y H O N R
P O R P O I S E S E H C N E B
```

ETHAN FOX AND THE
SHADOW PRINCESS EXCERPT

There was only one fish in the tank, swimming frantically in circles. But as Ethan got close, he could tell the fish was not a fish at all. It was a tiny porpoise blowing shape bubbles from its blowhole. A string of bubbles blew out and hovered mid-water before slowly floating towards the surface. As they rose, the bubbles morphed into letters spelling out the words: HELP ME!

"I've never seen such a small porpoise before," Ethan said.

"Why is he calling out for help?" Hayley asked.

"Um—oh yeah—about that," said Dakota. "There'za perfectly good explanation fer that."

Ethan and Hayley's eyes stayed glued to the small porpoise that turned towards them and stared . . .

"Is that—"

"What is Fin Drenchler doing in your fish tank?" Hayley asked in a stern, condemning tone. "Let him . . .

MEET THE SEERS

The Seers are the blue eyes peeking out from the desert sand watching Ethan. They are strongly connected to Creator Stravis and thus have a similar connection with the Hybrid Child, who is Ethan; and highly evolved. The Seers' leader is Hippocrates. His daughter is Adara.

In book #1, Ethan Fox and the Eyes of the Desert Sand, the Caretakers learned of the Seers existence after unearthing Starvis' journal. Also in book #1, Ethan had a dream and received the poem book, which was from the Seers; he wakes up with it in his bed.

In book #2, Ethan Fox and the Shadow Princess, the Seers speak to Ethan and return their gift to him—the poem book—by way of Jasper. And so, the Seers have reached out to Ethan once again.

ACTION

BENEATH

BLUE EYES

CHOSEN WORLD

COMMUNICATION

CREATOR

DESERT SAND

DIMENSIONAL

ENCOUNTER

FATE

FORTRESS

HIDDEN

HYBRID ONE

JASPER

OUTCOMES

PEERING

POEM BOOK

POWERFUL

PRESENCE

REACTIONS

RIGHTEOUS

SECRET

STRAVIS

WARNED

The Seers

```
C A B L U E E Y E S F R S T E
O S E M O C T U O O S E N N L
M U N G I H E R R O C R C E A
M O E U P O E T B R R O H D N
U E A L R S R L E R U T R D O
N T T J E E N T E N T A O I I
I H H A S N O I T C A E R H S
C G Y S E W S E A P A R R T N
A I B P N O R O F O R C S I E
T R R E C R R T N W A G I T M
I A I R E L L T N E C L V L I
O E D M E D E S E R T S A N D
N L O W A R N E D F I U R F S
O G N I R E E P L U O I T N T
P O E M B O O K L L N O S T E
```

ETHAN FOX AND THE SHADOW PRINCESS EXCERPT

"Stravis said not all the words were for him to understand. It appears they have finally found their intended audience."

"How is that possible?" Hayley asked.

"The Seers are multi-dimensional beings. They view all of time in an instant," Vanessa said. "They understand all possible outcomes of all possible actions and reactions. So it's not hard to imagine they were writing to both of you – even though you exist in different timeframes."

Ethan and Hayley stood in silence, pondering what they had learned.

"So what did Stravis ask of you and Odin?" Ethan asked.

"He gave us the location and asked Odin to investigate what was happening there. So Odin visited the site and witnessed the atrocities they committed . . ."

MEET THE SAYERS

The Sayers are devolved volunteered Seers. One by one, bare humanoids with enormous oversized blue eyes emerged from the desert sand accepting Stravis' offer—about twenty of them. They were bald and totally naked except for a golden swirly eye-shaped medallion embedded in each of their chests. Adara was chosen among them to be their leader. In fact, she lays down her life for her people and becomes the Shadow Princess.

Why the volunteer assignment? The Seers required certain skills only Caretakers possess to accomplish their plan—to give the Nibblewart prophecies to the Caretakers. So, the Seers enlisted Headmaster Odin's wife, Vanessa. Vanessa was asked to break the Caretakers most sacred rule. Thus, Vanessa created the Sayers. The Seers are a very evolved lifeform. The only way to create a humanoid from them is to devolve them.

ADARA

AWAKENED

BOOK OF CREATORS

CHEST

DAUGHTER

DESERT SAND

DEVOLVE

EMBEDDED

GIANT BLUE EYES

HIPPOCRATES

HUMANOID

LIFEFORM

MEDALLION

MISSION

NIBBLEWART

PROPHECIES

RELATED

SAYERS

SEERS

SHADOW PRINCESS

SWIRLY EYE-SHAPED

TRANSFORMED

VOLUNTEERED

WOMAN

The Sayers

```
S S E C N I R P W O D A H S G
B R T L S E T A R C O P P I H
O E R R E L A T E D M L A Z D
O Y A U A D E R B E I N W N M
K A W M D N E L D F T M A E V
O S E I A R S A E B T S K D O
F R L S R W L F L D T R E D L
C E B S A L O U O R A E N E U
R T B I I R E M E R R E E D N
E H I O M E R S A V M S D D T
A G N N Y I E T N N L E W E E
T U L E E D C H E S T O D B E
O A S E I C E H P O R P V M R
R D I O N A M U H L G I A E E
S W I R L Y E Y E S H A P E D
```

ETHAN FOX AND THE
SHADOW PRINCESS EXCERPT

"Do you know anything about these Sayers?" Brianna asked.

"No, only that they have giant blue eyes," Ethan said. "I'm mostly reading between the lines and making connections that may or may not be right."

"You're doing great. Keep going," said Hayley.

"Well, I–I think the Sayers and Seers are somehow related, but I'm not sure how."

"What became of them?" Damien asked.

"I don't know what happened to them after Adara disappeared. But a Caretaker woman was present when they rose from the desert sand. If we find out who she was, she might be able to tell us something."

"You may find your answer," Damien said. "Your Seer friends have more to say."

Wisps of golden whimsy wafted from the poem book as the pages turned to the next blank page, and a . . .

MEET THE SHADOW PRINCESS

The Shadow Princess can be seen as a dark silhouette of a young woman. She is pitch black from top to bottom and outlined by a glowing blue aura. Her face, body, and clothing, all consist of the same glossy substance that causes her shining yellow eyes and blue aura to cast a glow giving her a liquid sheen. A golden necklace wraps around her neck and is clearly visible against her blackness. A swirly eye-shaped pendant hangs from the chain against her upper chest. Her mouth moves like she is trying to speak but unusual sounds come out instead.

Before becoming the Shadow Princess, her name was Adara. She was the Seers leader, Hippocrates' daughter. Victor Qruefeldt tried to kill Adara as he sucked her into the black puzzle box; but her spirit lives on.

ADARA

APPARITION

BLUE AURA

DANGER

EYE PATTERN

FORTRESS

HIPPOCRATES

MEDALLIONS

NECKLACE

NEW YORK

NIBBLEWARTS

PENDANT

SAYERS

SEERS

SHADOW PRINCESS

SIGN

SILHOUETTE

SPIRIT

UNINTELLIGIBLE

UNSEEN ENERGY

UNUSUAL SOUNDS

VANISHED

WARNING

YELLOW EYES

The Shadow Princess

```
E F O R T R E S S A M H B B S
T N F L U P P P T P S I L L E
T S I G N D E I R P S P T U L
E T S U U G N R A A N P N E B
U V N R S N R I W R E O A A I
O A O E U I E T E I C C D U G
H N I G A N T T L T K R N R I
L I L N L R T F B I L A E A L
I S L A S A A K B O A T P I L
S H A D O W P R I N C E S S E
S E D I U I E O N O E S W L T
R D E M N T Y Y E A R A D A N
E L M N D M E W S A Y E R S I
E C D K S E Y E W O L L E Y N
S S D Y G R E N E N E E S N U
```

ETHAN FOX AND THE SHADOW PRINCESS EXCERPT

"Why did you call her the Shadow Princess?" Hayley asked, cutting him off mid-sentence. "Before, you referred to her as a woman in black – but this time you called her the Shadow Princess."

"Did you hear what Gruggins was shouting about when we arrived in the front room?"

"Not really. My mind was wandering. I was more worried about what I would say to Mom."

"He was angry with the Nibblewarts," Ethan explained. "They keep disturbing his naps, and all they talk about lately is the return of the Shadow Princess."

"Yeah, so what," said Hayley. "The Nibblewarts are always blabbering about something. Nobody listens to them or takes anything they say seriously."

"A truth that falls upon deaf ears is true to no one," Ethan said.

"Where did you come up with that philosophical . . ."

MEET THE NIBBLEWARTS

The Nibblewarts are the devolved Sayers. Since Victor Qruefeldt's attempt to kill Princess Adara with the puzzle box failed; he devolved the Sayers into Nibblewarts. The Nibblewarts have long hair braids that fall to the sides of their faces exposing big blue eyes and fat buck teeth. The Nibblewart high priest carries a miniature golden staff.

Nibblewarts believe grumplings symbolize good luck; so they have a tendency to follow Gruggins around—interrupting his naps. Gruggins calls them rock-eating roaches. They move in and out of The Residence from The Hall of Doorways negative door. At the Pyramids of Never, the Nibblewarts work in small teams eating straight lines into the rock to cut perfect blocks away from giant bolders—building Pyramids.

BONFIRE

BOULDERS

CARAVAN

CAVEMEN

CHAMBER

CREATURES

EATING

GOLDEN STAFF

GRUMBLE

HIGH PRIEST

LAUGHTER

LEADER

MAGICALLY

NEGATIVE DOORS

PAST

PROCESSION

PROPHECIES

PYRAMIDS

QUARRIED

TORCHES

TRIBE

TUNNELS

WAGONS

WHEELBARROWS

The Nibblewarts

```
W  M  G  D  R  O  C  R  E  A  T  U  R  E  S
H  A  F  P  R  O  C  E  S  S  I  O  N  A  D
W  G  S  C  I  Q  U  A  R  R  I  E  D  T  I
H  I  G  H  P  R  I  E  S  T  G  D  W  I  M
E  C  S  A  A  I  N  A  V  A  R  A  C  N  A
E  A  S  M  S  R  N  D  T  E  G  W  E  G  R
L  L  R  B  T  S  I  I  T  O  P  M  I  R  Y
B  L  E  E  Y  O  V  H  N  O  E  Z  E  U  P
A  Y  D  R  E  E  G  S  T  V  R  B  R  M  A
R  R  L  T  D  U  R  T  A  A  I  C  A  B  B
R  A  U  O  A  I  L  C  N  R  C  L  H  L  Q
O  G  O  L  D  E  N  S  T  A  F  F  U  E  Z
W  R  B  O  N  F  I  R  E  B  S  U  L  F  S
S  E  I  C  E  H  P  O  R  P  W  I  Z  N  T
L  E  A  D  E  R  U  H  S  L  E  N  N  U  T
```

ETHAN FOX AND THE SHADOW PRINCESS EXCERPT

"Yeah, well, I'll give them some of my goodwill, all right," Gruggins said and shook his fist again. "Always droning on about the Shadow Princess—"

The beeping of Damien's ELMO cut Gruggins off . . .

Hayley, Damien, Tinx, and Azron turned towards the study, but something had grabbed Ethan's attention, and he stood listening to Gruggins' rant.

"The Shadow Princess has returned," Gruggins said as the others walked away.

"Ethan, are you coming?" Hayley asked. Ethan backed his way towards the study but kept his eyes on Gruggins.

"The Shadow Princess delivered us from evil, the Shadow Princess will lead the chosen one, Shadow Princess this, Shadow Princess that . . ."

"If I hear one more word about the Shadow Princess or the Nibblewart prophecies—"

GREET THE RESIDENCE

Blue sky, a black-and-white checkered plane, and a tree-lined horizon frames the outside of the The Residence. Portal spheres float on the plane, held in place by colored electric fields. Blue for Atlantis, green for Ceres, red for Hades, and yellow for Zephyr—the elemental worlds. But inside was the front room of The Residence, the entrance to a world within our own. Book #1, Ethan Fox and the Eyes of the Desert Sand describes The Residence rooms, The Hall of Doorways, and so on. The Residence reminds Ethan of a haunted mansion, except clean and lived in.

In book #2, Ethan Fox and the Shadow Princess, we learn that The Residence is in one realm, the Caretaker City of Zen is through The Hall of Doorways, and Vanessa Ravenwood's home is outside of the realm of The Residence, upstairs, on the thirteenth floor.

CANDELABRUM

CANDLES

CARETAKERS

CHAMBERS

CHECKERBOARD

DEADWOOD

DIRECTORY

EARTH

FIREPLACE

GALLERY

HALL OF DOORWAYS

LIGHT BEETLE

MANSION

MAP ROOM

MARKET SQUARE

MEMORIAL

MIRROR

MOONGARDEN

PEDESTAL

PORTALS

PORTRAIT

REALM

SPECIAL QUARTERS

SPHERE REPLICA

The Residence

```
H C A C I L P E R E R E H P S
C A H M A P R O O M S D N E R
A R L A C N D O O W D A E D E
E T Y L M A D E L D N A C E T
R D R A O B R E K C E H C S R
A I E H M F E E L R T W O T A
U R L T E M D R T A E I I A U
Q E L R Y C E O S A B A R L Q
S C A A M L A M O L K R L I L
T T G E L A R L O R A E U M A
E O M I R R O R P R W T R M I
K R M A N S I O N E I A R S C
R Y P O R T R A I T R A Y O E
A E E L T E E B T H G I L S P
M O O N G A R D E N V O F T S
```

ETHAN FOX AND THE SHADOW PRINCESS EXCERPT

Nearly a year had passed since Jasper lured him and Hayley to The Residence and introduced them to the strange Caretaker world. . . .

They entered the front room, where Ethan's reflection stared back at them from the sizable mirror across the room. He remembered throwing a ball through the mirror and watching it bounce out onto the portal plane when he unlocked the portals.

"Well, kiddo," Gruggins said, "this is the end of the line for me. I'm beat after all the excitement. Time for a well-deserved nap."

"Where is everybody?"

"Dealing with the mess we just left, I'd imagine. Mush-mouth will be along shortly, I'm sure. You can wait here or in the study." The front door shut as Gruggins fluttered off Ethan's shoulder. He vanished into a tiny brown box on the table near the study door.

MEET THE CARETAKER CITY OF ZEN

The Caretaker city of Zen residents include Hayley, Vanessa, and the Wentworths. Access to the Caretaker city of Zen is through The Hall of Doorways. The city vaguely reminded Ethan of home—Manhattan; but without the car horns and sirens.

Hundreds of people in Caretaker robes walk about tending to their daily business. Lines of people wait in front of small telephone booth-like structures. They entered one by one only and disappear in a bright beam of light that strobes skyward from the top. These are part of the Caretakers teleport network into the human world. The teleport network is hardwired to specific locations throughout the world. Most Caretakers use them to travel to work daily, but others choose to live amongst the humans.

BUBBLES
BUILDINGS
CARETAKERS
CITY OF ZEN
CYLINDRICAL
DESTINATION
ELEVATION PODS
FLOATED
HARDWIRED
HAYLEY
HUMAN WORLD
LOCATIONS
ROBES
SCI-FI MOVIE
SKYLINE
SKYSCRAPERS
SOUNDS
STREETS
STROBED
TELEPHONE BOOTH
TELEPORT NETWORK
VANESSA
WENTWORTHS
WONDROUS

The Caretaker City of Zen

```
T E L E P H O N E B O O T H C
E Y D E S T I N A T I O N U Y
L E S S H T R O W T N E W M L
E L E V A T I O N P O D S A I
P A L L D E T A O L F E K N N
O H B E S K Y L I N E R Y W D
R L B A U D I T S D N I S O R
T O U S O E S F O V E W C R I
N C B S R B F O U G Z D R L C
E A E E D O I O N P F R A D A
T T S N N R L T D O O A P L L
W I E A O T J I S E Y H E A W
O O B V W S T E E R T S R F O
R N O E I V O M I F I C S N R
K S R E K A T E R A C O S T E
```

ETHAN FOX AND THE SHADOW PRINCESS EXCERPT

Hayley escorted Ethan down The Hall of Doorways to his room. She explained, she now had her own living quarters in Zen city, but would stay in her old room next to his while he was around. . . .

Ethan squinted as his eyes adjusted to the morning brightness, but they grew wider and wider as he slowly took in the sights of the wondrous Caretaker city. The scene reminded him of a sci-fi movie: there were no cars, but large transparent bubbles floated all about the skyline with people inside. They were standing at the end of a vast street, running straight down the middle of the city. Giant cylindrical skyscrapers lined the sides of the road and stretched skyward as far as the eye could see. Ethan furrowed his brow as he witnessed several bubbles hit and melt into the sides of the buildings.

"Elevation pods," Ethan said. "I rode in one at the Drone Wars."

MEET THE DRONE WARS

Drone Wars are the sport of Caretakers. A head-to-head battle of evolutioneer ability and wits. The Drone Wars are as much a game of chess as a show of raw brutality.

Most Caretakers wear formal attire to an event like the Drone Wars. The color combinations represent their elemental origins. For example, purple means one parent is from Atlantis, and one is from Hades.

Access to the arena seating is from the floater ports into elevation pods—giant bubbles floating skyward with people inside, taking them to their seats.

The evolutioneer platforms appear; where the contenders compete. Next, a call to battle. The first match is two first-year contenders. After several matches, more experienced competitors use larger drones which means more complex creatures and strategies.

ARENA
BARRIER
BATTLE RING
BOXES
CHAMPIONSHIP
COMBAT
COMPETE
CONFUSED
CONTENDERS
DRONE WARS
ELEVATION PODS
EVOLUTIONEERS
FLOATER PORTS
GONG RANG
HOLOGRAPHIC FACE
HOVERED
MATCH
PLATFORM
POUCH
RINGSIDE
SHOOK
SPHERICAL
STADIUM
VENDORS

The Drone Wars

```
C H A M P I O N S H I P R A H
O O O V D D M R O F T A L P O
N V S R S E S S M L E W A R L
T E F D R N D Y A T T A C I O
E R L R O B A T T L E R I N G
N E O O D P A O C A P E R G R
D D A N N G N R H T M N E S A
E C T E E H O O R A O A H I P
R O E W V L C N I I C O P D H
S M R A V D B U G T E H S E I
H B P R A N M T O R A R S D C
O A O S E X O B W P A V L M F
O T R D E S U F N O C N E O A
K S T A D I U M F A C S G L C
N R S R E E N O I T U L O V E
```

ETHAN FOX AND THE
SHADOW PRINCESS EXCERPT

"Wow, look at all the vendors," Ethan said. "Reminds me of the boardwalk." . . .

"Where is the arena?" Ethan asked. "Where does the match take place?"

"The arena is here. You are not looking in the right places."

Ethan scanned the room around him and slowly guided his gaze upwards. The room walls stopped about thirty feet up, but they did not end at a ceiling like most rooms. Instead, it continued up to an open night's sky filled with stars. Ten enormous concentric rings hovered in the sky several hundred feet directly overhead. The annuli grew wider as their diameters increased – and a giant empty circle of the sky filled their center.

"What is that up there?"

"That is the arena," Boris said as they gathered their refreshments. "Come, they are about to . . ."

WHO SAID THAT?

ALBERT
AZRON
BELLA WENTWORTH
BLAIR TRABBLEMORE
BORIS WENTWORTH
BRIANNA TANGLEWOOD
CADEN STANLEY
DAKOTA DRAKELAN
DAMIEN RAVENWOOD
DORKIN DRUMBLES
ETHAN FOX
GEORGE FOX
GRUBNER TROWEL
GRUGGINS MCGHEE
IRVIN MCGILLICUTTY
JASPER
JORDANNA RAVENWOOD
LINUS

MEDUSA
MELVIN MCGUILLICUTTY
MRS. MOONGARDEN
NEWTON
NIBBLEWART HIGH PRIEST
NICHOLAS KNIGHT
NORELL
ODIN RAVENWOOD
PIXIE-DEVILS
POE
ROMAN TRABBLEMORE
SHADOW PRINCESS
STRAVIS
THE FATES
TINX
VANESSA RAVENWOOD
WORDLY PAGEMORE

"No, you didn't."

"A Kraken's Fury."

"I almost got mine."

"I'll catch mine first."

"Wonderful day it is."

"CAW, CAW, CAW."

"What a rosy surprise."

"All hail the Grimlord."

"The out-door is missing."

"Harpies no like Ethan Fox!"

"You're such a n-nice b-boy."

"Look there. I think I see one."

"I tracked your portal beacon?"

"I've been meaning to stop by."

"Enough of the history lesson."

"Adara become Shadow Princess."

"Is that what you're looking for?"

"Guess I finally got yer attention."

"We know the drill. S-spill it already."

"I forbid you to return to the bunker!"

"Have you deployed our little friends?"

"He doesn't like the stench of mutants."

"The Grimleavers are honing their craft."
"He's probably afraid of his own shadow."
"Don't miss out on all the fun Ethan Fox."
". . . visions of eyes peering at me from . . ."
". . . a taletaddler named Pepper visited me."
"I thought we'd never find each other again."
". . . help you find the hidden desert fortress."
". . . your connection to Stravis . . . is strong."
". . . confused with my goofball of a brother."
"Still sore about that piece I wrote about you?"
"Yellow energy beam burst from the . . . mouth."
"The archive houses all pieces rejected by the Fates."
"I distrust the other Creators, especially Zamalador."

HOW WELL DO YOU KNOW THE STORY?

CHAPTER ONE
A BITE OF THE BIG APPLE

1. Name six favorite characters that Ethan quietly cataloged in his mind while in the taxi with his parents at New York's Time Square.

2. Who lured Ethan and Hayley to The Residence?

3. What was the name of the tall female vampire?

4. How old is Ethan?

5. What was the name of the game that George played on Ethan at their favorite Italian restaurant?

6. How many desserts did George eat?

7. Who stepped out of the swirling vortex that Poe created?

8. What caused Ethan to be separated from his parents on the way to their destination?

9. What creeps Ethan out?

10. Who did Ethan see standing between him and the trash bin?

11. What did Ethan encounter in the dark alley with the shadow woman?

12. Who came to escort Ethan back to The Residence?

13. How did Gruggins finally convince Ethan to return to The Residence?

14. What was the purpose of the beat-up old tire leaning against the fence at the back of the alley?

CHAPTER TWO
BACK TO THE RESIDENCE

15. What color was the box on the table near the study door that Gruggins vanished into?

16. What color is pyrodevlin Albert?

17. What frightens RGB?

18. Who oversees the Caretaker Arts & Literature archive?

19. What three cereal commercials did Irvin's face morph into?

20. How long was Hayley missing before she was reunited with her mother?

21. Where did Hayley move to outside of The Residence?

22. What was Bella Wentworth's good news?

23. What was the significance of the date when Victor Qruefeldt orchestrated his attack on the human world in New York?

24. What is Damien obsessed with?

25. Why would Stravis stay behind when the other Creators returned home?

26. Who are Ethan's birth parents?

27. What was the gift that Irvin brought to Ethan?

28. What was troubling Ethan after seeing that video of his encounter with Fin?

CHAPTER THREE
STRAVIS' BUNKER

29. What was the lie that Hayley told Wordly Pagemore?

30. What did Ethan spot on a shelf behind the desk of Wordly Pagemore?

31. Who is Mrs. Moongarden's right hand man?

32. Who is the newest CAGE member? And what does CAGE stand for?

33. Where did Ethan and Hayley book-travel to?

34. What transportation was used to transport Ethan, Hayley, Damien, and Tinx to Stravis' bunker?

35. How did Ethan, Hayley, Damien, and Tinx enter into Stravis' bunker?

36. What did Ethan find in Stravis' bunker? And what did it prove?

37. Who did Ethan and Azron encounter outside of Stravis' bunker?

38. What was the disturbance in the sand that was putting the *Sand Miser Dune* party in danger?

39. What do desert harpies hate?

40. How did Ethan defeat the desert harpies that were overcoming Azron?

41. How did Azron get all the glass shards the desert harpies pierced him with out of his arms and neck?

42. Where was Hayley's copycat?

43. What did Jasper say to Ethan atop Stravis' bunker?

44. How did the *Sand Miser Dune* party return home?

CHAPTER FOUR
CREATURES OF THE DARK REALM

45. Who was interrupting Gruggins' nap?

46. Who are the two Caretakers that Jordanna has been overly protective of?

47. What gift did Jasper on behalf of the Seers return to Ethan at *Sand Miser Dunes*?

48. Who are the two Caretakers that have now seen the Shadow Princess?

49. What did the wall pantry in the cafeteria remind Ethan of?

50. What did Ethan and Hayley eat in the Caretaker cafeteria?

51. Why did Ethan call the woman in black the Shadow Princess?

52. What did Ethan and Hayley encounter at the end of their snacks in the cafeteria?

53. What was the name of the poem that came to life in the cafeteria?

54. Who was Grandpa Odin?

55. Who is the retired dark master?

56. What is the name of Dakota Drakelan's red book with black lettering?

57. Who are Balder, Gilly, and Skronk?

58. Who was in Dakota Drakelan's fish tank?

CHAPTER FIVE
ESCAPE TO NEW YORK

59. Why couldn't Ethan get a hold of Hayley on her ELMO (Elemental Modulator) device?

60. Who was climbing the immense beanstalk called the skyclimber?

61. What was the name of the skyclimber?

62. Who did Azron and Nicholas rescue from the skyclimber?

63. What did Hayley want to show Ethan in the Moongarden?

64. What were the four symbols on the black rings of the spin dial (selection dial)?

65. What do the symbols represent?

66. Name the four elemental worlds, their colors, and their corresponding Creators.

67. Where are the four worlds located?

68. What world does the symbol on Ethan's palms represent?

69. Leaving the spin dial, what did Hayley and Ethan stumble upon?

70. What door did Ethan and Hayley enter to step onto the checkerboard portal plane?

71. When Ethan and Hayley escaped to New York, who did they initially run into?

72. In New York, who did Ethan and Hayley encounter next?

73. What is the name of the Shadow Princess?

74. Who can understand what the Shadow Princess speaks?

75. Who was George Fox's taletaddler?

76. What is a tether port?

CHAPTER SIX
THE DRONE WARS

77. Who was Ethan introduced to after returning back to The Residence from New York?

78. What are Drone Wars?

79. What was the title of the article Ethan found and read in *The Residential Daily Star* about deceased Headmaster Odin Ravenwood?

80. What was the article about?

81. At the Drone Wars, the Caretakers wore robes of every imaginable color combinations. What did the color combinations represent?

82. For example, what does the color purple represent?

83. What did Ethan order to drink at the Drone Wars?

84. Where was the Drone Wars arena located?

85. How did Ethan and Boris get to their Drone Wars seats?

86. After seated at the Drone Wars, who were the four Caretakers CAGE members that Ethan recognized?

87. Before the Drone Wars match began, who did Boris Wentworth leave to shake hands with?

88. What were the names of the first Drone Wars match first-year contenders?

89. What attacked Ethan at the Drone Wars?

CHAPTER SEVEN
THE ORACLE

90. The next morning after the Drone Wars outing, what did Boris Wentworth give Ethan?

91. What was the confrontation in the Map Room about between Jordanna and her two children, Hayley and Damien?

92. What does it mean when Ethan's palm symbols turn white?

93. What does it mean when Ethan's palm symbols turn red?

94. What does it mean when Ethan's palm symbols turn green?

95. What does it mean when Ethan's palm symbols turn yellow?

96. How did Ethan defeat his attacker at the Drone Wars?

97. What was it that ElMOs have built-in and what does it do?

98. Where did the jeweled dagger that Ethan pulled out of his pocket tote come from?

99. How did Ethan and Hayley unlock the iron door that was upstairs in The Residence leading to the Trabblemore chamber?

100. What did Ethan and Hayley find in the Trabblemore chamber?

101. Who did Ethan suspect was releasing the death scarabs?

102. Who entered into the Trabblemore chamber while Ethan and Hayley were hiding?

103. Who next entered into the Trabblemore chamber?

104. Who did Ethan and Hayley think Blair's father was working for?

105. Who did the swirly eye pattern on the yellow sheet – seen covering the painting on the easel when Ethan and Hayley were in the Moongarden ruins – remind Hayley of?

106. What was the name of the city that Hayley and her grandmother had a home in?

107. Where is the Caretaker city of Zen located?

108. Who had been to the hidden desert fortress of fate in the past?

109. Who built the pyramids?

CHAPTER EIGHT
PANDORA'S BOX

110. What was Damien working on in the basement in his new office, formerly Daavic's office?

111. After reading the **Pandora's Box** poem, where did Tinx, Hayley, Damien, and Ethan dash off too?

112. What did Ethan find in wood petrified Pandora's left front jacket pocket?

113. Why couldn't Ethan, Hayley, Damien, and Tinx use the same method of transportation to *Sand Miser Dunes*, book-travel, to go back to Stravis' bunker?

114. Where did the first leg of their trip on the way to *Sand Miser Dunes*, back to Stravis' bunker, take them?

115. Who was left behind?

116. What endangered their safety when the modified bubble journeyed to Stravis' bunker?

117. After the ELMOs malfunctioned because of the lasting electromagnetic activity from the hyperhole event, who navigated the bubble to Stravis' bunker?

118. After the towering shards of glass danger was over, what next did the party run into on their way to Stravis' bunker?

119. What did the bubble party see after clearing the top of the vanisihing dune?

120. Were the desert harpies surrounding the building?

121. Why did throwing a portal beacon through the bubble not pop the bubble?

122. What was the daydream that Ethan had in the bubble?

123. How did Ethan, Hayley, and Tinx locate the hatch to Stravis' bunker on their descent?

124. What greeted Ethan, Hayley, and Tinx as soon as they touched down next to the opening of the bunker?

125. What happened after Hayley approached the engraving in the stone wall, in Stravis' bunker, and slowly placed the metal key that they brought with them inside?

126. What did Ethan discover in Stravis' secret room that related to the Shadow Princess?

127. What was on the aisles of fully stocked shelves in Stravis' secret room?

128. What else did they find in Stravis' secret room?

CHAPTER NINE
A GRIM NEW START

129. Why was Bella crying?

130. Name the nine CAGE members.

131. What was the "need-to-know" CAGE meeting about?

132. How was Stravis' secret room described?

133. Where did CAGE agree to rehouse Stravis' laboratory to?

134. How did CAGE decide to go about relocating Stravis' laboratory to The Residence?

135. How was CAGE going to get to and fro – from The Residence to Stravis' bunker and back?

136. Why did Stravis build the lab?

137. Three of the elemental worlds are mentioned in Stravis' journals, which elemental world is not mentioned?

138. What is a habitat absorbing reflection trap?

139. Who did Ethan and Hayley meet at Market Square in an effort to help out Mrs. Moongarden?

140. Who pushed Ethan at Market Square?

141. How many seeds do skyclimbers release once every two hundred years?

142. Who were "The Four Cohorts" on the handwritten list?

143. What does "hart" stand for in the poem, **Mirror Mirror**?

144. What was Ethan's worst nightmare?

CHAPTER TEN
THE NIBBLEWARTS

145. Describe the Seers.

146. What was the synopsis of Ethan's dream when he saw the Seers in their full form?

147. Who was assigned to help catalog Stravis' journals?

148. What is a maelstrom?

149. What is the Alcove of Enigma?

150. What is significant about the Alcove of Enigma?

151. Who did Ethan and Hayley meet at the Alcove of Enigma?

152. Why wouldn't Dorkin go into the Alcove of Enigma room?

153. What did Ethan and Hayley find in the Alcove of Enigma room?

154. What secrets did the painting hold?

155. Where do the negative doors lead to?

156. Why did Hayley insist that Ethan had to stop following the Nibblewarts through the negative door?

CHAPTER ELEVEN
THE PYRAMIDS OF NEVER

157. What is a tether port?

158. Who did Ethan and Hayley get the tether port from?

159. Why was "apprentice" circled on "The Four Corhorts" list found in Odin Ravewood's top desk drawer, in his headmaster chamber, at The Residence?

160. What are dwindle-berries?

161. Who provided Ethan and Hayley with dwindle-berries?

162. Who did Ethan and Hayley witness at the pyramids?

163. What did Ethan and Hayley see him holding?

164. Who was the Shadow Princess before her transformation?

165. Who transformed her into the Shadow Princess?

166. What does the Shadow Princess want with Ethan?

167. What are the Nibblewart prophecies?

168. Where did the high priest Nibblewart lead Ethan, Hayley, and his tribe into?

169. What was the vortex actually?

170. What did Ethan and Hayley run into after coming through the vortex?

171. Who next did Ethan and Hayley have a run-in with?

172. How did Ethan and Hayley escape their dilemma?

CHAPTER TWELVE
THE SAYERS

173. After escaping the likes of Medusa, where did Ethan and Hayley tether port to?

174. What is a leap-letter?

175. Who created the most dangerous weapon ever created?

176. Who was the weapon created for?

177. What was the name of the weapon?

178. What did Hayley bring to Tinx when she arrived at The Grimleaver Atrocities Memorial?

179. Who was at Tinx's cousin's memorial?

180. Who is Brianna's sister?

181. How did Brianna know of Ethan and Hayley's encounter with her sister?

182. Who did Ethan and Hayley invite to their meeting with Tinx and Damien?

183. What did Ethan bring back with him before tether porting back to Dakota's house?

184. What was the name of the rocks?

185. Where are these rocks found?

186. What properties do these rocks contain?

187. What type of water is used to hydrate or grow such rocks?

188. Who is the "oracle" in **The Shadow Princess** poem?

189. What is the name of Vanessa's butler?

190. Who was Vanessa with in her castle, when Ethan, Hayley, Damien, Tinx, and Brianna arrived?

191. What most sacred Caretaker rule did Vanessa break?

192. Why did Vanessa break the oath?

193. What is a Sayer?

194. What did the Seers gift Vanessa with in return?

195. What mission did the Sayers sign up for?

196. Who was the Sayers' leader?

197. What happened to Princess Adara?

198. What happened to the Sayers?

199. Are the portal prophecies and the Nibblewart prophecies one and the same?

200. Where will the portal prophecies appear?

CHAPTER THIRTEEN
MEDUSA

201. What is significant about the Pyramids of Never?

202. Who reported visiting a construction site in the desert?

203. Where did the Map Room report the location of the construction site in the desert?

204. Where did the Map Room initially report the location of the great vanishing dune?

205. What was hidden beneath the vanishing dune?

206. Where is Brianna's sister, Medusa at?

207. What happened to the *Sand Miser Dune* portal?

208. Who was part of the plan to defeat Medusa?

209. Who were part of the mission to retrieve the portal prophecies from beneath the vanishing dune?

210. On the way to the mission, where did Tinx first book-travel to before flying the rest of the way?

211. When Medusa approached, what did Jordanna warn the others?

212. How did Ethan transform dying Medusa into her original serpeneze body?

213. Did Medusa die?

CHAPTER FOURTEEN
THE NIBBLEWART PROPHECIES

214. What was Medusa enslaved to protect?

215. The end of the corridor led to a clearing where two odd contraptions stood. Name them.

216. What was Heldrik Vonn Grim's signature?

217. When Damien asked to peek into the box, what was Dakota's warning to him?

218. What kind of creature is a dust goliath?

219. Describe the desert harpies.

220. Who did Jordanna summon to help with the dust goliath's demise?

221. What supplies did Jordanna request the summoned party to bring?

222. What are sand-peepers?

223. What are the gravity shoes for?

224. Why were the hydrosphere ejectors modified to select from one of two water sources: earthly and elemental water sources?

225. How does the selector switch on the hydrosphere ejectors work?

226. What are the energy coils for?

227. Who came up with the plan, how to defeat the dust goliath?

228. What was the plan?

229. What did the formed beast look like?

230. What finally defeated the dust behemoth?

231. What happened to the Hell-Giants?

232. When they entered the pyramid to retrieve the Nibblewart prophecies, who did they encounter?

233. What did the Shadow Princess tell Jordanna?

234. What was Adara's parting words to Hayley?

CHAPTER FIFTEEN
A GRISLY DISCOVERY

235. Who vouched for Dakota Drakelan, who was absent at the debriefing, keeping the Caretaker secret regarding the prophecies?

236. What measures were put in place to protect the portal prophecies?

237. Who are the Careguards?

238. Who is behind rallying Jordanna as headmistress detractors?

239. When Irvin put on his anchorman hat, what did he report from the human news story?

240. Name the seven cities that the Grimleavers are targeting and attacking all across the globe.

241. Who was Ethan inferring was Hayley's friend?

242. Why is Adara's connection to Hayley stronger now?

243. What was Adara's destiny?

244. Name the four names on Odin's list; he called them "The Four Cohorts?"

245. Who were "The Four Cohorts?"

246. Who was Drake Evans?

247. What happened to Drake Evans?

248. Who was Lindrew Scragmort?

249. What was the Great Exodus event?

250. What happened to Lindrew Scragmort?

251. What happened to Jason Crowley?

252. What became of the fourth cohort, Heldrik?

253. Why was the pyramid complex built?

254. What kind of gold was Damien using in his experiment? And what kind of gold should he have been using?

255. What was the findings of Damien's experiment?

256. Why did they use earthly water to hydrate the Ceresian bloating stone used to build the pyramid complex?

257. What purpose does the giant pyramid structure serve?

258. How did Ethan get into the Ravenwood chamber?

259. Who did Hayley go to meet in the Caretaker city of Zen without Ethan?

260. Who else went to the Caretaker city of Zen?

261. At first glance, why did Ethan think he saw a sizeable spider-like shadow in the Wentworths' residence?

262. Why did Hayley go to visit the Wentworths?

263. When Ethan and Tinx received a knock on Odin's chamber door, what did they find when they opened the door?

264. Who was the dead body?

CHAPTER SIXTEEN
THE DAY OF RECKONING

265. What was tucked behind Boris' lapel?

266. Who kidnapped Hayley?

267. What lured Ethan back to the Pyramids of Never?

268. When Ethan demanded Hayley, did Victor comply?

269. Did Victor know that Princess Adara was the Shadow Princess?

270. Was Victor alone when he lured Ethan to the Pyramids of Never?

271. Who are the Grimleavers?

272. Who is Norell?

273. What did Norell say?

274. After Ethan lunged at Norell for pummeling Hayley to the ground, what did she do to Ethan?

275. What did Hayley whisper in Ethan's ear?

276. What calming technique did Ethan use on himself?

277. What did Victor take from Hayley? And where did he put it?

278. What else did Victor take from Hayley?

279. Who did Ethan secretly bring along with him?

280. What did Gruggins do in secret?

281. What did Hayley demand back from Victor?

282. How did Victor respond?

283. What happened next?

284. Who arrived that caused Victor to grab hold of the portal beacon, and vanish?

285. Who appeared at Ethan's dying body?

CHAPTER SEVENTEEN
A KRAKEN'S FURY

286. What was happening on the museum break-in news?

287. What was missing from the museums?

288. What did the Caretakers molecular scan reveal?

289. Why was this a problem?

290. What important news did Dorkin Drumbles have that interrupted the CAGE debriefing?

WORDLY PAGEMORE'S

EARLY WORM
ACTIVITIES & GAMES

ANSWERS

WHO SAID THAT? ANSWERS

"No, you didn't." — Linus

"CAW, CAW, CAW." — Poe

"I almost got mine." — Albert

"A Kraken's Fury." — The Fates

"I'll catch mine first." — Newton

"All hail the Grimlord." — Norell

"Harpies no like Ethan Fox!" — Azron

"The out-door is missing." — Ethan Fox

"Is that what you're looking for?" — Tinx

"Wonderful day it is." — Dorkin Drumbles

"What a rosy surprise." — Mrs. Moongarden

"Look there. I think I see one." — Grubner Trowel

"You're such a n-nice b-boy." — Bella Wentworth

"I tracked your portal beacon?" — Nicholas Knight

"Don't miss out on all the fun Ethan Fox." — Jasper

"I've been meaning to stop by." — Irvin McGillicutty

"Enough of the history lesson." — Gruggins McGhee

"Guess I finally got yer attention." — Dakota Drakelan

"I thought we'd never find each other again." — Medusa

"He doesn't like the stench of mutants." — Caden Stanley

". . . a taletaddler named Pepper visited me." — George Fox

"Adara become Shadow Princess." — Nibblewart high priest

"We know the drill. S-spill it already." — Brianna Tanglewood

"I distrust the other Creators, especially Zamalador." — Stravis

"He's probably afraid of his own shadow." — Blair Trabblemore

"Have you deployed our little friends?" — Roman Trabblemore

"Yellow energy beam burst from the . . . mouth." — Pixie-devils

". . . confused with my goofball of a . . ." — Melvin McGillicutty

"The Grimleavers are honing their craft." — Damien Ravenwood

"I forbid you to return to the bunker!" — Jordanna Ravenwood

". . . visions of eyes peering at me from . . ." — Odin Ravenwood

". . . help you find the hidden desert fortress." — Shadow Princess

"Still sore about that piece I wrote about you?" — Boris Wentworth

"The archive houses all pieces rejected by . . ." — Wordly Pagemore

". . . your connection to Stravis . . . is strong." — Vanessa Ravenwood

TRIVIA QUESTION ANSWERS

CHAPTER ONE
A BITE OF THE BIG APPLE

(1)   Name six favorite characters that Ethan quietly cataloged in his mind while in the taxi with his parents at New York's Time Square.
(1) Spiderman, (2) Superman, (3) Ironman, (4) Godzilla, (5) King Kong, and (6) Harry Potter.

(2)   Who lured Ethan and Hayley to The Residence?
Jasper.

(3)   What was the name of the tall female vampire?
Norell.

(4)   How old is Ethan?
Fourteen.

(5)   What was the name of the game that George played on Ethan at their favorite Italian restaurant?
Crack Ethan up game.

(6)   How many desserts did George eat?
One and half; his and half of Betsy's.

(7)   Who stepped out of the swirling vortex that Poe created?
Victor Oruefeldt.

(8)   What caused Ethan to be separated from his parents on the way to their destination?
A bus crash.

(9)   What creeps Ethan out?
Zombies.

(10)   Who did Ethan see standing between him and the trash bin?
A dark silhouette of a young woman.

(11)   What did Ethan encounter in the dark alley with the shadow woman?
Small dragon-like creatures; miniature dragons.

(12)   Who came to escort Ethan back to The Residence?
Gruggins McGhee.

(13)   How did Gruggins finally convince Ethan to return to The Residence?
Gruggins resorted to casting a grumpling enchantment on Ethan.

(14)   What was the purpose of the beat-up old tire leaning against the fence at the back of the alley?
It was a portal beacon and their ticket to The Residence.

CHAPTER TWO
BACK TO THE RESIDENCE

(15) What color was the box on the table near the study door that
      Gruggins vanished into?
      Brown; in book #1, Ethan Fox and the Eyes of the Desert Sand,
Gruggins' green box was smashed when he was abducted.

(16) What color is pyrodevlin Albert?
      Red.

(17) What frightens RGB?
      Reddish marbles; firelyte capsules.

(18) Who oversees the Caretaker Arts & Literature archive?
      Wordly Pagemore.

(19) What three cereal commercials did Irvin's face morph into?
      (1) Trix, (2) Lucky Charms, and (3) Frosted Flakes.

(20) How long was Hayley missing before she was reunited with
      her mother?
      A century.

(21) Where did Hayley move to outside of The Residence?
      She now has her own living quarters in Zen city.

(22) What was Bella Wentworth's good news?
      Her husband, Boris Wentworth was found alive.

(23) What was the significance of the date when Victor Qruefeldt
      orchestrated his attack on the human world in New York?
      It was Ethan's birthday.

(24) What is Damien obsessed with?
      Stravis' journal.

(25) Why would Stravis stay behind when the other Creators returned home?
He is strongly connected to the Seers and helped them save the Hybrid Child (Ethan Fox).

(26) Who are Ethan's birth parents?
Alexander and Tiffany Sturgis.

(27) What was the gift that Irvin brought to Ethan?
A water pistol.

(28) What was troubling Ethan after seeing that video of his encounter with Fin?
It made him wonder, was it something he said that led to Fin's disappearance. Seeing himself fall into a trance like that made him feel somehow responsible.

CHAPTER THREE
STRAVIS' BUNKER

(29) What was the lie that Hayley told Wordly Pagemore?
She was studying for Caretaker training, and one of the questions asks about traveling to Stravis' bunker.

(30) What did Ethan spot on a shelf behind the desk of Wordly Pagemore?
Pandora's box; the petrified woman in the Moongarden was holding it.

(31) Who is Mrs. Moongarden's right hand man?
Grubner Trowel.

(32) Who is the newest CAGE member? And what does CAGE stand for?
Tinx; Caretaker Anti-Grimleaver Enforcement.

(33) Where did Ethan and Hayley book-travel to?
Sand Miser Dunes.

(34) What transportation was used to transport Ethan, Hayley, Damien, and Tinx to Stravis' bunker?
A giant sand slug.

(35) How did Ethan, Hayley, Damien, and Tinx enter into Stravis' bunker?
The heavy iron hatch, exposed a dark stairwell into the sand.

(36) What did Ethan find in Stravis' bunker? And what did it prove?
A hydration capsule, used by hydromorphs when they are away from water for extended periods. It proved that Fin Drenchler had been there.

(37) Who did Ethan and Azron encounter outside of Stravis' bunker?
Shadow spirit; Shadow Princess.

(38) What was the disturbance in the sand that was putting the *Sand Miser Dune* party in danger?
Desert harpies.

(39) What do desert harpies hate?
Water.

(40) How did Ethan defeat the desert harpies that were overcoming Azron?
He used Irvin's gift; the toy water pistol Irvin modified.

(41) How did Azron get all the glass shards the desert harpies pierced him with out of his arms and neck?
Tinx removed them with her tweezer-like front teeth.

(42) Where was Hayley's copycat?
On a secret mission.

(43) What did Jasper say to Ethan atop Stravis' bunker?
He said, Ethan's journey has only just begun.

(44)　How did the *Sand Miser Dune* party return home?
A portal beacon.

CHAPTER FOUR
CREATURES OF THE DARK REALM

(45)　Who was interrupting Gruggins' nap?
Nibblewarts.

(46)　Who are the two Caretakers that Jordanna has been overly
protective of?
Hayley and Tinx.

(47)　What gift did Jasper on behalf of the Seers return to Ethan at
Sand Miser Dunes?
Poem book; brown book with gold lettering.

(48)　Who are the two Caretakers that have now seen the Shadow
Princess?
Ethan and Azron.

(49)　What did the wall pantry in the cafeteria remind Ethan of?
The replicator in *Star Trek*.

(50)　What did Ethan and Hayley eat in the Caretaker cafeteria?
Spaghetti with meatballs, and pizza.

(51)　Why did Ethan call the woman in black the Shadow Princess?
Ethan overheard Gruggins complaining that the Nibblewarts
were constantly disturbing his naps. And all the Nibblewarts talked
about lately is the return of the Shadow Princess.

(52)　What did Ethan and Hayley encounter at the end of their
snacks in the cafeteria?
A tiny insect-like creature similar to a scorpion but different.

(53)   What was the name of the poem that came to life in the cafeteria?
Creatures of the Dark Realm.

(54)   Who was Grandpa Odin?
Odin Ravenwood; former headmaster, Jordanna's father-in-law, Hayley's grandfather.

(55)   Who is the retired dark master?
Dakota Drakelan.

(56)   What is the name of Dakota Drakelan's red book with black lettering?
Secrets of the Dark Realm.

(57)   Who are Balder, Gilly, and Skronk?
Tiny creatures that Dakota Drakelan rescued from the Dark Realm.

(58)   Who was in Dakota Drakelan's fish tank?
Fin Drenchler.

CHAPTER FIVE
ESCAPE TO NEW YORK

(59)   Why couldn't Ethan get a hold of Hayley on her ELMO (Elemental Modulator) device?
She may have blocked incoming messages.

(60)   Who was climbing the immense beanstalk called the skyclimber?
Azron.

(61)   What was the name of the skyclimber?
Lois.

(62)   Who did Azron and Nicholas rescue from the skyclimber?
A small evergreen trembling nomad.

(63)   What did Hayley want to show Ethan in the Moongarden?
The selection dial that Daavic showed them in book #1, Ethan Fox and the Eyes of the Desert Sand.

(64)   What were the four symbols on the black rings of the spin dial (selection dial)?
They are the same four symbols that made up the Creator's crest that they found in the lair of the spider gecko; found in book #1, Ethan Fox and the Eyes of the Desert Sand.

(65)   What do the symbols represent?
The symbols of the four Creators of Earth, one from each of the four elemental worlds.

(66)   Name the four elemental worlds, their colors, and their corresponding Creators.
(1) Creator Stravis from the elemental world of Zephyr, the yellow planet, (2) Creator Driveous from the elemental world of Atlantis, the blue planet, (3) Creator Vraitor from the elemental world of Ceres, the green planet, and (4) Creator Zamalador from the elemental world of Hades, the red planet.

(67)   Where are the four worlds located?
Outside of The Residence realm.

(68)   What world does the symbol on Ethan's palms represent?
Creator Stravis from the elemental world of Zephyr's symbol.

(69)   Leaving the spin dial, what did Hayley and Ethan stumble upon?
A painter's easel and canvas that stood on the beach ahead of them; the painting was covered by a yellow sheet with a black swirly eye-shaped emblem stamped on it.

(70)   What door did Ethan and Hayley enter to step onto the checkerboard portal plane?
The in-door; front door.

(71) When Ethan and Hayley escaped to New York, who did they initially run into?
Nicholas Knight.

(72) In New York, who did Ethan and Hayley encounter next?
The Shadow Princess.

(73) What is the name of the Shadow Princess?
Adara.

(74) Who can understand what the Shadow Princess speaks?
Hayley, with the help of her rift-key ring; it finally woke up.

(75) Who was George Fox's taletaddler?
Pepper.

(76) What is a tether port?
It is how one is transported into the future.

CHAPTER SIX
THE DRONE WARS

(77) Who was Ethan introduced to after returning back to The Residence from New York
Boris Wentworth.

(78) What are Drone Wars?
The sport of Caretakers; a head-to-head battle of evolutioneer ability and wits.

(79) What was the title of the article Ethan found and read in *The Residential Daily Star* about deceased Headmaster Odin Ravenwood?
The Troubling Truth Surrounding Headmaster Ravenwood's Latest Decisions.

(80)   What was the article about?

The appointment of Dakatoa Drakelan to the position of Master of Dark Studies.

(81)   At the Drone Wars, the Caretakers wore robes of every imaginable color combinations. What did the color combinations represent?

Formal attire; the color combination represented their elemental orgins.

(82)   For example, what does the color purple represent?

Purple means one parent is from Atlantis (blue), and one is from Hades (red).

(83)   What did Ethan order to drink at the Drone Wars?
Sugar-pickle soda.

(84)   Where was the Drone Wars arena located?

The 30 foot high walls did not end at a ceiling; instead, the arena continued up to an open night's sky filled with stars. Ten enormous concentric rings hovered in the sky several hundred feet directly overhead.

(85)   How did Ethan and Boris get to their Drone Wars seats?

Floater ports led them to elevation pods, which brought them to their VIP-seats.

(86)   After seated at the Drone Wars, who were the four Caretaker CAGE members that Ethan recognized?

(1) Brianna Tanglewood, (2) Damien Ravenwood, (3) Nicholas Knight, and (4) Azron.

(87)   Before the Drone Wars match began, who did Boris Wentworth leave to shake hands with?
Roman Trabblemore.

(88)   What were the names of the first Drone Wars match first-year contenders?
Artemis Klem and Reginald Simmons.

(89)   What attacked Ethan at the Drone Wars?
A massive black beetle-like insect; an enormous death scarab.

CHAPTER SEVEN
THE ORACLE

(90)   The next morning after the Drone Wars outing, what did Boris Wentworth give Ethan?
A small box with a red bow with the small reptilian garment frill from Boris' lapel.

(91)   What was the confrontation in the Map Room about between Jordanna and her two children, Hayley and Damien?
Jordanna wanted to assign a CAGE babysitter for Ethan and Hayley. The compromise was Tinx (Hayley's request) and Damien (his request) to oversee the group.

(92)   What does it mean when Ethan's palm symbols turn white?
White point out something that Ethan is not seeing.

(93)   What does it mean when Ethan's palm symbols turn red?
Red points to danger.

(94)   What does it mean when Ethan's palm symbols turn green?
Green to ward off ill intent; to ward off evil.

(95)   What does it mean when Ethan's palm symbols turn yellow?
Yellow when it is heaven sent; referring to Stravis.

(96)   How did Ethan defeat his attacker at the Drone Wars?
He spontaneously devolved an evolved creature back to its original form when his palm symbols turned green.

(97)   What was it that ElMOs have built-in and what does it do?

A proximity encoder; it produces a holographic result of something it earlier recorded.

(98)   Where did the jeweled dagger that Ethan pulled out of his pocket tote come from?

In book #1, Ethan Fox and the Eyes of the Desert Sand, while in the lair of the spider gecko chamber, Ethan found a pirate's remains. The skeleton wore tattered clothes and clutched a jeweled dagger in his hand; Ethan claimed it.

(99)   How did Ethan and Hayley unlock the iron door that was upstairs in The Residence leading to the Trabblemore chamber?

With Blair's holographic severed hand held up against the embossed symbol. This caused a red glow to appear beneath the hand – and the emblem slowly melted away to reveal the flat keypad. Next, Hayley stepped forward and tapped at the keypad to enter the symbols from the paper Blair's hand was holding.

(100) What did Ethan and Hayley find in the Trabblemore chamber?

A death scarab in a jar.

(101) Who did Ethan suspect was releasing the death scarabs?

Blair Trabblemore.

(102) Who entered into the Trabblemore chamber while Ethan and Hayley were hiding?

Blair, Caden, and Malik.

(103) Who next entered into the Trabblemore chamber?

Roman Trabblemore.

(104) Who did Ethan and Hayley think Blair's father was working for?

Victor Qruefeldt.

(105) Who did the swirly eye pattern on the yellow sheet – seen covering the painting on the easel when Ethan and Hayley were in the Moongarden ruins – remind Hayley of?
Vanessa Ravenwood.

(106) What was the name of the city that Hayley and her grandmother had a home in?
Caretaker city of Zen.

(107) Where is the Caretaker city of Zen located?
Within The Residence through The Hall of Doorways.

(108) Who had been to the hidden desert fortress of fate in the past?
Odin Ravenwood.

(109) Who built the pyramids?
Devolved Sayers – three foot tall cavemen creatures called Nibblewarts built the pyramids.

CHAPTER EIGHT
PANDORA'S BOX

(110) What was Damien working on in the basement in his new office, formerly Daavic's office?
Daavic's ELMO; Daavic's Elemental Modulator.

(111) After reading the **Pandora's Box** poem; where did Tinx, Hayley, Damien, and Ethan dash off too?
The Moongarden.

(112) What did Ethan find in wood petrified Pandora's left front jacket pocket?
A hand-sized metallic object; it is a key.

(113) Why couldn't Ethan, Hayley, Damien, and Tinx use the same method of transportation to *Sand Miser Dunes*, book-travel, to go back to Stravis' bunker?
Jordanna locked away the book.

(114) Where did the first leg of their trip on the way to *Sand Miser Dunes*, back to Stravis' bunker, take them?
The Glass Pillars of Nym.

(115) Who was left behind?
Damien.

(116) What endangered their safety when the modified bubble journeyed to Stravis' bunker?
Jagged crystal branches protruding out from the sides of the crystal pillars and the tips of the giant pillars.

(117) After the ELMOs malfunctioned because of the lasting electromagnetic activity from the hyperhole event, who navigated the bubble to Stravis' bunker?
Stravis himself by way of Ethan's palm symbols glowing yellow and spinning around directionally.

(118) After the towering shards of glass danger was over, what next did the party run into on their way to Stravis' bunker?
The great vanishing dune.

(119) What did the bubble party see after clearing the top of the vanisihing dune?
A tall stone building.

(120) Were the desert harpies surrounding the building?
Yes.

(121) Why did throwing a portal beacon through the bubble not pop the bubble?
Elevation pods are designed for planetary survey and passing portal beacons is part of that design.

(122) What was the daydream that Ethan had in the bubble?

He was no longer looking down at the building. He was inside. It was dark all around – and glowing yellow eyes slowly moved toward him. The Shadow Princess was motioning and speaking to him, but her words were unintelligible.

(123) How did Ethan, Hayley, and Tinx locate the hatch to Stravis' bunker on their descent?

The pole once again popped up to reveal the hatch buried beneath the sand.

(124) What greeted Ethan, Hayley, and Tinx as soon as they touched down next to the opening of the bunker?
Desert harpies.

(125) What happened after Hayley approached the engraving in the stone wall, in Stravis' bunker, and slowly placed the metal key that they brought with them inside?

It fit perfectly and made a satisfying clanking sound as the rock appeared to suck the key into place. Next, part of the rock wall melted away, exposing a yellow door with Stravis' symbol embossed on it.

(126) What did Ethan discover in Stravis' secret room that related to the Shadow Princess?

An extensive collection of swirly eye-shaped medallions like the one hanging from the Shadow Princess' necklace; only smaller, sixteen to be specific.

(127) What was on the aisles of fully stocked shelves in Stravis' secret room?

Samples of animals, vegetables, and minerals from the elemental worlds as well as Earth.

(128) What else did they find in Stravis' secret room?
A shelf full of yellow notebooks.

CHAPTER NINE
A GRIM NEW START

(129) Why was Bella crying?

As CAGE secretary, she was not invited to attend the exclusive CAGE meeting.

(130) Name the nine CAGE members.

(1) Jordanna Ravenwood, (2) Damien Ravenwood, (3) Alexander Sturgis, (4) Nicholas Knight, (5) Brianna Tangelwood, (6) Azron, (7) Tinx, (8) Hayley Ravenwood, and (9) Ethan Fox. Ethan is an honorary member; in book #1, Ethan Fox and the Eyes of the Desert Sand.

(131) What was the "need-to-know" CAGE meeting about?
Stravis' bunker briefing.

(132) How was Stravis' secret room described?

The best-equipped research laboratory Damien had ever run across. Stravis appears to have taken detailed notes, so Damien should be able to recreate everything Stravis did.

(133) Where did CAGE agree to rehouse Stravis' laboratory to?

At The Residence in Damien's basement office; formerly his twin brother Daavic's hideout.

(134) How did CAGE decide to go about relocating Stravis' laboratory to The Residence?

Restrict access to the front room and the study for a week. That allows enough time to bring everything in through the portal plane.

(135) How was CAGE going to get to and fro – from The Residence to Stravis' bunker and back?

Hayley wisely left a portal beacon so that they can use the portal plane and travel directly to the bunker.

(136) Why did Stravis build the lab?

To research peculiar interactions between elemental and earthly matter.

(137) Three of the elemental worlds are mentioned in Stravis' journals, which elemental world is not mentioned?
Zephyr.

(138) What is a habitat absorbing reflection trap?

Instead of capturing the image in a mirror, the glass absorbed the reflection and created a perfect copy of the environment.

(139) Who did Ethan and Hayley meet at Market Square in an effort to help out Mrs. Moongarden?
Irvin.

(140) Who pushed Ethan at Market Square?
Caden Stanley.

(141) How many seeds do skyclimbers release once every two hundred years?
Seven.

(142) Who were "The Four Cohorts" on the handwritten list?

(1) Drake Evans, (2) Lindrew Scragmort, (3) Jason Crowley, and (4) Heldrik Vonn Grim.

(143) What does "hart" stand for in the poem, **Mirror Mirror**?
Habitat Absorbing Reflection Trap.

(144) What was Ethan's worst nightmare?

Shards of broken glass covered the floor in the front room by the wall opposite the front door – and the giant mirror normally reflecting the portal plane was gone along with its empty frame. (The empty frame was a working replica of the portal plane.) Victor Qruefeldt did this with the Trabblemores help. The Grimleavers now have complete and total access to the human and elemental worlds.

CHAPTER TEN
THE NIBBLEWARTS

(145) Describe the Seers.

Bare humanoids with enormous oversized blue eyes emerged from the desert sand. They were bald and totally naked except for a golden swirly eye-shaped medallion embedded in each of their chests; big-eyed people.

(146) What was the synopsis of Ethan's dream when he saw the Seers in their full form?

A young Victor Qruefeldt had captured a woman and used a small black box that when open, wiry black strands shot out and enveloped the woman. She was dead. But something happened – she opened her eyes, and a bright yellow light glowed from within as a sheen flowed over her prune-wrinkled black skin, making her smooth again. The black apparition of the woman floated free of her restraints; she is now the Shadow Princess.

(147) Who was assigned to help catalog Stravis' journals?
Wordly Pagemore.

(148) What is a maelstorm?

A powerful whirlpool in the sea or a river; a situation or state of confused movement or violent turmoil.

(149) What is the Alcove of Enigma?
It is a specialized room in the Gallery.

(150) What is significant about the Alcove of Enigma?

All the paintings in that room have one thing in common. They were all determined to be significant by the Fates, yet the Caretakers still have no idea what they mean or represent.

(151) Who did Ethan and Hayley meet at the Alcove of Enigma?
Dorkin Drumbles.

(152) Why wouldn't Dorkin go into the Alcove of Enigma room?
That room is a den of inequity in his opinion.

(153) What did Ethan and Hayley find in the Alcove of Enigma room?
A canvas covered in a yellow sheet with a black swirly eye-shaped emblem stamped on it.

(154) What secrets did the painting hold?
The Nibblewarts are the rock-eating roaches, Gruggins called them. The little cavemen-like creatures were eating the boulders to shape them into rectangular stones to build the pyramids.

(155) Where do the negative doors lead to?
The past.

(156) Why did Hayley insist that Ethan had to stop following the Nibblewarts through the negative door?
They wouldn't have a way back to the present.

CHAPTER ELEVEN
THE PYRAMIDS OF NEVER

(157) What is a tether port?
A tether port is how the Caretakers transported Ethan into the future; it is how Ethan disappeared from the Caretaker world.

(158) Who did Ethan and Hayley get the tether port from?
Dakota Drakelan; Dakota got it from George Fox.

(159) Why was "apprentice" circled on "The Four Corhorts" list found in Odin Ravewood's top desk drawer, in his headmaster Ravenwood chamber, at The Residence?
It was circled because Odin knew Dakota Drakelan served as Heldrik's apprentice.

(160) What are dwindle-berries?

Linnie was Mrs. Moongarden's pet name for the itsy Bitzy bush, another of her ingenious creations. Each Itsy Bitzy grew up to ten dwindle-berries a day on every one of its pigtails. The fruit was highly valued due to its ability to shrink things, even people. One dwindle-berry will cause the near-halving of the consuming party, but the shrinkage is reversible by simply eating an equal number of shrunken dwindle-berries. (More about Mrs. Moongarden, the Itsy Bitzy bush, and dwindle-berries can be found in the Ethan Fox Chapter book: Mayhem in the Moongarden.)

(161) Who provided Ethan and Hayley with dwindle-berries?
Grubner Trowel.

(162) Who did Ethan and Hayley witness at the pyramids?
Jason Crowley.

(163) What did Ethan and Hayley see him holding?
A Heldrik Vonn Grim puzzle box.

(164) Who was the Shadow Princess before her transformation?
Adara.

(165) Who transformed her into the Shadow Princess?
Victor Oruefeldt.

(166) What does the Shadow Princess want with Ethan?
To lead the chosen one (Ethan) to the Nibblewart prophecies.

(167) What are the Nibblewart prophecies?
What was, what is, and what shall be.

(168) Where did the high priest Nibblewart lead Ethan, Hayley, and his tribe into?
A vortex; but not a death vortex.

(169) What was the vortex actually?
A time portal; they are back in present time.

(170) What did Ethan and Hayley run into after coming through
the vortex?
Pixie-devils.

(171) Who next did Ethan and Hayley have a run-in with?
Medusa.

(172) How did Ethan and Hayley escape their dilemma?
The tether port; it connects two points in time and space.
They've already moved back to the present time, but the tether port
is still connected to its location in space, which means it should
transport them to Ethan's dad's place in Manhattan unless Dakota
reprogrammed it.

CHAPTER TWELVE
THE SAYERS

(173) After escaping the likes of Medusa, where did Ethan and
Hayley tether port to?
Dakota Drakelan's house.

(174) What is a leap-letter?
Telegrams sent backward in time.

(175) Who created the most dangerous weapon ever created?
Heldrik Vonn Grim.

(176) Who was the weapon created for?
Daavic Ravenwood.

(177) What was the name of the weapon?
Heldrik Vonn Grim puzzle box.

(178) What did Hayley bring to Tinx when she arrived at The
Grimleaver Atrocities Memorial?
A small plate of cricket toast.

(179) Who was at Tinx's cousin's memorial?
Tinx, Ethan, Hayley, Brianna, and Azron.

(180) Who is Brianna's sister?
Medusa.

(181) How did Brianna know of Ethan and Hayley's encounter with her sister?
Brianna often sees through her sister's eyes.

(182) Who did Ethan and Hayley invite to their meeting with Tinx and Damien?
Brianna.

(183) What did Ethan bring back with him before tether porting back to Dakota's house?
Rocks.

(184) What was the name of the rocks?
Ceresian bloating stone.

(185) Where are these rocks found?
A form of rock found on Ceres; the green planet.

(186) What properties do these rocks contain?
When exposed to water, they expand, almost limitlessly depending on the size of the water source.

(187) What type of water is used to hydrate or grow such rocks?
Atlantian water used to hydrate them.

(188) Who is the "oracle" in **The Shadow Princess** poem?
Vanessa Ravenwood; Hayley's grandmother.

(189) What is the name of Vanessa's butler?
Melvin McGillicutty.

(190) Who was Vanessa with in her castle, when Ethan, Hayley, Damien, Tinx, and Brianna arrived?
Dakota Drakelan.

(191) What most sacred rule did Vanessa break?
Vanessa devolved a select few of Seers into Sayers – those who volunteered for the mission, about twenty.

(192) Why did Vanessa break the oath?
The Seers (the eyes in the desert sand) required certain skills only Caretakers possess. Caretakers do not have powers of creation. Since the Seers are a very evolved lifeform, the only way to create a "humanoid form" of a Seer – called a Sayer – is to devolve a Seer.

(193) What is a Sayer?
A Seer (an eye in the desert sand) transformed into a humanoid form; capable of communicating with the Caretakers.

(194) What did the Seers gift Vanessa with in return?
Second sight; she is an oracle.

(195) What mission did the Sayers sign up for?
The Sayers' mission was to bring the word of the Seers to the Caretakers. They were to deliver the portal prophecies described in the Book of Creators. In other words, to pass the Nibblewart prophecies to the Caretakers.

(196) Who was the Sayers' leader?
Princess Adara.

(197) What happened to princess Adara?
Princess Adara gave up her life to save her people, the Sayers. Victor Qruefeldt used the puzzle box to kill Princess Adara; but it didn't work. Her physical body is dead, in tombed in Victor's black box; however, her spirit is outside the box and her spirit is called the Shadow Princess.

(198) What happened to the Sayers?

Since Victor Qruefeldt's attempt to kill Princess Adara with the puzzle box failed. He devolved the Sayers into Nibblewarts.

(199) Are the portal prophecies and the Nibblewart prophecies one and the same?
Yes.

(200) Where will the portal prophecies appear?
In the Pyramids of Never.

CHAPTER THIRTEEN
MEDUSA

(201) What is significant about the Pyramids of Never?

The central pyramid holds the portal prophecies foretold by the Book of Creators.

(202) Who reported visiting a construction site in the desert?
Headmaster Odin Ravenwood.

(203) Where did the Map Room report the location of the construction site in the desert?
Northern Africa.

(204) Where did the Map Room initially report the location of the great vanishing dune?

The vanishing dune is in one of the protected realms. And not accessible from the human world.

(205) What was hidden beneath the vanishing dune?
The pyramids.

(206) Where is Brianna's sister, Medusa at?
In the pyramids beneath the vanishing dune.

(207) What happened to the *Sand Miser Dune* portal?
Jordanna had it destroyed.

(208) Who was part of the plan to defeat Medusa?

Dakota Drakelan and his friends; Balder, Gilly, and Skronk.

(209) Who were part of the mission to retrieve the portal prophecies from beneath the vanishing dune?

Jordanna, Brianna, Damien, Ethan, Hayley, and Tinx as well as Dakota, Balder, Gilly, and Skronk.

(210) On the way to the mission, where did Tinx first book-travel to before flying the rest of the way?

The Glass Pillars of Nym.

(211) When Medusa approached, what did Jordanna warn the others?

Remember, don't look into her eyes.

(212) How did Ethan transform dying Medusa into her original serpeneze body?

His palms glowed green, and he somehow understood what to do. He ran to Brianna's side and held his palms against her dying sister. The color of Medusa's skin changed beneath his hands – and a new pigment quickly swarm over her entire body bringing back her natural shade of greenish blue. The black nest of vipers transformed, too; returning to the same green tube-like worms on her sister's head.

(213) Did Medusa die?

Yes.

CHAPTER FOURTEEN
THE NIBBLEWART PROPHECIES

(214) What was Medusa enslaved to protect?

The cloaking device (the vanishing dune) and a complexed black box that scatters a lifeform into smaller ones.

(215) The end of the corridor led to a clearing where two odd
contraptions stood. Name them.

(1) A cloaking device and (2) a complexed black box; this
device scatters a lifeform into smaller ones – but the whole of the
original lifeform is still intact.

(216) What was Heldrik Vonn Grim's signature?
Black boxes.

(217) When Damien asked to peek into the box, what was Dakota's
warning to him?
Sure! If yer keen ta havin' another moon-shaped pupil.

(218) What kind of creature is a dust goliath?
They're from the elemental world of Zephyr, like a Hell-
Giant, only much bigger and made from wind and dust instead of
fire.

(219) Describe the desert harpies.
Those desert harpies are pieces of a larger lifeform; a dust
goliath. But most of its body is the vanishing dune itself.

(220) Who did Jordanna summon to help with the dust goliath's
demise?
Nicholas, Azron, and RGB (Albert, Linus, and Newton).

(221) What supplies did Jordanna request the summoned party to
bring?
Hydrosphere ejectors, gravity shoes, and sand-peepers for the
entire team at the site. In addition, she requested the team to bring
energy coils for Nicholas and Azron.

(222) What are sand-peepers?
A pair of silver glasses with horizontal slits for lenses; they
enable one to see in a sandstorm.

(223) What are the gravity shoes for?

Gravity shoes will keep one from getting sucked off the ground by the creature.

(224) Why were the hydrosphere ejectors modified to select from one of two water sources: earthly and elemental water sources?

Earthly water only serves to repel the desert harpies. Artisans on the elemental worlds craft durable goods using a mixture of Zephyrian dust and Atlantian water. The creature is made of Zephyrian dust.

(225) How does the selector switch on the hydrosphere ejectors work?

To use earthly water to repel the beast, then switch to Atlantian water to solidify it, or turn it to pottery.

(226) What are the energy coils for?

They are used to restrain deplorables.

(227) Who came up with the plan, how to defeat the dust goliath?

Ethan and Hayley.

(228) What was the plan?

Dakota will destroy Heldrik's device, which will cause the desert harpies to merge into a dust goliath. Once the harpies fully merge with the body, the vanishing dune will lift off the pyramid complex and allow Azron to open one of the rear exits. Next, the party will exit out the back. The monster should be in the largest pyramid at the center of the complex . . .

(229) What did the formed beast look like?

The creature looked like a tornado, with the upper half of a devilish sand monster growing from its center. It reminded Ethan of a pissed-off giant sandman with ram horns. The dust mass making up the creature's shape flowed like liquid through its body. The tornado sucked in any particles falling to the ground and replenished its form.

(230) What finally defeated the dust behemoth?

Dakota summoned two Hell-Giants per Ethan's request.

(231) What happened to the Hell-Giants?

The Hell-Giants act much like the firelytes in book #1, Ethan Fox and the Eyes of the Desert Sand. There, firelyte capsules when thrown to the ground, eprupted into small infernos that morphed into firelytes. In the scene in chapter four, the firelytes each grabbed a leg of a wooden end table, hoisted it up, and whistled in unison as they marched towards the fireplace. In the same way, the Hell-Giants slowly climbed to the beast's upper arms and cuddled them like a child hugging mommy, and melted into a log.

(232) When they entered the pyramid to retrieve the Nibblewart prophecies, who did they encounter?
The Shadow Princess, Adara.

(233) What did the Shadow Princess tell Jordanna?

The Nibblewart prophecies as foretold in the Book of Creators are now Jordanna's to protect since she is the Caretaker leader.

(234) What was Adara's parting words to Hayley?

Adara thanked Hayley for saving her. Adara bonded her soul to the rift-key to save her people from the evil one. When Hayley recovered it from the puzzle box, she freed Adara's soul from eternal damnation. Adara was the voice who spoke to Hayley through her ring.

CHAPTER FIFTEEN
A GRISLY DISCOVERY

(235) Who vouched for Dakota Drakelan, who was absent at the debriefing, keeping the Caretaker secret regarding the prophecies?

Alexander Sturgis.

(236) What measures were put in place to protect the portal prophecies?

(1) Nicholas updated the cloaking device; it is now a projector as well as a cloak. It projects a copy of the vanishing dune that is only seen from a distance – and at the same time, it cloaks the complex from those who pass by. (2) With respect to the indigenous lifeforms living in the protected realm, Nicholas also placed proximity detectors around the perimeter. If anything approaches by land or air, they will be alerted. A gnat couldn't get to within a mile of the complex without them knowing.

(237) Who are the Careguards?

Armed soldiers who Jordanna ordered to guard the portal plane at all times.

(238) Who is behind rallying Jordanna as Headmistress detractors?

Roman Trabblemore.

(239) When Irvin put on his anchorman hat, what did he report from the human news story?

Break-ins; each of the galleries in question exhibits artifacts shared from the same mystery collection. While neither the owner of the collection nor its origins are known at this time. Sources confirm pieces from the mystery collection have gone missing due to these break-ins.

(240) Name the seven cities that the Grimleavers are targeting and attacking all across the globe?

(1) Atlanta, (2) Boston, (3) Chicago, (4) Washington DC, (5) Berlin, (6) London, and (7) Rome.

(241) Who was Ethan inferring was Hayley's friend?

Her infinity ring; the Shadow Princess communicates telepathically to Hayley through her rift-key (infinity ring).

(242) Why is Adara's connection to Hayley stronger now?

Because her soul is now free ever since she has fulfilled her destiny.

(243) What was Adara's destiny?

To deliver the portal prophecies to the Caretaker leader; in this case it was Jordanna.

(244) Name the four names on Odin's list; he called them "The Four Cohorts."

(1) Drake Evans, (2) Lindrew Scragmort, (3) Jason Crowley, and (4) Heldrik Vonn Grim.

(245) Who were "The Four Cohorts?"

Gaylord's associates, according to Dakota Drakelan.

(246) Who was Drake Evans?

Drake Evans was a long-time friend of Gaylord's. When Gaylord became headmaster, Drake was his number one and consulted on his every decision.

(247) What happened to Drake Evans?

He went missing and Gaylord started to act irrationally.

(248) Who was Lindrew Scragmort?

He was the portal master during the Trabblemore administration. He oversaw the four portals during the Great Exodus and became Gaylord's number one after Drake Evans' disappearance.

(249) What was the Great Exodus event?

"A Great Exodus occurred, and creatures from the Caretakers worlds migrated to Earth in vast numbers. The Creators returned to fix the situation and prevent a repeat; the Creators locked the portals when they left. The lock will only open upon discovery of the portal prophecies as written in the Book of Creators." – excerpt from book #1, Ethan Fox and the Eyes of the Desert Sand.

(250) What happened to Lindrew Scragmort?

He, too, later went missing.

(251) What happened to Jason Crowley?

You could argue he went missing too, until someone tried to make a point by leaving his dead body on Hayley's grandmother Vanessa's doorstep.

(252) What became of the fourth cohort, Heldrik?

It is like he's disappeared from existence with no record.

(253) Why was the pyramid complex built?

The poem, **The Fortress of Fate**, clearly says, "A fortress built for wicked plans."

(254) What kind of gold was Damien using in his experiment? And what kind of gold should he have been using?

He used normal gold when the recipe calls for once-cloaked Leprechaun gold.

(255) What was the findings of Damien's experiment?

Minerals from Ceres react when they encounter once-cloaked Leprechaun gold. However, some minerals create a much more powerful blast than others.

(256) Why did they use earthly water to hydrate the Ceresian bloating stone used to build the pyramid complex?

The Ceresian bloating stone hydrated with Atlantian water, does not react.

(257) What purpose does the giant pyramid structure serve?
They could store things in a giant structure like that.

(258) How did Ethan get into the Ravenwood chamber?
Hayley had made Ethan a copy of her hand so he could enter Odin's chamber without her.

(259) Who did Hayley go to meet in the Caretaker city of Zen without Ethan?
The Wentworths.

(260) Who else went to the Caretaker city of Zen?
Ethan.

(261) At first glance, why did Ethan think he saw a sizeable spider-like shadow in the Wentworths' residence?
It was Bella Wentworth using all four of her arms to pick herself up off the floor.

(262) Why did Hayley go to visit the Wentworths?
She went to ask Boris about Heldrik Vonn Grim.

(263) When Ethan and Tinx received a knock on Odin's chamber door, what did they find when they opened the door?
Lying on the ground in front of them was a shriveled grey corpse.

(264) Who was the dead body?
Boris Wentworth.

CHAPTER SIXTEEN
THE DAY OF RECKONING

(265) What was tucked behind Boris' lapel?
A note from Victor Qruefeldt.

(266) Who kidnapped Hayley?
Victor Qruefeldt.

(267) What lured Ethan back to the Pyramids of Never?
Victor Qruefeldt's note instructing Ethan to meet him there; he had Hayley.

(268) When Ethan demanded Hayley, did Victor comply?
Yes; he threw her to the ground at Ethan's feet.

(269) Did Victor know that Princess Adara was the Shadow Princess?
No.

(270) Was Victor alone when he lured Ethan to the Pyramids of Never?
No; he had a whole army of Grimleavers coming.

(271) Who are the Grimleavers?
They comprise of vampires, trolls, ogres, and other dark creatures.

(272) Who is Norell?
A tall vampire woman with long black hair.

(273) What did Norell say?
All hail the Grimlord.

(274) After Ethan lunged at Norell for pummeling Hayley's back to the ground, what did she do to Ethan?
A cold wave of chills washed over his body as he struggled to move – but the harder he fought, the more frozen he became; it was called a freezing hex.

(275) What did Hayley whisper in Ethan's ear?
Calm yourself; Adara says calmness will free you.

(276) What calming technique did Ethan use on himself?
He closed his eyes and thought of when he first met Hayley on the beach. He remembered her grabbing hold of his hands and the butterflies he felt. A warm rush of energy swept through his body – and suddenly, he could move again.

(277) What did Victor take from Hayley? And where did he put it?
Her ring; the rift-key. He put it in the black puzzle box he held in his hand.

(278) What else did Victor take from Hayley?
Her copycat.

(279) Who did Ethan secretly bring along with him?
Gruggins.

(280) What did Gruggins do in secret?
Gruggins unbound Ethan's hands.

(281) What did Hayley demand back from Victor?
Her Tabby Cat.

(282) How did Victor respond?
He used the puzzle box and created a vortex to strike and kill Hayley; called a soul reaping vortex.

(283) What happened next?
Ethan launched himself in front of the vortex to save Hayley and he was struck instead.

(284) Who arrived that caused Victor to grab hold of the portal beacon, and vanish?
Jordanna and the rest of CAGE accompanied by an armed battalion of Careguards.

(285) Who appeared at Ethan's dying body?
The Shadow Princess.

CHAPTER SEVENTEEN
A KRAKEN'S FURY

(286) What was happening on the museum break-in news?

It appears they took similar items from each of the museums. They were thoroughly ransacked; speculation that they were looking for something specific. All the museums they hit had exhibits with items pilfered from Stravis' bunker during the Pandora fiasco.

(287) What was missing from the museums?

The only things missing were small rock collections.

(288) What did the Caretakers molecular scan reveal?

They were looking for a Ceresian bloating stone.

(289) Why was this a problem?

Stravis' research revealed peculiar alchemy between earthly items when they come in contact with certain elementals. A Ceresian bloating stone is one of those elementals, which means, Victor Qruefeldt now has all the material he needs to blow up a vast portion of the known universe – new weapon of mass destruction.

(290) What important news did Dorkin Drumbles have that interrupted the CAGE debriefing?

Dorkin informed Jordanna of an important new painting in the Gallery. The Fates were unanimous, calling the painting "A Kraken's Fury." In the lower middle portion of the scene, Hayley could see the body of a boy lay on the ground. She looked at his palm, and the symbol in its center gave off a dim yellow glow. Hayley faced the others and said, "That's Ethan! He's alive and needs our help!"

Author Photo © 2024 Edwin Wolfe

Eric Moeszinger—an acclaimed award-winning author and creative force behind the enchanting world of Ethan Fox Books—is a storyteller whose tales are steeped in the essence of his own life. Writing under the pen name E. L. Seer, the "E" representing Eric and the "L" a nod to his beloved wife Lori. Eric's literary journey began in the serene neighborhood of Sacramento, California, where rustic charm blended seamlessly with the spirit of exploration. From Sacramento roots to engineering, his journey culminates in inspiring stories that resonate and give back.

Explore the expansive multiverse of the Ethan Fox *Original Series* by visiting our website and blog, or by connecting with us across our social media platforms. And join us on a journey that glows with rare magic, unearthly wonders, and true friendships.

https://www.EthanFoxBooks.com, https://www.KidsStagram.com,

www.Facebook.com/EthanFoxBooks, ELSeerAuthor@gmail.com,

www.Twitter.com/@EthanFoxBooks, www.Instagram/@EthanFoxBooks,

www.Goodreads.com/user/show/133515145-e-l-seer